NIGHT VISION

NIGHTHAWK SECURITY - BOOK TWO

SUSAN SLEEMAN

1

Jenna Paine would do anything to protect her daughter. Anything. But she didn't think she'd need to prove it tonight.

Not this way. Not with strong fingers pinching the tender skin of her arm in near blizzard conditions outside her rental cabin. Twisting that arm behind her back. Forcing her toward the cabin in knee-high powdery snow.

She reached over her shoulder with her free hand and raked her nails over her attacker's face. Scraping. Gouging. The sumo wrestler of a man squeezed harder. Pain razored into her body and a moan erupted from deep inside her soul.

"Please don't," she begged for the first time since this unknown man surprised her. "I'll give you whatever you want."

"Shut up!" He shoved her up the back stairs of the mountain retreat, her feet dragging in the drifts of snow.

How could this be happening? She'd just stepped outside to get wood for the fireplace. It had seemed safe. Everything about this cabin had seemed safe. Now this?

She kicked hard and caught his shin. He spun her around and punched her in the face. Her head whipped back. She gasped the cold air. Breathing hard. Willing the shock and pain from her mind.

If only she could make a break for it. Try to run. To escape. But she'd never leave Karlie alone with this man. Her four-year-old was sound asleep in the master bedroom.

Please! Please, protect my baby girl from this lunatic. She can't handle this too. Not after losing her dad.

Just fifteen minutes before, Jenna had been so excited about the *Christmas in the Mountains* giveaway she'd won on a local radio station. Two full weeks in the cabin and Christmas just under a week away. Should've been fun. Now, she'd give anything to be back in her dingy one-bedroom apartment.

Her attacker shoved her over the threshold. She tumbled to the floor, her knees and shoulder taking the brunt of the fall. More pain. Agonizing. Sharp. She wanted to curl up. To protect herself from more pain. But she wouldn't give up. Not when Karlie needed her.

She shoved her boot in front of the door to keep it open. She doubted anyone was out in the snowstorm, but if they were, maybe they'd see the light spilling out of the doorway and investigate.

The man jerked her to her feet, wrenched the door closed, and thrust her into the first bedroom, his hand clamped on her arm. She eased away to look at his face. His dark eyes narrowed, his long chin jutted out. He spun, his gaze running over every inch of the room like a radar. He pulled her deeper inside the room and jerked open the nightstand and dresser drawers, his fierce grip bruising her arm. He checked the closet and uttered a long string of curses.

"Not here." He dragged her like a rag doll along with him into the hallway.

"What do you want?" she asked, desperation creeping through her words. "Name it. I'll give it to you."

He muttered something under his breath, but she couldn't make it out. He hauled her through three more bedrooms, searching and pawing through everything before marching toward the master. Toward Karlie.

Jenna's heart raced, and she dragged her feet.

He pulled harder, the heels of her boots scraping against the wood, the high-pitched sound grating on her nerves. He grabbed the knob. Paused. Twisted. He issued a grunt of satisfaction.

No. Please. Not Karlie.

He slammed his meaty hand onto the door and sent it flying inward. The wood banged against the wall.

Jenna's breath caught in her throat. She shot a look at the bed.

Empty.

Karlie, where are you?

The attacker gave her no time to think but dragged her past the closet and toward the master bath. A hint of light seeped under the closet door.

Karlie. It had to be her.

Lately, Karlie had taken to dragging her bedding and a flashlight into the closet at home. She snuggled under her blankets to look at her favorite books when she should be sleeping, eventually dozing off. Even after a year, she was still having a hard time over her father's sudden death from a heart attack. Camping reminded her of her younger days when she'd gotten along with Toby. Before he constantly nagged Karlie to get over her juvenile idiopathic arthritis, as if she had control over the autoimmune disease.

Her assailant's fingers tightened on Jenna's bruised arm. She winced but didn't cry out and give him the satisfaction of knowing he was hurting her. He shoved her toward the closet. She swung her body hard, forcing him to turn from the closet doors.

"Please," she said loudly, hoping Karlie heard. "What are you looking for? If it's a person, I'm alone here."

He grabbed the knob and whipped open the door. Jenna's breath stilled, and she glanced inside. Karlie had left the light on, but she'd huddled under a mound of blankets.

The creep ripped the blankets free.

Curled in a tight ball, Karlie's eyes were closed.

The creep grunted his frustration, closed the door, and quickly moved to the dresser drawers. Pawing through each one of them. He let out a long breath and marched Jenna down the hall and into the family room. He jerked out a wooden dining chair and shoved her into it.

She massaged her arm and watched him. He whipped out a long knife and eased closer, his eyes tight. He pressed the tip of the red blade into her throat.

The steel bit into her skin, the sharp sting excruciating. Blood dripped down her neck. She angled back, trying to get away.

He bent lower, his face inches from hers, staring at her with mean, ugly eyes. Spittle clung to the corners of his full mouth twisted in a nasty smirk.

Was this it? Was he going to kill her now?

Sweat beaded on her forehead. She tried to draw back.

"You move even a fraction of an inch, and I'll cut you." He released her as if she wasn't worth the trouble and started pacing across the cabin. He passed her purse on the table, upended it, and dug through the contents.

He was distracted, but for how long? Could she escape?

He swept her things to the floor in an angry swipe then began pacing again, his heavy boots thumping on the wood floor. He was dressed all in camo. Like a hunter. And she was the prey. His body was massive, as if he lifted weights all day long or was a bodybuilder of some sort. Or a monster, like Bruce Banner when his heart rate skyrocketed and he turned into the Incredible Hulk. Yeah, she'd think of him as the Hulk.

Step. Step. Step. He turned. Paced again. His quick movements stirred up the fresh pine scent from the tree she and Karlie had decorated just hours before. The attacker moved past the Christmas lights she'd strung around a door. Past a fire dying in the big stone firebox. She could barely believe the cozy space filled with plump furniture had gone from cheery and welcoming to terror and danger.

He slowed. The footsteps halting and uneven now.

Was he rethinking his plans? Could he be considering taking off and not hurting her?

Doubtful. She'd seen him. Could describe him to the police. He had to know that.

Oh, why hadn't she waited to go for wood in the morning?

She'd wanted to get a head start for tomorrow. For the big day planned with Karlie. Hitting the bunny slope early. Sharing large cups of hot cocoa at the lodge. Forgetting about the turn their lives had taken when Toby died and left them in debt and homeless.

Now this? Could she take any more?

Please, please, please. Protect us. Protect my baby. Help me to protect her.

Jenna could call 911 but her phone was across the room. Probably didn't matter. The deputies would likely be hard-pressed to respond in this weather. At least not quickly enough to save her and Karlie. Didn't matter anyway. She couldn't get to her phone.

The front door was her only escape as the creep stood between her and the back door.

Could she race across the room to that exit with her attacker nearby?

Possibly, but then what about Karlie? Jenna could circle around the back and get her daughter. But what might he do to Karlie before she reached her baby girl? No, Jenna couldn't risk it.

He muttered a curse then paused by the Christmas tree. Maybe he was looking for presents to steal. If so, he'd come to the wrong cabin. She had no money for presents other than trinkets for Karlie's stocking.

He jerked out his phone and thumbed the keys.

A text? He was sending a text or an email in the middle of all of this? Or, even crazier, looking something up on the internet? And what about Karlie? What was he going to do with her?

His phone rang, and he answered it. "Yo."

An angry male voice was coming from the other end of his call, but she couldn't make out the words.

"I had to secure the place first," the Hulk said. "Did a quick search but haven't had a chance to do a thorough one."

A spew of angry words filtered from the phone.

He scratched his chin covered in stubble. "What do you want me to do?"

Another long string of words from the man on the other end of the call.

"I can do that." He shoved his phone in one jacket pocket then pulled a thick roll of duct tape from the other one.

His eyes locked on hers in a bone-chilling glare. He moved toward her, ripping a long strip from the roll, the tape sucking against itself and echoing through the stillness. "Hands behind your back."

"Please, don't do this," she begged again. "I have money

6

in my purse. It's not much. Fifty dollars. You can have it. And I have a credit card too. Just take it and go." She didn't tell him that Toby had maxed out this card along with every other line of credit they had.

"I don't want your stinkin' money." He jerked her arms behind her back and secured the sticky tape around one of her wrists. It clung to every pore of her skin, and she tried to jerk her hand away, but he yanked her arm back.

"If this isn't about money," she said, looking over her shoulder at him. "Then what do you want? Why are you here?"

"Wasn't supposed to be...never mind." He shook his head, his expression angry as he stepped around her.

"Wasn't supposed to be what...me?" she asked, as she couldn't think of any reason someone would want to hurt her.

"Shut up. I need quiet so I can think," he said in response, neither a confirmation or denial. So what, then? His comment about searching made it obvious that he was looking for something, but maybe he was also looking for someone. But who?

Shawn. Yes, Shawn. Made perfect sense that this creep would be after her brother. He was a drug addict and had recently become involved in selling drugs. She hadn't seen him since Toby's funeral, but now, with her husband gone, she and Karlie were alone. So alone. She'd reached out to Shawn. Invited him to the cabin for Christmas to try to make amends.

And this is what it got her in return. Par for the course. A user for years, Shawn had worn out his welcome. If she hadn't been so desperate for family of any kind, she wouldn't have called him. But she was.

She eyed the attacker. "You're looking for Shawn, aren't you? What did he do?"

He dropped her wrist and clamped big, beefy hands over his ears, which were sticking out below a rolled up stocking cap. "Stop your yammering. I have to think."

"Maybe I can help you."

His eyes narrowed into tiny slits. "You wanna help me figure out how to get rid of you?"

She gasped. Jerked back. "Why? Why do you want to get rid of me? If this is about Shawn, I don't know anything about his business. And you...I don't even know you. I didn't do anything to you. Please."

"You seen me, didn't you? You'll go to the cops and then..." He shook his head and grabbed the other wrist.

This was it. She would die if she didn't do something. She had to get help. But how? She couldn't protect Karlie if she was dead. She tried to wrench free.

He cuffed her across the face, his meaty hand snapping her head back, her body following. Her shoulder slammed into a small table. It wobbled then tumbled to the floor, taking his attention.

Perfect. She could run. Now.

She jumped to her feet. Charged for the door. Flung it open. The icy cold air felt good. Cleared her mind. Her thoughts.

No. This was wrong. She'd let her fear of dying get to her. She couldn't abandon Karlie. She paused on the threshold.

What was she thinking? She wasn't. At least not more than the desperation of a woman who was about to die. She wouldn't run out on Karlie. Ever.

That left only one option.

She threw back her head and screamed from the bottom of her toes.

Brendan came to a stop and jerked the stocking cap from his head to listen.

He'd heard a scream. He was sure of it. But up here? In a family resort at Mount Hood? Maybe something he'd hear on his job as a partner with Nighthawk Security, but not up here. Right?

He cocked his head again. Another sound. Just down the road. A woman. Definitely a woman. This one less intense, and it was suddenly cut off as if a hand had covered her mouth and silenced her.

Probably someone just playing in the snow and whooping it up before the brunt of the storm settled on them and howling winds made it too treacherous to be out.

But could he afford to believe in *probably*? He never had. He'd stepped up whenever there was a question. And especially if a woman's life was on the line.

He took off running, adrenaline fueling his legs. His heavy boots whispered through the foot of powdery snow that had fallen today. The moon shone bright, illuminating his way up the curving mountain road. He rounded a bend just in time to see a cabin door slam closed. The sound reverberated through the tall pines and echoed across the wide clearing.

He raced for the long walkway to a large log cabin lit from inside. The pristine snow glistened in the moonlight. Not a single footstep had marred the perfection, but the porch held a small set of prints facing out.

Had a woman opened the door and screamed?

He shook his head. He'd come up here to get away from the tense life of protecting people and running investigations. Away from working crazy hours. Not having a day off for weeks. He needed a break. So why, after two days in seclusion, was he jonesing for some action?

Most likely the reason he was inventing this scream.

Still, he couldn't just walk away. He had to check it out.

He took the walkway, his hand automatically drifting to his hip, where he carried his sidearm at work. But, of course, he was on vacation and wasn't openly carrying. He did have his favorite pistol, a compact .380 Colt, in his pocket. That would have to do.

He knocked on the door. As he waited, he glanced up into the night sky. Snow pelted down from above and whipped sideways in the wind. The weather forecaster had predicted another ten inches or more tonight. Perfect powder for a day on the slopes tomorrow. If he could get to the slopes.

When no one answered, he knocked again and waited. Still no answer.

His concern mounted. If he were still a deputy, he would have enough information to believe that someone was in harm, and exigent circumstances would've allowed him to bust through the door to check on the occupant's welfare. But he wasn't a deputy anymore. Just a private investigator on vacation. If he barged into the place, he could be arrested for breaking-and-entering.

He and his brothers were still getting the Nighthawk Security agency off the ground, and that was the last thing the agency needed.

Muffled noises came from inside. Sounded like a scuffle.

Okay, so someone was home and ignoring him.

He heard what sounded like a heavy object being dragged across the room.

Enough with this speculating. If someone was in trouble, he could be wasting valuable time. He jumped down from the porch and went to the nearest window. He could still be arrested as a Peeping Tom, but hopefully the occupants wouldn't see him.

He planted his gloves on the icy sill and rose up on his

toes. A family room that was furnished exactly like his family's rental sprawled out before him. He glanced around the room, his gaze stopping at the far corner. His mouth dropped open, and he hung by his fingers. Staring. Processing the scene.

A muscular man was holding a knife to the throat of a woman duct taped to a chair. He reared back, lifting his arm, the knife paused in mid-air.

No! No!

Brendan banged on the window to draw the man's attention. He stopped, arm raised. Brendan didn't wait for him to move again but plowed through the snow. Up the steps. Tried the doorknob. Locked as expected. He slammed a boot into the door. The solid pine shook but held fast. Again and again, he kicked until the frame gave way.

Grabbing his gun, he barged inside. He aimed his weapon on the area where he'd spotted the man. He was gone, and the woman was attempting to stand with the chair affixed to her body.

"Brendan Byrd, former sheriff's deputy and Army Delta Force," Brendan said so she didn't think he was a thug too. "I'm staying just down the road on vacation."

"Please, help." Her frantic gaze connected with his. "My daughter's hiding in the master bedroom closet. The attacker ran that way. Hurry. Help her, please."

"Don't move," Brendan commanded as he crossed the room. Not like she could. Not tied to the chair, but he'd seen women do miraculous things when it came to saving their children. For all he knew, she would shuffle her way down the hall to her child.

A child. He had no time to waste here.

The cabin layout was identical to his family rental, and the master was at the end of the hall. He reached the hallway and whipped around the corner, gun at the ready. *Empty*. He started down the unlit space.

Even this far away, he could hear the chair banging against the floor in the family room as the woman tried to free herself. *Desperate*. She was desperate. Brendan got that. Lived it even, and had seen it in his family's eyes when his dad needed a kidney transplant. In his own eyes in the mirror.

Maybe he could erase some of this woman's fear by checking on her daughter. He cautiously moved toward the other bedrooms and two bathrooms, clearing them one at a time. Holding his breath, he burst into the master. The window was wide open, the screen pushed out. The suspect's likely escape route.

Brendan cleared the bathroom then went to the closet. The girl was tucked under a blanket, fast asleep, oblivious to the drama. Her soft blond curls lay against her cheek, and she hugged a stuffed plush snowman tightly against her chest.

Thank you. Thank you. Thank you.

He wanted to stay put and look at the precious child, safe and unharmed, when so often as a deputy he'd witnessed the reverse, but her mother still needed him. He closed and locked the window, double-checking to be sure the latches had caught, then raced back to the family room.

The woman had marched the chair almost to the hallway. Her terrified eyes locked on his. "Karlie."

"Is fine." He smiled to ease her mind, while his traveled to catching the perpetrator. "She's sleeping in the closet, and it looks like your attacker took off through the master bedroom window."

"Thank you, God." A rush of air came from her mouth, and her body sagged against the restraining tape.

He dug out the Winchester pocketknife his father had

given him on his sixteenth birthday and slashed through the tape at her back. He moved around front, catching sight of the bruise that was forming around her eye and cringing.

He gripped her hands and freed her wrists. "If you'll be okay alone, I want to trail the attacker. He's probably long gone, but it's worth trying."

"Sure. Go." She waved a hand.

He sliced through her ankle tape. "Do you have a flashlight?"

"I saw one under the kitchen sink."

"Lock yourself in the master with your daughter while I'm gone." He bolted for the kitchen and found the large light. He didn't want to leave them alone, but he had to try to nail this creep before he hurt someone else.

"Be back as soon as I can," he shouted and took off out the back door. He'd call the sheriff's office or ask her to, but a patrol car would take forever to get through in these horrible conditions if it even did, so that could wait. The suspect couldn't.

The biting wind sandpapered snow into his face, and he bent his head against the force. He moved as fast as he could along a single set of large boot prints quickly filling with huge white flakes, leading him into the woods. He lifted his feet high and clomped into the deep drifts. The wind picked up, howling so fiercely he could hardly see. He couldn't continue for much longer, or he'd risk getting stranded, which could mean sure death.

In a small clearing, he started to turn back, but snowmobile tracks caught his attention.

He dropped to his knees. The tracks were fresh for sure. Had to be their guy.

Not good. No way he'd catch up to a snowmobile.

He needed a forensic team, but no way they would arrive tonight. Deputies would have their hands full. This incident would be a priority under normal circumstances, but not when the deputies were out saving people stuck in the horrific conditions before they froze to death.

By morning, fresh powder would completely obscure the tracks and boot prints, and he needed to do something to preserve the evidence. He lodged the flashlight between his neck and ear, shone it on the tracks, then took pictures with his phone. Hopefully, they'd be clear enough to determine the make and model of the machine.

He followed the same procedure with the boot prints. Before moving again, he ran the light over the area. Something dangled from a low hanging branch. He moved closer. A piece of fabric. Navy blue. The attacker had worn a navy jacket. At least this was something to go on.

He carefully extracted the scrap to keep from damaging the cloth, pocketed it, and stepped down the tracks, hoping to determine the direction the attacker had fled. Reaching the private road that ran in front of the cabins, he paused to catch a breath from the strain of plunging through such deep snow and study the tracks that turned sharply north. The creep was headed for the unplowed main road. Headed for more potential victims.

Brendan couldn't stop the guy. Not without a snowmobile. He dug out his phone. Yes! A signal even in this storm.

He tapped 911. He might not be able to go after the guy himself, but he would do everything within his power to keep this armed and very dangerous man from hurting another defenseless person.

2

Jenna wanted to sweep Karlie into her arms. Hug her close. Smell the clean scent of her shampoo and never let her go, but her sweet child had such trouble sleeping lately that Jenna would settle for sitting next to Karlie and placing a hand on her back.

Jenna closed her eyes and focused on her daughter's regular heartbeat pounding beneath trembling fingers. She forced herself to take slow, steady breaths to ease out the adrenaline that was still coursing through her body.

In. Out. In. Out.

Despite the breathing, her anxiety clung to her and tears pricked her eyes. She touched her eye that was swollen from his punch. The nick on her neck inflicted by his knife.

He'd been about to kill her. Truly kill her.

She shuddered, the waves of fear rolling over her body.

If that man hadn't come along...no, she wouldn't go there. He *had* come along. A big, strapping guy who'd made an impression on her. He'd stood strong, confident, and intense. Once he'd told her that he was a former deputy and Delta Force, she trusted him. With him in the cabin, she believed she and Karlie would be all right.

Jenna let out another long breath. They were safe.

Or were they? Was she just putting her trust in another man because she was in a situation she needed to get out of? Just like when she'd married Toby.

Toby. Poor misguided Toby. He'd hurt her so many times. Not physically, but with harsh words. *That* she could deal with. But Karlie? Hurting Karlie? No, that was unacceptable, and when he turned his verbal abuse on their precious child, Jenna decided to leave him. Then he'd died. Suddenly, just like that. A heart attack at thirty-six in the arms of another woman. Such a freak thing to happen. Sudden. Jenna was unprepared. Now this. This horrible invasion. It was all too much.

Tears started rolling down her cheeks, and anger had her swiping them away.

She was sorry Toby had died. Honestly sorry, but other than the lack of financial support, her life was better now. Her love for Toby and their relationship had been over almost as soon as they'd married twelve years before. She'd thought she was in love, but it didn't take her long to see he was unstable and mean. She'd soon realized she'd only married him because her life at home was a mess, and he was her ticket away from the disaster that was her parents' marriage. Instead of finding freedom, she'd stepped into a similar situation of a verbally abusive husband.

"I'm sorry, my sweet, sweet child," she whispered and kissed Karlie's cheek. "Life will get better. I promise."

It has to.

But before she could convince herself, her thoughts drifted to Shawn. If it turned out he was the person the attacker was looking for, she didn't know how to explain to Karlie that another male in her life had failed them. Sure, he hadn't been in Karlie's life very much, but enough for her to grow fond of him.

Jenna heard footsteps coming down the hallway. Could it be the killer coming back? Her heart raced. She looked for a weapon. Anything to protect herself.

"It's me," the Delta guy called out.

She let out a terror-filled breath and quickly swiped away her tears. She was in charge of her little family now, and Karlie depended on her. That meant Jenna had to be strong at all times. Never let her guard down. And never instantly trust a man, not even Brendan. Be cautious. Even with him. And while she was at it, she would do her very best never to let anyone see her cry again. Especially not Karlie.

"I'm coming into the bedroom, ma'am." The man's voice preceded him as he poked his head around the corner.

She got up and gestured at Karlie. "She's managed to sleep through all of this," she whispered. "Mind if we talk in the family room?"

He held out his hand. "After you."

She eased past him and caught the scent of peppermint and a tangy aftershave, refreshing and pleasant. Sure, fine, he smelled good, but it didn't stop her unease from the attack. Especially not as she headed toward the room where she'd been forced into the chair, duct taped, and then nearly stabbed to death. She could still feel the tip of the knife against her skin.

Her head swam, and she paused at the entrance to take in the mess. The small table lay on its side. The vase and a ceramic eagle were both smashed on the floor from her struggle with the guy. The door was splintered and hanging by one hinge, but somehow Brendan had managed to close it. Snow had blown in and melted in small puddles on the gleaming wood floor. She would have to clean the room up, but she didn't have the strength.

The owners were going to demand she pay for the

damage, but with what money? She was only one survivor-benefit check from social security away from losing their apartment.

She couldn't go back into the family room, so she stepped into the adjoining kitchen with a large island overlooking the family room and turned to face Brendan. "Can I make you a cup of cocoa or tea?"

He stopped on the other side of the island and casually rested a hip against it. "If the attacker was in here, it's best to touch as few items as possible before we get a forensic team out here."

"He wasn't." Her legs still weak, she slid onto a stool. "Do I need to call 911, or have you taken care of that?"

"It's done, but the local sheriff's office can't get anyone up here tonight. Weather's too bad. He appointed me acting deputy and asked me to protect the scene until they could respond."

"And the man? I'm guessing since you're back so fast you didn't find him."

He nodded. "He'd stashed a snowmobile about a mile away. I tracked it to the main road. He's long gone, but I gave the sheriff a description and he put out an alert for him." Brendan put on his glove and reached into his pocket, withdrawing a blue scrap of fabric. "I found this on a branch. I thought it looked like his coat."

She studied it carefully, then nodded. "It's his. Made by Columbia. The logo was embroidered on the front."

"Columbia's such a big brand in these parts, I don't know if that'll help me with the investigation or not."

"I'm sorry," she said sincerely. "All of this must have ruined your vacation."

"Truth be told, I was getting a little bored anyway." His mouth turned up in a brilliant smile, captivating her.

She stared at him—her hero. She'd noticed his strength

when he'd broken through the door, but now she took in his incredible build that spoke to many hours in a gym. He had nearly black hair, stubble covering a wide jaw, and eyes the color of a crisp blue sky. His nose was broad, and he had a welcoming smile that had likely melted quite a few hearts over the years and was fast melting hers.

"I'll just grab some paper and a pen to jot down your statement while it's fresh in your mind," he said, thankfully oblivious to her thoughts.

She gestured at the table in the family room. "There's a notepad and pen by the phone."

While he collected them, she warned herself not to be distracted by this handsome man. Toby had come to her rescue, too, right after they got married. Her father had snapped and physically attacked her mother. Toby allowed her mom to live with them, and Jenna had put on blinders, seeing only a knight in shining armor. But a bitter, hard, cruel man lived underneath that coat of armor.

Still, he put a roof over her head and let her mother stay until she passed away from lung cancer. Shawn stayed with them, too, until his drug abuse became an overwhelming problem. After Karlie was born, Toby was smitten with her and was a solid father. At least, until six months before he died and Karlie was diagnosed with juvenile idiopathic arthritis. Toby took every opportunity to tell Karlie she was a faker. He constantly belittled her and told her it was all in her head and to get over it.

Sure, Karlie looked perfectly healthy to most people, but Jenna saw the swollen and red joints. Karlie's joint stiffness and pain were very real and inhibited her activities. Jenna's heart broke each time Toby criticized Karlie. Jenna had tried to make up for it by talking with her daughter afterward and explaining how it was hard for people to think someone was sick when most of the time they looked just fine on the outside. Others couldn't see the pain or the damage occurring inside her joints. Her father was one of them.

Brendan cleared his throat, and she looked up to find he'd returned and had taken off his jacket to reveal wide shoulders in a deep green sweater. He was watching her, his eyes filled with concern, an emotion that had always been lacking in Toby's eyes.

Her heart skipped a beat, and she felt a blush rising over her face.

"Ready for my statement?" she asked, her voice pitched too high and she hoped it didn't give away her unease.

He smiled again, but it was stiff and formal. "Maybe we should make an official introduction first. As I said before, I'm Brendan Byrd. I used to be a Multnomah County Deputy and served in Delta Force. Now my four brothers, also former law enforcement officers, and I have formed a protective and investigative agency in Portland."

"I'm Jenna. Jenna Paine."

He sat on a stool down the island from her. "Okay, Ms. Paine—"

"No. Jenna, please." The Paine name reminded her of Toby's death and all that entailed in their lives.

"Okay, then, Jenna." Another smile, less dazzling, but attractive all the same. "Do you have any questions about me that I can answer before we talk about the break-in?"

"You said protective and investigative agency. What exactly does that mean?"

"People whose lives are in danger hire us to protect them. And we also investigate things like missing family members, birth parents, criminal cases, et cetera." He leaned back in his stool. "We work out of the Veritas Center. Have you ever heard of it?"

She shook her head. "Sounds fancy."

"Fancy?" He smiled. "Maybe. Veritas means truth, which

is appropriate because it's a lab where science is used to find the truth. They started out with a main focus of running DNA for the public, but now they also work with law enforcement to process forensics. Our sister Sierra is the trace evidence expert."

"I never knew such private labs existed, but then, I've never needed law enforcement in my personal life, so I really never paid much attention to it." She thought of her dad's physical abuse of her mother and worked hard not to give away her unease.

"We often partner with them in our investigations, and they lease us space, not only for our agency, but we also live in an attached tower of condos."

"Must be convenient."

"It is." He sat forward and picked up his pen. "Now, if you're comfortable proceeding with my questions, go ahead and tell me what happened here. Don't leave anything out."

Comfortable with him? Yeah, way too comfortable for a woman who knew better than to trust a stranger. But he seemed legitimate in his professional life, so she could at least trust him with what happened in the invasion. She recounted every detail, including a vivid description of her attacker and each step he took. Brendan carefully watched her as if evaluating her every word, and it seemed like she was on trial, not a victim. If she hadn't already been shaking from the attack, his intense gaze might make her quake in her boots.

"You came in right as he decided to kill me." The memory of the creep standing over her with the knife sent a shudder through her body.

"And you're sure you didn't recognize him?"

"Positive. He told the man on the phone that he hadn't searched thoroughly yet, so I think he was looking for something or someone, but not me. He said it wasn't supposed to be and then let his sentence fall off. I wonder if he meant it wasn't supposed to be me."

"He could've broken into the wrong cabin, I suppose," Brendan said unconvincingly.

She jutted out her chin. "You sound like you don't believe me."

He said nothing but kept watching her, probably waiting for her to speak. To tell him what she was holding back. The only thing she was keeping from him was Shawn, and she wouldn't mention him because she had no proof he was involved.

"Let's suppose he really *was* looking for you." Brendan sat back and rested his hands on the counter. "Is there anyone in your life who might want to do you harm?"

"Harm *me*?"

"You seem surprised."

"I am. I mean, I don't get out of the house much except to run errands and go to church, so I really don't interact with people."

"You don't work?"

She shook her head.

"What about your husband?"

"He died a year ago."

"I'm sorry. That's rough." His voice had softened, and his warm, comforting tone wrapped around her. "This may sound insensitive, but I have to ask. If your husband is no longer supporting you, then how is it that you don't have to work?"

He was right, it was insensitive, but she'd answer anyway. "There was no big life insurance policy, if that's what you're getting at. We're simply trying to live off social security survivor benefits so I can continue to stay at home and care for Karlie. She has some health issues. For the moment things are working out, but it's looking like I'll need to get a job soon."

He flipped the notepad closed. "Okay, that's good for now, but please keep trying to think if there's anyone who might want to attack you. Unless there's something else you want to tell me, I need you to change clothes. Bag the ones you're wearing to preserve any evidence for our forensic staff."

"Okay," she said.

"And you mentioned scratching your attacker. I'll need to scrape your nails for DNA." She frowned, but he went on, "While you change, I'll look for something to put the cells in. You can put your clothes in a clean garbage bag."

She nodded, feeling wooden and stiff, like she'd exercised for hours. She turned to the cabinet under the sink and pulled out a white trash bag. "I'll be right back."

She stopped on the way to the master bathroom to check on Karlie then ripped off her clothing. Pain stabbed her body in so many locations she couldn't name them all, but she kept moving. The sooner she got this done, the sooner life could go back to normal. Normal. Ha! The terror of the night would live with her forever. And these clothes? She had no money to replace the jeans and sweater, but she'd never wear them again. So she was glad someone was taking them.

When she got back to the kitchen, Brendan had an envelope lying on the counter labeled with her name, the date, and time. The pocket knife he'd used to free her was in his hand. She set her clothing bag next to him, and he tied it closed.

"Your nails, next." He held out his hand.

He was going to touch her. His hand on hers. She hesitated.

"I won't bite," he joked and pointedly looked at her hand.

He smiled, accentuating his full bottom lip. Great. Even harder to ignore him as a man. He wiggled his fingers. She placed her hand on his palm, and the warmth of his touch sizzled through her as expected. His head shot up, and a spark of interest flared in his eyes for a moment before he looked back down.

So, he felt it too. *Not good.* Something she'd have to work hard to guard against.

He placed her fingers over the paper and gently scraped. She looked down on his hair the color of dark chocolate. Thick and full too. What would it be like to slide her fingers through the slightly wavy strands?

Seriously? A man just attacked you, and all you can think about is how attractive this guy is.

He finished her last finger and sealed the envelope, his expression now as closed off and guarded as hers should be. "Let's take Karlie and leave before we disturb potential evidence."

"Leave?" Jenna's voice pitched up before she got it under control. "I can't drive back to Portland in this weather."

"You can't stay here." He put the notepad in his jacket pocket. "In fact, it would be prudent to have someone with you at all times until we resolve this. Your attacker must know you can identify him. If he's desperate enough, he'll come looking for you. You can spend the night with my family, and we'll figure this all out in the morning."

Her fingers drifted to her neck. To the cut from the knife. Small. Barely painful, but a reminder of the attack. Of the evil eyes glaring down at her. The knife raised, ready to plunge into her chest.

Desperate? Yeah, the creep was desperate. And right now, other than her daughter and this stranger named

Brendan—this kind, tough, handsome guy—she had no one else who cared if she lived or died.

~

Brendan hadn't expected an argument from Jenna when he offered to share the family's cabin with her for the night, but the fire in her eyes—a calm blue color like Mirror Lake, which he'd stumbled across on one of his favorite outdoor hikes—and her hands seated on generously curved hips told him she didn't care for his idea one bit. But she had nowhere else to go, not unless she wanted to risk a drive down treacherous mountain roads to Portland, and he certainly wasn't going to allow that.

"I realize we're complete strangers," he said, thinking that was the reason that made her hesitate. "But my parents are staying there so we won't be alone."

Her only response was to bite her lower lip.

"Look," he said. "There's no way I'm letting you get in a car to head down the mountain at this time of night. If you insist on leaving, then I'm driving."

"I make my own decisions," she said, a cold, hard stare replacing the hesitancy in her eyes.

"I know." He lowered his voice and stepped closer. "I'm just trying to help. It's your decision, and I guess I can't stop you." *But I can follow you to make sure you don't run into trouble.*

She sighed. "You're right. I'm overreacting. Obviously I can't take Karlie out on dangerous roads."

"But?"

She flipped her wavy blond hair—he picked up a reddish hue, not that he was looking—back and lifted her shoulders into a hard line. "But I don't take charity."

"Charity? Who said anything about charity? I'm just

25

offering you a place to stay for the night because there aren't any other options. You can take off the minute the roads are clear."

She watched him for a moment then shook her head. "You must think I'm a nutcase."

"Nutcase, nah. Cautious, yes. Which is a good thing. I like caution." He smiled and received a little half smile that brightened her face and gave her a vitality that he liked. "If my parents weren't there and you agreed to stay the night with me, I'd have lectured you on personal safety. But they *are* there, so it's all good."

"I suppose," she said, still waffling. Maybe she thought he was lying.

He had to seal the deal. "Hey, it's like this. If I go back and tell my mom where I've been and that I didn't bring you and Karlie home...man." Just the thought of her irritation and disappointment made his insides quake. "She'd shove me out the door and make me come looking for you. Don't make me go back out into the cold twice. Please." He smiled again, this time making sure she saw the humor and maybe she would lighten up.

"I guess I can't make you have to deal with that." Her half smile grew, and her face brightened. Her cheeks, dotted with freckles, lifted.

The smile hit him like a punch to the gut, and his brain pretty much refused to function. To find a coherent thought. She was beautiful on the outside with her pale complexion and cute freckles, but she had a radiance glowing from inside too. That was what was holding his interest, and he wanted to get to know her.

Really? He wanted to get to know a woman. No. Get to know *this* woman. He hadn't had any interest in a relationship for a while. Eleven months, precisely. Not since the incident.

Her smile evaporated, and her eyes narrowed. He stowed his thoughts and took a few steps back, garnering a raise of a delicate eyebrow. He'd gotten his way. She was coming home with him, but with his attraction to her, he wished he'd come up with another solution.

Focus on the swollen eye, not the one with the calming blue and long lashes blinking rapidly at you. The bruise reminded him of the damage to this beautiful woman. Damage inflicted by a man's fist. The raw red color was already turning purple. And her wrists. He'd look at them—at the raised red welts from the tape.

Rage erased all other feelings. How could a man attack a woman for any reason? Get mad at her. Maybe wish he could understand her, but hit her? Never.

He swallowed down his anger so he wouldn't make the situation worse. "Once the roads are passable, I'll request a medic so we can get that eye looked at."

"No." She pulled her shoulders even higher. "No. I'm fine, and I can't afford to pay an ambulance bill."

"But it's—"

"No! I'm grateful for your help here, but I insist. No ambulance."

Stubborn. He liked that. "Okay, then, let's get out of here. Why don't I carry Karlie, and maybe we won't wake her up."

"I don't..." She paused and bit her lip again. "That would be very kind of you."

And that was very diplomatic of you.

"Would you like to pack a bag?" he asked.

She shook her head. "We never had a chance to unpack."

"So, if it's okay with you, I'll carry Karlie, get the two of you settled in the cabin, and then I'll come back for your bags."

"I can take them."

"No way we're going to dig out your car to drive down there, and we're talking nearly a mile trek through some very deep snow."

"I'll manage." That iron resolve had returned, and his respect for her grew.

He only wished he could trust her. He wanted to. In fact, as a man, he did, but as a former law enforcement officer... He didn't, not completely. When he'd questioned her about knowing her attacker, she'd looked away from him.

A very common sign that meant she was withholding something. What, he had no idea. But he didn't like it. Not one bit. He would get to the bottom of whatever thought had made her turn away. He had to if he was going to keep her and that precious daughter safe.

3

Jenna stepped in the door of Brendan's cabin, and she instantly felt the room was alive with a feeling she couldn't put her finger on. The smell of pine and woodsmoke from a crisp fire filled the space. A tree with colored lights matched the one provided for Jenna at their rental, though colorful presents were stacked under this tree. Hers was bare. The room held the same furnishings, too, but the place just felt different. Better somehow.

Uncertain how to proceed, she glanced at Brendan, who had his focus on Karlie, and she could swear she saw immense sadness. Why, she had no idea. She hardly knew him, but she felt a burning desire to find out what could put such a pained look on his face. Did he have children? A daughter?

She glanced at his hand. No ring and no sign of ever having worn one. So likely not married. Didn't preclude him having a child.

He suddenly glanced up, a shutter covering the sadness, and she could swear she saw gears shift in his brain before he smiled at a tall, slender woman with blond hair spiked in short little tufts lounging on the sofa. She came to her feet and rushed across the room.

"Brendan...son? What's happened?" she asked, worry etched in the lines around her eyes.

Brendan introduced Jenna. "My mother, Peggy Byrd."

Mrs. Byrd leaned closer to look at Jenna's eye. "Oh, my word. We need to get some ice on that eye." She took the bags from Jenna's hands and dropped them on the floor. With an iron arm around Jenna's shoulders, Mrs. Byrd led her toward the kitchen.

Jenna let herself be led, not sure at all what his mother had planned. She didn't question why her son had brought home a stranger and child in the night—the week of Christmas, no less.

"Brendan, get that young lady into bed while I tend to Jenna. She can sleep in yours and Aiden's room."

Jenna wanted to ask who Aiden was, but she kept quiet and let Brendan's mother take charge. For the moment—just for the moment—Jenna would relax and let someone else take over.

"Have a seat at the island." Mrs. Byrd released Jenna's hand. She retrieved a dishcloth and filled it with a Ziploc bag of ice, then rushed back across the room and handed it to Jenna.

She caught a hint of vanilla coming from the pleasant woman.

"Thank you, Mrs. Byrd." Jenna placed the icy coolness over the bruise and stifled a moan at the sharp pain slicing into her head.

"Please. Call me Peggy." The woman took a seat next to Jenna and gestured at the family room, where a man sat open-mouthed. "That's my husband, Russ. Our whole family should be here by now, but the snow kept the others home. Hopefully they'll get here tomorrow."

Jenna was just about to ask for more information on their family, but Brendan came into the room.

He joined them, resting his hands on the island. "Karlie's still out like a light."

"Thank you," Jenna said.

"Now, how about you tell me what's going on?" Peggy spoke to Brendan, patting the barstool next to her.

Jenna opened her mouth to speak, but Brendan took over before she could. He told the story of her attack, adding details that Jenna would've glossed over. The last thing she needed was these people feeling sorry for her and thinking she was a charity case. She'd had enough of that after Toby left them in debt. With no money to pay the mortgage, they'd lost their house and lived in a shelter until she took a few temp jobs and saved up enough money to get into their modest one-bedroom apartment.

Peggy tsked and shook her head as Brendan talked. When he finished, Peggy spun. "You poor thing. You must still be terrified."

Jenna wanted to admit she was, but she needed to be strong. "I'm okay."

"She's handled this like a real trooper." Brendan caught her eye and smiled.

The same smile as back at her cabin. It took the tough guy and made him seem vulnerable. Add that to the sadness she'd seen earlier, and she really wanted to know what made him tick.

"Well, sweetheart," Peggy said. "You don't have to worry about a thing while you're here. Let's get you settled in front of the fireplace with a cup of cocoa, then you can hop into your pajamas and get some sleep." She took Jenna's hand and tugged her to her feet.

Jenna didn't even try to refuse. Peggy was a take-charge person, just like her son. A trait that didn't bother Jenna with Peggy, but Brendan? That was another story. He was a man. A pushy, I-want-my-way man. Just like Toby had been. She may have thought Brendan seemed trustworthy, a good guy, but that was as far as she'd let her feelings go. She'd never return to a life of servitude like she'd had with Toby. Never. Toby had proved she could never know the real man lurking under a kind exterior.

Peggy cleared an assortment of board games from a comfy club chair and, after officially introducing her husband, whose smile reminded Jenna of his son's, she pointed to a chair. "Now you sit here, sweetie, and I'll get that cocoa going." She turned to the men. "And don't you pester her with questions. She's had enough for tonight, poor thing." She scurried into the kitchen, passing Brendan, who came to lean against the stone fireplace.

"Yes." Brendan met Jenna's gaze. "She's always like that."

"What?" Jenna asked.

Brendan's eyes creased with laughter. "I could see the questions in your eyes. Mom's a take over and ask questions later person."

"Nothing wrong with that," Russ said with a twinkle in his eyes.

"I didn't say there was."

"Why don't you come in here and put on some Christmas music," Peggy called from the kitchen. "The green CD. I'm sure you'll like it, Jenna. It's a collection of songs from various singers that we've had since the eighties. It always says Christmas to me."

"And we play it nonstop." Brendan groaned as he went to the kitchen, where a portable CD player sat on the counter.

His mother playfully waved a hand in the air. "You still have that stuffed Christmas moose, so you're not one to talk."

"And no matter how much you want to get rid of

Mooseltoe, I'll have him until the day I die." He slipped an arm around Peggy's shoulders and pulled her into a hug. They looked so happy together that jealousy bit into Jenna's stomach, and she had to look away. She stared into the roaring fire, crackling and hissing, and listened to soft strains of *Silent Night* fill the space.

She'd sung carols as a child, but not at home. Only when her father wanted some time without a kid in tow and dropped her off at Sunday school. But Christmas itself? Other than when she'd sneaked off to church, it had always been a big disappointment. So were other holidays growing up. Just a reason for her dad to get drunk and abuse her mother. Jenna would never let Karlie suffer that way. She'd made sure her daughter had memorable holidays. Had a real chance to learn about God and grow in her faith. Had gifts and made special memories.

If not for winning the cabin vacation, this year would've been a bust in the gift department. But now what? They couldn't stay here after tonight. They'd have to head back to their apartment and spend the holiday without a tree and only the stocking presents for Karlie.

Tears pricked Jenna's eyes, but she wasn't going to cry. She kept her gaze on the fire, enjoying the warmth wrapping around her, and only looked away when Brendan came back.

Peggy brought in a plate of sugar cookies cut out in Christmas shapes and frosted in bright icing. "Jenna will bunk in the same room as Karlie, and I'll reassign everyone tomorrow."

He turned to Jenna. "I'll take your bags to the room."

"Thank you," she replied, knowing with the set to his expression, it was useless to mention that she could carry her own bags.

"Thought you could use a little more sugar with your

33

cocoa." Peggy smiled sweetly then turned to her husband. "Do I need to ask if you want cocoa and cookies?"

Russ caught his wife's hand. "Only if you've suddenly gone senile and can't remember who I am."

"Oh, I know who you are all right." She laughed, then kissed the top of her husband's head and hummed on the way back to the kitchen.

"I'll help, Mom," Brendan said from the doorway.

They made quick work of filling trays with steaming mugs of cocoa, bringing them into the family room, and taking a seat. Jenna selected a Christmas themed mug, enjoyed the warmth permeating her fingers, and slowly sipped the rich chocolatey cocoa. More than once, she caught Brendan's gaze lingering on her. Questions lingered in his expression, but she was thankful he didn't interrogate her in front of his parents.

They started talking about board games, and she sat back to observe the banter among the three of them. She felt like she'd been transported to an alternate universe, one where families were perfect and life was trouble-free. But she was smart enough to know this family had to have their share of troubles or Brendan wouldn't have looked so sad. Maybe these people were using joy to cover something up. Like they were trying hard to hide something. If that was true, they were very good actors. Their joy felt genuine.

"Come on, love." Peggy stood and held out her hand to her husband. "With a day of skiing tomorrow, we should all be getting to bed."

"Don't need to tell me twice." Russ stood. "I can't wait to hit that fresh powder. *If* the slopes are open after this crazy storm."

Peggy frowned at Russ then looked at Brendan. "Can you clean up and put away any cookies you don't scarf down before you go to bed?"

"Sure. I won't be up long enough to eat them all."

"A first then." His mother laughed. "Jenna, your room is the second one on the left."

Jenna took the hint and got up to go to bed.

"Wait, Jenna." The words shot out of Brendan's mouth, garnering an inquisitive look from the others. "I wanted to have a word with you."

"Okay." She sat back down.

"In private." Brendan arched an eyebrow and made shooing motions at his parents, who were still lingering.

Peggy looked like she didn't want to leave, but she eventually followed her husband out of the room. Jenna had to smile at Peggy's protective mother-bear instinct. Jenna felt the same way about Karlie.

"What's so funny?" Brendan moved to a chair closer to her.

"Nothing funny. I just like your mom. She's so protective of you."

That made Brendan frown.

"You don't like that?"

"It's fine. Most of the time, anyway. But my dad recently needed a kidney transplant. Since then, Mom's taken things to extremes in the protective department."

Ah, maybe that was the reason for this guy's sadness. "That must have been so hard for all of you."

"My older brother, Aiden, donated his kidney, so all's good. But she sure doesn't want him to ski tomorrow if he makes it up to the cabin. I don't either. One wrong fall and..." He shrugged, but his sadness returned, pouring from his eyes like a physical ache before he pulled his shoulders back and cleared it away. "I wanted to ask you a few additional questions about the intrusion."

"Okay," she said, oddly feeling hurt that he wouldn't

open up with her. She assumed his sadness related to his dad, but honestly, it seemed like more than that.

"I've been thinking about your attacker," he said. "Give me the exact words he used when he talked to you."

She thought back to the moment. To their discussion. "He said, 'it wasn't supposed to be...' and then the last of his sentence drifted off. I tried to clarify that he meant me, but he didn't confirm it."

"So, he could have been saying something else."

"Like what?"

"Like it wasn't supposed to be hard, or this cabin, or even this way."

She gave it some thought, his words playing over and over in her head. "I suppose he could've meant any of those things."

Brendan clasped his hands together. "Maybe he really did go to the wrong cabin, and we need to be looking at the owners of your place or even nearby renters."

"Sounds like a good plan."

"There won't be anyone in the rental office at this time of night, and the storm has really picked up so I can't get through to check on the others."

"You think the attacker came back to do the job the right way?"

"I doubt it, but you can never be too careful. I'll have the office check on the neighbors first thing in the morning and make sure everyone is okay, then I'll do a background check on them." He stood. "But now, we both need to get a good night's sleep."

Did she? Her brain said yes, but her heart said no. Question was, which one was she going to listen to?

36

Brendan stood on the front porch, the empty coffee cup in his hands filling with snow still falling. The cold flakes landed on his face and melted in little droplets. The sun was rising somewhere behind thick clouds, but he could only see hints of light and his breath puffing before him. The forecast called for the clouds to give way soon and the snow to stop. Radio reports said the roads were still impassable, but, thanks to a ski resort tram, his parents could go skiing as planned.

A yawn caught him, and he considered going back in for what would be his fifth cup of coffee. It was going to be a long day after a sleepless night on the couch. He could've slept in one of his brother's rooms since they hadn't arrived yet, but he'd wanted to be by the door, just in case the attacker had somehow seen him move Jenna and Karlie to this location.

Even if the couch had been comfortable, he wouldn't have slept. Not with his mind filled with thoughts of protecting Jenna and questions about the attack. So he'd stayed up to get everything down on paper. Once the main roads cleared, the duty sergeant would hand the case off to a detective, and Brendan would have the facts to pass along, and he could resume his vacation.

Or could he? Jenna still needed protecting. Even if she was right and the attacker had targeted her by accident, she'd seen his face. Not something he would likely leave alone. The county wouldn't have the manpower to assign a protective detail to her, so Brendan needed to be there for her and little Karlie.

But even if the sergeant *did* have the staff, Brendan wanted to be the one to keep them safe. He couldn't put a finger on why it seemed so important at the moment, but it was. Enormously. Thinking of not being there for them made his chest ache. Probably a holdover from his days in

Delta Force and as a deputy, when his life was all about service to others. Or from his mom and dad, who'd taught him and his siblings to live their faith.

The door opened, and Jenna stepped out, leaving prints in the snow that had fallen since he'd been standing outside. She held a large mug of black coffee, and a column of steam rose from the mug. She wore a blue parka with white furry trim around a hood that framed a very pretty face. A face marred with a harsh purple-and-green bruise surrounding her eye and a red welt on her cheek.

His anger rose, and he had to swallow to keep it in check.

She stepped up next to him and stared ahead. He waited for her to speak, running his gaze over her, pausing at her hand. She no longer wore her wedding ring, but there was a telltale dent where it had once sat.

"I'm not leaving today, am I?" Sadness lingered in her tone.

"I'm afraid we're snowed in. The latest reports say it'll let up by afternoon, so the roads could be clear tomorrow."

She took a sip of her coffee. "Forecasters didn't predict this much snow."

"They're often wrong," he answered, their meaningless chitchat getting to him. "Time for me to get back to work."

"Back to it? What time did you get up?"

"Early," he said and left it at that. "I've called the complex office. They require a warrant to release the owner's and renters' information, but they're checking on the other residents to be sure they're all safe. I'll get going on that warrant, and then I'll make a few calls."

She glanced at him. "Calls for what purpose?"

"First, I want to find out if other home invasions occurred in the area."

Her eyebrow went up. "Sounds like you've really thought this through."

"Couldn't sleep last night." He turned to face her and waited until she looked up at him. "Before I do anything, I have to ask a few more questions, and I need you to be completely honest with me."

"Okay."

"Yesterday. At your cabin. When you told me what the attacker said, you looked away like you were hiding something. I need to know what that something is."

"I..." She bit her lip, something he'd noticed her do several times now. "You really must've been a good deputy."

"The best." He grinned to lessen her unease, but he didn't miss the fact that she'd sidestepped his question. "So, you didn't tell me the truth, then?"

"I told you the truth."

Right. The answer he'd expected, but his gut said she was still keeping something from him. So he waited for her to speak. A tactic he'd learned in law enforcement. Remain silent and guilty people were often so nervous they blurted out the truth.

He eyed her for extra measure.

She didn't say a word. Just sipped her coffee.

Okay, maybe he was wrong. Maybe she was on the up-and-up. He'd still keep his eyes open for what she was hiding. Maybe hiding something like Tristen did. Because secrets like that could end up with someone dead.

For now, he'd move on. "Did you think of anyone who might want to harm you?"

She shook her head hard, the snow that had fallen on her reddish-blond hair whispering away. "No...no. Not me."

"Are you sure? Maybe someone you owe money to?"

She took a long breath and let it out, the moisture tinting the air white. "I've got debts to pay off. Big ones, thanks to

Toby. Since I didn't work, I didn't think I had a right to question him about how he managed our money. And besides, there was always enough for whatever we needed. But then he died, and I found out he'd taken out a second mortgage and forged my name on the documents. Worse yet, he was seriously behind on both mortgages. Without his salary, I didn't have any money to make the payments, so we lost the house. I'm working on paying off all of his debt now, but it's slow going."

Brendan fisted his hands. How could a man leave his wife in a situation like that? Sure, he understood that people had to go into debt at times due to things beyond their control, but it sounded like Toby might've been living beyond his means. And now, Jenna was stuck with picking up the pieces.

"That must've been hard to go through while mourning the loss of your husband," he said, working hard to hide his anger over her situation.

"The hardest part was seeing Karlie's disappointment when she had to leave her room and swing set in the backyard. But I tried to make the best of it." Jenna closed her eyes for a moment. "Helped me get over losing Toby when I found out he died in the arms of another woman. Turns out he'd been cheating on me for a year."

Another strike in the guy's book for Brendan. "You've been through a lot."

She met his gaze and held it. "You don't know the half of it, but let's just say that having this guy attack me when I'd won the holiday at this cabin was a low blow. I wanted Karlie to have a good Christmas, but now..."

His anger climbed up his throat, and he had to swallow hard to keep his fury out of his voice. "You can stay here as long as you want."

"I'll be gone as soon as the roads clear."

Her decision didn't sit well with him. "That's not a good idea. You need protection. We can provide that for you."

"We?"

"My brothers and I. We do this for a living. We can keep you both safe."

"No." She shook her head hard, her wavy hair flying in all directions. "You know I can't pay you, and I won't take—"

"Charity. I know. You said that before. But you need to think of Karlie. Her life must be worth accepting help under any condition."

Her full lips dipped in a frown. "You don't play fair."

"I'm not playing, Jenna." He locked gazes with her. "You're still in danger, and you need someone to be with you and Karlie twenty-four/seven. If not us, then someone else. But on behalf of my brothers, I'm offering to provide that protection until we find your attacker and to investigate at no cost. We won't stop until he's put behind bars and can't hurt either of you again."

She swallowed, drawing his attention to her delicate throat with the harsh red nick from the knife. The anger over her attack raged full in his gut again. What was with all of this anger? Sure, he hated it when a woman or child was threatened, but he was almost taking this personally. It was just a job.

"You're right. I'd be thankful for your help." She held his gaze, but her intensity wavered. "You said 'investigate.' How can you even begin to do that when we're stuck up here in the snow?"

"I have contacts in Portland who'll do some leg work for me, but before I get started, is there anything else I need to know?"

"About what?"

"You. Your past. Anyone else who might be targeting you."

"I've told you everything you need to know."

"You're sure?"

"Seriously, what's with this third degree?" She crossed her arms. "I'm not lying to you, but I get the distinct impression that you think I am."

"All my years in law enforcement have left me suspicious," he said, which was true, but after Tristen lied to him the week before she died, his trust level was at an all-time low, especially when it came to beautiful women.

"You don't have to be that way with me. I won't lie to you."

"Okay, then." He held up his ice-cold mug. "I could use another cup."

She nodded. "I should head in too. Karlie will need breakfast."

He opened the door and waited for her to enter. She set down the mug, shook the snow off her coat, and hung it on a peg by the door. Her eyes were sparkling, and her cheeks rosy from the cold. Despite the bruise and welt, her beauty shone through.

"Just one thing." She lifted her chin. "I'm not letting you do this investigation alone. I need to be involved, please don't make those calls without me."

Far be it from him to stand in her way. So many things had gone wrong in her life, and he wouldn't make things worse for her. Though honestly, it would be better for both of them if he worked alone. Alone and far, far away from those eyes that looked straight through him while at the same time sending his heart racing.

4

Jenna didn't wait for Brendan to hang up his coat but turned to his mother, who was in the kitchen taking a raspberry cream-cheese coffee cake from the oven. The sweet smell saturated the air, and Jenna's stomach rumbled. She'd already asked Peggy for the recipe and would make it for a special occasion for Karlie as she loved raspberries.

"I'll just check on Karlie," she said so his mother wouldn't think she was rude as she scurried through the room and away from Brendan.

She could feel Peggy's questioning gaze following her. Jenna really didn't need to check on her daughter playing in the den with Russ, but she couldn't look Brendan in the eye. She hadn't lied to him. Not really. Sure, she hadn't told him about Shawn, and he could be the key to this whole intrusion. But she didn't have one bit of proof that the incident was related to her brother. And no matter how far Shawn had gone down the wrong path in life, he was still her brother, and she owed it to him to give him a chance to explain before she dragged him into this mess.

She stopped short of the door to the den and tapped Shawn's name in her phone. The call rang and rang. Not surprising. He often partied in the night and was rarely awake in the morning.

"It's Jenna," she said after the beep. "Call me the minute you get this message. It's urgent."

She wished she'd gotten ahold of him, but she would keep trying. She stowed her phone and put on an overly bright smile for her daughter, who was concerned about Jenna's black eye. Jenna had made up a story about falling while getting the wood, and Karlie seemed to buy it.

Jenna went into the den. Russ could've knocked Jenna's socks off when he volunteered to play Legos with Karlie. He'd said their daughter, Sierra, had recently gotten married, and he was hoping for grandkids soon. But it'd been so long since he'd had a small child at home that he was out of practice.

Jenna found the pair seated on an area rug, bent over a colorful pile of Legos. Karlie's blond head was perched next to Russ's salt-and-pepper buzz cut. With the way he carried himself and the haircut, she suspected he was former law enforcement too.

Karlie looked up. "Look, Mommy. We're building a cabin just like this one. Even has a Christmas tree."

Jenna squatted beside them. "It looks just like it."

She frowned. "Wish we could've stayed in our own cabin. I liked our tree better."

"But if we *had* stayed there, you wouldn't get to play with Mr. Byrd."

"And I'm the best ever." Russ grinned, reminding her so much of Brendan that she didn't know if hiding out here was any better than facing Brendan.

"I s'pose." Green brick in hand, Karlie looked at him. "But you don't do the bricks right all the time. I haveta tell you how."

Jenna knew Karlie's dissatisfaction was more about

Karlie wishing they could have the extravagant Christmas seasons they'd had when Toby was alive than leaving the other cabin, one more reason for her mountain of debt. But that was something to think about later. Her attacker and how they would get off this mountain safely were far more pressing matters.

She stood and ruffled Karlie's hair, sending up a whiff of her favorite strawberry shampoo. "I'm going to go help get breakfast ready. I'll call you when it's finished."

"Then can we go skiing?" She peered up at Jenna, her eyes hopeful.

"We'll see." Jenna had promised Karlie a day on the bunny slope learning to ski. Jenna didn't want Karlie to know about the attack, so she couldn't explain that she needed to stay here to help Brendan find the attacker. She would have to figure out a way to tell her sweet daughter that skiing was out of the question. And Jenna had to make sure that the others didn't discuss the attack in front of Karlie either.

"Guess I should offer to help too." Russ got up. "See you in a little bit, munchkin."

Karlie's face screwed up in question, looking just like her father. "What's a munchkin?"

Russ smiled at her. "An adorable little girl like you."

Karlie smiled and threw her arms around Russ's leg to hug him. He blushed but scooped her up for a hug. He was going to make such a wonderful grandfather. She wished Karlie had loving grandparents, but they'd all passed away.

Jenna left the room and joined Brendan and his mother. Their conversation stilled, and uncomfortable silence filled the air.

Russ joined them, his gaze going between his family members, as if he was picking up on whatever it was Jenna

45

was missing. She didn't have time to figure out what she'd walked into.

"Before Karlie gets out here," she said, taking advantage of the lull in the conversation. "I'd like to ask that no one mentions the attacker in front of her."

"Russ is the most likely one to spill the beans." Peggy gave him a pointed look. "Do your best, okay?"

He shook his head. "I can keep a secret."

Brendan snorted.

Russ mocked offense. "Well, I can."

"We know, dear." Peggy grinned then clapped her hands. "Now, let's get the French toast made so we can hit the slopes."

"French toast and skiing on the same day." Brendan rubbed his hands together. "What's better than that?"

"I don't know." His mother grinned. "Becoming a grandma would beat it hands down."

"*That* is no secret for sure," Brendan said.

They laughed, and Russ grabbed Peggy in a hug. This was the kind of marriage Jenna had dreamed of. Instead, she'd gotten a sullen man who rarely talked and made all the decisions, ruling over them and claiming he was only doing as the Bible said. Being the man in charge of his household.

Brendan poured a cup of coffee. "I'll be taking a pass on skiing to start an investigation into Jenna's attacker."

Russ held out his cup for Brendan to fill. "Thought you were on vacation."

"Never mind his vacation," Peggy said. "We raised him right, and that means that if someone needs his help, he's going to offer it." She looked at Brendan. "We'll be at the lodge all day. Maybe you can join us later."

"We'll see." He filled Jenna's cup without asking her.

She wanted coffee, but she didn't like him making decisions for her, no matter how small. She'd had enough of that the twelve years she was married.

"To tide you over until the French toast is ready." Peggy slid a platter with the gooey coffeecake to Jenna. "Of course, you and Karlie will join us for skiing."

She could honestly say she would love to spend the day with this family. They were so upbeat and cheery, and Jenna loved their sparring because it was good-natured and not filled with unspoken animosity like she'd shared with Toby. It would be good for her to see more of their successful marriage to prove that the love Jenna had always dreamed of really existed and their behavior wasn't just show. Plus, Karlie was expecting to ski. But, if Jenna had learned anything in life, it was that you couldn't always have what you wanted and had to make the best of things.

She picked up a small piece of the coffee cake. "I appreciate the offer, but I want to help Brendan with the investigation. I'll give Karlie something to keep her busy in the bedroom while I work on the investigation."

Peggy came around the island and took Jenna's hand. "I know this is important to you, and I won't argue, but would you consider letting Karlie join us? I'll personally stay on the bunny slope and keep my eye on her all day."

"Then she won't have any fun," Brendan muttered with a laugh.

Peggy tweaked his nose. "Ignore my misguided son. I'll make sure Karlie has fun."

Jenna was so tempted. "It's enough that we're already invading your holiday. I don't want to impose even more."

"Please let her come with us," Peggy said. "I taught all my boys how to ski and, if she doesn't know how, I would love to teach her too. If you don't mind."

"It would be wonderful if Karlie got to go skiing like I

promised." Jenna looked at Brendan, who was scowling. "Is it okay with you?"

"Sure," he said, but his body language sent a different message.

Why would he possibly want Karlie to stay here? Did Brendan not want to be alone with her? *Wait, alone.* They were going to be alone.

Peggy clapped her hands again. "Then it's settled. Karlie will spend the day with us. If the two of you finish your work early, you'll come up to the slopes too. And maybe the rest of the family will be able to get here by then too."

"One thing you need to know," Jenna said, keeping her focus on Peggy. "Karlie has juvenile idiopathic arthritis. She hasn't had a flare-up recently, but you never know why or when one will happen. She doesn't like to tell me when she doesn't feel good because she knows I'll make her rest. So if you could keep an eye out for her getting tired, I would appreciate that."

"Oh, my," Peggy said. "That just breaks my heart. Of course I'll keep an eye out for that. Anything else I should watch for?"

"Limping or running a fever. If that happens, the joints in her fingers will likely swell too."

"The poor little thing. I'm going to add her and you to my prayers. It's got to be so hard to see your child suffer like that." Peggy put her arm around Jenna and squeezed. "We'll take good care of her. I promise."

"Thank you." Jenna smiled up at Peggy.

"Now, to get that French toast going." She grabbed a Christmas themed apron lying on the counter. "Russ, you heat the griddle and I'll get the batter mixed."

Peggy pulled out a barstool and took Jenna's hand. "And you, honey, will have a seat and relax. After all, you have to spend the day with Gruffy Brendan." She winked at him.

"Nicknamed by his siblings when he was crabby. A well earned name."

"I'm not crabby."

"Then why the frown?"

"I'm not frowning."

"Yes, you are," Peggy and Russ said in unison.

"I'm gonna get started on my work." Shaking his head, he took his coffee to the family room.

He obviously wanted to be alone with his thoughts. Jenna would give him until after breakfast to think through whatever he was pondering. Once Karlie and his parents left for skiing, Jenna would be at his side, demanding to be included in the investigation.

Thankfully the ski resort ran their snow tram through nearby neighborhoods or Brendan's parents would never have made it through the snowdrifts that Brendan was plowing through toward Jenna's rental cabin. He, and Jenna right beside him, needed to search the area for the knife as it was the strongest lead they could find.

They hadn't been out long yet, and his face was already chilled from the sharp wind, and he was having a hard time breaking through the drifts of powdery snow. They were almost up to Jenna's thighs. He would suggest she walk behind him to take advantage of the space he'd cleared, but he wanted to be able to see her at all times.

His phone dinged. He dug it out and glanced at the screen, his heart dropping. "Oh, wow."

"What's wrong?" Jenna asked, her words coming out between labored breaths, but she kept on battling the snow.

"One of my contacts found another recent home invasion in the metro area. Was a few weeks ago, but the description of the perpetrator sounds like the guy who attacked you."

She glanced up at him. "Did anyone get hurt?"

Brendan hated to answer, but she needed to know the truth. "A guy was killed. Thomas Steele. He's the brother of a Portland police officer I know. I worked an investigation with her once."

Breathing hard, Jenna's steps slowed. "Do you really think he was killed by my attacker?"

"Not sure, based on the info in the text. My guy is trying to get any additional details."

"And I don't suppose you'd want to bother his sister at a time like this."

"Not until I have something that might link the crimes. Still, I'll keep it in the back of my mind as we work the investigation." He fired off a thank you response to his buddy and started walking again.

He could see from a distance that his temporary method to secure the cabin door had held. Even the biting winds last night hadn't blown it open. The snow had stopped falling an hour ago, and the sun broke through heavy clouds to glisten on the pristine white blanket. A gorgeous scene, but for Brendan, the sunshine didn't erase the horrible event that happened in this cabin last night.

He headed for the back yard, and the closer they came to the building, the more Jenna shivered. He stopped and looked her in the eyes. "Are you sure you want to do this?"

She nodded and lifted her chin. "I won't let the actions of a man dictate my life. Not ever again!"

Wow. That was a heated response. One he hadn't expected. There had to be a story behind her statement, but he wouldn't probe. At least not now. Later was another thing. They'd worked together all morning doing internet research and making phone calls and had gotten to know each other better. He really was coming to like and respect her. If he was ever tempted to date again, she'd be tops on his list. After that comment though, he doubted she was into dating anyone right now.

They moved around the cabin, and he stopped to face her. The sun glinted in his eyes, and he lowered his sunglasses from his head. "We'll start under the window and work in a grid pattern. Side-by-side, straight ahead, then turn and come back, so we know we've covered every inch. Got it?"

"Yes."

"If you find a place where the snow is too deep for you to reach the ground, just holler and I'll work the area."

"Was that a short joke?" she asked with sudden mischief in her eyes.

He had no idea how she'd switched from being terrified to joking, but he'd seen all morning long that she was trying hard not to let this situation derail her.

"Short joke? Nah. Just an observation." He chuckled.

She joined in, but her laughter was nervous, as if she was covering up her unease. He wanted to finish this job and get her back to his parents' cabin, where she felt safer.

"Let's get started," he said, and together they inched through the snow.

The recent snowfall came in at about twenty-five inches, but some of the drifts were four feet high. The powder soon covered their arms and chests and even Jenna's chin from bending forward and sweeping their hands through the snow.

"You said the sister of the guy who died is a cop, right?" she asked.

He nodded. "Londyn Steele. Her Dad was once a police officer too. He recently retired. Bighearted couple. Churchgoers. They would have given anyone the shirt off their backs, and this is what they got. A son murdered."

He stopped for a moment. "I have to wonder where God is in all of this. I mean, the Steeles are amazing people. I know they have several children. All grown-ups now, but still, how are they handling this?"

"We can't always figure out how or why God works," she said with conviction. "My pastor keeps telling me God doesn't give us what we can handle. He helps us handle what we're given."

He shook his head. "Easy to say, but life is hard. Some days very hard."

"I don't think it's easy by any means. I struggle every day with things thrown my way." She watched him with such intensity that her gaze felt like a physical touch.

She brushed the snow from her chin, but her glove was covered with fluffy powder and only made it worse. She pulled off her glove and used her hand. "Does your comment have something to do with the look I saw on your face last night?"

"What look?"

"When we got to your parents' cabin. You looked really sad."

He thought back to their arrival. He'd glanced at the tree and remembered last Christmas without Tristen. He'd thought he'd learned to hide his feelings to keep his parents from worrying about him and ruining this year's celebration, but maybe not. "You caught that, huh?"

"Guess I could be a good detective too." She smiled.

He didn't feel like smiling back or sharing his thoughts.

"It's okay," she said. "You don't have to talk about it if you don't want to."

Her wounded gaze made him feel bad for keeping quiet. "I was thinking about how you trusted me to bring you to my parents' cabin. Then I saw the Christmas tree. My girlfriend died last year around Christmas. Unlike you, Tristen put her trust in the wrong guy, and he killed her."

Jenna shoved her hand in her glove and looked at him. "What happened?"

He resumed searching to keep her from seeing how much Tristen's loss still affected him. Not in a romantic way. He'd come to terms with that loss, but in the way that a guy feels when he failed to protect a woman he cared for. "We'd been dating for a couple of months when she showed up at my place with a bruise on her cheek. She said she'd fallen in the shower and hit a grab bar. I believed her. I didn't know her prior boyfriend was violent and that he'd tried to get back together with her. She turned him down. He got mad and hit her. She probably didn't tell me about it because she knew I'd take the guy's head off." He stared ahead at the mounds of glimmering snow.

"When she went home that night, he was waiting for her on the stairway outside her apartment. According to the boyfriend, she said she didn't want to be with him. He slammed a fist into her jaw, and she fell backward down a flight of stairs. Broke her neck. She held onto life for two days in the hospital while I prayed nonstop for her to make it. She didn't."

"I'm so sorry, Brendan." Jenna pushed through the snow and touched his arm, but it didn't thaw the anger and grief that was as frozen in his heart as the miles and miles of snow surrounding them.

He looked at Jenna then. "If only she'd told me the truth. I would've insisted on watching out for her, and she'd be alive."

Jenna's eyes drew together, and her forehead furrowed below her knit cap. "This is why you were so adamant last night about me coming with you, and this morning about me telling you everything."

He nodded. "And it's why I don't trust very many people anymore. People lie. I saw it all the time when I was in law enforcement, but with Tristen, it was personal."

"You were dealing with an unusual group of subjects in law enforcement. People who would do anything to stay out of jail."

"Tristen wasn't facing jail time." He clenched his fists. "I should've known she was keeping something from me. I should've followed her. Watched out for her."

Jenna stepped closer and looked up at him. "You couldn't watch her twenty-four/seven for the rest of her life. That's God's job."

"So tell me this." He locked his gaze on her. "Where was God when this guy beat her up? When she laid in that hospital bed for days? He sure wasn't with Tristen, and He hasn't been with me since then. Of that, I'm certain."

5

Hypocrite.

Who did Jenna think she was, telling Brendan that he needed to trust God to look out for people when Jenna felt the same way he did? Where had God been when she was attacked? When Karlie was diagnosed with a chronic illness? During Jenna's horrible marriage?

Sure, Jenna didn't suffer physically, but God could've heard her cries and stopped the mental anguish she'd endured long before Toby's death. He could heal Karlie. And Toby didn't have to die, did he? He didn't have to leave them penniless. She and Karlie didn't have to become homeless, living in a shelter, until she started receiving her benefits.

Jenna had hit rock bottom in that shelter. She'd called out to God then. Day and night. Especially at night when she'd held Karlie in her arms and tears poured out over their situation. But like Brendan, she hadn't felt God's presence. And if last night was any indication, He was still silent. Meant everything was up to her, and the weight of carrying such a burden was dragging her down.

She and Brendan had so much in common. Both had

experienced great difficulty, and both felt God hadn't responded. Maybe He'd put them together for that very reason. To help each other figure things out.

Is that it? Is that Your plan?

Brendan had started sweeping through snow with a renewed sense of urgency and she pawed through it next to him, hearing only the whisper of the powdery flakes and nothing from God. She knew He wasn't an on-demand God like so many things in life today—open the internet and order up your answers to your problems and get them instantly. But it had been years since she believed He was hearing her.

Brendan suddenly stood up, his gaze alert. "Do you hear that?"

"What?" she asked, her heart kicking into high gear.

"A truck." His hand drifted to the gun he'd holstered at his waist. "Maybe a snowplow. Let's go see."

"But our search," she said.

"It'll be here when we get back, and it's perfectly obvious where we moved the snow so we can pick up right where we left off. Stay in the same path we took earlier to disturb as little of the scene as possible." He gestured for her to go first.

She didn't want to argue more. Sure, she didn't like being told what to do, but this man knew how to keep her safe, and if he wanted her to come with him, she would. She followed the footsteps toward the road, and he was right behind her.

By the time they rounded the corner of the cabin, a large snowplow pushing away mounds of snow had slowed on the road, the diesel engine idling loudly until the motor stilled and two men slid down. A black SUV stopped behind it, and two women and three men piled into the snow. All dressed in snow gear, they surveyed the area.

"No way," Brendan said from behind her. "I can't believe they made it up here."

"They?" Jenna pivoted and was surprised to find him standing so close.

"My siblings," he said, sounding proud.

"Did you know they were coming today?"

"They were supposed to be here last night, but the storm kept them away. I figured they'd get here as soon as the roads were cleared. Didn't figure they'd bring their own snowplow." A genuine smile crossed his face. "Let's go welcome them to the neighborhood."

For some reason, she was nervous about meeting them. If they were anything like Brendan or his parents, they'd be nice and welcoming, but she felt an overwhelming desire for them to like her.

He gestured at the path, and they eased through the remaining snow to the road. The group stood watching, their gazes sharp and appraising, reminding her of the way Brendan had acted when he'd questioned her.

Brendan cocked his head. "I wasn't expecting you before the roads were plowed."

"We couldn't risk losing evidence." The woman with blond hair and bangs shifted her focus to Jenna.

This woman sounded pleasant enough, but honey-brown eyes locked on Jenna with an intimidating force. The urge to back off hit Jenna, but she stepped forward instead.

"You must be Jenna. I'm Sierra." She clamped a hand on Brendan's arm. "This big lug's only sister and trace evidence expert at the Veritas Center."

She jutted out a hand to Jenna, her grip tight, but Jenna held her own, earning a look of respect from Sierra.

"Let me introduce the rest of the family." Sierra moved back to the ones who'd gotten out of the SUV with her and placed her arm around a very intense dark-haired man. "This is my husband, Reed. He's an FBI agent."

With his inky-black hair and wide jaw, he fit in with the Byrd brothers quite well.

"Nice to meet you," he said and smiled.

She smiled and was going to say something but Sierra moved on.

"And next is Aiden's fiancée, Harper. Take pity on her and Reed, as they chose to join our crazy family. The rest of us had no choice."

Harper had reddish brown hair that fell in soft waves to her shoulders, and she wrinkled her nose. "You can't help who you love." She laughed, and so did the others.

Sierra moved on to a guy who looked a lot like Brendan. "Our parents did us a favor and named the boys in alphabetical order. This is Clay. Before they started Nighthawk Security, he was an ICE agent."

"Nice to meet you." He smiled but it seemed like he had to dig deep to find it.

"And next we have Erik. He's a former Portland police officer." Despite his confident stance, his sandy blond hair—the same color as Sierra's—made him look more like a beach bum than a cop.

"Hi." He planted his feet a little wider apart.

Sierra moved down the line to the guys from the plow truck and tapped the arm of a man who looked gruff and world-weary. He was the only guy whose hair covered his collar, where the others had short, crisp cuts.

"This is Drake. Former US Marshal. He specialized in fugitive recovery."

He gave her a brusque nod. Jenna could easily see him hunting down a fugitive.

"And last," Sierra said, moving to the next man and slipping her arm in the curve of his. "This is the old guy of the family. Aiden. He thinks he's the boss of us. Maybe because of his age or because he was an ATF agent for so long that he believes he's far superior to all of us."

Aiden was built with wide shoulders, square jaw, and dark hair. Jenna could easily see him flashing an ATF badge.

"Or," he said, knuckling Sierra on the head, "it's because I'm just plain smarter than the rest of you combined."

The group groaned, and Jenna knew she should be intimidated by such a strong show of force, but she felt something else coming from them too. The same warmth and genuineness that their parents had exhibited, and she immediately liked the Byrds. Even Drake, who still hadn't moved much.

"You were all in law enforcement," Jenna said.

"Except for me." Sierra's gaze softened. "Our dad is the best dad ever so we..."

Her voice broke and tears glistened in her eyes.

"That's okay, Sis." Aiden's arm went around his sister, but he kept his focus on Jenna. "Dad was a career deputy. Top-notch detective at the end. We wanted to honor him by following in his footsteps. Fortunately, there was a law enforcement job that fit each of our likes."

"Though there's no accounting for Sierra's love of every-thing science," Clay muttered, but a smile curved his mouth, and the heaviness from Sierra's eyes lifted.

Jenna hated that these strong people had almost lost their dad, but she was now certain that with all of them here, they would find her attacker, and he would be held accountable.

Aiden glanced at his watch. "I'd like to take a moment to review the case, but the light will be gone soon, so we should get to looking for that knife. We can process the cabin later."

Brendan widened his stance. "I'm acting as deputy for the county, and I can't let you into the cabin."

Aiden took a step forward. "We'll be going inside."

"Not until after Sierra processes the place from top to bottom." Brendan pulled back his shoulders and stared Aiden down. Jenna loved seeing Brendan holding his own, but at the same time, she hated his stern look. It reminded her of Toby's dictatorial ways.

Sierra stepped between them. "Let's leave that until later where we can talk somewhere warm and comfy. Right now, I need to get started inside."

"And I could use help searching for the weapon in all of this snow." Brendan didn't take his eyes off Aiden. "Jenna and I started a grid search by the cabin. Follow me back there, and we can continue."

"I brought wood like you asked to fix the door," Clay said. "You want me to do that first?"

Brendan nodded at his brother, who headed for the truck.

Reed took Sierra's gloved hands. "I know you'll be late, so I can walk Harper back to your parents' cabin if you'd like."

"That would be great." Sierra looked at Harper. "Assuming you want to go."

"Your mom hinted at cookies and cocoa by the fire, so you bet I want to go." She laughed.

"I'll need to keep the SUV for my equipment in the back," Sierra said. "But you're welcome to take the snow-plow." She laughed.

Reed shook his head and kissed her forehead. "My little smart aleck."

"Always." She wrinkled her nose.

"Want me to help carry?" he asked.

"Thanks, but I don't know what I'll need until I shoot the

scene." She gave him a kiss on his cheek then went to the back of the SUV, lifted out a camera, and hung the strap around her neck.

Aiden turned to Harper, his irritation gone and a beaming smile directed at her. "Do you want your bag now, or can it wait?"

"Wait." She clapped her hands on her arms and did a little dance. "I just need to get out of the cold."

"Now come on," he said. "You're an Olympic downhiller, and we just got back from Sweden, which was much colder. How can you not handle this little bit of cold?"

"Must be the thought of the hot cocoa and fire waiting for me." She gave him a quick kiss. "See you later."

She walked off with Reed, and Aiden joined Brendan. The tension clung between them as they returned to the back yard. She didn't know if this was normal or because Brendan was keeping Aiden out of the cabin. Everyone fell into line, and she smiled when she realized they were in alphabetical order. She assumed this behavior was left over from their childhood. They silently started parting the snow and inched forward.

Jenna glanced at Brendan to judge his mood. His movements were efficient and graceful. Even as a big guy, he moved with an ease that drew her to him. He had a confident swagger, and yet, she could remember the compassion and sorrow over the loss of his former girlfriend in his eyes. He seemed to be a great guy. The complete package, and she'd be lying if she said she didn't feel this buzz of awareness between them.

The group reached the end of the grid and turned to start back the other direction. Brendan looked up and caught her eye. A moment of unfettered attraction passed between them, and she sucked in a breath but couldn't seem to let it go.

How was she going to survive this investigation without falling for this guy when all she wanted right now, other than finding her attacker, was a happy daughter and a life free of complicated relationships?

~

Brendan watched the sun make a fast dash toward the horizon, blanketing the area in near darkness. They'd only just finished searching the outside but didn't find a lead. No red-bladed knife. No knife at all. Just a ton of snow, and Brendan's fingers were icy cold.

He looked at the team. "I'll check in with Sierra, and then we'll head down the hill."

"I need to get the snowplow off the road." Drake dug in his pocket for keys. "I'll have to run it up to the cul-de-sac to turn around."

Clay's forehead furrowed. "I need to load up the tools and leftover wood from the door. Then I'll follow Drake with the SUV."

After fixing the door, Clay had joined the search, and he seemed more somber than usual. Brendan needed to make time to check in with his brother to see if something happened.

Brendan faced Jenna. He wanted to keep her by his side, but taking her inside the cabin where she'd been attacked would be cruel. He would send Aiden, but Brendan wanted to see firsthand what Sierra had located. "Stay with Aiden. He'll watch out for you."

"I sure will," Aiden said, looking at Brendan like he wanted to be giving the orders. Their agency was so new that Aiden had tried to run every gig, and Brendan and his brothers had let him. At first. But now they were gradually finding their roles in the company.

Brendan took one last look at Jenna then went inside.

Sierra was on the floor by the chair where Jenna had been bound, taking close-up pictures of the duct tape.

"We're done out there," Brendan said. "Found nothing. You good to call it a day."

She shook her head. "I want to finish this place tonight."

"Then how about dinner with the family, and I'll come back up here afterward and be your lowly assistant."

"Are you kidding me? You in servitude to me?" She got up, stretching her back, her eyes twinkling. "I'm all over that."

She put on her ski jacket and slipped her arm in the curve of his. They walked to the door, and Brendan admired Clay's handiwork in repairing the doorjamb.

"Clay did a good job." She dug an official seal for the door out of one of her many bags on the floor.

"We can even use the lock again, which means you can keep your supplies safe, and we can protect the scene."

"Make sure to thank him. For some reason he's been kind of testy today." Sierra affixed the seal to the door, warning people to stay out.

"I noticed that. I'm going to check-in with him when we get back to the cabin."

"I'd ask him about it, but you guys just blow me off when I do."

"That's because you don't just ask, you pester us until we talk."

"Well," she said, "if you wouldn't all clam up—"

"Umm, hello, we're guys, in case you haven't noticed."

"I've noticed. Trust me."

Brendan looked at the road. "Deputies should be able to get through by morning."

"Don't be too sure. Not everyone has a snowplow." Sierra

winked, and the truck roared into action as if Drake knew they were talking about him.

Brendan looked at the vehicle. "How did you get that truck anyway?"

"Drake knew a guy."

Brendan swept the snow off the porch with his boots. "Of course. Drake knows a guy for almost every purpose."

Brendan started down the steps but, when Drake shifted into gear, Brendan heard another engine humming. He looked at the SUV, but Clay wasn't in the driver's seat yet. Brendan searched the road.

"What's up?" Sierra asked.

"Another engine running." He leapt from the porch and charged through the snow toward Jenna and Aiden.

"Take cover. Now!" Brendan yelled, but the closest cover was the SUV, and Clay had hopped in and was pulling away.

Aiden spun as if searching for the best solution.

"The tree," Brendan shouted. "Now! Move!"

Aiden grabbed Jenna's arm and started towing her toward a large pine tree.

Brendan had nearly reached them when a snowmobile roared out of the woods heading straight for Jenna. Brendan picked up speed, pulling his boots through the deep snow as fast as he could move.

He kept going. One struggling step at a time. But everything seemed to play out in slow motion in front of him.

The machine roared ahead. Aiden shoved Jenna behind the tree. The snowmobile raced in front of Brendan. He launched himself into the air, aiming for the helmeted driver. He hit the guy with his shoulder and reached out with his arms to drag the driver off the machine.

The driver hung on, and Brendan fell into the snow face first. He rolled to his back in time to see the driver wobble and nearly tip the snowmobile before righting the machine and roaring off.

Brendan watched in disgust as it zipped across the road and into the distance. No way he could catch the snowmobile. It plowed through drifts like a hot knife through butter and flew up a hill.

Jenna charged out from behind the tree, her eyes narrowed. "Are you all right?"

"Fine," Brendan said, though he wouldn't talk about his pride. That was smashed to pieces. He'd almost had him. Almost didn't cut it.

"I'll grab my camera and take pictures of the track," Sierra called out.

Brendan brushed off his face, the angry swatting of his hand mimicking his internal frustration, and pulled out his phone to snap some shots of his own. "To compare to the one last night."

"You think it was my attacker?" Jenna asked, sounding breathless.

"Same jacket. Size and build were right too. Helmet kept me from seeing his face, but it was him."

Jenna shuddered.

"We need to flag Clay down and let Jenna ride down to the cabin with him," Aiden said.

Brendan didn't need to be told how to protect Jenna, but his brother was right. "You go ahead and wave him down."

Aiden fired Brendan a testy look—likely irritated at being ordered to do anything by his younger brother—and strode out to the road. He and Aiden had learned in spec ops to embrace their alpha male side and had butted heads in the past, but not to this degree. Maybe Brendan was being too sensitive to his brother's attempt to direct things. Maybe Brendan was stifling Aiden's ideas. Brendan should watch for and control this crazy need to be in charge, as it would take everyone's help to keep Jenna safe.

"I don't know what I would've done without the two of you," she said, her gaze following Sierra.

His sister returned with her camera, placed markers by the tracks to indicate size, then started snapping pictures.

Brendan looked at Jenna. "We need to up our protection plan and not let you go outside anymore."

"You're going to confine me to the cabin until I can go home?" Her frown said she didn't like the plan.

"Yes, going home isn't a wise move, either. We have to assume your attacker has figured out where you live by now. We'll take charge of your movements to keep you and Karlie safe."

She eyed him. "I'm not going to give you carte blanche. I do have a life to live."

"But you didn't plan to be anywhere but here until after Christmas, right?"

"Right."

"So you can stay with my family until we find this guy."

"I'll think about it."

"Done." Sierra hung her camera around her neck and pocketed her markers. "Too bad you didn't have any markers last night so we had a scale comparison for the other track."

The plow truck rumbled down the road, the SUV behind it, and Aiden waved Clay to a stop.

"C'mon." Brendan took Jenna's arm and rushed her through the snow to get her into a vehicle and safely back to the cabin.

He practically shoved her into the back seat, and she gave him a pointed look. He backed out to see if Sierra was coming with them.

"Cool it," his sister whispered as she approached. "Your manhandling is scaring her even more."

He slid in next to Jenna and took a long look at her. She was gripping her gloved hands together and biting her lip. Sierra was right. He was coming on too strong.

"Everything will be all right," he said, but she didn't look convinced. "I promise I won't let anything happen to you or Karlie."

She arched a brow but didn't say anything.

Right. She didn't trust him. Maybe that was his fault for sharing how he'd failed Tristen. Maybe Jenna didn't think he was up to the job. Or maybe she had other reasons for not trusting him. For all he knew, she could even be thinking about something else. He'd thought she'd been holding something back, but could she actually be involved with this man who tried to kill her? She'd admitted she needed money. Could she be doing something illegal to get some cash, and it'd backfired on her?

He wanted to question her, but not when she was so upset. For now, he'd call the duty sergeant and update him on the snowmobile. When Brendan finished his call, Clay swung the SUV into the driveway next to the giant snowplow.

Brendan got out and offered his hand to help Jenna down. She ignored it and climbed out on her own. Something was going on with her. Maybe, as Sierra said, he'd just come on too strong. But one thing was certain. If he was going to keep Jenna safe, he would need to get to the bottom of this thing she seemed to be hiding. And he needed to do it soon.

6

Outside the SUV, Jenna became a human sandwich. Brendan came up on one side of her and Aiden on the other. Clay fell in behind. She had a trio of protection, and she was grateful, but she felt guilty. Like she was taking their protection under false pretenses. She should have told Brendan about Shawn. She should tell him now. She just couldn't be a traitor without talking to her brother first. She would give him one more call. If he didn't get back to her by morning, she'd reconsider her stance.

They stepped into the cabin, and a spicy aroma competed with the wood smoke from the fireplace, where a raging fire crackled and welcomed them home.

"Mommy!" Karlie ran across the floor in her stocking feet. She slid to a stop and bumped into Jenna. "I missed you."

Jenna dropped to her knees and scooped her daughter up in her arms. Her sweet child smelled like a mixture of wood smoke and the fresh outdoors.

Jenna leaned back and brushed Karlie's hair from her face then rested her hand against her forehead, just to be sure she didn't have a fever. Her temperature felt normal. "Did you have a fun day?"

"I learned to ski. Nana taught me."

Peggy joined them. "I hope you don't mind. I told her to call me Nana. Mrs. Byrd got old real fast, and if I ever have grandkids"—she paused and gave Sierra a pointed look as she stepped in behind Jenna—"I want them to call me Nana. It's what I called my grandmother. And she's going to call Russ Papa."

"That's fine." Jenna smiled to ease Peggy's discomfort, but inside she felt a sense of loneliness over the fact that all of Karlie's grandparents had died.

Karlie slipped free and took Peggy's hand. "We had the bestest fun. I want to go back tomorrow. Can I, Mommy? Please. Can I?"

"We'll see."

Karlie frowned. "That usually means no."

"I can't go to the slopes, and I don't know if Nana wants you tagging along all day again."

Karlie looked up at Peggy. "You do want me, don't you?"

Peggy lifted Karlie into her arms. "Of course I do, sweetie."

"See, Mommy. I knew she did."

"If it's too much I can keep her with me," Jenna said.

Peggy waved her hand. "Never. It's great practice for when we have—"

"—our own grandchildren," Sierra finished for her mother and grinned.

"Well, it is." Peggy frowned at Sierra. "And even if it isn't, Karlie's a joy."

"I'm a joy, Mommy." Karlie's little shoulders lifted higher.

Jenna tweaked Karlie's nose. "I already knew that, honey."

Peggy set her down. "Now everyone get washed up for dinner."

"Excuse me for a minute." Jenna headed for the hall bathroom. She turned on the water to cover her voice and called Shawn. She got his voicemail again. "Seriously, Shawn, if I don't hear back from you soon, I'm going to call the police. So call me."

She used the facilities and cleaned up for dinner, then changed into dry clothes. Feeling much more sociable, she pulled her shoulders back and returned to the dining area, where leaves had been added to the already long table, and Christmas dishes and silver shone under the sparkling light above. She almost laughed at the stark contrast between the rustic antler chandelier to the formal place setting, but she thought it might offend Peggy, and Jenna would never want to do that.

Most of the family was already seated, but Clay and Drake were carrying food to the table, and Brendan stood by the door talking on his phone. He'd changed out of his wet clothes too. He'd put on dark jeans with a body-hugging turtleneck that outlined his sculpted physique. As with everything she'd seen him wear, these clothes were ironed and wrinkle-free. Maybe that lingered from his military days.

From what she could hear, he was having a conversation with the sheriff reiterating the report he'd made earlier to a sergeant about the snowmobile rider who'd tried to run her down.

"Mommy, over here," Karlie waved from near the end of the table. "Nana said we could sit next to her, and she's going to sit at the top so she can get more food."

Jenna smiled at her daughter. "I'm going to help carry in the food, and then I'll sit by you."

Karlie pouted. "I want you now."

"I know, but it'll just be a minute."

"You go ahead and sit." Peggy placed a large pot of chili on the table. "You're a guest, and we've got everything under control."

Jenna thought to protest, but she took a seat. Her hip connected with the chair, and a bruise from hitting the tree ached under the skin. Her arm hurt, too, but she was alive, and for that alone, she felt immense gratitude for this family.

Gratitude you're going to repay by keeping a secret from them.

"What's wrong, Mommy?" Karlie slipped onto Jenna's lap. "You have your sad face on."

"Do I?" Jenna searched for an answer that wouldn't worry Karlie. "I guess I'm sad that I missed seeing how good of a skier you became today."

"Nana took videos for you."

"That was nice of her."

"She's nice."

"I know, honey. I can tell."

Brendan came to sit next to her, smiling at Karlie. "Did you have fun today?"

"Nana taught me to ski." She puffed up her chest.

Brendan grabbed a plaid cloth napkin and put it on his lap. "She taught me to ski too."

Karlie's eyes narrowed. "But you're big."

"She taught me when I was little like you."

"That must've been a really long time ago," she said seriously. "You're old like Mommy."

Brendan laughed. "It *was* a very long time ago. Mom taught all of us to ski."

"Mom who?"

"Nana. She's my mom."

"Nu-uh." Karlie shook her head.

"Uh-huh."

"Nana," Karlie called out. "Are you his mom?"

Peggy nodded. "I'm a mom to most of the people here."

Karlie's eyes widened. "Wow."

"Okay," Peggy said. "Let's pray."

Everyone joined hands and Russ prayed for their meal.

At the end, Peggy looked up. "Dig in, but save room for cookies."

"I just wanna have the cookies," Karlie said.

"But you like chili and cornbread." Jenna scooped chili into Karlie's bowl.

"Not as much as Nana's cookies." When she looked at the table settings, her frown turned to a smile. "I like having pretty dishes."

"Then let's see you empty your bowl so you can look at the pretty design on the bottom," Jenna said.

"But be careful," Brendan warned. "The chili will be hot."

Karlie gave a serious nod, reminding Jenna of how she should act when Brendan gave her a direction to keep her safe.

But how far would Brendan's desire to protect them go? Seemed like he would stop at nothing, and she sure hoped it didn't come down to him risking his life.

Every seat in the cabin's living room was taken, so Brendan stood by the fireplace. Karlie was the only person missing. Jenna had given her a bath and put her to bed fifteen minutes ago, then settled in with his family as if she'd been a part of it for years instead of less than a day.

She sat with her hands clasped in her lap, her cheeks still red from the cold. Vulnerable was the word he would use to describe her if he had to stick to one word. But if he could have two, the second would be strong. She was an enigma for sure, but at the same time, he found her intoxicating. Couldn't stop thinking about that look they'd shared out in the snow earlier today. Powerful. He'd known her for, what? A minute or two? And he was a goner.

He took a better look at the whole package. In the firelight, her wavy hair was dark bronze at the roots, blending into a lighter blond on the tips. The color looked natural, but what did he know about a woman's hair coloring. She'd changed into a fitted green sweater and skinny jeans with dressy boots before dinner. She looked elegant and rugged at the same time.

How did she manage that? To be a contradiction all the time? Only piqued his interest more.

"If you're ready, Jenna," Aiden said from his seat on the fireplace hearth next to Harper. "We'd like to get started with our questions."

She nodded, but her chin trembled. Gone was the strength, and her vulnerability cut him to the quick. He inched closer to her before he knew what he was doing and froze.

"Don't worry. We don't bite." Sierra patted Jenna's knee then looked across the room at Drake, who sat with his arms crossed. "Drake looks like he does, but honestly, he's a real softy underneath that gruff exterior."

"That's enough, Sierra," Drake warned.

She waved at him and peered at Jenna. "I'm the only girl, so all these guys think they can boss me around." She leaned closer. "Between you and me, I don't usually listen to them."

Aiden gave Sierra a tight look, his warning to move on clear, then he faced Jenna. "Tell us about yourself."

"Okay," Jenna said. "But I don't know what you want to hear."

"Just tell us what you might say when you first meet someone." Sierra took out a notepad. "We'll jump in if we want more information."

"You know I have a daughter. Karlie's four. My husband, Toby, died about a year ago, and both sets of Karlie's grandparents are gone. We live in a small apartment. I don't work. Took a few temp jobs until we started receiving survivor benefits from social security. I'm hoping we can get by on that until Karlie is school age, and even then it's my dream to homeschool her when it comes time. Toby had racked up a lot of debt, so I'm paying that off, and we don't have money to do most things. We stick to free stuff, like the park, library, and hikes. The library is Karlie's favorite. She could look at books nonstop if I let her." Jenna fell silent for a moment. "That's about all I can say."

"We were all homeschooled," Sierra said.

"And look how great we turned out?" Erik puffed up his chest in an exaggerated pose.

The family laughed. Jenna seemed uneasy, but she joined in. Brendan liked seeing her relax a bit though that nervous undercurrent lingered.

He waited for the laughter to die down and met her gaze. "You know, with all seven of the guys here carrying, that you and Karlie are safe with us, right?"

She nodded, but it wasn't convincing.

Harper looked at Jenna. "You really can trust them. They won't let you do anything where you could get hurt. Nothing. Trust me. I know. I had a stalker and hired them to protect me. They set the rules, and I had to follow them."

Aiden took Harper's hand. "Rules for your own good."

She gave him a loving smile. "Oh, I know, but still. It was

a bit overwhelming, so I know how you feel, Jenna, and we can talk later if you want."

"Nothing to talk about." Clay crossed his arms. "We don't make rules up just because we like them. They're in place for your safety."

"We really haven't talked about that," Brendan said. "With the snow, we didn't think anyone was out and about, but after the attempt today, we need to adjust."

"And things will be different now that roads are being plowed," Drake said. "Tons of people will be heading up here to ski, and your attacker could easily hide among them."

Trust Drake to bring up the downside. Brendan gave his brother a *cool it* look.

"If you don't have extra money, how did you afford the cabin?" Drake asked gruffly, clearly not taking the hint.

"I won it in a radio contest."

"Nice bit of luck," Erik said.

"It was, I suppose. Until the attack." Jenna took a breath. "It was supposed to be Karlie's Christmas present." Jenna looked at Peggy. "And thanks to you, you're letting her enjoy it despite the attack."

"The little miss should have a perfect Christmas, and I'm going to make sure that happens." His mother set her jaw, and Brendan knew she would succeed at all costs, something he respected about her.

"No offense," Jenna said. "But I hope we'll be gone by Christmas. Because that means this creep who attacked me will be behind bars, and it'll be safe to go back to our cabin or home."

His mother slid forward and took Jenna's hand. "Even if the boys capture him, I'd like to invite you to finish out your vacation right here where we can pamper you both. That is if you want to."

"Thank you. I'll think about it." Jenna smiled. "I can never repay you all."

His mother waved her hand. "No repayment needed. You and Karlie are a joy to have around."

Jenna withdrew her hand and held her arms tight to her body.

His mother instantly nurtured whoever the boys or Sierra had brought home as kids, and she was doing the same thing now. Her attention could be overwhelming if a person wasn't used to such affection.

"Sierra," Brendan said, drawing them back to the investigation. "Do you have an update on the forensics?"

"Not much yet. I did compare the snowmobile tracks from tonight to the ones you took pictures of, and they're a match. I don't know the make and model yet."

"It was a Polaris," Brendan said. "I saw the name on the side, and I know you couldn't miss that it was red."

She nodded. "Which should give me the info I need, and then we can check local dealers."

"I'll do that," Clay volunteered.

"Thanks." She looked at Jenna. "I need to take your prints and get a hair and DNA sample from you and Karlie for elimination purposes."

"I can get hair from Karlie's brush if that works," Jenna said.

"Perfect." Sierra smiled, and Brendan saw the resemblance to their mother. In fact, he hadn't realized it before, but Sierra had the same mothering personality too. He'd always just thought of her as a pest when she butted into his personal life, but she really did have their best interest at heart, and he needed to give her a break. At least some of the time.

"Once I finish collecting samples," she said, "I'll need to get back to the lab to process everything."

Reed frowned but didn't say anything. Brendan knew he thought Sierra worked too much, but then, as an FBI agent, Reed worked long hours too. Brendan didn't know if their mother's dream of grandchildren would ever come true.

She took Reed's hand. "Sorry, honey. I know we were going to relax here, but..."

"But you have to go back to the city tomorrow. I get it."

She kissed his cheek. "Thank you for being the best husband ever."

He pulled her in for a hug.

Drake mocked gagging, and the others laughed.

"Careful boys," their mom said. "Hopefully, you'll all get married someday, and payback can be tough."

Sierra's expression turned mischievous. "You know it."

"Let's get back to the topic at hand," Brendan said.

"One thing no one mentioned was that the attacker's knife has a red blade," Jenna said. "I'm guessing that's unusual."

"It is," Brendan said. "Anyone familiar with red-bladed knives?"

"Grady would know," Sierra said and looked at Jenna. "He's the weapons expert at Veritas. I'll text him." Sierra started tapping on her phone.

"Tell us more about Toby," Aiden said.

Jenna's eyebrow arched. "Why?"

Aiden withdrew his arm from around Harper and sat forward. "Brendan said there was a similar home invasion. We have to wonder if the two are connected. Especially since Toby left you in debt and likely needed money. But why? Was his job in trouble or something else? Like gambling. Or even borrowing from a loan shark. His former work could be that connection. Or his hobbies. Or friends."

"He didn't have friends or hobbies. None. Unless you consider watching any one of endless sports shows a hobby." Her tone had turned sharp and irritated. Brendan wondered about the marriage, the stories she hadn't shared. Not that it was his business. "And he was an investment broker at a Portland firm. Wilman Investments. But don't ask me for details about what he did on the job. I couldn't tell you. He never talked about his work."

Brendan's mind raced with questions too personal to raise in front of the others. He jotted down the information she'd shared in his small notebook. He would question her about Toby when they were alone and share pertinent details with his brothers later.

Sierra looked at her watch. "I need to finish up the cabin. And remember, Brendan, you're helping me."

He groaned. "I must've been crazy when I offered."

"Not a momentary thing." Erik grinned.

Sierra's phone dinged. "Grady says a few companies make red-bladed knives. He'd need to see the actual weapon or a picture of it to be of any help."

"I'll keep that in mind in case it's recovered." Brendan looked at Aiden. "Will you take charge while I go with Sierra?"

He sat forward. "Sure thing."

Brendan turned his focus to Jenna. "Please stay in the cabin and listen to Aiden's directions if something should come up."

Her eyes widened. "You think my attacker will come here?"

"Not likely, but we have to be prepared for anything." Brendan clapped his hands. "That's it."

"Despite the sparring, I liked sitting in on your meeting," his dad said. "I miss real work."

"Being an industrial security guard is real work."

His dad rolled his eyes and got up. "C'mon, Peg. Let's

leave the younger generation to do their thing and get a good night's sleep."

She let him pull her to her feet. "Anyone need anything before I hit the hay?"

"They're grown, Peg. Quit babying them."

"We don't mind. Not at all." Erik laughed and held up his glass. "But I can get my own water."

He stood, and Clay did too, following his parents.

"Can I talk to you for a second, Clay?" Brendan called after him and joined him in the back of the room. "What's up with you, bro?"

"Up?"

"You've been a grouch all day."

Clay crossed his arms. "Can't a guy have a bad day?"

"Most guys can, and it's no big deal, but you? You're never like this. At least not since..." At the tightening of Clay's eyes, Brendan shut up. He was about to mention a time about a year ago when Clay was lead on a joint op between ICE and the FBI where an older gentleman had been killed. Though Clay had been cleared of all wrongdoing, he blamed himself and had moped around for several months. They never found the killer, and Brendan knew Clay still worked the investigation in his free time. Even after leaving ICE.

"So what's up?" Brendan moved on.

Scratching his neck, Clay stepped closer. "It's Grace."

"The friend Harper set you up with?" Brendan asked, glad it was as simple as woman trouble, but that could actually be the hardest trouble of all. "I thought you two were good."

"*Were* is the operative word." Clay rubbed a hand over his jaw. "We decided to be exclusive. Then I caught her with another guy."

"Aw, man. That's rough."

Clay nodded. "I thought we had a good thing going, but I guess not. And on top of that, I have to figure out how to tell Harper about the break-up. I don't want to trash her friend, but I also don't want this to be a thing in the family, you know?"

Brendan looked at Harper, who was still sitting on the hearth with Aiden's arm around her. "Sure, I get it, but I don't think you need to worry about Harper. She's a straight shooter, and she'll understand. Just tell her the truth."

Clay arched an eyebrow, reminding Brendan of their dad when they were trying to get away with something as kids. "You really think it'll be that simple?"

Brendan nodded. "But be sure you do it with Aiden there. If he thinks you hurt Harper, you'll never live that down. I mean never."

Clay rolled his shoulders. "Maybe I should tell him first."

"Yeah, maybe, but then Harper might be mad that you talked to him about it first. Together, neither of them can go down that road."

"See," Clay stated firmly. "I told you it was complicated."

"Whatever you decide, do it before Grace talks to Harper. If the woman cheated on you, I doubt she'd have a problem lying about the breakup."

Clay stared across the room at Harper and Aiden. "Guess I'll tell them right now and hope it doesn't ruin our vacation."

"Good luck, man." Brendan clapped his brother on the back.

He crossed the room like a dead man walking.

Sierra quickly kissed Reed and joined Brendan. "You ready to be my slave?"

"Ready? No. But I'll do it." He grinned at his sister.

She punched him in the biceps, and he slung an arm around her shoulders and knuckled her head.

She escaped from him and wrinkled her nose. "Seriously, Brendan, I'm an old married woman, not your sister to pick on."

"You'll always be picked on and you know it. How else can we show you we love you?"

She headed for the door and grabbed her parka. "Um, how about say, 'I love you, Sis.'"

"That's just not how we roll." He slipped into his boots and jacket.

The moment he opened the door, the cold air whipped in carrying the smell of a wood fire. Most people would be hunkered down in front of their fireplaces, not going out on a night like this, but the Byrds weren't most people. Their parents taught all six of them to be exceptional in everything they did, and they all tried to make their parents proud. To emulate the way they lived their faith.

Sierra produced a flashlight and shone it down the steps. He trailed her through the snow that was flattened from the earlier trips to the cabin.

"Let's walk off that dinner if you don't mind."

"Okay with me." Brendan patted his stomach. "Got to keep my six-pack."

He laughed, and the sound rang through the quiet night.

She rolled her eyes. "Everything okay with Clay?"

"Will be." He raised his voice to be heard over the howling wind.

She glanced up at him. "You're not going to tell me more, are you?"

"It's his thing to tell if he wants to." Brendan lowered his head against the snow gusting in icy shards. He kept his head down all the way to Jenna's rental cabin, where he used his pocket knife to slit the seal Sierra had affixed to the door.

Sierra inserted the key and twisted the lock. "You hear from the sheriff's office today?"

Brendan nodded. "Detective Grant should arrive as soon as the roads are clear. I don't know him, do you?"

"No." Inside, Sierra shed her jacket and hung it on a chair. "But then we don't tend to get a lot of forensic requests from Clackamas County."

"Let's hope he's competent." Brendan knew no matter the guy's investigative skills, he and his brothers would keep on the case. "And maybe he can help push through the warrant for the names of the owner and nearby renters. The clerk said the judge wanted more probable cause. He didn't buy the attacker hinting at making a mistake was enough to approve giving out so many people's private information."

"Judges are getting more demanding when it comes to privacy issues these days."

"True that," he said. "Now, what do you want me to do?"

She held out evidence bags. "First, label these with the case number. You can find it on the other bags. Then as I call out, you can bag the samples and fill in the information."

He took the bags. "And here I thought you were going to give me some dirty work."

"I haven't ruled that out yet." She grinned at him, slipped into her Tyvek suit and gloves, and got down on the floor near the tipped over chair.

He sat at the table and labeled a few bags.

"How much do you know about Jenna?" Sierra asked.

He paused, pen in the air. "What do you mean?"

"Seems like you've bought her story without question, and that's not like you." Sierra picked up a hair with a tweezer and held it out for him to bag. She gave him the details to add, and he sat back down to fill it in.

"You usually zero-in like the sniper you are and get to

the point," Sierra continued when he'd hoped she would let it drop. "With her, you seem to be ignoring the point altogether."

He capped the Sharpie. "You think Jenna's lying?"

"She seems like she's legit, but you haven't even mentioned running a background check on her. At the very least, you should do that."

His thoughts went to Tristen. If he'd completed a background report on her, would she still be alive? Or was that just wishful thinking? Maybe even if he'd done the report the old boyfriend wouldn't have shown up. So would Brendan then be blaming himself for not doing as thorough of a job as he should? Would he blame himself no matter what had happened?

"Hello." Sierra waved a hand. "Where'd you go?"

"Tristen."

Sierra frowned. "I don't see the connection."

"If I'd done a background check on her, I would've learned about the abusive boyfriend, and I might've been able to stop him from killing her."

"You don't do background checks on girlfriends, do you?"

"That would be creepy."

"Exactly. So there's no comparison."

Wasn't there? He was attracted to Jenna. Maybe more than attracted. Looking into her background would be just as creepy as checking on a girlfriend.

"Oh, I see." Sierra lifted her chin and eyed him. "You have feelings for Jenna."

"No. Not feelings."

"Then what?"

He shrugged.

"You're attracted to her."

He nodded.

She sat back. "How in the world did I miss that?"

Because he was doing a good job of hiding it. At least he hoped he was. "This stays between us. Aiden gets even a hint of it, and he's going to pitch a royal fit."

"Hello. Just bring up Harper."

"He'll say when we were assigned to Harper's protection detail that he managed to keep his professional and personal life separate."

"But we all know that's not true. He's just blind."

"Exactly. So he can't see how he behaved and will let me have it. So keep quiet on this, okay?"

A wide smile crossed her face. "This is so wonderful. You haven't been interested in anyone since Tristen. That's been a year, and since you weren't very serious, I thought you might be dating by now."

"Can we please change the subject?"

"Only after you answer one question for me."

He nearly groaned.

"Are you going to pursue Jenna?" Sierra asked.

"She doesn't seem interested," he replied to avoid the real question.

"Since when would that stop you?"

Yeah, since when?

Since Tristen died and he learned that he couldn't trust people he cared about to be honest with him. So maybe that background check on Jenna was in order here. She'd probably freak if she learned he'd asked Erik to run it, but it was the right thing to do for the investigation. And maybe the right thing to do to keep her alive.

7

Jenna woke in the middle of the night to the sound of the wind buffeting the cabin. The snowstorm had definitely ended, but high winds continued, not unusual for the area. Or so Russ had told her. They'd been coming to the cabin for ten years now and had been snowed in many times.

She loved that the Byrds had traditions. Not so, her family. Some Christmases they didn't even have a tree. Depended on how sober her dad was and if alcohol had consumed all their money.

Grr. She didn't want to bring up all these old memories. Served no purpose.

She quietly slipped down from the bed so she wouldn't wake Karlie next to her or Harper in the other bed. Once Peggy knew Jenna was staying, she'd reassigned rooms, giving Sierra and Reed their own room and putting the brothers into the other two, sharing bunk beds as well. She could just imagine Brendan with his long legs cramped up in one of the smaller beds. All the brothers would have problems, but only Brendan came to mind.

Another thought she didn't need to be having. She slipped into a fluffy fleece robe and warm slippers and crept out of the room. Her feet stuttered to a stop. Brendan was lying on the couch, a plump pillow beneath his head and a heavy quilt over his body.

What was he doing out here? She didn't want to wake him. She'd sneak into the kitchen for a glass of water and head back to her room and hope she could go to sleep.

She tiptoed across the space.

"Couldn't sleep?" he asked.

Shocked at his voice, she spun. "Sorry. Did I wake you?"

"No." He sat up and ran a hand through his hair sticking out at odd angles.

She wanted to tame those wayward strands. Seriously? Bad idea. Really bad idea. She gestured to the kitchen. "I was just going to get some water."

He slid out from under the quilt and went to the fireplace. He grabbed the poker and, resting one hand on the mantle, stuck it into the flames, the muscles under his turtleneck rippling. Mesmerized by his smooth movements, she forgot all about her water, and continued to watch when he didn't know she was looking at him.

They'd just met, and yet, something about him felt familiar. Was it because he reminded her of Toby, or that he had that same goodness and homey vibe his family radiated? She'd always wanted a big boisterous family like his. Was that why she was attracted to him? Had it already gone beyond the physical? Because, man, he was a good-looking and fit guy.

He pulled the screen closed and turned toward her. The flames flickered in his eyes. Barefoot below jeans that hung low on his hips, he padded across the room. "It's close enough to dawn that I'm going to start the coffee." He clicked on the pot. "Thankfully, Mom prepares it the night before so it's ready, or we'd have to suffer with my coffee-making skills."

"Each machine is different."

"Right." He grinned. "I could've blamed it on the coffeemaker."

He reached into the cupboard, took out a big covered container, and lifted out a giant frosted Christmas tree.

"Mom's cookies. Don't tell on me." He winked at her.

She loved his playful mood and wanted to see more of it. "Only if I can have one too."

He held out the container and gave her a conspiratorial smile. "They go really well with coffee."

She selected a smaller star with yellow frosting and colorful red and green dots, and decided she would stay up for a while.

"Wimp," he said. "I thought you'd be brave enough to take one of the big ones."

She rolled her eyes and bit the star. The crisp cookie crumbled in her mouth as the frosting melted on her tongue. She wanted to scarf it down but saved the rest for when she had her coffee.

He snapped the lid closed and put the cookies back, then leaned against the counter and crossed his feet at the ankles. He shoved his free hand into his pocket, looking relaxed and at home.

The coffee gurgled in the background, the fire crackled, and her heart thundered so loudly she thought he must hear it pounding. The room was illuminated by flames from the fire and the twinkling white lights on the tree. His face was shadowed, all sharp lines and angles. And his bare feet made her imagine mornings with him, and how different they might be than the ones she'd shared with Toby, often hungover and crabby.

"You're staring," he said.

"Sorry. I didn't mean...I was..."

"Hey, it's okay. As long as you like what you see."

He was flirting with her. Seriously, flirting, and her face flushed.

"I embarrassed you," he said.

"I...I..." She shrugged.

"I'm a pretty direct person. Guess it comes from so many years as a sniper."

She gaped at him. "You were a sniper? As in a person who killed other people?"

"I was." He pushed off the counter and rested his free hand on it. "Does that bother you?"

"I don't know. I mean, I've never met a sniper." Thoughts raced through her head. "What's it like?"

He didn't answer right away but seemed to ponder what he wanted to say. "It's a stressful job for sure. Your team's lives depend on you, so there's a tremendous amount of pressure not to miss." His fingers tightened on the edge of the counter.

She was terrified of guns and never wanted them in her life, but Toby had been a hunter so guns were part of their lives. The same would be true if she were with Brendan. He had to like guns to have been an expert at shooting them. Shooting at people and killing them.

She almost gasped when she thought about it. "Do you ever feel guilty about killing people?"

His eyebrow shot up. "Now look who's being direct."

"I'm sorry." She rested a hand on his arm. "Don't answer if you don't want to. I understand."

He looked at her hand. She snapped it back.

"I don't mind the question. There's no guilt. People misunderstand the job. I went ahead of my unit to eliminate the enemy combatants who planned to kill our troops. And then served on overwatch to keep my eyes on the enemy to make sure our guys were safe. Hundreds of U.S. troops are alive today because of my skills with a gun. So I count it an honor to have served the soldiers and their families in that capacity."

He took a long breath. "And as a deputy, I prevented the loss of life when a tactical response was required. The most memorable incident was when a woman and her three children were taken hostage in a home invasion gone wrong. I can sleep easy at night thinking about them because I was there when they needed me."

She let it all sink in and realized how amazing this man was. His compassion and caring allowed him to do a difficult job to save others. He was truly a hero. "Thank you for serving in that capacity. Like you said, there have to be so many families who are thankful their soldiers came home alive from combat thanks to you."

He gave a sharp nod and turned to the coffee pot that was gurgling its last gasp. "Do you drink it with cream and sugar?"

"Just black." He poured two cups, not putting anything in either.

He handed her a mug, a smile on his face. "Now the cookie."

She bit her star and sipped the coffee, the sugar melting in her mouth, as she thought about him. How could he go from the intense sniper to a cute flirt in the blink of an eye? It was like he was two men in one. So was Toby. And the second guy she'd met with him was horrible. But she just couldn't see Brendan having a dark side. Or maybe it was just wishful thinking.

"See," he said. "Nothing better than Mom's cookies and coffee."

"I'll have to get her recipe."

"Do you like to bake?"

She nodded. "Bake and cook. I used to have a large garden and chickens when we had a house. I loved growing

89

organic foods for Karlie. Now, I can't afford them. I'm not complaining. Honest. Just stating a fact. Organic produce is too expensive."

"You sound so much like my mom. She always has a garden and chickens too. She preserves a lot of food and used to say when we were younger that was the only way they could feed five boys on a detective's salary." A fond smile found its way to his face. "It was our job to weed the garden and take care of the chickens. I can't tell you how many eggs I collected."

"Did you like it?"

"When I was a little kid, yes, but around middle school I was too cool to garden." He chuckled and took a big bite of his cookie.

"I really miss it. Gardening was a hobby as well as an escape."

"From?"

"Life's pressures," she said, being purposefully vague.

"Then I hope someday you can have your garden back." He blew on his coffee. "I bet if you asked my mom, she'd give you a patch until then. She's always saying the garden's too big for the two of them now and gives away a lot of her produce."

Jenna nodded, but this felt a lot like charity, something Jenna hadn't needed to accept until now, and a heavy sandbag of worry for her and Karlie's future pressed down on her shoulders. She couldn't let him see that. "I'll bet they didn't have cookies like this when you were in the army."

"Mom would've sent them if I could've told her where I was deployed. But it was all confidential."

"Do you miss it?"

"Some days, but I wouldn't want to go back through the transition to civilian life again, that's for sure."

She sipped on her mug. "Why's that?"

He looked hesitant to answer.

"It's okay," she said. "You don't have to tell me."

"It's..." He shook his head. "When you're in, you're trained to act with violence. The opposite is true in civilian life, and you've gotta get used to that again."

"But there must've been some things as a deputy that were similar, right?"

"Yeah, sure, but there you're trained to deescalate and violence of any kind was the last resort. And in the army you're a closer part of a team, and you learn to rely on everyone. It's not about you, you know? But then, boom. You're out and back in civilian life and this family you've been counting on for years is gone. Your mission is totally changed. It breaks you down. Thankfully, I had my real family. A lot of guys who don't have that support don't make it."

She set down her mug to pick up the star. "Don't make it?"

"Some take their own lives. It's a big thing. Almost fifteen percent of all adult suicides are vets."

She swallowed the bite of cookie that had turned to sawdust in her mouth. "I didn't know."

"A lot of people don't. But, like I said, I had my family and a job. So I had a purpose. Now I have the agency and my brothers counting on me. That's a great thing to have."

She took a long drink of the strong coffee. "Seems like you really love it."

"I do. We formed the agency because of Aiden's missing kidney. Figured if we could get him out of the ATF he'd have less chance in sustaining an injury that would take out his last kidney."

"That was quite a sacrifice."

He shrugged. "It's what you do for your family. Be it blood or a team like Delta."

She stared at him then, unable to comprehend that blood relatives really did sacrifice for each other, let alone guys who weren't related. Of course, she'd give everything for Karlie, but her experience with her family was another story.

Brendan suddenly came alert. "You hear that?"

"No. What?"

"A snowmobile. Moving fast. Our direction." He set down his mug. "Get Karlie and take her to the bathroom where there aren't any windows."

Fear settled into Jenna's body with a sharp ache, and she was frozen in place.

"Go. Now!" He took her shoulders and pushed her in the right direction.

That was all she needed. She rushed across the room and looked back to see him grabbing his gun from a holster on the sofa and then putting on his boots.

As he reached for the doorknob, her heart skipped a beat. "Be careful, Brendan! Please be careful!"

Brendan waited until Jenna disappeared in the hallway, then looked out the peephole in the door. The machine wasn't on them yet, so he slipped out and squatted behind a small pine in a large pot on the porch. He held his gun at the ready, his heart thudding like a drum.

He could be wrong. This might not be a threat at all. But he wouldn't take a chance with Jenna's life. He peered through the wind-driven snow and saw the machine approach. No headlights. *Okay. Fine.* He was right. No one would ride without lights unless they were up to no good.

The snowmobile rumbled closer. One rider. Black

helmet. Large build. Male. Fit Jenna's attacker. And the machine was a red Polaris.

The man slowed in front of the cabin and grabbed something from between his knees. He lifted his arm and hurled the item at the porch. It landed with a loud thud and rolled a few times to come to a stop six inches from Brendan's foot. A brick with paper wrapped around it

The snowmobile roared off. When it was out of sight, Brendan grabbed the brick and opened the computer generated message.

She can't hide. Give her up or the next time it won't just be a brick. The whole family will be sorry.

Brendan wanted to crumple the note and toss it away before Jenna could read the message, but it was evidence. He carried it inside and shoved it in an evidence bag from Sierra's kit. He was about to stow the bag until after breakfast, but Jenna poked her head in the room. He shoved the bag behind his back.

"I heard the door close. Is everything all right?"

All right? No. Far from it. "You're safe to come out. I hope you didn't wake Karlie."

"She's an early riser anyway." Jenna gave a wobbly smile. "I'll just go get her."

"Great," he said, thankful that the child would join them, giving him a reason to not tell Jenna about the message just yet. He hid the bag then refreshed his coffee and sat at the island. How would he tell her? The thought of giving her more bad news after the terror she'd been through put a pain in his chest.

Footsteps raced over the wood floor, and Karlie, big smile on her pudgy face, zoomed into the room. She was clutching the same stuffed snowman as when he'd found her in the closet, and she climbed up on the barstool by him.

"Hi," he said, giving her a genuine smile.

"This is Olaf. He's from *Frozen*. Did you watch *Frozen*?"

He shook his head.

She frowned. "How come?"

He glanced at Jenna, who was silently crossing the room. "Because I didn't have a special little girl like you to watch it with."

"I'm special. Mommy says so all the time. We can watch it together."

He loved her enthusiasm and hated to disappoint, but... "I don't have it here."

"I do. In my suitcase." She smiled. "I'm hungry. Nana said she was going to make her famous chocolate chip pancakes." Karlie frowned. "I don't know what famous means."

"It means special too."

"I wish she would get up."

"Now, Karlie, you have to be patient." Jenna settled on a stool.

"Actually." He pushed off his stool. "I know how to make them."

"You do?" Little Karlie's eyes widened as if he'd just admitted he was Superman.

"Nana taught me when I was a boy."

Karlie jumped off the stool. "Can I help?"

He could never say no to that adorable face, a miniature of her mother's. "Sure, but I think you better set Olaf down so he doesn't get dirty."

She gave a serious nod and placed the stuffed snowman on the stool next to her. "Don't worry, Olaf. I'll give you some pancakes too."

"Okay," Brendan said. "Let me get the ingredients out and a big bowl because I know you can eat lots of them."

"What are 'gredients?" she asked.

"The things that go into the pancakes, like flour and eggs."

"I want to mix the 'gredients."

"You can, and you can even help me measure them."

"Did you hear that, Mommy? I get to measure."

"I did." Jenna's smile for her daughter was glorious and shot right to Brendan's heart. The love he saw between them was just like his mother's love for him. Jenna and Karlie might not have much money, but they were rich in the most important thing.

Brendan set the bowl and measuring cups on the counter near Karlie.

She grabbed the biggest cup and mimicked measuring and pouring. "I like to measure my sand. I'm good at it. Right, Mommy?"

"The best."

He set the ingredients on the island. "We need to start with the flour."

He opened the canister, and Karlie got on her knees on the stool. Jenna reached out to help, but Brendan wanted her to relax, so he stepped behind Karlie and helped her level the cup. "Okay, dump it in the bowl."

She got most of it in the bowl, and he added just a bit more to replace what she'd spilled.

"We have to make enough for everyone so we need to do two more cups of flour." He started to help her.

She pushed his hand away. "I'm a big girl. I can do it."

She had her mother's stubborn nature. "Okay, but did you see how I sliced off the extra with a knife?"

"Uh-huh. I can do it."

And to Brendan's surprise, she did. Mostly anyway. He'd never been around kids much, but he had to admit to enjoying teaching Karlie how to make the pancakes. Karlie stirred and got flour all over her hands, face, and fuzzy pajamas, but Jenna just smiled as she looked on, so he figured it was okay.

"Done," he announced.

Karlie swiveled and threw her arms around him. "I like you a whole bunch."

"Honey, you're getting Brendan all dirty," Jenna said.

She pulled back.

He smiled at her and pressed a hand over her soft curls. "I don't mind one bit. I like you bunches too."

"What do we have here?" His mother came into the kitchen. "I can say I wouldn't mind waking up to the sight of the three of you every year on our trip."

"Mom," Brendan warned.

"What? I'm just saying." An innocent look on her face, she waved her hand as she often did. "Now scoot. All of you so I can have my coffee and finish up the breakfast."

"Can we watch *Frozen* now?" Karlie's hopeful gaze melted Brendan's heart the rest of the way.

"We sure can," he said before Jenna could weigh in.

"Yay! I'll get it." Karlie flew off her stool and ran down the hall.

Jenna looked up at him. "You don't have to watch."

"I haven't seen an animated movie in years. Looking forward to it."

Karlie ran back into the room, a fuzzy blanket draped over her arm and DVD in her hand.

"Walk," Jenna said.

Karlie slowed, but her steps were a cross between running and skipping. She tucked Olaf in her arm by the blanket, then grabbed Brendan's hand and tugged him to the living room.

She handed him the DVD. "You can put it in. But be careful. It belongs to the library."

He complied and sat on the couch to turn on the TV. She

climbed up in his lap and settled back with her blanket and Olaf tucked up by her face. Tenderness for her bloomed in his heart, and the raw emotions shocked him. How could a little four-year-old wrap him around her finger in just minutes?

Jenna joined them, a look of consternation on her face. "You don't have to let her sit on your lap."

"I don't mind."

"He likes me," Karlie said. "He said so."

Jenna gave Brendan a what-are-you-gonna-do look, and they shared a genuine smile that brightened eyes that he'd mostly seen troubled. He wasn't prepared for the pure sweetness of her smile, and his heart took a tumble. He had to remind himself to breathe.

"Anyone want coffee," his mother asked, pot in hand. She glanced between them. "Oh, oh my. I guess I'll go back to the kitchen."

"No," Jenna said quickly. "It's not what you think."

"If that's what you say." A beaming smile came from his mother, and she backed out of the space as the movie previews ended and *Frozen* began.

Brendan was going to have a hard time living this down with his mom. She would be all over the thought of him and Jenna as a couple. A ready-made grandchild would be just to her liking. Especially one as adorable as little Karlie Paine.

8

Jenna clutched the warning letter in her hand, her mind at a loss for words as she stared at the brick in the plastic evidence bag. What did she say to Brendan? How did she respond? Or how did she act in front of his brothers? Her attacker really wanted to kill her. Enough to demand they give her over to him.

"Why?" she finally got out as she handed the letter enclosed in a plastic bag back to Brendan. "What did I do?"

"At the very least, you've seen him, and he can't risk you identifying him," Aiden said.

"And it looks like he's not going to give up," Drake stated.

"He will when we stop him." Brendan's forceful tone left no doubt that he planned to succeed. "And to do that we need to get the drone up in the air and take a look around. Follow the snowmobile tracks as far as we can."

A vehicle rumbled up the road. Jenna's heart lurched, and she shot a look out the front window.

"Stay put." Brendan locked gazes with her for a moment then went to the door. "It's the detective."

Jenna let out a breath, her heart still tripping fast. She

was a basket case, and she didn't think she'd recover until her attacker, now brick thrower, was in custody.

Brendan slipped into his boots and swung the door open. A rush of cold air flowed in, cooling Jenna when the threat had already frozen her in place. She looked around the room at the family of protectors, who had various versions of frustration on their faces. She wanted to trust them. To believe they had this under control, but could she trust anyone anymore? At all?

And that included God. Why did He allow the attacks and now this warning? She couldn't come up with a single way the situation was good for her or Karlie. Other than meeting this family, but that was just a temporary thing. As soon as it was safe to leave, she'd be out the door and heading back home.

She heard Brendan's confident tone as he introduced himself to the detective on the porch. A detective. It was one thing telling Brendan and his family about the attack. Another thing altogether talking to an official law enforcement officer. She mentally prepared herself for the coming inquisition.

The chubby detective, with silvery buzzed hair and narrowed grayish-brown eyes, lumbered in behind Brendan, who introduced everyone.

Detective Grant scratched his head as if he didn't want to deal with this group. He zoned in on Sierra. "Thank you for stepping in and preserving the evidence. I got your email with the report, and that's all I need right now."

"Good." She gave him a genuine smile. "Let me know if you have any questions."

He shrugged out of his drab green parka, revealing a pale blue dress shirt and black striped tie. "I'd like to talk with Ms. Paine alone."

"I'll be staying," Brendan said, his tone brooking no argument, and Grant didn't argue.

"We can all find something to do and let you talk here." Aiden stood.

"Just be quiet so you don't wake Karlie from her nap," Brendan warned.

Jenna's mouth fell open before she snapped it closed. Everyone was casting suspicious glances at her and Brendan. She would normally be embarrassed at letting others see her attraction to Brendan, but surprise and warmth from his consideration were her only emotions. Karlie had obviously made an impact on him this morning, and Jenna didn't know how she felt about that. Her daughter needed strong male role models in her life, but Jenna didn't want her to get attached to Brendan when their connection was temporary.

The family members disappeared down the hall.

Grant plopped down on a plump chair across from her and took out a notepad and pen. "Go ahead and recount what happened with the attacker."

She told her story, quick and matter-of-factly, while Brendan rested on the arm of the sofa beside her. Seemed like he was there to protect her from the detective, or maybe just for moral support.

"And that's it?" Grant's eyes locked on her, mining for information she didn't have to give.

"I went after the suspect and found a snowmobile trail," Brendan said. "I took pictures, and the track matches the one from a man who tried to attack her yesterday and then pitched a brick at the house this morning." Brendan shared the rest of the incident.

Grant kept his gaze pinned on Jenna. "Tell me why this guy attacked you."

Jenna clasped her hands together. "I have no idea."

He didn't seem to buy her answer. Suspicious just like Brendan had been at first, but he seemed to have mellowed.

"Can you describe the attacker well enough for us to have a sketch made?" Grant asked.

She nodded. "I think so anyway."

"I saw him too," Brendan said.

"Good," Grant said. "I'll have to get someone from the state to come up. Might take a day or two."

Brendan settled his hands on his thighs. "Or we could call Kelsey Dunbar at Veritas. She's their anthropologist, but she does sketches too."

Grant frowned. "Can't pay for that?"

"No worries," Brendan said. "I'll take care of it."

Jenna looked up at Brendan. "I can't let—"

"It's okay." He smiled. "Kelsey's a friend and colleague. I'm sure she'll do it in return for a short ski trip. I'll call her when we're finished here."

Grant got up. "Let's go walk the scene. I'll ask my other questions there."

Go back to her cabin? Her gut cramped, and she wanted to run and hide in a closet like Karlie had done. But Jenna wasn't a child and couldn't hide from difficulties in her life. She stood.

"I'll ask my mom to watch Karlie." Brendan headed down the hall.

Grant stared at Jenna, his gaze had an edge to it, making her uncomfortable. She knew what he was doing. He was trying to get her to blurt out something she might be hiding from him. Something like Shawn.

That wouldn't happen. She hurried over to her jacket and boots and took her time putting them on. Her shaking fingers fumbled with the zipper, and it snagged on the fabric. She tugged to no avail.

When Brendan returned, she was still struggling.

"Let me help." He reached out before she could object, and their hands brushed.

That awareness of him replaced her fear with a wonderful warm feeling for the flash of a moment. He was so close she could touch his rugged jaw. She wanted to. Just to see if such a kind and compassionate man was real or if she was making him seem like more because he was her hero. A real life hero. Maybe she was letting her gratitude make him into a superhero.

"There." He got the zipper moving and stepped back to put on his jacket. "Mom's good with watching Karlie."

Slipping his hands into heavy gloves, Grant joined them. "How old is your daughter?"

"Four."

"At her age, if she did see the attacker, she won't likely remember him, which is good."

Jenna nodded, but she heard footsteps and spun to see Clay and Erik enter the room.

Brendan looked at Grant. "I'm bringing our drone to get an aerial view of the scene. If it's okay with you, my brothers will be coming along to help."

Grant eyed the men. "Fine by me as long as they don't get in my way."

"You won't even know we're there." Clay smiled at Grant, and the detective seemed to relax a notch.

Jenna was beginning to think Clay was the family peacemaker.

"And we'll also be driving there to protect Jenna," Brendan said, no peacemaking vibe in his tone at all.

Grant's eyebrow went up in an arc, but he didn't respond. Just opened the door and stepped out. The gusty wind had died down, and a light but cold breeze blew into the cabin.

She started to follow Grant, but Brendan held up his hand. "Clay will check out the surroundings first."

Clay grabbed a pair of binoculars on a hook by the door and exited. She'd noticed he seemed to be a gung-ho guy or just lacked patience. She wasn't sure which yet.

Grant looked back. "You coming or what? I've got a backload of things to do from the blizzard."

"Go ahead," Brendan said. "We need to do a quick threat assessment first."

He shook his head and lumbered down the steps to his vehicle.

Jenna looked at Brendan, whose gaze was watchful. "Clearly he thinks your actions are overkill."

"I honestly don't care what he thinks or if he has to wait. Your safety comes first for us, and it will until the attacker is behind bars."

His adamant tone both scared her and made her feel better. "I appreciate everything you're doing, but I don't want to make Grant mad over having to wait."

"He'll get over it."

But he could take it out on me and badger me until I give him Shawn's name.

Grant drove off in his car. How odd that he'd taken his car when he'd shaken his head over her being driven.

Clay turned midway to the SUV and nodded.

"Straight to the vehicle. No stopping." Brendan cupped her elbow and led her to the vehicle's back door.

Erik drove them up the hilly road, the tires crunching over snow left behind by the plow. Grant had arrived and tapped his foot on the cabin porch and pointedly looked at his watch.

When the SUV stopped, she reached for her door handle.

"Not so fast," Brendan said. "Let Clay get the place open first."

Clay wasted no time, but slid from the vehicle and marched through the snow. He pushed the door open and suddenly drew his gun.

"What's happening?" she asked, her eyes fixed on Clay stepping through the doorway.

Grant followed, gun drawn.

"We won't know until Clay reports." Brendan sounded calm, but she saw the worry in his eyes, ramping up her own concern.

She watched. Her breath held. Time seemed to stop. She glued her gaze to the door.

Please don't let anyone be hurt.

She counted. Waiting for Clay to come back outside.

When he stepped onto the porch and shoved his gun into his holster, she blew out a breath. He charged out to the vehicle. His eyes were tight, and she didn't know what to think, other than that something bad had happened.

He opened the vehicle door. "You're not going to like this. Place has been ransacked. Totally torn apart."

Brendan knew Jenna was strong. She continued to prove it. Walking through the ransacked cabin with Grant, where she relived the night of the attack, proved it. Sure, her voice trembled, as did her body, but she persevered. Brendan almost didn't make it. He'd hated to see her so upset and wanted to stop the interview several times. He didn't, though. No point. Grant would just keep coming back to ask additional questions. Still, Brendan didn't know how much more Jenna could take before breaking down, and now that they were back in the family room of the cabin, where everything was strewn about and furniture tipped over, it wouldn't hurt to push Grant along.

"If you don't have any other questions," Brendan said pointedly to the detective. "I'd like to get Jenna back to my parents' place."

Grant frowned. "I'm done. For now anyway."

Footsteps sounded on the porch. Brendan spun and reached for his sidearm.

The door opened, and Erik stepped in, holding the drone's controller with the attached iPad.

Brendan let out a silent breath. "What's up?"

Erik held up the controller. "I thought you and Detective Grant would want to see what we recorded less than a mile from here."

Brendan didn't like Erik's serious tone. "Do we have a potential threat?"

"Didn't see any active threats, but we can't rule them out."

Brendan turned to Jenna. "I need you to go into the hall bath and lock the door. Don't come out until I say it's safe."

"But I—"

"Go. Now." He firmed his shoulders.

Her lips pressed together. "I told you I want to be a part of the investigation."

He didn't back down. Couldn't back down. Not with her safety on the line. But he could be nicer about it. "Please, Jenna."

Maybe it was his use of her name, but her shoulders relaxed. She turned and marched into the hallway, each step ringing out against the tall ceiling and telling him that she was frustrated. He didn't want to make her life harder, but better frustrated than dead.

He waited until he heard the lock click into place. "Okay, Erik. Show us the video."

He brought up the feed. "I'll fast forward to the footage you need to see."

The video raced ahead and suddenly slowed. The camera hovered high in the sky, but dropped down and zoomed in on the ground.

Brendan sucked in a sharp breath, his eyes glued to the large male lying on his back, a red-bladed knife protruding from his chest.

9

Brendan followed Grant's footsteps in the deep snow toward Jenna's attacker. Her dead attacker.

Brendan couldn't see the body yet, but Clay stood near a band of crime scene tape strung between trees. Wind whistled through the clearing, sending the yellow plastic fluttering and trying to break free.

Clay looked up from his phone. "As you can see, I set up a perimeter and cordoned off the scene. Grant's with the body, and he asked me to keep everyone out."

Brendan eyed his younger brother. "Not me."

Clay lifted his chin. "Yeah, you too."

"Sorry, bro." Brendan lifted the tape and ducked under it. "No way I'm staying out."

Clay shook his head. "I told Grant you wouldn't listen. He said just be sure you follow his footprints. Also, the ME is delayed due to road conditions, so I asked Dad to bring up the canopy he always keeps in their SUV to erect over the body."

"Good job," Brendan said. "Let me know when Dad arrives."

"I also called Sierra. She was heading into town to process the other forensics, but I told her to turn around."

"Thanks, man." Brendan looked at his brother. "Now why did I ever think you were annoying?"

"Not a clue. I'm far too charming to be annoying." Clay quirked a smile.

"Hey, how did your conversation go with Harper and Aiden?"

"Good. Great actually." He let out a relieved breath. "I knew I liked Harper, but she just proved what a special person she is. She totally understood, and Aiden thanked me for coming to them together. I didn't tell them it was your idea, of course." He grinned.

"Of course not. And I'll never tell. Well, maybe..." Grinning, Brendan followed the path up the hill, but the moment he laid eyes on the body lying beside the snowmobile track, his good mood vanished. He and his brothers often joked around on the job to deflect the stress, but there was nothing funny about a person losing his life. Even if it had been Jenna's attacker.

Waves of undulating snowdrifts stretched out as far as Brendan could see, disturbed only by fallen pinecones from the trees above. Well, and a dead body. A very dead body.

Brendan lifted the binoculars he'd snagged from Drake and searched the wooded area ahead of him, trying to find any danger that might linger. Tall pine and maple trees cast shadows below, and an ominous feeling chilled Brendan. This killer was smart. Not a hint of having been at the scene except for the snowmobile tracks that Brendan believed would match the tracks they'd already photographed.

Grant stood over the body and didn't look up when Brendan reached them. The victim's face was a blotchy red. Eyes blank. His head was turned to the side and deep scratches ran down the visible side of his face, like fingernails had gouged his skin. Jenna's nails? Likely. His mouth hung open as if he'd been surprised in death. Maybe he'd been joyriding with a partner. A buddy. Fellow tough guy. Then bam, he got a knife in the chest. His own knife, as the red blade by the hilt indicated.

Brendan could definitely ID the guy as Jenna's attacker. No questions asked. On the one hand, Brendan was glad they'd found the guy. On the other hand, this wasn't over, and they were now looking for a killer.

"He's the guy who attacked Jenna," Brendan told Grant.

"You sure?"

"Positive. I saw him holding a knife over her and then fleeing the cabin."

"We'll need Ms. Paine to confirm."

Brendan figured Grant would require Jenna to weigh in, but there was no way Brendan would bring her out here in the open for the killer to take a potshot at her. But Brendan had to play this down if he wanted Grant to agree. "If it's all right with you, I'll take a picture and show it to her."

"Sure, fine. A long as she gets a look at the guy."

Brendan approached the victim and snapped a close-up of his face. Seeing the lifeless body took Brendan back to some of his Delta and law enforcement days. Not good days for sure. The ones that involved a body were hard to handle and overcome.

He shook off the tightness forming in his chest and took a wide view of the scene instead of focusing on the loss of life.

"Looks like he arrived on snowmobile." Grant squatted, and his legs disappeared in the snow. "No footprints, so he had to be dumped from the machine."

Brendan agreed. To a point. "Depending on how long he's been here, boot prints could've been filled in by blowing snow. We've had some strong wind."

Grant stood and brushed his legs off. "We'll have to wait for the ME to tell us how long he's been dead. The freezing temps will make that determination more difficult."

"How long before the ME arrives?"

"Today, I hope."

"My dad's bringing up a canopy with lights in case we go into nightfall."

"Oh, we will. No question. Hopefully your sister can get the forensics done before then." Grant clapped his hands on his arms. "Freezing out here. Can I count on one of your men to hold the perimeter while I make some calls in my car?"

"Sure thing."

Grant's bushy eyebrows rose. "And they'll keep everyone out this time?"

"Everyone except me, but I'm done here. And we'll put up the canopy for you."

"Just make sure you don't disturb anything."

Brendan didn't need the warning, but he nodded so Grant would leave him alone and he could get back to Jenna sooner. They made their way back to Clay, and Grant kept going to his car.

Brendan waited until Grant was out of earshot then looked at Clay. "Okay. So what else am I gonna find on the video that you and Erik didn't want Grant to know about?"

Clay lifted his chin. "How do you know we have something else?"

"Brothers, remember? I can read both of you." A simple explanation but the reading of others actually came from Brendan's time in the army. They were taught to work as a team. Look out for the good of their fellow soldiers. Do that, and the team would operate better. That ethic had stuck with Brendan, and he'd never been a lone wolf like Clay tended to be.

As the middle brother, he'd often been left alone when they were growing up. Brendan hung with Aiden and Drake with Erik. Clay needed to work hard to get attention or be included. Made him more outgoing and at times aggressive, as he was used to exerting his rights. That had changed a bit since Aiden got engaged, and Brendan and Clay had hung out more often.

All irrelevant right now, when Brendan had to keep his focus on the mission. Something else the army had taught him. "So, what did you find?"

Clay cued up a copy of the video on his phone and held it out. "We trailed the snowmobile tracks for a few miles. Took us here."

Brendan followed the drone footage. "A tent campground?"

Clay nodded. "It's a couple miles away. It's closed for the season, but there's a tent set up. No vehicles but this."

He zoomed in on the video showing the bright orange tent and a red Polaris snowmobile Brendan recognized parked right next to it.

He looked up. "That's our guy's hidey-hole."

"Exactly." Clay grinned. "And no telling what we're going to find there."

Brendan felt the excitement of a strong lead building in his gut. "We need to get over there ASAP."

"You telling Grant?"

Brendan shook his head. "He might not have banned me from this scene, but he'll call in reinforcements before going into the campground. He won't let us anywhere near it."

Clay arched an eyebrow. "He could charge you for obstructing his investigation."

"I haven't officially been asked to stand down as the acting deputy. I can infer that my temp duties are done from Grant's arrival, but it's a fine line that I'll walk for as long as I can. And even after I'm told to stand down, that's not going to stop me. I'll get to the bottom of Jenna's attack no matter what, and that now looks like it includes finding a killer." Brendan curled his hands into fists. "How did the roads look from the drone?"

"Passable until you get into the campground. Then we'll have to hoof it."

"Then I should get going." He met Clay's gaze. "I promised Grant someone would stand sentry here."

"Not me." Clay stowed his phone and raised his shoulders into a hard line. "I want in on the campground. Get Erik to do it."

Brendan felt a sudden chill and shoved his hands into his pockets to warm them up. Of the brother's, Clay lacked the most patience and standing duty here would sorely test that, but Brendan couldn't cater to everyone. "We can't always give him the grunt jobs or he's never going to get more experience."

"We can start with that tomorrow." Clay chuckled.

Brendan was about to respond when he caught sight of their dad, a boxed canopy perched on his shoulder, struggling through the deep snow.

Clay's eyes brightened. "We'll ask Dad to stand duty. He'll be glad to do it."

"I'm down with that. It'll give us an extra man at the campground." Decision made, Brendan slogged through the snow to help his father.

He was huffing and puffing, and he dropped the canopy. "Never carried this thing through such deep snow. I hauled it all the way up here. You boys go ahead and put it up."

"After we do, will you stand guard and keep everyone except Sierra out of the scene?" Brendan asked.

"If you want me to." He tried to sound nonchalant, but the gleam in his eyes said he was glad to be back in the law enforcement game, even if he *was* acting in the grunt job of officer of record.

Brendan picked up the box and put it on his shoulder. "Dang, Dad. This thing *is* heavy."

He grinned, looking just like Clay had a moment ago, only older. "Told you."

Brendan turned to the crime scene, slid the box under the fluttering tape, and unpacked it right inside the perimeter to keep from disturbing the area around the body. He and Clay assembled the structure and hauled it up the hill and into place over the body.

Clay paused to stare at the dead man. "You think that's the knife Jenna was threatened with?"

"Not often you see a red-bladed one like that, so yeah, I do." Brendan started down the hill, trailing the extension cord behind him and ducking under the tape. Clay slipped under the perimeter next to him.

His dad eyed the cord. "Hope that reaches the cabin."

"Looks like it will," Brendan said, hoping he was right. "We have an errand to run. Be back soon."

His dad frowned. "Not going to loop me in, huh?"

"I don't want you to have to lie to Grant when he asks where we went." Brendan grinned at his dad.

"One of *those* errands." His dad winked and clapped Brendan on the back. "Good luck."

"Thanks." Brendan glanced toward the dead guy on the hill. "We just might need it."

Jenna stood by Brendan inside the door of his parents' cabin. She pondered everything he'd just told her about their plan to raid the campground while Aiden stood watch over her and Karlie at the cabin. He'd also shown her a photo of the man who'd died so she could confirm he was her attacker. She nearly dropped to the floor at the sight of the knife protruding from the man's chest. And now Brendan was going to go after the killer.

The thought made her heart ache.

"I don't like you heading into danger," she whispered for his ears only and took his hand. "I might've only known you for a few days, but please come back safe and sound. Karlie and I need you."

His eyes widened, and she waited for him to say something, but he didn't speak. Not a word. He simply clutched her hand and held her gaze for a long moment.

How could she have said something so foolish? She needed him. Sure she did. To keep them safe, but her comment had implied more. Was she starting to feel something for him? Had she let her guard down and allowed her emotions to rule?

And what did Brendan think about her statement? If his startled expression told her anything, it said he didn't want that *more* she was suggesting.

"You know," she said, backpedaling. "You've been in charge of everything, and we need you to keep it up."

"Right." He didn't look away but rested his hand on the doorknob, as if wanting to escape.

"Not that I want you to stay safe just for that," she babbled on. "I mean, I don't want you or anyone else to get hurt. You've all been so good to us."

She grabbed his hand again. "Let's pray for your safety before you go."

Great, now she was using prayer as a diversion. What was going on with her?

She held tightly to his hand and offered a sincere prayer for his safety. For everyone's safety, and that they would find a lead to help them bring in the killer.

Killer. Seriously, she was praying about a killer. In her life. Unbelievable.

She ended the prayer and squeezed his hand.

He smiled at her, a cute lopsided number that revealed a dimple in his cheek and sent a jolt straight to her heart. "Thanks. And I'll tell the others you prayed for them too."

"Please let me know the moment you can about what you find and if everyone is fine."

"Sure thing." He turned the knob and watched her for a long moment before stepping out.

When the door closed, worry nearly smothered her. Not an emotion she'd ever felt this deeply before. Sure, she'd been distressed, and she worried for Karlie's health and when they'd lost their home, but Jenna never experienced this visceral ache of concern.

"He'll be fine," Aiden said. "They all will."

She spun to look at him. "How can you be so sure?"

"Brendan was a Tier 1 operator when he served in Delta Force. Tier 1 Special Units are closed teams. Membership only by invitation. They're the best of the best operators."

"He didn't mention that."

"No guy on the team is going to tell you that. They're tops in their units. Yet, most of them think they're just average Joes doing their jobs."

"Just like you," Harper said, joining them and taking Aiden's hand.

He smiled at her but waved off her comment. "Brendan will come back just fine. He's faced far more dangerous foes and lived to tell about it."

Jenna had thought highly of Brendan before, but now she had a special appreciation for his skills. And his humility. Even more, she wanted to get to know him, but first he had to return safe and sound from hunting down a killer.

10

The sun beat down on the tent, and the fabric nearly glowed with the bright orb in the sky behind it. Brendan and his brothers had been watching the campsite for thirty minutes now without even a hint of activity. By the time they'd arrived, the snowmobile was gone and they'd seen no movement inside the tent. Not good. Whoever killed Jenna's attacker could have taken the machine and could still be in the area. Brendan had to find out what or who was in that tent and get back to the cabin to make sure she wasn't his next victim.

Brendan turned to his brothers. "I'm calling the surveillance. We go in as planned."

Planned meant tactical vests. Helmets. And assault rifles. And Brendan on overwatch with his rifle.

"Firing at any occupants in that tent is the last resort," Brendan said. They had no legal right to fire on anyone other than in self-defense. Raiding someone's tent and harming them would be classified as aggravated assault, and shooting the occupant would mean serious prison time.

"We also need to be mindful of the potential evidence here," he added. "And be careful not to destroy it."

"We know what we're doing, bro." Clay rolled his eyes and glanced at Drake and Erik. "I lead. They follow. You take overwatch. Let's move."

Brendan didn't like leaving the breach in his brothers' hands. Not that it was unusual for him. He'd often played the role of sniper, removing himself from the direct action in the army and as a deputy and should've been comfortable hanging back, but he wanted to be firmly in charge of everything to do with Jenna.

Clay stood and looked at Brendan. "You need help getting up, old man?"

Time for Brendan to roll his eyes. He got to his knees then duckwalked to a nearby mound and slithered through the snow on his belly. Under a large spruce, he propped the rifle tripod on the mound and sighted his scope on the tent.

"Target in sight," he said in his comms unit. "You're a go."

Clay waved Drake and Erik forward, and they eased out of their positions behind a solid cinderblock bathroom. They had to lift their knees high to break through the thickly crusted snow but methodically crossed to the camping site. Clay halted in front of the zippered opening. Drake moved past him to take up the far side. Erik took the backside in case any occupant managed to flee. With only one entrance, that was unlikely, but he could always cut through the nylon and squirt out the back.

"Come out with your hands where I can see them," Clay called out.

Brendan kept his focus on the zipper, memories of hours behind the scope in Afghanistan and Iraq plaguing him.

"No movement," Clay said into his mic. "Going in."

Brendan's gut cramped. Unlike a building with windows, the tent had zero interior visibility, and Brendan couldn't keep eyes on Clay. Once he stepped into that tent, Brendan could do nothing to protect his younger brother.

The pull of the zipper through the comm unit sounded like a harsh rasp in the still of the day. Clay split the opening with his rifle and stepped in.

Brendan waited for a report. A clock sounded in his head, each tick raising his concern.

One. Two. Three...ten...twenty.

"No occupant," Clay announced on the comms.

Brendan let out his breath. They might be safe now, but adrenaline still pounded through his body. "Erik and Drake keep watch. Clay open the flap so I can see inside."

Clay tied the flap back. Brendan ran his scope around the space and made a mental inventory. A sleeping bag lay on top of a small air mattress. A plastic bin of food items sat on the floor, a backpack nearby. And a stump of wood held aluminum foil, two spoons, a candle, lighter, and drugs that Brendan recognized from his time as a deputy.

"Heroin," he said into his mic, though Clay was likely familiar with it too, but he wanted his brothers to hear what was going on. "Guy was a user."

Clay squatted by the stump and pointed at balled up aluminum foil discarded on the floor. "Either he's been here for some time or he had company."

"Two spoons says company to me."

"Yeah, using in tandem." Clay stood. "The drug use might help us figure what he was looking for at Jenna's cabin. Though she doesn't appear to be into drugs."

"Look in the backpack," Brendan said and Clay opened the pack. He pulled out a pair of jeans and T-shirt along with a roll of duct tape.

"Could be the tape used to secure Jenna," Brendan said.

Clay dropped the items back inside and reached for a wallet. He removed the driver's license and held it up to give Brendan a clear look. "It's Jenna's attacker, all right."

Clay turned the license around and snapped a picture. "Guy's name was Lonny Odell. Lived in Gresham."

The eastern most suburb of Portland wasn't far from their location.

"We need to check out his place," Clay said as if reading Brendan's mind.

Clay looked at Brendan. "Still want to keep Grant out of this?"

"Until after we get a look at Odell's place. We can head over there right away." Brendan ran his scope over the campsite. "Firepit's been cleared of snow. Feel the burnt wood and ashes."

Clay stepped out and squatted by the pit. "It's cold. No one's been here for a while. Or at least no fire's been lit."

"Gather around," Brendan said.

His brothers cautiously made their way over to Brendan's location. He remained behind the scope. "The killer could still be in the area, though no sign of that. Now that we have Odell's name, Erik, I want you to use the new skills you learned from Nick and run background on the guy."

Nick Thorn, the Veritas Center's cyber expert, had given Erik an intensive course on completing a deep dive on people. The team no longer had to count on Nick all the time. He was far too busy with paying jobs to keep dropping things for the Nighthawk team.

"And a check on Jenna," Brendan added at the last minute.

"Jenna?" Clay asked. "You think she's keeping something from us. Or lying?"

"We have to do our due diligence on every client, right?"

"'Bout time," Drake muttered.

Brendan looked back at his brother and wanted to punch him but held his anger in check. Drake was right. It *was* about time Brendan did his job in that area.

Erik glanced between the pair of them. "Glad to get out of this cold and see what I can do."

"And let me guess," Drake said, his tone sarcastic. "You want me to stand watch here in case the killer returns."

"Exactly." Brendan resisted smiling at what could be perceived as payback for his comment when it wasn't. He just thought Drake would do a good job. Brendan put his rifle in the case and slid down the incline. "Also, give Sierra a call. Ask her if she can get her assistant out here to process the tent."

"Grant's not going to like that," Drake warned.

"I know." And Brendan didn't care. He had to do what was right to find the killer. "I'm heading over to Odell's place with Clay. Should only take a couple of hours. If we need Sierra there, too, I'll let you know."

Drake didn't look happy about being left behind, but he nodded.

Erik opened his mouth, and Brendan knew his baby brother planned to comment on how nice and dry he would be in the cabin while Drake froze his tail off in the snow. Brendan didn't want to deal with the result, so he slashed a hand across his neck to tell Erik to hold his tongue and shoved Erik in the direction of the SUV.

Clay followed and they drove straight to the cabin to drop Erik off. Brendan ran inside to update Jenna. Due to his snowy boots, he remained by the door, but Erik brushed past the family gathered around the dining table playing Monopoly to grab his laptop from the coffee table and head down the hall. He was either going to the den or his room for quiet. With Karlie missing, Brendan suspected she was playing in the den or napping.

Jenna rushed up to him, seeming out of breath. "You're okay?"

"Yes," he said. "We're all fine. No one was in the tent, but we did get your attackers' ID." He held out his phone with the driver's license picture that Clay had taken. "Recognize the name?"

"Lonny Odell." She shook her head but kept her focus pinned on the screen. "Never heard of him."

Aiden joined them and looked at Lonny's scowling photo. "Looks like a real character."

"We also found drugs and paraphernalia in his tent," Brendan said. "I think it's heroin."

Jenna didn't say a word, but continued to stare at the photo. Brendan didn't want her to keep looking at the man who attacked her, so he locked his phone.

"I'm sorry you had to see him again," he said.

She worried her bottom lip between her teeth and stared over his shoulder as if deep in thought. Or maybe her thoughts had returned to the other cabin, and she was reliving the attack.

"Clay and I are heading over to Odell's place." He looked at Aiden. "You good to watch things here."

Aiden nodded. "FYI, I saw the ME's van arrive a few minutes ago. They'll be loading up the body."

"Medical examiners. Body." Jenna clasped her arms around her middle. "This is all surreal, and we still don't know why this man came to my cabin and who killed him or why."

"I'm wondering if it's drug related." He looked at her, waiting for her to claim she didn't use drugs, but she didn't say a word. Nothing.

Was she dodging this topic? He had to come right out and ask. "Do you use drugs, Jenna? Is that how he might know you?"

She jerked back. "I can't even believe you'd ask me that. I thought you'd gotten to know me well enough to know that couldn't be true."

He didn't want to hurt her, but she still didn't answer his question. "Sorry, but do you?"

"No." Her firm tone and clear eyes declared she was telling the truth. She turned away and went to sit on the hearth by the fire, her arms still protectively circling her waist.

Karlie came running into the room and slammed into Brendan's leg. "You're back. Wanna play?"

Another member of the Paine family who he was going to disappoint in less than a minute. He took a knee so he could look her in the eyes. "I do, but I have to go out again."

She frowned, looking so much like a miniature version of her mother that it tore at his heart. "When will you be back?"

"Just a couple of hours."

"Coupla hours is a long time." She spun to face Jenna. "Is a coupla hours before my bedtime?"

"Yes."

Karlie faced Brendan then and placed her hands on both sides of his face. The touch of her soft little fingers against his skin melted his heart, and he was smitten with the four-year-old, even though he had no idea what to do with a child other than make pancakes.

She held his gaze. "Promise you'll play with me."

"Promise."

She pulled her hands free and ran over to her mother. "He's going to play with me when he gets back."

Jenna didn't look all that impressed and still seemed to be a million miles away. He wanted to ask about her thoughts, but not in front of the others, who were watching him as if he'd grown several heads.

"What about dinner?" his mother asked.

Brendan stood. "We can grab something in Gresham."

She tsked. "You're going to miss a most excellent pot of vegetable soup and fresh biscuits if I do say so myself."

He really hated missing his mother's home cooking, but he hated Jenna being in danger far more. "Save me some?"

"I'll try but you know your brothers." She wrinkled her nose.

"Dad not back yet?" he asked.

"He's too busy playing deputy to come home." She shook her head, but her tone was loving and understanding, as she'd been for so many years.

"Drake won't be here either," Brendan said. "He's on a stakeout."

"In this weather?" His mother shook her head. "Tell me you left the SUV with him."

"Sorry. We need it."

She pressed her lips together. "Then tell me where he is, and I'll get something warm down to him."

"I'll write down the address, but send Dad or Erik." He grabbed a notepad and pen on the counter. "I don't want a suspect spooked by someone who doesn't know how to safely approach."

"Maybe that will get your father home." She chuckled.

He wrote down the campground information and looked at Aiden because he couldn't bear to see the disappointment in Jenna's expression again. "I'm out of here. Call me if anything out of the ordinary happens. I mean anything."

He strode to the door, and, despite knowing he'd be sorry, he turned to look at Jenna. He'd expected disappointment. Not the worry in her eyes that grabbed at his emotions, and he wanted to stay. But he had a job to do, and in the long run, leaving her behind was for her own good.

With gloved hands, Brendan raised the window of the modest bungalow in an older neighborhood in Gresham and climbed in. As Clay slipped in behind, Brendan shone his flashlight over the kitchen, finding it surprisingly spotless. He hadn't expected a bachelor with a drug habit to be so neat. A dish rack held clean dishes, and not a crumb lingered on the wood countertops. Magnets clung to the refrigerator holding receipts and photos. Nothing stood out as important, but he took photos of everything.

Clay ran his light over the gleaming vinyl floor. "I thought the place would be trashed, what with the drug use and all."

Brendan couldn't agree more. "Maybe it wasn't his stash."

"You could be right. We should soon find out. If he was a user, he's bound to have left paraphernalia, maybe drugs, around here."

Brendan stepped into the hallway and Clay followed. They turned right for the living room. Neat and tidy too. Nice furniture. Some expensive-looking artwork. Massive flat-screen and surround sound system on the far wall.

Brendan let out a low whistle. "Either this guy had a great job or he was into some seriously illegal stuff that paid well."

"No sign of drugs." Clay moved back into the hallway.

Brendan followed him, his flashlight beam merging with Clay's when they crossed paths.

They stepped into an office, and Brendan went straight to the computer. Clay took a bookshelf holding covered beige boxes and started pawing through them with gloved hands. Brendan woke up the computer and sat in the chair. They might not be leaving physical fingerprints in the place, but just by waking up the computer, he was leaving a digital print behind. Sure, it didn't track to him, but it would tell a forensic examiner that someone had been on this machine after Odell's death. As a deputy, Brendan would never have touched the computer, but he wasn't a deputy any longer, and his worry for Jenna compelled him to act.

He scanned the screen for email. Found nothing. Looked in the menu. Nothing there either. No banking information or statements. He checked the internet browser and the guy had cleared his history. A sign that he was paranoid about anyone finding out what he'd been up to, and it would take computer techs to recover the data.

He opened the address book and took a picture of Odell's contacts and phone numbers. Several were doctors, and there was a long list of food delivery places. No sign of parents or siblings. No one at all with the same last name.

Brendan looked up. "He might not have any next of kin. Or if he does, he doesn't keep their contact info in his address book."

"He might know their phone numbers."

"But how many people today actually know anyone's number? Not the majority for sure."

Clay's eyes widened. "Look at this." He held out a small black notebook. "It looks like some sort of code."

Brendan took the book and flipped it open. The first page held dates down the left side of the paper, five-digit numbers in the middle, each with a corresponding five- to six-digit number on the right side. The numbers started at ten thousand and went up to one hundred thousand.

Brendan flipped the page. "Two pages of numbers."

"The round numbers on the right make me think dollars."

"If so, he's had a regular income, which would explain his pricey possessions."

"Income from what? No signs of drugs." Clay peered around the room. "Maybe he's a dealer. Maybe he wasn't the one sleeping in the tent. Maybe that was a client, and it was his drugs we found."

"Sounds possible. Except the dollar amounts are too large for a small street-corner dealer. Maybe it's not income. Maybe these are the dates he received a supply of drugs, and the number is what he paid for the stash."

Clay arched an eyebrow, looking like a pirate behind the beam of his flashlight. "If he sold a hundred grand in drugs, he must have cash stored somewhere."

"I'll take pictures of these pages, and then let's tear this place apart to find the money." Brendan snapped the photos then started through boxes with Clay until they'd completed searching every inch of the shelves. For the most part, they found receipts and old banking records.

"No current bank statements and there weren't any on his computer either," Brendan said. "And no history of logging into a bank."

"Maybe he only uses cash." Clay narrowed his eyes. "After all, if this book really is a cash journal, he'd have to go into a bank to deposit the money to use it any other way. And he'd have to be careful to keep the amount under the fed's limit."

Brendan knew Clay was referring to bank requirements to report withdrawals and deposits of cash exceeding ten thousand dollars. "I don't remember seeing a credit card in his wallet. And there wasn't anything on his computer to suggest any online purchases, so he could be on a cash-only basis."

"Erik might find more in his deep dive."

Brendan nodded. "Let's keep looking."

They went to the master bedroom, searched drawers, the closet, and nightstand to no avail. In the third bedroom, Brendan sat on the bed to check the nightstand and hard lumps protruded from the mattress beneath him.

He tore off the bedding and unzipped what appeared to be a soft-sided waterbed mattress. He flipped the cover back. "Well lookie here."

Clay stepped across the room and shone his light on the bed. "Cash. A boatload of it."

"Actually a mattress load, but yeah. Big bucks." Brendan took a picture of the cash then closed the cover and remade the bed. "Question now is, how did he get the money and does it have anything to do with Jenna?"

11

Jenna sat with Karlie in front of the blazing fire, the glorious warmth on her back radiating through her body, but not easing out the chill that hadn't gone away since Brendan departed. She was coming to like being with him and coming to like him. No, that was wrong. She was more than liking him. She had feelings for him. No matter how much she'd warned herself not to fall for him, she was well on her way to doing just that.

She sighed, drawing Peggy's attention from where she sat with Russ on the sofa. The remaining family members were seated in the other chairs in the cozy room.

Her eyes narrowed. "Is everything okay?"

"Fine," Jenna answered. It was the truth, after all. She and Karlie weren't in danger right now and were enjoying the Byrds' hospitality. The vacation wasn't what Jenna had planned. Nothing like it. But there were wonderful moments among the terror. Jenna just needed to embrace them.

Peggy stood. "I think it's time for hot chocolate. Who wants some?"

"Me. Me." Karlie jumped up, a big grin on her face.

"Me, please," Jenna corrected.

"Please." Karlie's smile evaporated.

Jenna felt bad for ruining her daughter's joyful moment, but Jenna had to correct Karlie so she learned to be appreciative and polite.

Jenna pushed off the warm brick hearth. "I'll help."

Peggy waved a hand. "You're a guest."

"A guest forced on you during your holiday. The least I can do is not give you extra work." Jenna looked at the others. "Anyone else want hot chocolate?"

"You know we do." Russ grinned, his smile slightly lopsided, like Brendan's. "I can't imagine anyone turning you down."

Jenna looked at Harper and Aiden, who both nodded.

"I should ask Erik too," Jenna said.

"That would be nice, sweetheart, and Karlie can be my big helper." Peggy held her hand out to Karlie, who skipped over to her.

Jenna's heart lightened in seeing her daughter skipping without pain. Even with all the changes in her normal schedule, she hadn't experienced any ill effects on her health, and for that Jenna was grateful. She offered a prayer of thanks as she went down the hall to the den and knocked on the open door. "Your mom is making hot chocolate. Would you like some?"

Erik looked up from his computer and ran a hand through his hair, and for the first time she saw a bit of Brendan on his brother's face. It was the eyes. The same color, but more than that, the same expressive way of channeling his feelings through them. "I could use a break anyway."

"Things not going well?"

He closed his laptop. "I'm striking out on Odell's background search. Hardly finding anything. I don't want to admit defeat and have to call Nick for help."

"Nick?"

"The cyber expert at Veritas. He's a whiz when it comes to the internet. He taught me how to do a solid background check, but I'm coming up empty-handed."

"Then a break is just what you need. Plus, I'll bet your mom will add some of her cookies to the offer."

"Cookies?" He hopped up and smiled. "Why didn't you say so?"

He laughed, and she found herself smiling all the way to the kitchen. She liked all of Brendan's brothers, but Erik seemed to be the easiest going. The others were more complex. Or maybe he just hid the complexity better.

Karlie was sitting on the edge of the counter, a smile on her face, chocolate smeared on her cheek. She was talking and talking, telling Peggy about what she liked to do and about how Olaf liked to do the same things.

Jenna thought to rescue Peggy, but she looked happy too. Sounded like Aiden and Harper were going to get married in the spring, so maybe Peggy's odds of having those grandchildren would increase. But it seemed like Harper and Sierra both loved their careers too much to take time out for children.

Jenna's thoughts traveled to Brendan. Did that mean Peggy would pressure him for those grandchildren? And would he give in to the pressure to marry someone so he could fulfill his mother's wishes?

No. Not Brendan. He knew his own mind, and no one was going to pressure him into anything. Especially not marriage.

The SUV cut through the snowy roads, heading up the mountain, and Brendan would soon be back at his family's rental cabin. Couldn't be any sooner, as far as he was concerned. He wanted to be by Jenna's side to be sure she remained safe.

He checked his phone, looking for a missed call or text. Nothing.

Clay glanced at him from the driver's seat. "You're going to burn up your battery if you keep checking."

Clay was right, but Brendan wouldn't bother with a response except to glare at his brother.

"What?" Clay shook his head. "You got it bad for Jenna, is all I'm saying."

"And how would you know that?"

"You mean besides the way you're jonesing to get back to the house to check on her?"

"Yeah, besides that. Assuming that's what I'm doing."

"You are. Plain as day."

"And what else?" Brendan couldn't wait to hear his answer.

"You didn't do a background check on her right away. You just trusted her and offered our services. For free, no less. I can't see you ever doing that with any other client."

"Is that all?" Brendan shook his head. "She has a little kid for Pete's sake. What did you expect me to do? Leave her at a cabin with a busted-down door in a blizzard while I looked into her past? You'd have done the same thing."

"Sure, but once I got back to our cabin I would've done a background check. Or had Nick do it. Kid or not, I wouldn't just trust her. Unless...well, you know the unless."

Clay spoke the truth. Brendan got that. He *should've* ordered that background report early on. And as he'd told Sierra, he didn't do it because he'd thought it would be creepy. If he'd found a guy in danger instead of Jenna, he would've checked the guy out before letting him step foot in his parents' cabin. So now not only was he under Jenna's spell, but he was probably a sexist when it came to protection too. A woman versus a guy under attack. Brendan's protective instincts kicked in for a woman. Not so much for most guys.

And they were kicked in high gear right now. Telling him something was wrong. But what?

He peered out the window. A snowy blanket covered everything as far as he could see—most of it untouched— and the cabins were dark. The storm had likely kept most people away, but by tomorrow he would expect lights spilling out many of the cabin windows, along with trees lit by twinkling lights. At least that was what he'd experienced in the past years.

Christmas was only four days away, though he hadn't thought much about the holiday since he'd discovered Jenna being held at knifepoint. Her throat cut. Her eye blackened.

His phone chimed. Heart racing, he looked at the screen. A text from Drake.

Sierra's assistant Chad is here. No sign of anyone else.

Brendan replied. *Can you stay until Chad is done and report back?*

Can do.

Brendan was about to thank Drake when his phone rang. Seeing Grant's name, Brendan considered ignoring the call. But he needed to update the detective on Odell's house and the tent. Now would be as good a time as any. Especially since Chad was at the tent, and Brendan wanted Sierra to process Odell's place too.

"What can I do for you, Detective?" Brendan forced himself to sound glad to hear from the guy.

"Seriously, you're gonna play dumb with me?" His tone rose an octave.

"Dumb?"

"You take off, and even with your sister here, you don't come back? Only one thing would be keeping you away. A lead."

"Two, actually." Brendan fessed up to searching the tent, gave Grant Odell's name, and described his house.

A long breath of air sounded through the phone. Grant was likely waiting for Brendan to say more, but he would wait the guy out. Maybe let Grant get a little of his irritation out before going on.

"I could've been working on background on Odell all this time," Grant finally said. "But no. You don't think it's important enough to tell me. I just might haul you in for obstructing justice."

Brendan had expected Grant to threaten arrest, but Brendan would do the same thing again if it meant getting closer to stopping the killer. "I was never officially relieved of my acting deputy role, so the search was well within those parameters."

Grant swore under his breath. "A technicality."

"Still, I was acting in an official capacity. Besides, we wore booties and gloves and left everything right where we found it."

"Is this the way you roll? Because if it is, we can end our association right now."

"I'm sorry. We had to follow the leads." Brendan waited for the guy to keep yelling at him.

"Consider yourself officially relieved of your acting-deputy status." His tone was deadly calm. Far worse than hearing his anger.

Brendan understood Grant's fury, but it wouldn't stop Brendan from following leads wherever they took him.

"See that?" Clay pointed ahead.

Brendan leaned forward. In the distance, a small headlight cut a sharp beam through the dark. An engine sounded. A snowmobile.

"Sorry. I gotta go. I'm almost at my parents' cabin, and I'll head up to see you after we check in here." He shoved his phone into the dash holder and grabbed his night vision binoculars to peer out the front window. "Looks like the same machine Odell used. Two riders. Headed for our cabin."

Brendan swallowed hard and tapped Aiden's icon on his phone. When his brother answered, Brendan put him on speaker. "We're almost at the cabin. Spotted a snowmobile approaching you. Same model as Odell used. Two riders. Nearly there."

"Already on the porch watching the progress," Aiden said.

"Good. Good. And Jenna?"

"In the bathroom. Dad at the door."

Brendan let out a breath. "Make sure she stays there. After the threatening message it's probably best to move everyone out of the living room."

"We've got this."

Brendan knew in his brain that his brothers and dad were more than capable of protecting everyone, but his heart was another matter. "Stay on the line."

"Will do."

"Step on it, Clay." Brendan raised his binoculars again.

Clay pressed the gas pedal, but the SUV fishtailed, and he had to ease off. The SUV continued up the road, but the snowmobile seemed rocket-propelled, shooting forward at a much faster clip. Brendan zoomed in on the driver. He was a big guy. Burly. The passenger. Slight. Could be a woman or man. Both wore helmets, and Brendan couldn't tell. Nor could he make out any distinguishing features even with his night vision binoculars.

The machine pulled up even with the cabin.

"Snowmobile is slowing by you, Aiden," Brendan reported, his stomach tightening.

"Trust me." Aiden sounded irritated. "I have eyes and my weapon trained on it."

Brendan wanted to trust his brother. Trust God. But everything was out of Brendan's control, and he hated that. Hated not being in charge. Hated not being able to protect them. Watching a fight was so much harder than being in one.

Please. Please. Please. Keep her safe.

The snowmobile engine wound down, and the machine stopped. The driver pivoted toward the passenger, grabbed him by the jacket, and hurled him into a snowbank at the side of the road.

"Passenger down," Aiden said.

Brendan kept his binoculars on the person lying face down in the snow. "Not moving. Could be dead."

"Or it could be a trap," Clay warned. "Guy faking it so one of us checks on him."

The driver turned back to his machine and roared directly toward their SUV. The loud engine ramped up higher, the growl shattering the silence. He raced ahead as if playing chicken with them. Daring them to run him down. He suddenly saluted and banked into a sharp turn, the machine's track lifting. He leaned into the turn, coming to his feet, balancing the snowmobile, and making the turn without an accident. He roared off into the woods.

Brendan looked through the binoculars again, following the machine's disappearance into an area out of Brendan's view.

"We should check on the rider," Aiden said. "Even if it's a trap, we'd hear the machine coming back to warn us."

"Not if he came back on foot," Clay said.

"We can't ignore the person down." Brendan lowered his binoculars to glance at Clay. "Pull up right beside the body. I'll use the vehicle for cover."

"I'll send Erik out to watch the area where the snowmobile headed," Aiden offered.

"Perfect." Brendan glanced at Clay, who was still concentrating on driving. "Get Drake on the phone and tell him to be on the lookout for the snowmobile."

"Roger that." Clay made the call.

Brendan crawled into the back of the SUV to retrieve a ballistic vest, slide into it, and fasten the Velcro.

"Drake says all is quiet," Clay reported. "But he's freaking cold and ready for someone to relieve him."

"We'll take care of that after we see to this guy." Brendan struggled back to his seat, hitting his head on the overhead light. He was pretty agile, but a guy his size wasn't meant to be crawling around an SUV.

Clay slowed, and the tires crunched over deep snow as the vehicle bumped into place next to the person, who hadn't moved a muscle since being dumped. Clay shifted into park.

Brendan eyed the downed rider as he opened the door. "Watch my six."

"Roger that." Clay drew his sidearm.

Brendan lifted his own weapon and slid down to his knees, the door and SUV protecting him on two sides but still leaving vulnerable spots. Hopefully Erik and Aiden had those covered. Brendan nudged the rider and kept his gun trained on the body. No response.

He shoved the body until it rolled over. The person's arms splayed out, giving Brendan full view of his hands. No gun. No knife. No movement. And a better look at the shape. The rider was definitely a guy.

Brendan had received basic medic training in the military and eased closer to feel for a pulse. The guy moaned and tried to say something, but Brendan couldn't make it out. "He's alive. We need to get him inside."

"How do you want to do it?" Clay asked. "I'd have you put him in the SUV but with the other vehicles in the drive, I can't get you much closer."

"He's not a big guy," Brendan said. "I can toss him over my shoulder, but I need everyone's backup."

"Erik's in place," Aiden said. "And we've got you from here."

"I still have your six," Clay said.

"Then let's do this." Brendan hefted the guy onto his shoulder and drew his gun again. "I'm moving."

He pushed to his full height, his knees arguing with the extra weight. His mind went back to the many similar rescues he'd performed in Delta. But those were different. He was often under fire from insurgents. Still, he had a team behind him back then. He had a top-notch team now too. Especially thanks to the many hours of tactical training and practice at Gage Blackwell's compound in Cold Harbor.

Brendan took a step and shifted the body for better balance. His next step, his boot plunged into knee-high snow. He lost his balance but quickly recovered and looked for a better path. He could sidestep to the driveway, but that would put him more in the open. Nothing for it but to go through the snow. He lifted his leg and plunged it in. He listened for any upcoming attack. Heard only a soft wind blowing and an owl hooting in the distance.

He powered through the drifts to the steps where Aiden waited, his rifle lifted.

Aiden kept his focus on his rifle but used his free hand to open the door for Brendan. "I'll stay out here until I'm sure we're clear."

Brendan tromped inside and his mother poked her head into the family room. "All clear?"

"Yes," Brendan said and set the guy on the sofa.

His mother came into the room. "Who's that?"

"Not sure. He was dumped out front from a snowmobile." Brendan lowered the guy onto the couch and removed his helmet. "Call 911. He needs medical help."

His mother made the call as Brendan took off the guy's helmet. He had long dirty-blond hair and a slender face with freckles covering his cheeks. Brendan felt for a pulse again. Slow and thready. He unzipped the man's ski jacket and searched for any wounds.

Brendan lifted one of the man's eyelids. Found a pinpoint pupil. Likely a drug overdose.

"Ambulance is on the way." His mother set her phone on the table. "Who do you think he could be?"

"No idea. I'll check for ID." Brendan unzipped the first jacket pocket found nothing. Second pocket, he lifted out a small plastic container. Inside, he found heroin, a cooking spoon, and syringes. He held the kit out for his mother to see. "Looks like he OD'd."

His mother gnawed on her lip. "So there's nothing we can do for him?"

"Other than to pray that the ambulance gets here in time to administer NARCAN, no." *And perform CPR if he stops breathing,* Brendan didn't add as he hoped that wouldn't happen.

"What's NARCAN?" his mother asked.

"It's a drug called Naloxone. It'll immediately reverse the effects of an opioid overdose. We carried the nasal spray when I was a deputy. Saved many lives that way. Medics will have an IV version, and it'll work even faster."

He took off the guy's jacket and checked his arms. Needle marks crawled up his sallow skin.

The door opened, and Brendan spun to find his brothers entering.

"Update?" Aiden demanded.

Brendan showed his brothers the drug paraphernalia. "Mom called 911. I need to search the rest of his pockets for ID."

He handed the kit to his mother, who held the box with trepidation, and he rifled through the guy's pant pockets. He pulled out some change, a matchbook, and a folded piece of paper.

He unfolded the paper. It said. *Leave what I want on the dining table in your cabin, Jenna, or you're next.*

His gut cramped, and he held the paper out for the others to see.

"So this guy really *is* looking for something," Clay said. "But what?"

His mother knelt next to the guy and checked his pulse. "Shouldn't someone get Jenna to see if she knows him? The message makes it sound like she might."

Brendan gawked at his mom. He'd forgotten all about Jenna. How could that have happened?

"I'll go." He strode quickly across the wooden floor, his boots leaving puddles of snow behind. He could already hear his mother tsking over the mess and see her handing him a mop to clean it up. He didn't want to do any mopping, but right now he just felt blessed to have a mother who'd always cared enough to steer him and his siblings in the right direction in life, so they didn't end up in a snowbank clinging for life.

He entered the hallway where his dad stood with Harper. "You're cleared to join Aiden if you want, Harper," he said.

She nodded and stepped down the hall.

Brendan turned to his dad. "Is Karlie still with Jenna or did she go to bed?"

His dad tipped his head at the bathroom door. "She's been chattering away since they went in. Don't know how Jenna can handle the nonstop babbling all day long." He chuckled.

"Would you mind taking the chatterbox into the den?" Brendan told him about the guy. "I want to see if Jenna knows him."

"No problem." His dad opened the door and held out his hand. "Hey, munchkin. Come with me, and we'll finish our Candyland game."

Karlie looked up at her mother. "He calls me munchkin. He says it means he likes me. I like him too. Can I finish the game?"

"Sure, but then it's bedtime."

"Aw, but I was gonna play *Go Fish* with Brendan." She stubbed the toe of a white sneaker into the wood floor for emphasis, making Brendan smile. She was a mini-Jenna and cuteness overload.

"You can play in the morning," Jenna said.

"Wanted to do it tonight." Her face downcast, she grabbed the outstretched hand and dragged Brendan's dad behind her.

"She's really getting off her schedule." Jenna frowned.

"Is that such a bad thing for a few days?"

"Maybe not for a healthy kid but with her JIA, she really needs to get a consistent amount of rest or it could flare-up."

"And what happens then?" he asked, as he knew nothing about the disease.

"Since it's an autoimmune disease it causes her joints to swell and be painful." Jenna twisted her hands together. "She also gets extremely fatigued. Beyond what words can describe."

Just the thought of the child suffering put a sharp pain in Brendan's heart. He couldn't imagine seeing it. Worse yet, being a parent and seeing his child suffering. He didn't think he could convey his sadness over her illness but he would try. "I'm sorry that she has to go through that. That you have to see it. Must be tough for both of you."

Jenna nodded. "I wish I could take it from her. I'd much rather suffer myself than watch her in pain."

"Not having kids, I don't know how you feel, but I can imagine it." He would do whatever he could while they were together to make sure the pipsqueak didn't get overtired and suffer a flareup.

Jenna eyed him, her gaze mining, for what he didn't know, but she suddenly looked away. "So, what's happening that you didn't want Karlie to see?"

He should've known Jenna would pick up on his hidden agenda. "The snowmobile driver dumped a guy out front who looks like he suffered a heroin overdose. We're waiting on the ambulance."

Her eyes got big and round. "Does he have any ID?"

Brendan shook his head. "But there's a note in his pocket that makes us wonder if you know him. The guy who dumped him is the man who killed Odell, connecting this to you. And the note was personal. Like he hurt this guy so you would give in and give him what he wants. So I'd like you to take a look at him to see if you know him."

Her face paled, the heavy smattering of freckles on her cheeks standing out. "Okay."

Something about her hesitancy gave Brendan a moment of concern, but when he gestured for her to go ahead of him, she marched straight into the family room.

"Cover him with a warm blanket," his mother directed from beside the man.

Erik tossed Aiden a heavy quilt that the family had used

to snuggle in for as long as Brendan could remember. His grandmother had made it as a gift for his mother's bridal shower, and they always brought it along to the cabin.

Jenna stepped around the corner of the sofa, Brendan right on her heels. She gasped and wobbled. "No. Oh, no."

Brendan supported her by the elbow. "You know him, then."

"Yes." She dropped down to her knees by the man and took his hand. "It's my brother."

She brushed his hair back from his forehead and lowered her voice. "Oh, Shawn, why? I knew you had something to do with this. I just knew it."

12

A light breeze could knock Brendan over. Poof. Just like that.

It wasn't the fact that Jenna had a brother. Sure. Fine. She didn't tell him about that and it stung, but the rest of her announcement? That her brother was likely involved in her attack and she hadn't told Brendan? That was almost unforgivable.

How was he supposed to protect her if he didn't know all the facts? Her actions were just like Tristen all over again.

He took several breaths to calm his anger before he said something he would regret and locked his focus on Jenna. "What do you mean he had something to do with this?"

She turned to look at him, probably because his words had come out between clenched teeth, the anger palpable.

"I'm sorry. I know I should've told you. But I couldn't get my brother in trouble. Just couldn't." She fell back on her haunches looking deflated. "It probably feels like I betrayed you all, but I didn't lie about anything. I only withheld information about Shawn. Shawn Nelson is his full name. He was supposed to spend Christmas with Karlie and me, but he didn't show up."

"And you weren't worried?" his mother asked, her tone far gentler than Brendan's had been.

"Worried, yes, but not in the way most people worry about a missing relative. Shawn's done this for years. He's been in and out of our lives. Mostly out for the last five years. But when Toby died, I wanted to reconnect with my only other living family member. So I invited him to spend Christmas with us."

Sounded like a legit explanation, but Brendan was still hurt, and he shoved his hands into his pockets so she didn't see him fisting them in anger. "And you think the killer might've been looking for Shawn?"

She nodded and looked queasy. "After a long history of drug use, he recently started dealing too. It's the sort of thing that might make someone come after him, right?"

"Yes." Brendan wanted to ask additional questions, but his mother was giving him the stink eye. Fine. He'd hold back for now. After all, Erik was supposed to be doing that background check on Jenna and would uncover details about Shawn too, and Brendan could then ask the questions left unanswered.

Jenna's gaze flitted around the room. "Is he going to be okay?"

"Of course he is," Brendan's mother said.

Brendan stepped closer. "Let me check his pulse again."

Jenna scooted out of the way, and he knelt down. He touched Shawn's clammy skin and found the pulse to time it against his watch. "Fifty-five."

"Is that bad?" she asked.

He gave a sharp nod but didn't tell her that brain damage could be an issue if Shawn's pulse fell much lower. She didn't need that extra worry.

"Where's that ambulance?" She jumped up and raced to the door to open it and peer out.

Before Brendan could go after Jenna, his mother did. She closed the door and put an arm around Jenna's shoulders. Despite Brendan's anger, he wanted to replace his mother's arm with his own arm and provide that comfort Jenna so needed. Was he being a fool? An idiot who was falling for another woman who kept secrets? Did she keep other things from him too?

"Worrying isn't going to get them here any faster," his mother said.

"I know but, I have to do something." Jenna's panicked voice washed away the last of Brendan's anger.

How could he stay mad at her when she was so worried about losing her brother?

"Why don't we pray for him?" Brendan's mother suggested.

Jenna's lips pressed together in a grimace. Didn't she think prayer could help?

His mother wasn't put off but took Jenna's hands and bowed her head. The others joined her, and she offered an eloquent plea for Shawn's healing.

Jenna looked up, tears swimming in her eyes. "Thank you."

His mother gave Jenna a hug, and Brendan hated standing by and watching.

"There," his mother said. "I hear the sirens now. The medics will give Shawn the NARCAN that stops the effects of the drugs, and he'll be fine."

Jenna jerked open the door and started to step out.

"Stop!" Brendan bolted after her.

She looked up at him with troubled eyes.

He couldn't let her unease sway him. "Your life is still in danger."

"But I want to wave the ambulance down."

"I'll go." Clay raced past them before she could argue.

"Come inside," Brendan said, softening his tone. "Please."

She took a long look at the road then stepped into the cabin. Brendan let out a silent breath. "You should know, even after the NARCAN, Shawn will still be transported to the hospital and probably kept overnight for observation. At least that's what I've experienced as a deputy."

Jenna looked at Brendan's mother. "You all have done so very much for us, and I hate to even ask this, but would you watch Karlie while I go with Shawn to the ER?"

"No! You're not going to the hospital." Brendan didn't like that his tone came out harsh and unyielding, but he couldn't let Jenna put herself in danger, even *if* her brother was ill.

Everyone pivoted to look at him.

"I'm sorry," he said. "That was harsh. But it's not safe for you to go with him."

"I'm going." Jenna planted her feet, looking much like Karlie when she'd stubbed her toe into the bathroom tile.

The sirens whirred closer, and panic that she would ignore him and leave with the ambulance nearly made Brendan issue another demand. He counted to ten before speaking. "This could all be a trap to lure you out of here."

"He's right," Erik said, but she seemed to ignore his comment and moved past him to the couch.

"I can't let my baby brother go alone." She dropped to the floor by Shawn and took his hand again but eyed Brendan. "You wouldn't sit back and let your siblings go through this alone."

He wanted to say his siblings wouldn't be in this position, but drug addiction could happen to anyone regardless of their background. "You're right, I wouldn't, but I can defend myself. You can't."

She raised her chin and kept her gaze pinned to him.

His mother stepped closer. "Why don't I go with Shawn tonight? Then, if he's admitted, you can visit tomorrow after the boys have time to plan."

Brendan wished his mom wouldn't call them the boys in front of a client, even if Jenna wasn't a paying client. Made them sound like little kids when they were grown men with multitudes of experiences between them. But she had a good suggestion.

Jenna looked at him. "Will you promise to take me to the hospital tomorrow?"

Promise? Could he? "*If* I can come up with a safe plan."

She stood. "Not *if*. Promise you'll take me, or I'm going with Shawn now."

"Fine. I promise." Brendan didn't like that he sounded so churlish about it, but his job was to protect this stubborn woman, and she'd just gotten him to promise something that could very well cost her life.

Jenna's heart hammered as she watched the medic inject NARCAN in Shawn's vein. She held her breath. Waited. Nothing. No response. Her heart fell, and she eyed the medic. "It's not working."

"Give it a second," he said, but his eyes were narrowed.

She tapped her foot and tried not to lose it in front of everyone. But, come on. Her brother was potentially at death's door, and she couldn't do a thing to help him.

God, please. I know I haven't felt Your presence lately, but be there for Shawn. He needs a miracle.

A hand touched hers, and she glanced down to see Brendan's strong fingers brushing against her skin. She didn't care if nearly his whole family, the medics, and a sheriff's deputy were standing nearby. She clutched his fingers for dear life and clung to the warmth.

The medic rubbed his fist over Shawn's chest. "Come on, fella. Are you with us? Come on. Come back."

Shawn suddenly gasped and sucked in a deep breath.

"There you go," the medic said. "You're back."

Relief flooded Jenna's body, and she nearly dropped to the floor, but Brendan supported her with a strong arm around her back. She didn't know what she would do without him here. If Shawn had shown up like this at her cabin she would've freaked out and panicked. Maybe wasted time before calling 911.

"Hey." He blinked a few times. "What's going on? Where am I?"

Jenna moved forward. "Someone dumped you off of a snowmobile, and you were unconscious."

"Sis?" Seeming dazed, he sat up and looked around. "Is this your cabin?"

"No. It's down the road. These are my friends. The Byrd family."

Looking exhausted, he lay back against the arm of the sofa.

"Do you remember what happened?" the medic asked.

"Not really."

"What drug did you take?"

"I didn't—"

"Save it." The medic held up a hand. "You OD'd, and I gave you NARCAN. It'll help you if the doctors at the hospital know what you took."

"Not going to the hospital," Shawn grumbled.

"We have to transport you."

"No can do." He started to swing his legs down, but the

medic stopped him and looked at Jenna with a plea for help in his eyes.

She moved forward. "You have to go, Shawn. You almost died."

"But I..."

"Go. For me." She took his hand. "Please. I want to make sure you're okay."

He glanced around as if looking for any other choice. "If you go with me."

"I can't. Someone is trying to hurt me, and it's not safe if I go."

Shawn's forehead tightened. "Hurt you? I don't understand."

"She was attacked," Brendan said. "Maybe by one of your associates. His name is Lonny Odell."

Shawn's mouth fell open.

Jeanna's heart dropped. "You know him?"

Before he could answer, the medic stood. "This can all wait until later. We need to get him transported."

"Yeah, later," Shawn said as the pair of medics helped him onto the stretcher.

The burly deputy stepped forward. "I'll be confiscating your contraband." He locked gazes with Shawn. "Maybe you can use this as a wake-up call and make different life choices going forward."

"I will." Shawn sounded earnest, and Jenna knew he meant it. Now. But later? She'd heard this too many times to think he'd actually follow through.

The deputy looked skeptical as he stepped back, but Jenna didn't care what the law enforcement officer thought right now. At least he wasn't arresting Shawn.

She snagged her brother's hand. "Peggy is going to come with you. She's the mother to all the guys here and a special person."

His mother moved closer. "Hi, Shawn."

He looked less than impressed. Of course, their mother had been a nightmare. Peggy's mothering skills would only highlight their own parents' deficiencies.

He forced a smile her way. "Hey."

"Don't give her any grief," Jenna said. "And I'll see you tomorrow if they keep you. If not—"

"If not." Peggy took over. "One of my boys will come get you and bring you back here."

Jenna smiled at Peggy. "Thank you."

She waved a hand and held out her phone to Jenna. "Put your number in while I get my jacket. Then I can send you regular updates without having to go through Brendan."

Jenna entered her number and gave Peggy a warm smile when she handed back the phone.

Jenna pushed Shawn's hair back and kissed his forehead. "Get well, Shawny."

He frowned at her. "How many times do I have to tell you not to call me that? I'm a grown man."

"You'll always be my baby brother."

"We have to go." The medic rolled the stretcher out the door.

Brendan shared a look with his mother that Jenna couldn't decipher, but Peggy swept Jenna into a hug, bringing tears to Jenna's eyes. Tears for Shawn. For herself. For both of them and their tough childhood.

Peggy released her and walked out with the medics. Jenna stood staring after them, her body seemingly frozen in place. Brendan closed the door.

Jenna supposed she was in shock. Not only had her brother almost died, but it looked like he knew her attacker. And maybe even knew a killer. Something she would get to the bottom of tomorrow when she talked to him. Of that, he could be certain.

Brendan thought for just a moment that he should go after Shawn and question him, but the guy needed to recover tonight, and Brendan would question him first thing in the morning.

"I don't know how much time you spend with your brother," the deputy said to Jenna, "but if he doesn't get clean, you should get your own NARCAN spray."

"How would I do that?"

"In Oregon, anyone can get it from a pharmacist without seeing a healthcare provider first. Falls under our Good Samaritan laws. You can also thank those laws for keeping me from arresting your brother for possession of this." He held up Shawn's drug kit with the heroin.

Brendan really *was* thankful for the deputy's arrival, but he was a young guy who seemed like he might give Jenna a stern lecture. Something she didn't need. Not when she was already distraught.

"We appreciate you coming out, Deputy." Brendan headed for the door to let the guy out.

Shoulders back, he marched to the door and gave a final look at Jenna as if she were the problem.

"Thanks again." Brendan waited for him to step out and closed the door.

Harper took Aiden's hand. "I think we should let Brendan and Jenna have some privacy to discuss this."

"But why?" Aiden sounded perplexed.

"I'll explain it in the den." She dragged him from the room.

Clay looked at Erik. "Guess we should take a cue too."

"Gonna be crowded in the den," Erik muttered as he followed Clay.

Jenna watched them for a moment, then went over to

the fireplace and stared at the flames. Brendan didn't mind being alone with her. He *did* mind seeing Jenna looking so desolate, and he would do just about anything to make her feel better, but what could he do?

He approached her, and she turned to look at him, her eyes dark with grief.

"I'm sorry you had to go through that," he said. *Right.* How trite did that sound when he felt like pouring out his heart to her, which he'd never done, not even to Tristen. So why Jenna?

She gripped the thick mantle on the fireplace. "I expected him to OD at some point, but I could never have imagined the actual impact of seeing it."

Karlie came running into the room, taking Jenna's attention. The child was brimming with energy, and her eyes were bright for such a late hour.

"Time for *Go Fish*." She grabbed Brendan's hand and started tugging him out of the room.

"Karlie." Jenna's warning tone stopped the child in her tracks. "I said that would have to wait until morning."

"Aw, Mommy," she whined.

Jenna knelt by Karlie. "I wish you could stay up, but honey, you know what happens when you get overtired."

"I hate JIA." She pouted.

"I know you do. I hate it too."

"Can Brendan read me a story? Please. I'll get ready fast. Promise. I'll even brush my teeth good."

"Yes, if you do get ready fast *and* if Brendan agrees."

She turned those big eyes up to him, and he was forever wrapped around her little finger. "Sure thing, little bit."

"And we have our prayers that we don't want to forget." Jenna stood.

Karlie's expression turned serious. "We haveta pray

every night. And during the day too. Mommy says God likes to hear from us."

"I'm sure He does." Brendan loved how Jenna was raising Karlie by setting a good example.

She skipped off, and a tight smile crossed Jenna's face. "Thank you for agreeing. I hate to keep imposing."

He didn't think but took Jenna's hand. "You're not imposing. I truly like Karlie. And you. So I'm glad to do it."

Jenna frowned and looked down at their hands. "I'm not free to get involved right now, so if you're hoping..." She shrugged.

Not free. His heart dropped. "Is there someone else?"

"No. No one." She looked back up, and their gazes collided. "And that's the way I want it."

She turned and walked away, leaving him wondering if she truly meant that or if she just didn't want to be with him, and she was just saying it to let him down gently. He very much wanted to find that out. No, he *would* find that out. Later. But now he needed to read a book to a four-year-old. Something he'd never done. Ever. But he'd had a lot of books read to him as a kid so he knew how to do it. In theory anyway. In practice was another thing.

He waited until Karlie came running into the room dressed in her Christmas footie pajamas. Her face was pink from washing, her eyes still eager but starting to droop. Taking his hand, she tugged him into the room shared with her mother and Harper.

Karlie grabbed a book called *God Gave Us Christmas*, the bright blue cover with a bear sitting in the snow inviting him to open and read it. She jumped into bed, tugged up the quilt, and patted the bed beside her. He sat next to her, and she circled her arm in his, pulling him closer and laying her head on his shoulder.

His heart melted. Poof. Like that. Into a big old puddle of

goo. She was so sweet and precious, ignorant of all the hard things life could include, things he'd witnessed, and he found himself wanting to protect her from any harm. From all the pitfalls of growing up that he knew she would have to go through.

She handed the book to him. "I told Mommy I wanted books for Christmas. I want to read them over and over instead of taking them back to the library."

"Which books do you want?"

She started naming them, but after a long list that he tried to memorize, her eyes drooped, and she tapped the book in his hand. "Read, please."

He opened to the first page and started the story of Little Cub. He reached the middle of the cute story and glanced at Karlie. Her eyes were drooping, nearly asleep, and it made him smile with contentment.

"Read more," she said, barely awake.

He continued on to the end, enjoying the book as much as Karlie seemed to. He closed it and eased out of her arm to gently let her head rest on the big fluffy pillow.

"Thank you." Jenna's whispered voice came from the doorway. "I'll take it from here."

He nodded and found himself very reluctant to leave them. He backed to the doorway, watching Jenna tucking Karlie's hair behind her ear and kissing her daughter's forehead.

He stepped into the hallway. As he closed the door, it seemed like he was closing himself out of their life when he wanted more than anything right now to be included.

"Oh man," Clay said from the end of the hallway. "You've got it far worse than I thought."

Brendan wanted to tell his brother to mind his own business, but why, when he spoke the truth? Brendan had not only developed feelings for Jenna but also for the pipsqueak who called Jenna mommy. He'd always admired men who married women with children, but he'd never thought he'd be one of those guys. He didn't get it until tonight. Not that he had plans to marry anyone, but to find out where his feelings for them went? Yeah, he wanted to do that for sure. Even if the outcome might not be in his best interest.

13

Brendan found Sierra kneeling in the snow where Odell's body had been discovered, a tweezer in one hand and a small vial in the other. The lights from the canopy glimmered off her white Tyvek suit. She'd put it on over her ski wear, stretching the fabric tight. She looked like the Stay Puft Marshmallow Man.

She looked up at Brendan, her cheeks rosy, her breath visible. "About time you got here. I've had to listen to Grant complain about you for far too long."

"Sorry. A lot has happened." Brendan shared about the tent and Odell's house and the money. And then Shawn.

"Oh, no," Sierra said. "Is Jenna okay?"

"I honestly don't know, but she's a strong woman. She'll get through this."

Sierra looked at him long and hard as if he were evidence she was trying to puzzle out. "She's someone you don't want to let out of your life."

"You sound like Mom."

"That's not a bad thing. When it's not directed at me." An impish smile he remembered from their childhood crossed her face.

"Exactly." He grinned. "I thought Reed would be with you."

"I figured you'd want the DNA from Odell's body processed as fast as possible, so I sent him back to Veritas with the knife and samples for Emory. I just got a text from him. He's back at the cabin."

"I'm gonna owe him big time for that trip, but thanks for thinking of it."

She deposited the item clasped in her tweezer into the vial and closed it. "He also took the potential DNA samples I recovered from the cabin. Could be Odell's or not, since it's a rental. The trace on Jenna's clothing and the nail scrapings are a better hope."

"Even if the samples return Odell's DNA, it's really no value to us. We have his ID now, and he's dead, so he won't stand trial."

Sierra tsked. "How many times do I have to tell you guys? Forensics is the hard science behind your investigations. You can't actually prove Odell attacked Jenna other than your eyewitness accounts."

"Yeah, but—"

"But nothing. Eyewitnesses get things wrong all the time. Even former lawmen like you."

He gritted his teeth so he wouldn't snap at her. "I'm not wrong."

"Then Jenna's fingernail samples and any touch DNA we locate on her clothing will prove that."

He didn't want to continue down this path. "It'll be more helpful if you find DNA that tells us who killed Odell."

"I've recovered a few samples that could do that. I just need to get them to Chad, and he'll transport them to the lab for Emory to get started on." She stood and brushed off her knees. "But here's something you should know. I overheard the ME talking to Grant. Odell was stabbed in the ear too. Not with a knife. Something like an ice pick."

"Two stab wounds," Brendan said as he processed the news.

"The one in the ear is the one that killed him. ME said it likely went straight into his brain. He hasn't seen anything like it since his military days."

"You think we're dealing with a professional hit here?" he said more as a way of processing. "Would be something a black ops guy might do."

She shrugged. "That's your area of expertise. I'm just the messenger. Gotta wonder though, what the point of the knife was."

"I don't know. Maybe to distract us from the real wound. Or just sending a message of some sort. Like it looked more dramatic." Brendan needed to think about this, but if a black ops guy was after Jenna, the risk to her life just grew exponentially. "Any prints?"

"Not here. But I lifted a ton in the cabin. Oh, and it would be great if we recovered the roll that the duct tape came from. I can match the edges."

"We saw a roll in the tent, and Chad will likely grab it," Brendan said. "Are you staying the night or going back?"

"If you want me to do Odell's place, I'd like to wait until morning. I'm beat, and I want to spend at least a few hours with Reed on this vacation." She chuckled.

But he caught the fatigue in her eyes, and he felt bad for ruining the time she should've had to recuperate from her very busy schedule. "I'm really sorry to spoil your time off. Is Reed upset?"

She shook her head. "He's very understanding. Just concerned that I don't get too worn down."

"I'm glad you two found each other. You seem happy."

"We are." A secretive smile stole across her face. "Very."

"Something you're not telling me?"

She opened her mouth to reply but pointed over his shoulder instead. "Danger, Will Robinson. Danger. Grant's approaching."

He rolled his eyes over her *Lost in Space* reference that their dad used all the time, and took a breath to prepare for Grant's arrival.

The detective stomped closer, exaggerating his steps. "You're not keeping your sister from working, are you?"

"I'm just stretching," Sierra said before Brendan could reply.

She always had his back, and he had hers. Was a hallmark trait of the family even when they were kids and fighting with each other. Pick on each other? Fine. Someone outside the family try to pick on them? Not cool.

"If it's okay with you," she continued, "I'd like to process Odell's house for you too. After you visit and earmark the items you want me to concentrate on, of course."

"He told you then." Grant glared at Brendan. "Figured he would. And yeah, might as well keep all the evidence in one place."

"Would it be okay if I waited until morning?"

Brendan liked how she was making Grant think he was in charge here when she wasn't even being paid to do the work.

He nodded and changed his focus to Brendan. "Now finish telling me about Odell's place."

Brendan shared every detail he could think of, including the ledger and discovered cash.

Grant let out a slow whistle. "Where does a guy like Odell get that much cash?"

"Wish I knew. Doubt it's legal though." Brendan stared at the blood-soaked snow and thinking of the ice pick turned his veins to ice. He had to up his search for this killer, and do it fast, before this possible black ops guy ended someone else's life.

~

Jenna didn't know what to focus on. Her brother's near death experience and hospitalization or the investigation into her attacker, now dead at the hands of a killer. Either topic left her nearly breathless with anxiety, and she couldn't enjoy the plate of cookies and hot cocoa Harper had served to the family in front of the fire.

Russ had gone to bed, and Harper and Aiden were snuggled under a Christmas-themed blanket on the sofa. Drake sat on the hearth, still warming up from his sentry duty, Jenna suspected. Erik remained in the den doing background research. Clay and Reed both reclined in comfy chairs, their phones in hand. And of course, Brendan was with Sierra, and it felt odd to be with his family when he was gone. Odd but not uncomfortable. They'd been very welcoming.

Jenna already knew it was going to be hard to say goodbye to the Byrds. Karlie would likely have an even more difficult time. She'd been basking in their compliments and kind comments. They adored her, and she was returning their admiration.

Jenna sighed and was about to excuse herself to go to bed when the door opened. The men all shot to attention, but Brendan stepped inside and stomped his boots on the rug then slipped them and his jacket off.

"Cold out." He nudged Drake aside and stood in front of the fire that was snapping and crackling with a fresh log.

Reed looked up. "Sierra say how long before she's done?"

"About thirty minutes."

Reed shoved his phone into the pocket of his cargo pants. "She's not alone up there, is she?"

"Grant's with her."

Reed came to his feet. "I think I'll go walk her home."

Jenna loved how protective these men were. Not in an overbearing way, but in a way that spoke to the love of their family.

"Can't be apart for even an hour, huh?" Clay grinned.

Jenna waited for Reed to get mad, but a soft smile claimed his lips. "Not if I can help it."

He headed for the door.

That was the kind of love Jenna had always wanted. A man so besotted with her that he wanted to be with her all the time, and yet gave her space to be who she wanted to be. Funny, though. She had no idea who she wanted to be besides mother to Karlie and a good Christian. Maybe that was enough, but maybe she wanted more. She'd had no time to figure that out. With struggling to just put food on the table, she'd been too exhausted to think about more than getting through each day.

"Mind if I get Erik, and we go through our leads to plan our next steps?" Brendan asked.

Clay sat forward, his fatigue seeming to evaporate. "Go for it."

"Agreed," Drake said. "It's way too quiet up here, and we need to do something other than just sit here in our rockers and get old."

Aiden nodded, but he glanced at Harper.

"I'm not sure I can help other than giving Jenna moral support," Harper said.

"Sometimes that's the best kind of support there is." Brendan squeezed Jenna's shoulder as he left the room.

She was glowing warm from the fire, and the blush stealing up her face was heating her up even more. But if the others noticed Brendan's soft touch, they didn't comment on it. She sure noticed though. It felt intimate. Like they had a connection and he wanted to remind her of it.

He returned with Erik, who grabbed a giant snowman cookie from the plate.

"I don't know how you guys can eat so many cookies and still stay in shape," Harper protested. "I have to watch everything I eat, and then I still have a few pounds I can lose."

"Lose?" Aiden arched a brow. "Your shape is perfect. Wouldn't change a thing."

"Yeah, but you don't have to fit into my compression tights." She grinned up at him.

"Would be weird if I tried." He laughed and drew her close to kiss her on the nose.

Erik groaned. "Oh man, that's a sight I don't even want to imagine."

"Yeah, you could never unsee it." Drake mocked a shudder.

They all laughed, and Jenna found herself joining in and wishing that, after she and Karlie were safe, they could still be friends with the Byrds.

Brendan moved to the head of the group. "Too bad I don't have a whiteboard to keep track of our notes."

"Karlie has a big sketchpad and markers," Jenna suggested. "I could get that."

"That would be great." Brendan gave her a glowing smile.

She lurched to her feet before she blushed under his attention again and hurried to her bedroom. She took a moment to tug Karlie's blanket up to her chin and kiss her cheek. Jenna worried about Karlie all the time. Toby's negativity had taken a toll on her, and now here she was with such positive and warm people only to be jerked away from them in the very near future to go back to the dismal apartment.

"No," she whispered. "Don't think about that. God will provide what we need, and we can be happy with just the two of us."

She grabbed the sketchpad and markers lying on the lower shelf of the nightstand and hurried back to hand them to Brendan.

He'd brought a straight-backed chair into the room and propped the pad up then squatted to scribble the word Forensics. "Sierra told me she hasn't had a chance to process any of the evidence, including fingerprints from the cabin. And you all know Reed has taken DNA and the knife to Veritas. After it's processed for prints and DNA, Grady will check it out. Maybe he can give us a lead. And hopefully, the duct tape I found at the tent will match the pieces found at the cabin."

Drake narrowed his eyes. "This is all good, but none of it helps us find who killed Odell and is likely the mastermind behind Jenna's attack."

Brendan took a long breath. "Just bringing you up to speed. The big news is that Odell was stabbed twice. The chest wound we knew about but the injury that killed him was in his ear. An ice pick-like tool that the ME thinks went straight to the brain."

Aiden let out a low whistle. "You thinking we're dealing with a black ops guy."

"Could be."

"What does that mean?" Jenna asked.

"That you have a seriously bad dude after you," Drake said.

She gaped at him.

Brendan fired a testy look at Drake. "Don't worry, Jenna.

You're safe with us." He shifted his focus to Erik. "Any hint that Odell is former military."

Erik shook his head. "Doesn't mean the killer isn't."

"Search for any connection between Odell and the military."

"Will do."

Brendan jotted that on the board. "In other news, Sierra's recovered promising samples from the murder scene and will process Odell's place in the morning. That could always provide us with something to go on."

"Nothing timely," Drake continued. "DNA is going to take at least twenty-four hours, and the prints could take that long for Sierra to get through too. We need something we can act on now."

Brendan frowned at his brother. "I'll question Shawn in the morning. He might be able to help." Brendan looked at Erik. "What can you tell us about Odell?"

"He's single. No job."

"None?" Clay asked.

"Nope."

Clay shook his head. "Then we're even more hard-pressed to explain the cash we found in his house other than he got it by illegal means."

"Hopefully Sierra can pull some prints other than Odell's from the money," Brendan said.

Drake leaned forward. "Probably covered in prints with how often money is handled, but doesn't mean they'll belong to Odell's killer."

Jenna could see Brendan was getting frustrated with Drake's continued comments, but he couldn't refute his brother's statements because they were true. Frustrating, but true.

"What about priors?" Brendan asked Erik.

"Rap sheet lists breaking-and-entering and assault with a deadly weapon."

Clay let out a low whistle. "I wouldn't have wanted to run into him in a dark alley."

Jenna saw Brendan's face pale as if the news was really sinking in and the thought of what could've happened to her if he hadn't come along made him queasy. It sure did her.

"What about next of kin?" Brendan asked.

"Parents are deceased. Have been for three years. Didn't find any siblings."

"There were some photos on the fridge," Brendan said, "but I'm not sure if they're family or not. I snapped pictures of everything and will forward to you, Erik, for possible facial recognition."

Erik nodded.

"I'm thinking one might be a girlfriend," Clay said. "That house was too clean for a normal bachelor."

"Hey," Brendan said. "Some guys are just neat like me."

"I said 'normal.'" Clay laughed, and his brothers joined in.

When the laughter died, Erik said, "FYI, the house he's living in was inherited from his parents. He's behind on the taxes."

Clay shook his head. "And yet he has a mattress full of cash. Sounds like he's afraid to spend it. Or he doesn't care if he loses the house, but I would find that hard to believe. Even in his less desirable neighborhood there's value in the place."

Drake leaned back and put his arms behind his head. "Maybe it's not his money. Maybe he's holding it for someone else."

"What about other finances?" Brendan asked Erik.

"No checking or savings. One credit card maxed out."

Clay shook his head. "Still, I ask. Why risk losing the house and having a maxed-out credit card with all that cash sitting around just waiting to be spent?"

"We answer that question," Brendan said, letting his gaze move from person to person, "and we find that lead we're so desperate to locate."

14

In the darkness of her bedroom, Jenna peered at the text from Peggy. The screen on her phone glowed brightly in the dark and announced the time as three a.m. Peggy was still awake and sitting at Shawn's bedside. All his tests so far checked out negative for any long-lasting damage, but the doctors planned to run additional neurological exams in the morning. On the bright side, he'd asked for help with his addiction—something Jenna felt immense relief over—and they'd started him on an opioid replacement therapy, so he was resting comfortably.

Jenna owed Peggy so very much and told her so in her reply to the text. But Jenna wanted to do more. She needed to find a way to repay this very generous woman. But how? That was the question Jenna had to answer. Couldn't be anything that cost much. She'd have to keep thinking about it.

Her thoughts turned to Shawn. Had her prayers for him finally been answered? Would this be the time that he kicked the habit? She hoped so, but right now she just needed to embrace the fact that he came back from the overdose.

Thank you, Father. For watching over him.

She wanted to believe God was watching over her too. Helping to keep her safe. Maybe by putting the Byrd family in her life. But was it just a matter of Brendan being in the right place at the right time, or was God really there, watching over them? A question she'd asked a lot lately as her life had spiraled out of control. If He *was* there, she still didn't feel Him at all.

She glanced at Karlie and smiled. Her precious daughter was the greatest gift Jenna had ever received. Any amount of hardship in being married to Toby had been worth having Karlie. And without the negativity in Karlie's life now, she could grow into a well-adjusted adult without all the baggage Jenna and Shawn carried. To become someone like the Byrd siblings, who seemed comfortable in their skin. She wasn't dumb enough to think they didn't have problems, but she could never see one of them berating a child as Toby had done.

The sight of Brendan reading to Karlie came to mind. Her little body snuggled up against his powerful arm. The juxtaposition of big tough guy and his gentle care of Jenna's adorable little girl was almost more than Jenna could handle. He would be a good father. She knew that innately. But he'd also demonstrated that in his gentle and considerate actions. And yet, no matter her attraction to him, no matter his displayed kindness, she still didn't know if she wanted a man in her life right now. She wanted to prove she could stand on her own two feet. Not just subsist on the social security checks as they were doing now, but make her own way in the world.

But did she want that if it meant Karlie missed out on having a father? On not having a provider in the family and the things a little bit more money could buy? Would she forgo the security of a husband if that were an option? No.

Jenna needed to do the right thing for Karlie. But what was right for Karlie? Was it Brendan?

Jenna's phone went dark, the room along with it, until just a tiny pinpoint of moonlight pricked through the blinds. Her mood shifted to darkness too. To Shawn. To Odell. To the killer.

Arrgh. She didn't want to think about any of that. She lay down. Plumped her pillow. Shifted. Tried to get comfortable. Shifted again. The bed felt rock hard. Like a cinderblock mattress.

Sighing, she swung her feet to the floor and slid into her favorite fluffy slippers. She'd seen a box of chamomile tea in the kitchen. She would brew a cup, then maybe she would be able to drift off.

She crept out of the room over the creaky wood floor, trying her best not to disturb Karlie or Harper. Probably an unnecessary precaution. As tired as Karlie had been when she'd finally given in to sleep, she likely wouldn't wake for anything.

In the hall, Jenna passed the other bedroom doors, making sure to move as silently as possible. She reached the living room, glowing embers in the fireplace were casting a soft orange color over the room. She rounded the kitchen corner and ran smack dab into a wall.

"Careful," the wall said.

She reached her hands up to steady herself and pressed them against the rock-hard muscles of Brendan's chest. She should remove her hands, but she let them linger, enjoying the solid feel of his body. She was starting to couple his physical strength with his reliable and steady personality.

"Don't tell me," he said, his tone light as he held up a large Christmas tree cookie. "I've got you hooked on these and you came for one too."

He grinned, that lopsided number that made her knees go weak.

"No. Tea." She reluctantly removed her hands and went to the electric kettle. The pot already held water, so she plugged it in and reached for the tea bags. She couldn't quite grab the container so she raised up on tiptoes. Still couldn't reach.

A big hand crossed over hers and grabbed the box for her.

"Chamomile," he said. "Means you couldn't sleep."

She took the box, this time being careful not to touch him. "Too much going on in my head."

"What's the latest news on Shawn?"

She ripped open the package and dangled the tea bag in a mug as she updated him on the last text from his mother. "Have you figured out how I can go see him?"

"Have you ever had the desire to ride in a snowplow truck?" His tone was far more casual about this trip than before.

"Uh, no."

He smiled. "Too bad. After tomorrow, you could've crossed it off your bucket list."

She unplugged the tea kettle before the whistle woke others and found herself smiling along with him. She hadn't often seen this lighter side to his personality, and it appealed to her. Very much.

"I've been working on the transport plan." He jerked a thumb over his shoulder at the coffee table holding a notepad and laptop. "We can go through the details in the morning when we know if you'll be going."

Just the thought of her brother made her frown.

"What did I say?"

She looked up from her cup, surprised to find insecurity in his gaze. She'd never seen that before. Did this have to do with his comment about liking her? The way she'd brushed him off?

Even if that was what put the uncertainty in his eyes, she wasn't going to bring it up. "As much as I love Shawn and want him around, I'd rather he went into rehab. I've never been able to convince him to do that. He keeps saying he doesn't have a serious problem."

"Maybe the overdose will convince him to get help."

"Yeah, maybe." She poured water over her teabag. "You want some?"

"Now you sound like my mom. She's always trying to get us to drink tea, and no one but Sierra will take her up on it." He mocked an exaggerated shudder and bit the treetop off his cookie. He chewed slowly, looking like he had something else on his mind. "Tell me about Shawn."

"What about him?" She looked at her cup, dunking the bag until the water turned a golden brown.

"Anything you want to share." He chomped another bite of the cookie and leaned against the counter, crossing his feet at the ankles. It was then that she finally noticed he was wearing green camo pajama bottoms and a long-sleeved green knit shirt that, if she hadn't felt the muscular chest, easily revealed his toned body.

She jerked her attention to the mug and blew on it, the steam rising into the chilly room in a swirl of white as the fire died and plunged them into darkness.

"Want me to bank the fire, and we can sit in the family room for a while?" he asked.

"Sure." Probably a bad idea, but he seemed interested in Shawn, and maybe it would help her sleep if she talked about her brother.

Brendan led the way across the room. "Just shove my bedding aside if you want to sit on the couch."

"You're still sleeping out here?"

"I want to be by the door." He grabbed a huge log and chucked it into the fireplace.

The wood quickly caught, flaring into a bright flame, and he jabbed the log with a poker, moving it around and sending up sparks.

She sipped her tea and watched his fluid movements, appreciating the work it must take for him to stay in such good physical shape. He came to sit next to her on the couch, settling into the corner and propping one leg on the cushion. She made sure to look at his face when she wanted to admire the strength in his legs.

"So tell me about Shawn," he said.

She took another long sip of tea and set her mug on the big coffee table. "He's younger than me. Seven years. Seven years that made a huge difference in his life. Before he was born my parents were pretty happy. But my mom didn't want a second kid. One was enough for her. My dad wanted a son. So he somehow messed things up for her, and she got pregnant. I never heard the details. Didn't want to. But she blamed him for having another child, and they started fighting all the time. About everything. You name it, they fought about it. Even over the weather. One would say too hot. The other too cold. Just to fight, I think."

She took a long breath and shook her head. "Shawn never knew the good years. I at least had those memories to fall back on. Plus, Mom didn't want him, so she basically refused to love him. I raised him more than she did. Then both my parents started drinking and doing drugs, and life got really ugly, including my dad turning abusive. There was no money for food. We got kicked out of so many dumpy apartments. Even spent some time living in Dad's van. When I graduated, I got a scholarship for a community college. That's where I met Toby."

She fought back the memories to tell the story without

breaking down. "I hadn't dated at all before that. So he swept me off my feet, and I thought I was in love. Turns out I was in love with the idea of getting out from under my parents' roof. One night my dad physically assaulted my mom, and he would've gone for me that night too if Toby hadn't intervened." She met Brendan's gaze. "Sort of like when you saved me from the attacker. Except Toby turned out to be a bigger problem than my parents. Verbally abusive and mean."

Brendan gripped his legs so tightly his fingers turned white. "Is this why you don't want to get involved with a guy?"

She didn't expect a discussion on Shawn to head this direction, but maybe it was good to clear the air on that front too. "That's part of it. I have trust issues. I don't know if I can ever trust a man again. But just as important, I've never been on my own. I want to prove that I can make it alone."

He searched her gaze. "I get it. Why you don't trust guys. I hope you've seen the guys in my family are all honorable men." He sat forward. "We wouldn't mistreat a woman. Never. I hope you can see that too."

Yeah, she could, but... "I think I can. But Toby put up a good front at first too."

"We're not putting up fronts." His gaze darkened, then he blinked the darkness away. "If you don't believe me, just think about my mom. Would she allow any of us to be a scoundrel?"

Peggy's kind and sincere face came to mind, and the image lightened Jenna's heart. "No. I don't believe your mother would allow such a thing. Not Ever."

~

173

Brendan tamped down a flash of anger when Jenna compared him to her deceased husband. Sure, Brendan wasn't perfect by any means, but his mother had taught him —taught him and all of his brothers—to treat women with respect, and they would never disrespect a woman.

He looked at Jenna. "Can you tell me anything else about Shawn?"

"Like what?"

"Who are his friends or who he hangs with?"

"I don't know anything about his life. Not only did I not want to know what he was up to, but he never came around and the few times he did, he just asked for money. I turned him down and he left." Tears filled her eyes. "So no, I don't know a thing about him except his number for a phone I pay for on my plan so I at least can contact him if I need to."

She fell silent, and he wondered what she was thinking about, but he would wait for her to tell him if she chose to do so.

She looked at him. "Can you think of something special I can do to thank your mom for everything she's done for us?"

He wasn't ready to change the subject. Not when he wanted to prove himself to her. To convince her that not all men were like her father or Toby or even her attacker or his killer—the man who'd dumped Shawn like trash—but Brendan could understand why she remained leery. His only option was to continue to show her by his actions that he was a good man. And pray for her.

But now he needed to answer her question. "I know if Mom were here, she would say she doesn't need anything special."

"Like you and your brothers. Protecting us and wanting nothing in return."

"Is that so hard to believe?"

"For me, yes. Everyone in my past except Karlie and my pastors has expected something in return for any kindness shown me." She stared down at her hands.

He shouldn't even think about touching her, but her utter look of defeat grabbed hold of him, and he took her hand in his. Her skin was as soft as the microfiber cloths he used to polish his weapons, but, despite the delicate fingers, she gripped his hand back with a fierce desperation.

He wished she'd look up, but he'd continue anyway. "You've been hurt. Been treated wrong. And yet, you're this amazing woman with a deep inner strength."

She shook her head and continued to look at their hands.

He crooked a finger under her chin to lift her eyes to his. He found them glistening with tears.

"I'm sorry." Her voice was so soft he almost didn't hear her. "Since the attack, I seem to be fighting tears all the time."

"Of course you are. It was a traumatic experience. Even strong people like you would respond with a roller coaster of emotions."

"Even you?" She challenged him by raising her chin higher. "You're all put together. Know what you want. How to get it. Decisive."

She really didn't know him, did she? His fault. He didn't let her see anything but the things he was able to control. "In cut and dried stuff like the job, I'm good, but I think I mentioned that I have issues with trust too."

"Tristen, right," she said, her gaze riveted to his.

"Right. Having gone through that helps me understand how you feel." He paused to get his words just right so he didn't offend her. "But here's the thing. You're letting your experiences color your feelings now. You probably think I'm doing the same thing with Tristen. The thing is, we can see the problem in other people, but we just can't seem to get past it in our own lives."

"Yeah, you're right, and seeing others struggle with the same thing makes me feel like less of a failure. Which should help me move on, but..." She shrugged.

"I've struggled with the trust issue for some time now, but you?" He held her gaze. "You're making me want to let it go. To see if this thing we have could go somewhere."

Her fingers slackened as if she wanted him to let go, but couldn't. She took a deep breath then eased it out. He could tell he wouldn't like what she had to say and prepared himself for the bad news.

"I like you, Brendan. I really do." She let go of his hand. "But I'm not there yet, and no amount of talking is going to change that."

He didn't want to end this conversation. He wanted more. Felt a burning need to make her want to get involved with him. The thought scared him, but for the first time in a year, he wasn't going to run from his emotions. He wouldn't stop talking about it like she'd asked. Instead he would do something to hopefully sway her mind in his direction.

He slid closer. Cupped the side of her delicate face and ran his thumb over her freckles. He met her gaze.

"I don't want to talk anymore, either," he whispered. "I want to kiss you. Would that be okay?"

Her expression waffled, every emotion flashing in her eyes before she closed them, her long lashes resting on her skin. She gave the smallest of nods that, if he hadn't been studying her so intently, he would've missed.

He drew her closer. Lowered his head as blood rushed into it, and he forgot everything but her lips as he kissed her. They were warm and soft and encouraging. Alive with emotions that fired inside him, and he was lost. Plain and simple. He was lost. For now. For good. And he wanted more. Much more.

He deepened the kiss. She slid her hands up his chest and around his neck, drawing him closer, and his heart thundered at her touch. He wanted to go on kissing her, but his brain flashed a warning. Was he taking advantage of her?

She didn't want a relationship.

The thought iced his veins, but before he could pull back she snaked her fingers into his hair, the warm feeling from her touch taking over his thoughts.

He somehow had to gain control again and stop this all-consuming kiss. Even if it was the very last thing he wanted to do.

He lifted his head, and her eyes slowly opened.

"We..." he said, but couldn't find the rest of his words.

"Shouldn't have done that," she said for him.

"Not what I was going to say, but, yeah. You're right."

"What were you going to say?" The words whispered out between the lips he still wanted to kiss.

"That the kiss was amazing, and we have a special connection," he admitted, bracing for her rejection.

She rested her fingertips on her lips, and he had the urge to replace them with his own. "But like I said, we shouldn't have done it. I'm not interested in dating right now, and we need to keep things professional."

He took both her hands in his. "That's not what your kiss said."

"I know. I..." She sighed.

He was putting pressure on her, and she didn't need that right now. "How about we just enjoy the fire together?"

"I should—"

"Just for a few minutes. It'll help you relax so you can sleep."

"You could be right." She withdrew her hands and swiveled to face the fire.

He already missed touching her, so he circled an arm around her shoulders and moved closer. Surprisingly, she laid her head against his chest. He leaned his head down to rest on her soft hair tickling his cheek.

He watched the flames licking at the wood, consuming it. That's how he was starting to feel with Jenna. Like she was beginning to consume his emotions, and he couldn't get enough of her company. He'd never set out to find a woman to share his life with. Had been running from it, in fact. But now he was done running.

Had God put her in his life to stop the running? To make him reevaluate the important things in life?

No matter the reason, he relished the feelings. Relished being able to share something as simple as a fire with this amazing woman.

Her body relaxed, and her breathing evened out.

He peeked at her. She'd fallen asleep.

He really should work on the transport plan, but he wasn't about to move and wake her up when she needed sleep. Or maybe he was just using that as an excuse to keep her by his side, where he was beginning to think she belonged for good.

15

"Mommy, there you are," Karlie's high-pitched voice broke through Jenna's sleep.

She blinked several times to come out of the peaceful slumber.

"No fair. I didn't get to have a sleepover." Karlie hurled herself into Jenna's arms. "I was scared without you."

"Sleepover?" Jenna was suddenly aware of the warm body next to her. She crooked her neck to find Brendan looking down at her with an amused expression on his face.

She glanced at the rustic bear clock above the fireplace. Seven a.m. *Oh, my goodness.* She did indeed have a sleepover. Not an intended one, but she'd fallen asleep next to Brendan. The heat of a blush stole up her face.

Brendan eased to the edge of the couch. "Since Mom's at the hospital, I'll make the coffee and see what I can scrounge up for breakfast."

Karlie grabbed his arm. "Member we're going to play *Go Fish*."

"Right after we eat." He tweaked her nose.

"I can help." She hopped down and took his hand. "Mommy says I'm the best waffle maker ever."

"Then we should have waffles for sure."

She tugged him to his feet, and he gave her a tender smile that melted Jenna's heart. That was exactly the way she'd once hoped Toby would look at his precious daughter, but he only found her faults and harped on those. Just like he'd done with Jenna.

She forced those memories away and stood. "Would you mind if I took a shower? I can come back after that and set the table."

"No worries." He lifted Karlie onto a barstool and ruffled her hair. "I have an AI helper here."

Her eyes narrowed. "What does AI mean?"

"The very best."

She swiveled to look at Jenna. "Did you hear that, Mommy? I'm the very best."

"You are indeed." Jenna hugged her daughter and wished she wasn't so in need of positive reinforcement, but after Toby's negativity, she craved encouragement. Hopefully, without the constant disapproval in her life, the need would fade over time.

Jenna kissed the top of Karlie's head. "Be right back."

"What no kiss for me?" Brendan's smile turned mischievous.

Karlie looked up at her. "Kiss him, Mommy. Everybody should get a kiss when they ask for one."

Jenna wanted to argue with her daughter, but she didn't want to make her feel embarrassed for her suggestion, so Jenna stepped over to Brendan. Planning to kiss his cheek, she rose on tiptoes.

He swooped an arm around her back and gave her a hard kiss on the mouth that spoke of so many possibilities.

"I think Brendan likes you too, Mommy," Karlie said.

"Brendan does indeed like you." He tweaked her nose like he'd done with Karlie.

Another kiss. *Really? Really?* Had she lost all common sense? After last night, she knew where it could lead, and kissing him today only made her want to go there again. Was she falling for him, or was she simply craving the positive like Karlie?

Jenna pushed against his broad chest and slipped out of his arms. As she walked away, she touched her lips. The memory of his kisses were almost as strong as the real thing, and her heart pounded.

Sure, she liked kissing him, but just as much she loved the cheerfulness and fun between the three of them. She could easily imagine mornings like this in the future. She wanted to sit down on a stool and join in the waffle making, which was precisely why she left the room.

She ran the shower cooler than normal, and, despite Brendan's assurance that he didn't need her help, she didn't linger under the beating spray. Karlie could be a handful in the kitchen, and Jenna wanted to be available in case things went wrong.

Yeah, that's why she was rushing back out there. Sure.

She put on dark jeans and a warm red sweater. She hoped the color might put her in a Christmas mood, which was why she'd packed it in the first place. She didn't like to dress in colors that drew attention, but Toby had given her this very expensive cashmere sweater one year. Ever practical, she would wear the sweater until it wore out, even if it had been a gift from him.

She towel-dried her hair and combed through it, the waves already starting to form. She'd once spent hours straightening her hair, but now she just let it do what it wanted. She had little money for fancy haircuts and wore it in a simple style that only needed an occasional trim.

She glanced in the mirror. Satisfied she looked presentable, she went back to the family room. She came to a sudden stop when she found Karlie sitting on the counter, her legs dangling over the edge as she concentrated on scooping flour from a container. Brendan looked at her, a fond expression on his face.

Karlie dumped the scoop into the bowl and gave him a radiant smile. "I did it and didn't spill."

"That's the best flour scooping I've ever seen." He held up his hand for a high five.

She raised her arm and leaned forward, but lost her balance and plunged off the counter. Brendan scooped her up before she hit the floor. She threw her arms around his neck and held on.

"I like you the bestest," she said. "Can you be my friend forever?"

He gave her one of those crooked smiles. "I'd like that, little bit. I really would."

"Let's tell Mommy so she makes a playdate."

"Brendan's kind of old for playdates," Jenna said, hating that it brought a pout to Karlie's face.

"Nu-uh. If he can do sleepovers, he can do playdates."

Brendan laughed, deep and sincere, and joy filled Jenna's heart. "Can't argue with that logic," he said.

Jenna couldn't either, and more than that, she didn't want to. Playdates in the future sounded like great family fun.

Erik stumbled into the room running a hand through his messed up hair. "What's for breakfast?"

"Waffles," Karlie announced. "And I'm helping make them."

She squirmed down and looked up at Erik. "You should have some coffee first. When Mommy looks like you do, she drinks coffee."

Jenna resisted rolling her eyes. "Can I get some for you, Erik?"

"Please, and the blacker the better. Some of us didn't have anyone to snuggle with in the night." He gave his brother a pointed look. "Came out for a glass of water and spotted you two."

"They had a sleepover," Karlie announced.

Erik tossed back his head and laughed. Jenna's face colored, and she rushed past Brendan to get the coffee.

The comment didn't seem to bother Brendan, and he shrugged. "Let's get this all mixed up, little bit."

He lifted her back onto the counter, and she picked up a spoon but winced. Jenna glanced at her hands as she passed, seeing red and swollen joints. Jenna handed the cup to Erik then felt Karlie's forehead. "You have a fever, honey."

"I know. But I wanna have fun."

"I'll get some Tylenol." Jenna glanced at Brendan to be sure he was okay with watching Karlie.

He gave a firm nod, and she went to their room to grab the children's Tylenol. She hoped this wasn't the beginning of an arthritis flare-up, but Jenna suspected her little sweetheart was in for a few days of pain and an overall sick feeling.

When Jenna returned, the waffles were sizzling in the waffle maker, steam rising up the sides, and Brendan was alone watching them. Karlie had gone to the couch with Erik, where they'd turned *Ask the StoryBots* on the TV. The bots were talking about how eyes see. Jenna gave Karlie the Tylenol and sat beside her. "Uncle Shawn is sick too. He's in the hospital, and I'll be leaving after breakfast to visit him."

Karlie finished chewing the tablets and looked up. "Can I come?"

"Not this time, honey. But if he doesn't come home today, you can visit another time."

Karlie didn't pout but gave a tired nod, telling Jenna just how badly her daughter was feeling.

Jenna stroked her hair. "After this show is over and you've had breakfast, I want you to take a nap."

Karlie frowned. "Aw, do I haveta?"

"You know rest is important when you're in a flare-up."

"It's not fair."

"I know, honey." Jenna gave her a hug and held her close to try to make up for the disease racking her little body. She'd already grown slower than most children and was smaller than a typical four-year-old, and she'd also suffered joint damage, which would be with her for the rest of her life, even if the disease did go into remission. Something Jenna prayed for daily. Sometimes hourly.

Karlie wiggled free and turned her attention to the show.

Jenna went to the kitchen, where Brendan had his phone perched between shoulder and ear while trying to wrestle a waffle from the iron. She waved him off and took the fork from his hand.

He smiled his thanks, that grin doing nothing but sending her heart into a tailspin.

"Thanks for your cooperation," Brendan said into his phone. "Now, I'd also like to have Shawn moved to another room."

He had to be talking to someone in charge at the hospital. He held the device away from his ear, and Jenna could hear the person speaking loud and quick, but she couldn't make out what he was saying.

"I understand the cost of moving him," Brendan said. "But isn't it better to incur the cost of cleaning a room than having a potential life-threatening incident?" Brendan's voice bordered on irritated. "The PR from such a thing would be far costlier."

Jenna couldn't hear the response, but Brendan's shoulders relaxed. "We'll keep in touch."

He shoved the phone into his pocket, and she turned her attention to pouring batter into the waffle pattern.

Brendan stepped closer to her. "Mom texted that they're keeping Shawn again tonight. That was the hospital administrator. He's going to move Shawn to a new room."

She glanced at him. "Why move him?"

"If our suspect has discovered Shawn's location, the last minute move should confuse him. At least for as long as you're at the hospital."

"Thank you for arranging that." She closed the waffle iron, releasing a burst of steam, and looked up at him. "When did you come up with this plan?"

"While you were sleeping."

"You didn't get any sleep?"

"I nodded off just before Karlie came in."

"I hope she hasn't been a pest for you."

"Pest? Nah. I like spending time with her." He shook his head. "If you would've asked me a few days ago what I thought about kids, I would've said I didn't know. Never been around them. Other than my younger brothers, and we weren't too many years apart."

"And now?" She held her breath, as his answer seemed extremely important.

"Now, I would say that, if they're all as adorable as Karlie, I'm all for them." He chuckled.

Her heart burst with joy at his answer. "You haven't seen the challenging times, though. She can pitch a big fit when she doesn't get her way."

"I still think the good must outweigh the bad."

"Definitely. And especially on days like today. She's headed into a flare-up, and I would do anything to take that away from her." She looked over at Karlie, whose eyes were drooping. "She needs to have a quiet day."

"I'm hoping Dad will watch her while we go to the hospital. If not, one of the guys will."

"I appreciate that. She'll probably sleep a lot, so it should be an easy day."

His focus moved across the room to Karlie. "Must be hard to see her suffering."

"You don't know the half of it." Jenna bit her lip to keep from crying. "I keep asking God why He's burdened her with this disease, but there's no point. I never get an answer."

He met her gaze, a tenderness in his eyes that was hypnotizing. "I don't know if this will help. I mean, it did for me when I separated from the army. I was stuck in the why. Why did everything seem so messed up? I didn't get an answer either. I even turned away from God. But then, our family pastor told me if I didn't find a way to move past my issues, it would only bring more pain."

He'd nailed her feelings right on the head. "That's where I am right now. So how did you get out of it?"

"At the urging of my pastor, I made a list of my why questions, and then he told me to turn them into how questions. How is an action word. It helped me do something instead of feeling sorry for myself and getting bitter. I slowly moved back toward God. Started to believe His promises again. Even when things were tough. It brought me hope. And honestly, saved my life."

"It really worked?"

"Yeah. Until Tristen. I got lost again, and I need to listen to my own words."

"Maybe I'll try it too," she said and meant it. "The whys have only exhausted me, so this sounds like something that could help."

"Something smells good." Russ came into the room. "Even *if* your mom isn't here."

Brendan gave his dad a jab in the arm, and Russ laughed.

Jenna loved seeing this family spar so good-naturedly. Her thoughts went to why she and Shawn had endured such a hard life growing up with parents who were less than desirable role models.

No. Don't ask why. Try Brendan's suggestion. Ask how.

How could she end the legacy her parents left behind? That one was easy. At least most of the time. Use what she'd learned about how *not* to be a good parent to be the best mother Karlie could hope for. And that meant Jenna needed to keep her faith strong. To trust God had their best in mind. Which meant she needed to find some time to talk to Him. Not just the quick little prayers she'd uttered of late, but real concentrated time in His word and before Him. Maybe then she would begin hearing His voice again.

Brendan took over the waffle iron and removed a steaming, golden brown waffle that made Jenna's mouth water.

"That for me?" Russ asked.

"We should let Karlie and Jenna eat first."

"Right. Guess my manners went to the hospital with your mom." He winked at Jenna.

Brendan chuckled. "Would you be able to watch Karlie while we transport Jenna to the hospital?"

"She's not feeling real well." Jenna explained.

"Glad to do it," Russ said, but he didn't look happy about it as he grabbed a cup of coffee.

"If it's too much of a bother, I can figure something else out," Jenna said. "I know it's an imposition."

"No imposition. She's fun." He leaned back against the counter and blew on his mug.

"Then why the frown?" Brendan asked before Jenna could.

"When you reach my age, you'll get it."

Brendan narrowed his eyes and paused with the batter cup over the griddle. "What does that mean?"

"Means one day you're a valuable asset to people in the law enforcement field, and the next thing you know you're babysitting." He held up a hand. "Not that babysitting is a bad thing. I'll enjoy the time with her. I just don't like being put out to pasture when I can still hold my own."

"You do still hold your own on the job."

"Not the same thing." He waved a hand. "Listen to me grumbling. It's just when I see you guys get geared up and head out, I miss the action, is all."

Brendan squeezed his dad's shoulder. "I can't imagine what it's like being left behind."

"You won't have to for a few years yet, but the transition period after separating from the army is a good comparison."

Brendan frowned. "Then it really stinks."

Russ gave a sharp nod and looked at the griddle. "Let's get more of those waffles made so I can build up my energy for babysitting."

Brendan looked at Jenna. "You'll want to get Karlie so you two can eat before my brothers scarf everything in sight."

Jenna laughed, and so did Russ. "They're not quite *that* bad, but they can put away the food. A cop's salary isn't the highest, and I remember times when Peggy and I wondered if we were going to have enough money to feed all of them. But God always provided."

Jenna could totally understand his statement. She only had one tiny mouth to feed and there were days Jenna didn't eat so Karlie could have the food and other things she needed. Like physical therapy to improve and maintain muscle and joint function and occupational therapy to improve her ability to perform daily living activities. Jenna couldn't even imagine trying to feed six kids, five of them growing boys.

"You have your transport plan finalized?" Russ slid onto a barstool and rested his mug on the counter.

"Yeah." Brendan handed the maple syrup to Jenna.

"Want to run it by me?" Russ asked.

Brendan's eyes showed a hint of irritation, but he washed it away. "Sure."

As Jenna prepared Karlie's plate, they talked about the ride to the hospital and how they were going to send out decoy vehicles while transporting Jenna in the snowplow truck. Once they were sure no one was tailing them, they'd converge in a designated location where Jenna would move to their armored SUV. Then all five of the guys would circle around her and escort her to Shawn's new room.

Her stomach knotting, she went to get Karlie. She couldn't believe all the prep needed just to get her safely to the hospital. She could hardly wrap her head around all the work and the things that had happened this week.

How did she, in a few short days, go from a stay-at-home mother just trying to feed her child to a woman who needed five bodyguards to keep her alive?

16

The big truck rumbled down the highway toward the hospital under dazzling sunshine, the whole vehicle vibrating under them. Jenna had never ridden in such a big truck, and her mind would normally be fascinated by the new experience, but every time the wheels hit a bump, Brendan's knee touched hers, and she couldn't quit thinking about the kisses. Last night's were different from the one this morning, but they both said one thing. He was not only interested in her, but also committed to pursuing where that interest led them.

Could she do the same? Could she forget what Toby had done? Said? Put away her trust issues? Forget asking why and just embrace the how? She wanted to. Desperately. But would she want to tomorrow or the next day, or were her feelings just a fluke that she would get over when she remembered the pain from the other men in her life?

You have seven men showing you that not all men are bad. What more do you want?

Wait, was that God speaking or just wishful thinking?

"Exit two miles ahead." Brendan leaned over to look at

Drake behind the wheel, bringing her back to the present. Back to the danger. Back to the fear.

She peeked at Drake and then Brendan to see if they had a clue about her thoughts, but their sharp gazes were pinned on the road and the mirrors. Searching. Seeking potential danger to prevent any harm to her. They'd both dressed in black tactical pants and more of those body-hugging shirts they liked to wear, their guns at their hips, which all helped her feel more secure, but still. Someone wanted to hurt her. Maybe kill her. Some fear was natural, right?

"Our exit's two miles ahead." Brendan's phone chimed, and he grabbed it. "Text is from Detective Grant. ME says Odell's official cause of death is a basal subarachnoid hemorrhage caused by the weapon he still thinks is the size and shape of an ice pick."

Jenna touched her ear and couldn't even imagine the pain. "That must've been a horrible way to die."

"And painful," Drake muttered.

"And even more of a reason to take care today." Brendan shoved his phone into his pocket and clenched his hands.

Jenna resisted gasping at the intensity of his tone and the sharpness of his movements.

"Take the next exit," he told Drake, his gaze pointed back out the windows.

As the vehicle rumbled off the highway and down a steep ramp, she took another look at him. He was concentrating so hard that he didn't know she was watching. He really was an amazing man. Strong. Both physically and mentally. A man of honor. Of service to his country. Loyal to his family.

He would make a fine father and husband. She knew that. He wasn't a poser like Toby had been. A man to turn to alcohol and drugs like her dad and Shawn. And surely a man who wouldn't be found on the wrong side of the law.

And of course, he was something to look at. Not that appearance was the most important thing, but it sure didn't hurt that she was attracted to him.

But she couldn't forget her desire to be on her own, could she? Or forget how she'd been hurt in the past and open her heart for more pain?

Or maybe a chance at that happiness she'd always wanted?

She dismissed the foolish emotions that she'd let take hold since Brendan Byrd walked into her life and focused on staying safe and seeing her brother.

Drake drove the truck to a parking lot where Clay sat behind the wheel of their SUV and Aiden was in the driver's seat of their parents' big Suburban, Erik in the passenger seat. Drake came to a stop nearby, the big truck lurching forward with the movements.

Brendan opened the door then pivoted and caught her watching. She blushed, but he gave her hand a quick squeeze and hopped down to look up at her. "Straight to the SUV."

She slid to the edge of the seat then moved down to the metal step. Brendan grabbed her by the waist and lifted her down. She'd been committed to being in control and watching for someone who wanted to harm her, but one touch erased that from her mind, and she nearly swooned. Seriously. A woman her age and with a child, swooning over a man. She'd never had the urge to do so in her life. So why now of all times?

Aiden stood next to the open back door, aviator sunglasses hiding his eyes, but she knew he was being extra watchful. She got into the SUV, and Brendan climbed in after her, Drake her other side. Erik and Aiden marched to their vehicle and took off.

"Let's move," Brendan said.

Clay shifted into gear and got them heading down busy streets in a suburban area of Portland. A few miles down the road, Brendan turned to her.

"We're almost there," he said. "I need you to listen to everything I tell you when we arrive. No questions. No discussion. Just act. It's all about your safety. Nothing else. Okay?"

She nodded. "Do you really think the guy who killed Odell will be there?"

"He didn't follow us," Drake said. "I guarantee that."

"But he could've followed the ambulance last night and be waiting," Brendan said. "Even if Shawn's changed rooms, we need to act as if this guy is nearby. We won't be using the main parking garage, so we'll have a bit of hike to the towers. We'll surround you, and I need you to stay within our circle."

"I can do that." Her words declared a confidence that she didn't feel.

At the hospital entrance, Clay parked behind Aiden, and Brendan stepped out in front of her. Drake to her left. Erik moved into place at her right. Aiden and Clay hurried behind her. All the men were shoulders back within a few inches of each other in height and were strongly built. She felt like a football surrounded by players in a huddle, the players willing to protect the ball at all costs.

They marched like a little army into the building and down a long hallway. She peeked between them at the people staring as they passed. She could easily imagine the sight they presented. Brendan took them on a route that involved several turns, his movements confident and sure.

She'd known they would be. First, it was his nature to be

confident, but second, he'd spent the rest of the night while she'd slept in his arms planning the route and the early morning hours calling hospital staff to be sure his plan would work and they would be safe. He put her first. Above everything, as did his brothers right now.

Thank you for these men. I am so blessed by their care.

In a courtyard area with a fountain sprinkling water, Brendan punched the elevator button, and a door slid open. They entered the elevator, and the men pivoted around her in formation so Brendan remained in front. Jenna turned too, memories of marching band coming back, and she could almost hear her middle school director calling out to pick up her feet. She laughed.

"What's so funny?" Brendan asked, not sounding happy with her humor as he glanced back at her.

"I was just thinking about how we must look to others. They have to be wondering what's going on."

Brendan's forehead tightened. "That's not important now. Focus on your safety and only your safety."

He was right of course, but his stern reminder and look stole Jenna's smile.

"Hey, lighten up, bro," Clay said. "You're coming on kind of strong."

Brendan worked the muscles in his jaw. "The threat is real. How can you come on too strong for that?"

Clay arched an eyebrow. "We can be vigilant and still not snap at each other."

"I didn't snap."

"Um, yeah, you did," Erik said.

Brendan looked at Jenna. "Sorry. I didn't mean—"

The door opened, and he jerked his attention back to the front. "Okay. We're a go. This is the most dangerous part of the transport, so be alert."

He stepped out, and everyone followed. They

marched down a hallway that smelled of antiseptic cleaner. Long gone was her humor. His attitude had her shaking with fear. She glanced at the room numbers, watching as they counted down. Five rooms away, a man darted into the hallway and slammed into Brendan.

He grabbed ahold of the man's arms and restrained him against the wall while the formation changed around her, Aiden shooting to the front to fill the slot Brendan had vacated, moving so fast, it was clear that they'd practiced such a drill.

"Hey," the guy said. "What gives?"

"Keep moving," Brendan told Aiden. "I'll catch up once I clear this guy."

"Clear me." The man glared at Brendan. "Do I look like some kind of crook to you? I'm just visiting my sister. Needed to refill my coffee."

Aiden got them moving again, but she saw the guy hold up a mug, and Brendan released him. "You slammed into me."

"So? Is that a crime nowadays?"

She didn't hear Brendan's reply, but as they reached Room 621, he brushed past them and looked at her. "I need to clear the room. Wait here."

Brendan knocked on Shawn's door and pushed it wide open and Jenna caught sight of her brother and Peggy.

"You again," Shawn said.

Looking tired, Peggy got up. "Hi, son."

"Just checking out the room before Jenna comes in to visit," Brendan said, his voice as sharp as a piercing bullet.

"Don't bother," his mother said. "We're alone, and everything has been calm."

Brendan ignored her and looked behind a bunched up curtain, then in the bathroom. He crooked his finger for

Jenna. She didn't hesitate but brushed past him. One of the brothers closed the door behind her.

She shrugged out of her jacket and rushed over to Shawn to take his hand. "How are you?"

"Okay. The drugs are stopping the crazy withdrawal issues."

She rested on the side of his bed. "That's such good news."

"C'mon, Mom," Brendan said, his tone less guarded. "Let's give them some time alone."

Jenna let go of Shawn's hand and went to the end of the bed to scoop Peggy into a hug. "Thank you for spending the night. I'll never be able to repay you."

"Make my son happy, and that would be more than enough repayment," she whispered.

"What?" Jenna pulled back.

"Just what I said." She tipped her head at Brendan. "He's worth getting over whatever is keeping the two of you apart." Her voice was still soft, she obviously didn't want Brendan to hear her.

He linked arms with Peggy then looked at Jenna. "Let me know when you're ready for me to talk to Shawn."

Never.

"Sure thing," she said.

He left the room with Peggy, and Jenna waited for the door to close before turning to Shawn. "Now, tell me exactly what's going on, and don't even think of lying to me."

In the hallway, Brendan released his mother's arm and searched every inch of the space he could find, but his mind wouldn't let go of the sight of Jenna in her red sweater and skinny jeans. When she'd stepped in the family room, he'd had to fight hard not to gawk at her. But man, red was her color. Made her face come alive and her lips coated with some kind of shiny gloss, were nearly begging him to kiss her again.

"You've got this in hand," Clay said. "And Jenna will be awhile, so why don't I take Mom to the cafeteria for some coffee."

"Good idea," she said.

Brendan didn't want to be a man down but Clay was right. He could be gone for as long as it took to have a cup of coffee. "Stay on your comms, and be ready to hightail it back if I need you."

"Understood." Clay took their mother's arm. "C'mon. Let's wake you up."

She looked up at Clay. "I look that bad?"

"You never look bad, Mom. Not ever."

"Ah, ever the family diplomat." She gave Clay a fond smile as they set off.

Brendan faced Drake. "I want you at the north end of the hallway."

"Roger that." He strode away, his posture telling Brendan he was mission-ready.

"Erik, you have the south side."

"You got it." He headed the other direction.

"Aiden, you're with me."

Aiden stepped closer to the door and took a wide stance. "How long you plan to stay here?"

Brendan looked at his watch. "If Jenna doesn't come out in fifteen minutes, I'm going in."

"You don't like this much," Aiden said.

"Not at all."

Aiden quirked a brow. "It's much better than a ski slope."

He was referring to when they'd protected Harper, and

she continued to train for her ski competitions even when a stalker was out to get her.

Brendan knew the two situations didn't compare at all. He could control this setting far more, but he didn't have feelings for Harper. "It feels as bad."

"You've fallen for her."

"Yeah," Brendan said, as there was no point in denying it. "And for Karlie. Never thought I would think a kid was great."

"Probably wouldn't with just any kid, but she's Jenna's child."

"Yeah. Yeah. Makes sense."

Aiden gave Brendan a hard look, and Brendan knew what was coming next. He braced himself mentally and physically. "Just say it."

"Just don't let your feelings get in the way of the job."

That was far less dictatorial than Brendan has expected his brother to be. "I'm doing my best."

"If it gets too much, let me know, and I'll take over."

"Ha! Like you would've let me take over Harper's protection detail."

Aiden grinned. "Guess that wouldn't have happened."

"No way." Brendan felt his worry lighten a notch, but he ignored the ease and kept his focus on his duty.

They stopped talking and did what they did best. Kept a person in danger safe so they could go about their life. Brendan envisioned every possible bad scenario that could occur while the time ticked by slowly.

Brendan got an email from Detective Grant, who'd been successful in getting a warrant through for the cabin renters and owners. Brendan wouldn't look at it now when his focus needed to be on protecting Jenna, but he forwarded the email to Erik to research the names on the list when they got back to the cabin.

Finally, near that fifteen-minute mark, the door opened, and Jenna stepped back, her eyes wary. "We're ready for you."

Brendan hated seeing her upset and didn't want to make it worse, but he had to question Shawn. Still, he could go easy on him. Brendan looked at Aiden. "Report anything out of the ordinary, and I mean anything."

"Roger that." He sounded nonchalant, but his usual penetrating expression was lodged on his face.

Brendan followed Jenna into the room. Shawn was sitting up higher, the covers pulled up to his neck. His eyes, the same color as Jenna's, were just as wary as hers. Maybe more so. His blond hair coloring and freckles really did make him resemble Jenna, and Brendan couldn't believe he'd missed the connection at first. Probably had due to the fact that the kid's hair was matted with sweat, and his skin was as pale as the snow outside.

"Hope you're feeling better," Brendan said, trying to sound cheerful.

"Yeah, man. I'm good." Shawn crossed his arms, and Brendan caught sight of the needle marks as he moved. "What do you want to know?"

"You indicated that you know Lonny Odell."

"Maybe *know* him isn't the right word. I ran into him at Heavenly Burgers and Brews."

"The restaurant near the ski resort?" Brendan asked.

Shawn nodded. "I was on my way to stay with Jenna and Karlie. But the heater in that thing I call a car doesn't work, so I stopped to warm up."

Made sense. In the Portland area, a person could get by without a heater, but not up in the mountains.

"So you ran into him there?" Brendan asked.

"Yeah...I mean...well, I sat by him at the counter, and we got to talking. One thing led to another, and well..."

"Well, what?" Brendan asked.

Shawn arched an eyebrow. "You're not a cop anymore, right?"

"Right."

"So, I had some good quality heroin and was into trying it out. Figured that would warm me up, you know?" He chuckled.

Brendan forced a smile when all he wanted to do was grab the guy and knock some sense into him. "So you went somewhere to shoot up."

He nodded, that wariness came back not only in his eyes but in the tense set to his posture. "He had a snowmobile, so we took it to his tent. He was set up in a state park, and he had a back entrance through the woods. The guy was crafty. Gotta give him props for the free lodging."

"Did you ask him why he was living in a tent?"

"He said there was this cabin he was supposed to raid and look for something."

"Did he say what?"

"If he did I was too far gone to remember. But I do remember he was broken up about something to do with the cabin. He started to mention a woman and kid then clammed up. I didn't have a clue then that he could be talking about Jenna and Karlie, or I would've done something about it."

If you weren't too stoned to act. "What day was this?"

"Monday. Late in the afternoon."

"And then what happened?"

"This other guy came to the tent. I think Lonny called him Sal, but I'm not sure. Whoever he was seemed really peeved about something. And mad that I was there too. He asked who I was and what I was doing there. I told him my name and that I was on my way to stay with Jenna. That seemed to make him madder."

Shawn paused and shook his head. "Then he said he was leaving and demanded Lonny come with him."

"And did he go?"

Shawn nodded. "But I gotta say this Sal guy was rough looking. Scars on his face. Leather jacket. I'm surprised Odell went with him."

"And you? Did Sal threaten you?"

"Nah, he told me to get moving as soon as I was able. I wasn't able for like a long time." He paused and took a long breath. "Then I didn't have a car. So I figured I'd spend the night. If Sal didn't come back, I could use his little heater and a warm sleeping bag."

"Did you spend the night?"

Shawn nodded. "Neither of 'em came by in the morning, so I found some snowshoes and started hiking out of there. But then Sal came roaring up on a snowmobile and offered me a ride back to my car."

"Did he take you back there?"

"We headed in that direction, but then we stopped in the woods on the way. Said he had to take a leak. That was when he told me Lonny had gone hiking. Before he left, he'd told Sal that I claimed I had some good product. He laughed and said his was better, so I told him to prove it. He handed over his stuff and told me to sample it. So I did. It was so pure, man. The high it was like...man, there're no words for it."

Brendan gritted his teeth to keep from saying anything. This guy was suffering from an addiction and needed help. Brendan had seen guys in the army with the same struggle. Good guys. Great guys. Great soldiers wanting to escape the realities they'd seen. Brendan knew telling Shawn off wouldn't help.

"Anyway," Shawn continued. "I think after I was out of it,

he must've given me another hit, and that's what knocked me out."

"Sounds like it," Brendan said. "He didn't give you his name?"

"Nope."

"You mentioned he had scars and a leather jacket. Can you describe him more?"

"He was big. Maybe six-three. Two-twenty. Had a weird beard. It was real skinny on the sides and connected to a narrow strip of hair he left on his shaved head. So it looked like the beard went all the way over the top of his head. Just plain odd."

And something that could help us find him.

"Do you know anything about this note?" He held out his phone with a picture of the note they'd found in his pocket.

He looked at it and flashed his gaze to Jenna. "Does he mean you? That you're next?"

"I don't know," she said. "But they found it in your pocket."

"Mine?" He gaped at his sister. "Is this about me and the drugs? Did I bring this danger to you?"

"I don't know. Did you?" Brendan asked before she had to answer and point out that her brother might indeed have played a part in what was going on. "The guy obviously wants something. Do you know anything about that?"

Shawn shook his head, but his expression was masking nervousness.

Brendan let go of his Mister Nice Guy routine and eyed Shawn. "There's something you're not telling us. It could be important. It could keep your sister alive. So whatever it is, fess up."

"It's just..." He glanced at Jenna then stared out the window. "I borrowed some money from a guy. Thought I could pay him back right away, but..." He clasped his hands and moved his head side-to-side in sorrowful arcs. "He's been after me. That's why I came up here."

He shot a panicked look at Jenna. "I mean, I wanted to see you, Sis, but...his goons were gonna hurt me real bad if I didn't disappear. Maybe they followed me. Maybe he's the one who dumped me at the cabin, not this Sal guy. I don't know. I just don't know."

Brendan wanted to light into the guy for potentially putting Jenna and Karlie in danger, but what good would it do? Shawn had already done the damage, and it was between him and Jenna.

"Can you forgive me?" He reached out for her hand, and she let him take it. "I'm such an idiot. I keep hurting you. I don't mean to. You know that, right?"

She nodded, but Brendan could see the anguish in her eyes.

"I'm going to get better. This is a new start. Just wait and see."

Typical behavior for a drug abuser and Jenna had likely heard this same thing many times. Brendan's experience told him that most users meant it. They didn't want to hurt the ones they loved. The drug controlling them caused the behavior. Brendan took a moment to offer a prayer for Shawn. For Jenna. For Shawn to succeed this time, and for reconciliation between them.

"I know it'll stick this time," Shawn declared.

Jenna leaned down and hugged her brother. "I'll help in any way I can."

"You wouldn't happen to have some spare cash lying around." He chuckled, but his expression said he was serious.

"I'd help you if I could, but since Toby left me swimming in debt, I'm not even making ends meet for me and Karlie."

She barely got out the statement before her voice choked up.

The anguish in her tone cut right through Brendan. He wished he could fix all of her problems. Not just the issue of keeping her safe. But she would never accept financial help. That he was sure of. So it was best to get back on track with the interview before he let his feelings take over and he offered something that could offend her.

He looked at Shawn. "What's the name of this guy you owe money to?"

"Cedrick Pulliam."

"And where can we find him?"

"He hangs at a bar in Portland most nights." Shawn shared the name of a bar known for brawling and assaults.

"Is there anything more you can tell us about either Odell or Sal?" Brendan asked, winding down now.

Shawn shook his head. "I think the bartender at the restaurant knew Lonny. Maybe they know Sal too."

"Okay, thanks," Brendan said. "We'll head over there. One more thing. Could you describe this guy well enough for a sketch artist?"

"Sure. Yeah. I can do that."

"And you should know that Detective Grant will want to talk to you."

"I didn't think I was in trouble for this."

"You're not. It's about Odell's attack on Jenna."

"Oh, right. Good." He blew out a breath.

"In the meantime, we'll station a guard outside your door. We'll rotate guys every twelve hours. If the sheriff's department finds enough manpower to station a deputy here, then we'll pull our guy."

Shawn arched a brow. "Why are you doing this for me?"

"You're Jenna's brother," was all Brendan said. He'd do anything to keep her from suffering additional anguish, and he was really starting to care for her. Not that he was going to let the first time he confessed how deep his feelings were for her be in front of the brother. Nothing romantic about that at all.

"Excuse me." He stepped away to press the button on the mic cord resting on his chest. "You on your way back up yet?"

"Heading for the elevator now," Clay replied.

"Roger that." Brendan released his mic. "As soon as Clay returns, we'll get going."

"Tell her thanks for me," Shawn said, earning a surprised look from Jenna. "She seems like a great mom." Brendan was surprised by Shawn's pensive tone.

Brendan wished that no child had experienced the upbringing Shawn and Jenna had faced. He wished that he could somehow go back in their life and change that, but he also knew that their childhoods were what had made them who they were. Good or bad, God could step in and use it all to bring good from the pain.

Even the pain of losing Tristen. All Brendan had to do was look for the good, and maybe then, he could let go of the guilt.

"Any idea when you're going to be released?" Brendan asked.

"They're trying to find a rehab program for me first. Don't have insurance, so I need one that doesn't cost anything. Guess most of the free ones have mile-long waiting lists. I'm not holding out hope and they'll cut me loose if they can't find one."

Jenna grabbed Shawn's hand. "Don't think that way. Now that you're serious about this, I know God will come through for you."

"I can look into it," Brendan said. "I have some contacts from my time as a deputy."

"That would be great." Jenna gave him the glowing smile that lit her eyes and transformed her into the most beautiful woman he'd ever seen. He knew it wasn't because of her physical features, which were nice, but from the inner glow that was radiating from her personality.

He wanted to do anything and everything he could to not only keep her safe but to make her happy. If she would let him, but that was a *big* if.

17

Brendan was turning out to be even more amazing than Jenna had thought. He'd been kind to Shawn in the interview when a lot of people would've been judgmental and written Shawn off as a lost cause. And then he'd offered to look into finding a rehab place for Shawn and post someone at his door at all times. No charge. Just because. And so Drake had stayed behind.

She knew Brendan's reason. At least she thought she did. He had feelings for her. She was in the same position with him. In fact, she'd purposefully sat closer to him than she needed in the back seat of the SUV on the way back to the cabin. His mother sat on Jenna's other side, and she kept looking at the two of them. She had eagle-sharp perception, and Jenna knew the woman was picking up on the vibe between them.

The best part was that Peggy seemed glad for it. An odd occurrence for Jenna. She wasn't used to being accepted for who she was. She was more used to being judged. If Peggy had found Jenna wanting, she would've sat between Jenna and Brendan, as she was also a fierce mother bear.

She leaned over Jenna and looked at her son. "What are the plans now?"

Brendan explained about visiting the restaurant. "We'll head over there right after we drop you off." He looked at Jenna. "Unless you want to check on Karlie."

"That would be great if it fits in the plan." She was so amazed at his continued kindness and stared into those bottomless eyes.

"Is something wrong with our sweet Karlie?" Peggy asked.

Jenna managed to drag her gaze from Brendan to look at his mother. "Looks like her arthritis is flaring up. She had a fever this morning. Plus, her joints are swollen, and she's tired."

"That poor little thing. I wish I was there to take care of her. A child needs a woman's touch when they don't feel well."

Brendan snorted.

"What?" Peggy looked at him. "You don't think that's true?"

"I think that's kind of old-fashioned thinking. Men today are more sensitive to feelings."

Peggy shook her head. "All I know is when you boys were sick you wanted your mother."

"Dad wasn't exactly all warm and fuzzy."

"But he couldn't have loved you more."

"Agreed." Brendan sat back and watched out the window.

Peggy gripped Jenna's hand tightly. "You don't have to worry. Russ and I'll take good care of her while you're gone."

Jenna gave Peggy a sincere smile. "I appreciate that."

"I'm honored that you would trust us."

"Are you kidding?" Jenna shook her head. "Look at the

amazing men and woman you raised. If Karlie grew up to be anything like them, I'd be overjoyed."

"They are pretty great." Peggy smiled. "And I think you favor one of them over the others."

"Mom," Brendan warned. "Don't start."

"What?" She cast Brendan an innocent look. "I'm just telling the truth."

"Truth or not, we've arrived, and we need to concentrate on safety."

"Okay." Peggy smiled. "I can talk to Jenna about this later."

Jenna knew the tenacious woman wasn't going to let the topic go, and oddly enough, Jenna didn't mind. She liked Peggy. If Jenna ever married again, and that was a *big* if, she'd love to have such a wonderful mother-in-law and grandmother for Karlie. The last bit would be a huge blessing. One Jenna could surely embrace.

Brendan got out but looked back into the SUV. "You're clear to move, Jenna. Mom, wait until we have Jenna inside, and I'll come back for you."

"But I'm not in danger."

"We can't be too careful." He had that all-male tough-soldier look on his face and in his posture.

Even Peggy didn't seem keen to argue and sat back. "I can wait."

Jenna slipped out, and the cold bit into her face. The sun had come out, but the temperature had dropped since the snow had stopped falling. A normal turn of events, but she didn't face this kind of cold in the city, and the sharp wind made her take a breath.

"You okay?" Brendan asked.

"Just shocked by the cold."

"Let's move." He took her arm and led her straight past Erik, who'd arrived with Aiden, and opened the door.

She stepped into the warm room and found an adorable sight that melted her heart. Russ was fast asleep on the couch. Karlie was in his arms, her head on the armrest and sound asleep too.

"Would you look at that." Brendan shook his head. "I'll go get Mom."

Jenna slipped off her coat. She wasn't going to wake either Karlie or Russ and wouldn't stay long, but she didn't want to adjust to the warmer inside air with her coat on and be even more chilled when she went outside.

The door opened, letting in a rush of that arctic air along with Peggy and Brendan.

Peggy stood watching Russ and Karlie, tears glistening in her eyes. "I never thought I'd see a day like this." She looked up at Brendan. "Have I mentioned I want grandchildren?"

Brendan rolled his eyes. "Maybe once or twice."

"I don't want to wake them." Jenna looked at Peggy. "Can you just give Karlie some Tylenol when she wakes up if she's spiking a fever again? It's in my cosmetic bag in the bedroom along with a thermometer."

"Of course I will. Now don't you worry." Peggy hugged Jenna. "It's our pleasure to care for her."

Tears pricked Jenna's eyes at the kindness and love she felt from this woman. Jenna blinked to wash them away before Brendan saw her go all blubbery and questioned her. Once feeling able to look at him, she lifted her gaze to him. "Ready to go?"

He nodded, stepped out, and looked around, even though his brothers were still on duty. She slipped into her jacket and zipped it closed.

Brendan faced Aiden. "Once we have Jenna safely in the vehicle, I want you to stay here to protect Karlie."

"Will do."

"Means no hanging out with Harper in the den."

Aiden eyed his brother. "I do know how to stand duty, you know."

"I know. Just making sure."

Aiden shook his head. "Let's get Jenna in the SUV."

Brendan crooked a finger at her, and she stepped out next to him. The biting wind hit her even harder after the brief warmth of the blazing fire, and she shrugged her jacket higher. She took a final look back at Karlie.

Father, please stop this flare-up before it gets worse, and please, please keep her safe. I couldn't bear it if anything happened to her.

Erik and Clay had scoped out the restaurant interior, making sure no threat existed before they helped Brendan escort Jenna inside and then remained at the door. Brendan felt welcome the moment he stepped through the door of the place with a gleaming wood bar that ran down one side of the large open room. A hanging metal fireplace surrounded by comfy chairs took up the middle of the room, and the other side held dining tables. Scarred but polished wood floors coupled with rustic wood walls made the space seem homey and inviting. And the savory smell of sizzling burgers cooking on an open grill on the far side of the room left his stomach growling.

Jenna looked up at him. "This place is amazing. We should have lunch."

"Normally I would agree, but my brothers are standing guard outside in the cold, and I wouldn't want you to linger in a place where you could be compromised."

"Yeah, sure. Makes sense." She sounded so disappointed that Brendan grabbed her hand.

"When this killer's behind bars, we can come back and

have lunch. Just the two of us." *A romantic lunch*. Something he would never say to a client, so he held his tongue.

"Deal."

A date. She'd agreed to a date. Had she even realized it? He squeezed her hand and released it. "Let's go talk to the bartender."

They stepped up to the guy who Brendan put in his early forties. He had a long reddish-brown beard and hair pulled back in a ponytail, and he wore a black shirt with the restaurant's name and logo screen-printed on the fabric.

"What'll you have?" A ready smile crinkled the skin around his eyes already creased with wrinkles.

"We were hoping to speak to the manager," Brendan said.

"You're looking at him. Homer Manning." He shoved out his hand. "Owner, barkeep, janitor. You name it. I do it." His smile widened.

Brendan introduced himself and Jenna as he shook hands with Manning.

"What did you need?" he asked.

Brendan wasn't going to beat around the bush. "We hoped you might know Lonny Odell."

"Lonny, sure. He's a regular. Why do you want to know about him?"

"He was found dead near our cabin, and we believe he attacked my friend here."

"Dead? But I just saw him Saturday night. Dead...man... that's rough." His smile evaporated, and he took a long breath as he planted his hands on the counter. "But Lonny, attack someone? Nah. I don't see it."

Jenna crossed her arms. "I saw him, up close. It was him."

"I did too," Brendan said. "Caught him in the act."

"Then he must've been forced to do it. He's like this big gentle giant."

"He wasn't gentle when he held me prisoner and raised a knife to my throat." Jenna lifted her chin and touched the knife wound.

"I'm sorry. Wow. Man, I mean wow." He shook his head. "Just can't wrap my head around it."

"Was he connected to the military at all?"

"Not that I know of. Why all the questions? You cops or something?"

"Former." Brendan lifted his shoulders into a hard line. "Now I own an investigation and protection agency with my brothers. We know this guy was here on Monday afternoon. Did you see him?"

"Monday's my day off, so no."

"Do you know anyone Odell used to hang with?"

"He knew most of our regulars, but I don't know if they hung out."

"There's not one person who stands out?"

"No." Manning balled up the rag he'd been using and dropped it on the counter.

"What about a guy with a shaved head and strange looking beard?"

"Strange how?"

"Thin on the sides and connected to a thin strip of hair on his shaved head so it looks like the beard goes all the way around to the other side."

"Hmm." He tapped his chin. "Well, not really. There was a guy I didn't know talking to Lonny Saturday night. The side of his beard was thin but he was wearing a stocking cap so I couldn't see the hair."

Sounded like the guy Shawn described, and Brendan needed more info. "You didn't hear his name?"

"I dunno. Maybe Sal. Or Al. Or Lonny could even have

called him pal. It was really busy that night. People partying before being stuck inside from the storm."

Sounded like their guy had been here, and the video camera above the bar could've captured him. "What about security footage? Can we take a look at it?"

"Gotta think about my patrons' privacy." The guy grabbed the rag again and started wiping the already gleaming bar.

"We'll be discreet with anyone we talk to, and we won't tell them where we got the lead."

"I don't know, I—" He shook his head and tsked.

"Please," Jenna pleaded. "This other man is threatening me and my four-year-old daughter. Please help us."

He sighed out a long breath. "Okay, fine. Let me get someone to watch the bar, and I'll show it to you."

He stepped out from behind the bar and crossed over to a tall blond waiter in a matching T-shirt and jeans. They held a short conversation, and then the two of them returned.

"Follow me." Manning took keys from his pocket as he headed for a door on the back wall. He stopped a few times to talk to diners and inquire about their food. His interaction was well-received, making Brendan wish he and Jenna could sit down and have that burger in the friendly guy's restaurant.

He led them into a small office with stacks of cardboard boxes containing napkins and toilet paper on one wall and a desk pushed up against the other. Behind it sat a credenza with a computer monitor and other electronic equipment.

Manning sat at the credenza. "I'd offer you a seat, but as you can tell there's only the one chair."

"No worries," Brendan said. "We're fine standing."

Manning clicked around with his mouse until his hand

stilled over a file dated for the prior Saturday. He started the video playing then fast-forwarded to late in the day.

"There," he pointed a finger at the screen. "Is this your guy?"

Brendan squinted at the image. "Can you take a screenshot and text it to me?"

"Hold on." Manning created a screenshot. "What's your phone number?"

Brendan handed Manning a business card with his contact details, and Manning tapped it into a message app on his computer.

Brendan's phone dinged, and he checked for the photo. "Perfect. Now can you let it run?"

"Can do." He clicked play again.

Brendan watched the feed carefully, looking for any possible lead. Finding nothing, he looked at Manning. "Can we look at Monday afternoon, now?"

Manning frowned but located the file and played it. When Shawn came on the screen, Brendan leaned closer. Shawn and Odell got up and left together, and Brendan noticed Jenna tangling her hands together and was frowning.

"I'd like a copy of Saturday night's video from the moment this guy enters the building through his departure, and this one from Monday too."

Manning looked up. "How do you want me to get it to you?"

"Email. Address is on my card." Brendan turned his attention to his phone and forwarded the still shot to Drake, asking him to show it to Shawn to see if this was the guy who drugged him.

"What are you doing?" Jenna asked.

He told her while Manning pushed back from the credenza. "Video is on its way to you."

"Hang tight while I confirm the contents." Brendan opened the email and tapped on the video. He started the first video playing, and fast-forwarded to near the end. Glad to see that he had what he needed, he moved on to the second file. When he was certain it was all there, he shoved his phone into his pocket. "Do you have cameras in your parking lot?"

Manning shook his head. "Come back in a few months, though, and we will. Been a few issues outside, and we want to cut things off before they become big problems."

Brendan didn't bother telling him that he didn't expect this guy to be on the loose in a few days let alone a few months. "Is there anything else about this guy that you can tell us to help us find him?"

"Sorry. Can't think of anything."

"Might there be someone else who would've interacted with him on Saturday?" Jenna asked.

Manning shook his head. "As you can see in the video, he hung at the bar for the entire time. But I can ask around. He might've talked to someone on the way in or out." He tapped Brendan's card on his knee. "If I hear anything, I'll let you know."

"Time is of the essence here." Desperation deepened Jenna's tone.

"Then I'll ask around today."

"Would you get back to me either way?" Brendan asked, so if Manning struck out, Brendan could check this item off his To-Do list.

"Sure thing."

Brendan's phone dinged, and he grabbed it to look at the text from Drake.

Shawn confirms that this is our suspect.

Brendan pumped a fist up and showed the screen to Jenna.

She met Brendan's gaze, hope now lightening her expression. "How do we find him?"

"I'll have Nick run this photo for facial recognition. Hopefully by the time we get back to the cabin, we'll have a name and address so we can bring this guy to justice."

18

Dinner at the cabin consisted of a savory beef roast with potatoes, carrots, onions, and turnips and a thick gravy that had Jenna's mouth watering before they all sat down together at the big table. Peggy had told Jenna she'd grown all the vegetables in her garden, and they'd had a fun chat about gardening while Peggy took a big crusty loaf of bread from the oven, the aroma filling the air. Jenna savored each bite of the peppery roast and fresh veggies, but she couldn't keep from looking at Karlie, who barely touched her food. Even her bread remained untouched, and she loved bread. She sat, hands on her lap, her head down.

Jenna touched her forehead. No fever. "Are you tired, honey?"

She nodded. "I wanna go to bed."

Her request told Jenna far more than anything else. Karlie only asked to go to bed when she was sick.

Jenna looked at the others. "Would you all mind if I get Karlie settled in bed?"

"Of course not." Peggy got up and came to squat by Karlie. She reached for Karlie's hands.

Karlie cried out in pain.

"Oh, no." Peggy clutched her chest. "Did I hurt you?"

Karlie nodded.

"Let me see your hands, honey," Jenna said.

Karlie held them out. Her joints were swollen and red, the same fingers on both hands, which was a hallmark sign of rheumatoid arthritis and JIA.

"Oh, sweetie, I'm so sorry I hurt you," Peggy said. "I would never want to do that."

"I know. Mommy does sometimes too, and she doesn't mean to." The sad resignation in her young daughter's voice broke Jenna's heart.

"Let's get you to bed. A good night's sleep will make things better." Jenna encouraged Karlie, but honestly, it would only help to reduce the fatigue. The joints would have to resolve with time. If they didn't in a day or two, Jenna would call Karlie's rheumatologist.

Karlie got up and limped toward the bedroom. JIA often affected knees in kids, and unfortunately, Karlie suffered from pain in those joints as well.

"How about I carry you to your room?" Brendan offered.

Karlie looked up at him with sad puppy-dog eyes. "Please."

He hurried over and knelt by her. "Tell me what to do so I can be careful not to hurt you."

She gave him a tiny smile. "I can hold my hands out like this." She stiffened her arms. "And you just haveta be careful of my knees."

"Okay. I can do that." He gently scooped her up from behind so her legs dangled.

She kept her arms out and gave him a serious look. "You did good. I want you to carry me every night."

Jenna suddenly wished for the same thing for her precious child. A father who didn't make fun of or belittle her, but one who looked at her with the same tender gaze in

Brendan's eyes. Jenna had been the only one who'd looked at Karlie that way until this family came into her life. It was almost as if Brendan and his family loved her, but that wasn't possible so quickly, was it?

He strode across the room, and Jenna followed. In the bedroom, he gently lowered Karlie onto the bed, his gaze fixed on her. Here was this big macho guy who'd fought in wars, patrolled dangerous streets, and was built like a tank, and yet, right now he looked as vulnerable as Karlie.

Jenna's heart clenched over how a guy like Brendan could humble himself for a little girl. Tears pricked Jenna's eyes, but she swiped them away and got out Karlie's pajamas.

"I'll let you get ready for bed, but one question first," Brendan said to Karlie. "Does your nose hurt too?"

She giggled. "No, silly. Noses don't get JIA."

"Then do you mind if I give your nose a kiss?" he asked.

She looked up at him, her eyes swimming with unshed tears. "Yes, please."

He kissed her nose and, even with sore joints, Karlie laid her fingers on his face. "I love you, Brendan."

He blinked a few times and stared at Karlie as if he didn't know how to respond.

Jenna stepped in with the pajamas. "I'll be out after I get her settled."

Brendan stood. "Good night, little bit."

"Night." She gave him a tired smile. "Can we play *Go Fish* again tomorrow?"

"We can play anything your little heart desires."

She looked like she could barely manage the weak smile crossing her face and laid back so Jenna could help with her pajamas. Jenna gave Brendan a big smile, and he gently cupped her cheek, then left the room.

"Do you love Brendan too, Mommy?" Karlie asked as she slipped her feet into her jammies.

Jenna didn't answer, but in her heart she was beginning to think she *was* falling in love with the man. For once, the thought didn't bring any pain, only a warm fuzzy feeling deep in her soul.

~

Sadness filled the room when Jenna returned. Brendan was probably fueling it, as he felt helpless to help little Karlie and he'd told them so. He was a take-action kind of guy, and he couldn't do a thing for her except love her and pray for her.

Jenna forced a smile. Brendan knew she was trying to alleviate the sadness, but everyone hurt for Karlie.

"We should go ahead and have dessert," his mom said. "I'll make sure to save some for when Karlie feels better."

"I'll help you," Jenna offered.

For once his mother didn't turn Jenna down. Maybe she knew it was better for Jenna to keep busy. They went to the kitchen together, and Jenna returned with a peppermint ice cream cake. His mother carried in the plates behind Jenna.

The cake was one of Brendan's favorite desserts, and his mom always served this dessert three days before Christmas.

"Looks amazing," Jenna said as she sat.

"Just wait." Brendan smiled at her. "Tomorrow night we'll have a Snickers trifle. And on Christmas Eve, Mom bakes a gingerbread cake. Then on Christmas Day, we get a red velvet and white chocolate cheesecake."

"Is it the same every year?" Jenna asked.

"Part of the family traditions." He patted his stomach. "I always have to double my workouts, but it's worth it."

Jenna looked longingly at the dessert, but he didn't think it was because of the food. He thought she wanted a family with traditions too. He'd never really appreciated them, but seeing things through her eyes, knowing her past, he thought he understood how she might feel.

What would it be like to share the same traditions with a wife and child? Someone like little Karlie, who seemed so excited about most everything, and grateful too? Even when she was suffering.

He didn't know how Jenna handled seeing her child in pain, knowing she couldn't take it from her. He wasn't Karlie's father, and he could barely stand to see the little tike hurting. Anger over the whole situation built in his gut.

Why God? Why let an innocent child suffer this way?

He thought about his talk with Jenna. About not asking the whys. Brendan shouldn't be asking either, but come on, it was an obvious question.

Obvious and useless.

He needed to focus on *how* questions.

Like, how could he make it better?

He could find who killed Odell so Jenna's and Karlie's lives could go back to normal. And while Karlie was with his family, he could make sure she was comfortable and had fun.

"You're not eating your peppermint, and it's your favorite," his mother said. "Something wrong?"

"I was thinking about finding this killer. We're waiting on facial recognition, but other than that we don't have much to go on."

"There has to be something," his dad said.

Brendan took a bite of the smooth dessert, the peppermint tingling in his mouth, and shook his head.

"Then do what I did when I was a detective." He set

down his fork and took a sip of his coffee. "Go back to the beginning and start over."

Jenna looked at Russ at the head of the table. "Start over, how?"

"Look at the attack." He cupped his mug. "In essence we have a home invasion, right?"

"Right," Jenna said.

Erik leaned forward to look at Brendan. "Hey, wasn't there another home invasion you mentioned?"

"Yeah, a PPB officer's brother was killed a couple of weeks ago."

"That happen nearby?" Clay asked.

"Same county as here," Brendan said, and mentioned Oregon City, the Portland suburb that was an hour away.

"But you think it was connected to Jenna?" Erik asked.

Brendan shrugged. "Just two home invasions in a short time in a city where it doesn't happen often."

"Could be a coincidence," Aiden said.

"You know what I say about that," Russ said.

"There's no such thing as coincidences," Brendan said, along with everyone else in the family, including his mom. Even Harper and Reed joined in, proving Brendan's dad said this far more frequently than he thought.

They broke into laughter.

His dad shook his head, pretending to be offended, but his mouth quirked up at the corner.

Erik dropped his fork, jumped to his feet, and bolted from the room.

Everyone watched as he disappeared and then returned with his laptop in hand. He started typing.

Russ looked at Jenna. "When you checked in for your stay at the cabin, did the person say anything odd?"

"Only that the place wasn't usually available this week, but the owners emailed and said to rent it out. The rental agent has a sister who works at the radio station, and they were looking for a holiday package, so she called her sister right away."

"Yes!" Erik pumped his fist up. "I was right. The cabin is owned by Gene and Iris Steele."

"Seriously?" Brendan sat up and dropped his fork on his plate.

"What is it, son?" his mom asked.

"Londyn Steele is the officer whose brother was killed in the home invasion," Brendan said. "His name was Thomas."

His father's eyes narrowed. "Steele with an E at the end?"

Brendan nodded, wondering where his dad was going with this. "They're not related to Emory Jenkins—formerly Steele—the DNA expert at Veritas, if that's what you're thinking."

"Not that." He waved a hand. "We're talking about Steele Guardians, right?"

"Yeah, Londyn's dad owns the company."

"Along with Gene's brother-in-law, Hugh," his dad clarified. "I know them both. They're retired PPB officers, and Gene's only son was running the business. Must be the guy who was killed."

Jenna looked at Erik. "How did you know about this?"

"The email Brendan sent to me from Detective Grant."

"What email?" Jenna asked.

"I forgot to tell you. When I was waiting for you to talk to Shawn, I got the list of renters and owners from Grant. Sent it to Erik to check out the names."

"Which I did," Erik said. "I read down the list that's in alphabetical, then started at the top to research. I hadn't made it this far down, but remembered the unique spelling."

"We need to talk to the Steele family about Thomas's

death," Brendan said. "Since I know Londyn, we'll start with her first thing in the morning."

Jenna gave a firm nod and the conversation came to a close. The somber mood dampened what should've been a Christmas celebration. He regretted bringing his whole family down even further with the discussion of Thomas's death and the danger to Jenna. But it might've brought them the lead they needed to move forward.

He pushed back his chair. "I'll do the dishes."

His mom watched him with narrowed eyes for a moment then got up. "I'll help you. Everyone else split. The fire needs stoking. Take your mugs if you want more coffee, and I'll make a fresh pot and bring it in. Maybe we can play Pictionary when we get done in the kitchen."

Brendan grabbed dessert plates and watched as many of his family members took their mugs to sit by the fireplace. His mom marched into the kitchen and grabbed the coffee pot to fill with water.

He brought the first stack of plates into the kitchen and opened the dishwasher.

She looked up from the sink. "What's troubling you, son?"

"Nothing."

"That wasn't a *nothing* look on your face earlier."

He shrugged.

She turned the water off. "Tell me, or I'll badger you until you do."

She was the most wonderful mom, but right now she was a very irritating mother. "I was thinking about how this investigation is ruining the family's Christmas celebration."

"Nonsense." She grabbed the coffee canister and started scooping aromatic grounds into the filter. "We have the privilege of saving Jenna and her child from certain danger at a time of year when we are thankful for the birth of a baby come to save the world. We can celebrate that. And celebrate that God gave you boys the skills to protect her."

"Yeah," he said, smiling at her. "Good way to look at it."

She took his arm and stopped him from loading a plate. "I think you're blinded to reality right now. Too many emotions that you need to sort out."

He couldn't deny it, but he didn't have time to sort out emotions. He had a woman and child to keep safe. A killer to find. And a free rehab place to locate.

"See." His mom released his arm. "There you go again. Off into another world."

"Sorry. I was just thinking about Shawn. I need to make some calls and find a free rehab facility for him."

"Then shoo. Go do that now, and I'll finish up here."

"You sure?"

"Don't look a gift horse in the mouth. I may never excuse you from dish duty again." She chuckled but suddenly sobered and grabbed him in a hug. She was a tall woman, but still, she rested her head on his chest. "You'll figure it out, son. And when you do, I know the whole family will be blessed."

After several fun games of Pictionary, everyone had gone to bed except Brendan, who was in the den, doing what, Jenna didn't know, but she wanted to wait up to see if he'd learned anything. Problem was, her eyes were closing in front of the fire. She should hit the hay, but the warmth felt so good. As if it could melt the chill that entered her body every time she thought about Shawn and the killer. And Karlie too.

Jenna closed her eyes and prayed for her daughter's health. Prayed that she would be well for Christmas and could celebrate the day. No matter where they were, they would find a church service and celebrate the day. Maybe Shawn would even be well enough to join them.

Oh, Father, I know I'm not deserving of anything, but could this please be the time that Shawn faces his addiction and works toward recovery?

"You sleeping?" Brendan's voice came from above.

She opened her eyes to find him standing over her, blocking the fire, the flames leaving him shadowed, his face even more chiseled than normal. More handsome and mysterious. Captivating, and she couldn't pull her gaze away.

She had feelings for this incredible man, and it was time she admitted it. She swallowed hard and forced herself to look over his shoulder.

"Praying," she said once she found her voice.

He sat next to her, and she caught a whiff of his woodsy scent. A smell she was coming to associate with him. He was close. Too close. Way too close.

She scooted back. He lifted an eyebrow and watched her without a word.

"What've you been up to?" she asked, taking another scoot back for good measure as the firelight dancing in the dark set a romantic mood she needed to do her best to avoid.

"Calling in a favor." He faced her and tucked one leg under the other. His knee bumped her leg, firing off her senses, and she almost jumped.

"Favor for what?" she got out from a throat that was quickly drying up.

"I'm trying to find that rehab facility for Shawn. Nothing certain yet, but it's looking good."

Excitement burned in her stomach. "For free?"

"Yep, absolutely free. And it's a great place with a good success rate."

"Thank you. Oh, thank you." She threw her arms around him and hugged him close.

"Don't get too excited yet. It's not definite and their opening isn't until the first of the year." He dropped his foot to the floor and pulled her even closer. "And we should hold off on telling Shawn until it is."

"Of course," she said, but barely noticed the conversation as she was busy reveling in his arms holding her tightly, his masculine scent. The feel of his hair brushing her neck. Of him. The man she could see getting involved with. But was this right? Was she wanting him in her life for what he could do for her, Karlie, and Shawn? For his family? For a safety net?

Or did she truly want a man in her life at all?

She didn't know, and it wasn't fair to him to lead him on. She pushed back and straightened her shirt. "Sorry. I just got so excited for Shawn. And with not having a place to go before Christmas he can—wait. I can't invite him to stay here. I know your mom said she would bring him back here from the hospital, but she probably didn't think about it being Christmas. We'll go back to my cabin."

Brendan's smile evaporated. "That's not safe."

"Shawn will be with us."

"He's in no shape to be your protector. He could relapse, for all we know."

She wanted to deny it, but Brendan could be right.

"He'll stay here. I know Mom and Dad will want that."

She knew the same thing. His parents were amazing, and they seemed very willing to live their faith and help the less fortunate. But she didn't know if she could ask more of them. They were already watching Karlie again in the morning so she and Brendan could interview Londyn Steele.

Brendan stood and tugged her to her feet. "Time for

some shuteye. And don't worry about Shawn. I'll ask Mom and Dad in the morning."

"I am so indebted to your family."

He got a funny look on his face.

"What's wrong?"

He didn't speak for the longest time but then tucked a stray strand of hair behind her ear. "Unless I'm crazy, there's something serious developing between us."

She gave a nod of acceptance. Not a big one. Just a hint of her agreement as she didn't know where this conversation was going.

"And I just realized. How will I ever know if you're developing feelings for me or if you're confusing it with gratitude?" He took a deep breath, his chest rising. "I can't risk getting hurt again. I barely survived the last time."

She wanted to take his hands. Hold them tightly and reassure him that her feelings were pure, but she didn't know that they were, and she wasn't about to move forward with him until she knew it was this strong, wonderful man alone that she was craving.

19

As much as Jenna wanted to talk to Londyn Steele right away, she wasn't available in the morning, so Jenna spent time with Karlie, who was feeling a bit better, while Brendan watched the videos from the restaurant over and over looking for any lead. He didn't find anything, and after they ate a hearty lunch of clam chowder and another loaf of the crusty bread, they headed into the city and central office of the Portland Police Bureau.

Londyn turned out to be intimidating and welcoming at the same time, and Jenna didn't know how she did it. She met them at the front door wearing a conservative black suit that fit her athletic body perfectly, and her crisp white shirt looked starched to perfection. Her hair was a unique nutmeg color with blond highlights. Jenna felt dowdy in her worn jeans and the old green sweater.

"Long time." Brendan shook hands with her. He didn't at all seem intimidated or interested in how nice Londyn looked. "This's our client, Jenna Paine."

Londyn offered her hand to Jenna, and Londyn's nails, pristine in a French manicure, had Jenna hesitating before offering her hand, ragged nails and cuticles and all. "I'm so sorry to hear about your brother."

"Thank you." She gestured at the table in the conference room.

"So detective, huh?" Brendan sat near the head of the table facing the door.

Jenna took a seat next to him.

"Maybe not for long." Londyn pulled out a steel-and-vinyl chair on the other side and sat.

Brendan arched a brow, and that intense inquisitive look Jenna had seen so often tightening the muscles in his jaw, fixed on Londyn. "Why's that, if you don't mind me asking?"

"Looks like I might need to take Thomas's place in the family business." Londyn's eyes clouded for a moment before she drew in a long breath and crossed her arms. "You think your investigation is linked to Thomas's murder?"

"Maybe."

"Go ahead and tell me about it." Londyn took out a small notepad like the ones Jenna often saw in movies and TV cop shows.

Brendan gave a concise description of Jenna's attack and the subsequent investigation. "So you see, the cabin is owned by your parents, and your brother was stabbed. Jenna was held hostage with a knife. And the description of the man seen near your brother's house fits with Jenna's attacker."

Londyn pursed her lips. She'd coated them with a very light pink lipstick. Her makeup was perfect, like everything else Jenna was starting to think about this woman, but maybe it was all a façade. After all, Jenna suspected Londyn had to prove herself in what was still mostly a man's world. If she took over her father's company, she'd likely be dealing with men more than women there, too, as Steele Guardians provided security guards for many large companies in Oregon and Washington.

"And get this," Brendan continued. "The knife he carried was red-bladed."

Londyn dropped her pen and locked gazes with him, a spark in her eyes. "Red. You're sure?"

"Positive. It was recovered from Jenna's attacker when he was murdered."

"One of the security cameras at Thomas's house captured a red-bladed knife. His killer made sure to avoid most of the cameras. But when he slipped in the back, he was holding the knife out, and the camera caught it."

"Wow," Brendan said. "That wasn't something that was shared with me."

"We're keeping it on a need to know basis." Londyn leaned forward. "Where's the knife now?"

"At the Veritas Center being processed for prints and DNA and examined by their weapons expert. If you can get a sample of Thomas's blood or DNA report to them, and they find a match on the knife, it'll prove a connection."

She sat back, her eyes glazing with tears and revealing a very vulnerable woman who'd just lost her brother to a horrific death. "If you're right, Thomas's killer is dead."

Brendan nodded but didn't speak.

Londyn closed her eyes and shook her head. "I was sorely looking forward to putting him in prison to rot for what he did."

"How is your family holding up?" Jenna asked.

Londyn opened her eyes and placed her hands flat on the table. "My parents are distraught. I have two sisters, and Thomas was our only brother. And he was the oldest so he was a natural to move into the business. My sisters and I are completing our mandatory law enforcement experience before we can consider joining the company."

"Mandatory law enforcement experience?" Brendan asked.

"You'll probably think this is weird, but our dad and Uncle Hugh started and still own the business. They swear they were successful because they were patrol cops first. So they made it a requirement for me, my siblings, and our cousins to put in five years in law enforcement before we could work there."

"But you've been at PPB longer than that, right?"

She nodded. "I love my job and planned to stay here, but with Thomas gone, that could change. My cousin Clare's an FBI agent, and she's joining the company in a few weeks for sure. After she determines the company's needs, our younger sisters and I might need to step in."

Jenna didn't know how Londyn could seem so calm. Maybe came from the horrific things she must regularly see on the job. "This has to be a very hard time for you all. I lost my husband suddenly. I understand at least a bit of what you're going through."

Brendan gave Jenna a look she couldn't interpret. She thought it was a mix of surprise and curiosity, but she'd told him about Toby, so how could he be surprised?

"Thank you, Jenna. It is...shocking." Londyn shifted her gaze to Brendan. "When will the knife DNA be back?"

"Later today at the soonest," Brendan answered. "My sister Sierra is the trace evidence expert, so I can lean on her and Emory, too."

Londyn nodded. "Glad it's at the Veritas Center. We couldn't ask for a better place to run the DNA."

Jenna had heard enough praise for this lab from Brendan and his brothers, and now Londyn, that she really wished she could see the place.

"How do you want to proceed?" Londyn asked.

"We've been working with Detective Grant with

Clackamas County on the attack and murder," Brendan said, knowing that Londyn would realize the metro county included Mount Hood too. "Maybe you could get together with him and discuss the investigation. I can head over to Veritas and check in on the forensics. Move them along if they've stalled. And hopefully you can get a DNA sample or the results for any samples that have been processed for Thomas over to them ASAP."

"No need. Thomas's DNA will be in the database from his time as a police officer here."

"Oh, right. The five-year thing."

"Exactly." Londyn stood. "I'll run Grant down and see what he's got in the works and let him know you and I spoke. I'll also loop in the detective in charge of Thomas's investigation."

"You should know." Brendan scraped his chair across the floor as he got up. "Grant's not happy with me because I followed a few leads before telling him about them."

"I would expect no less of you." Londyn grinned, but it quickly disappeared as if she felt like she shouldn't be happy. "Just don't do the same thing to me, or I'll be more than unhappy."

"I'd never do that to you. Not when it's your brother's murder we're investigating." He shifted his focus to Jenna. "Hang tight while I get Clay to bring the vehicle around front."

Jenna leaned back to watch him talk into his mic. He took a few steps, stopped and spoke to Clay, then took a few more steps and paused to listen.

Londyn also made a call, arranging a contingent of officers to meet them in the lobby. Jenna had no idea why, but she would just follow Brendan's instructions, so she didn't bother asking.

"Roger that." Brendan shoved his phone into his pocket

and spun, the soles of his tactical boots squeaking on the tile. "We're a go."

"There's something else you should know," Jenna said to Londyn as an afterthought. "My attacker tore your cabin apart. Ripped up mattresses and damaged other things. I can't pay you back right away, but I will over time."

"Don't worry about that. Our renter's insurance will cover it." Londyn opened the door, the steady hum of voices filtering in.

Feeling a huge measure of relief, Jenna followed Londyn back to the elevator, and they whisked down to the ground floor. When they stepped through the locked door, Jenna spotted a large group of officers on the sidewalk talking to Erik.

Brendan eyed Londyn. "What's going on?"

"I lost a brother. I'm not going to lose someone else on my watch. I thought we'd set up a wall to the car. Make sure Jenna was safe."

Jenna blinked away her surprise. "Thank you."

"No worries." Londyn poked her head outside and instructed the uniformed officers to take their positions.

They formed a column of protection, two deep, leaving a space for her to walk between them to the vehicle idling at the curb.

Despite the extra protection, Brendan stepped out to look up and down the street then shook hands with Londyn again. "Thanks for your help."

She waved her hand. "I'm the one who should thank you for bringing this to my attention."

"Glad to do so." He motioned for Jenna to step out.

She smiled at Londyn. "Thanks. And again, I'm so sorry for your loss. I'll pray for you and your family."

Londyn gave a sad nod. "Thank you. That's the best thing anyone can do."

Jenna wished she could lessen Londyn's loss, but only time and hopefully faith would bring her through it. Jenna exited the building, the temperature outside a good twenty degrees warmer than at the cabin, and a hint of sizzling beef from a nearby restaurant filled the air. She smiled at the officers as she passed them, but their attention roved like radars, looking for danger. She couldn't even put into words how blessed she felt to have so many men and women in uniform willingly giving of their own life so she could get to her vehicle safely.

She slid in, and Brendan entered behind her. Clay was at the wheel, and Erik took the front seat. Aiden had stayed at the house watching over Karlie, and Drake was still at the hospital with Shawn, but a deputy was scheduled to relieve Drake soon.

"Straight to the office," Brendan instructed Clay.

He had the vehicle in gear already and stepped on it. Jenna didn't speak, as the guys had their gazes fixed out the windows while Clay mingled the SUV with the city traffic and soon had them exiting onto a treelined street in the sparsely populated area. He pulled into the front parking lot for the Veritas Center.

At the sight of two glass towers glistening in the sun, Jenna's mouth dropped open. They were connected at the top by a glass bridge and a ground floor building at the bottom. "Wow. This is amazing."

Brendan smiled. "Wish we could take credit for it, but Emory inherited the building from her grandfather and built the business with five other partners. We just work and live here. Labs and offices are located in the tower on the left. The right tower holds our condos."

"Cool," she said and thought about how much time they must save not having to commute to work.

"The Veritas team lives here too. Except Emory. She and

Blake bought a house when they had a baby. One of the partners, Kelsey Dunbar, and her husband Devon, are expecting now, and I think they might move out too."

Clay pointed the SUV into a parking garage, where he used his fingerprints to gain access. They had to do the same thing at the door on the top floor to enter the building.

Brendan pulled it open and looked at Erik. "Go pick Drake up and come back to the office. Tell Clay we'll meet him in the office in a few."

"Will do." Erik headed back to the SUV, not complaining about being sent on a flunky's errand.

"Great security," she said as she passed Brendan, where he was holding the door open for her.

"It's topnotch. We'll go straight to the first floor to get a security pass for you. Every visitor needs one, and you can't go anywhere in the building without it or without one of us accompanying you." At the elevator, he used his prints to summon the car, and he took her down to the lobby to get her pass, and then back up to the fourth floor of the other tower, where a hallway sign said *Trace Evidence Lab*.

Long windows filled the wall, and Jenna could see into the room with machines around the perimeter and lab tables in the middle. Sierra sat behind one of the tables, and a man and woman sat at another. Brendan opened the door, releasing a strong chemical odor.

Sierra looked up. "This is a surprise."

Brendan crossed the room to her. "We had to go to PPB, so thought I'd stop in and check on the forensics and DNA."

Sierra looked at Jenna. "Translated, he's come to try to speed us up. But if anyone should know we can only go as fast as our machines allow, it should be one of my brothers." Her tone was filled with humor.

"Wait, what? I thought you all were superheroes and

could leap tall buildings in a single bound," Brendan said. "Surely you wouldn't let a simple machine slow you down?"

He laughed, and Sierra joined him. Jenna could easily imagine the two of them growing up and sharing fun times. And Jenna loved how less intense Brendan seemed to be since arriving at the lab. The change probably had to do with the lab's tight security, where he didn't need to worry about her safety as much.

"So when will we have DNA?" he asked.

"You'll have to ask Emory that, but sometime today I should think."

He waved a hand over her table. "And what have you located for us?"

She went to a locker on the wall and came back carrying several plastic evidence bags. She set them all down except the one holding the knife. "First, Grady said there isn't anything unique about the knife other than the color, and this model is popular, so there are too many retailers to be able to trace the purchase."

"And you? Did you find something?"

"Three types of blood. Most of the blade was coated with Odell's blood, but I found another sample right here at the hilt." She pointed to where the blade met the handle. "And then again, another mixed sample at the tip."

Jenna touched the small wound on her neck. "Could that be my blood from when he assaulted me?"

"Could be. I need your sample for comparison. We can do it right now if you'd like. And I can swab your mouth for your DNA, too."

"Okay," she said, though having her finger poked wasn't high on her list of things she wanted to do.

Sierra put on clean gloves then reached under the table and lifted out a basket containing lancets and pipettes wrapped in plastic. She ripped open a package. "If you'll stick out your finger."

Jenna put out her index finger and winced.

Sierra eyed her. "I haven't poked you yet."

"I know, but I'm kind of squeamish about blood."

"Then sit. I don't want you passing out on me and getting hurt."

Jenna slid onto a stool and rested her arm on the cool stainless steel table.

Sierra gave her brother a pointed look. "Come on, dude. What are you waiting for? Take this opportunity to hold her hand."

Brendan rolled his eyes, but Jenna soon felt his warm hand envelope her free one dangling by her side. She loved the feel of his skin. Rough, and yet, he held her hand as gently as he might a flower. She focused on how well their hands fit together. On the skin to skin contact. The warmth and strength he imparted.

"Done," Sierra said.

Jenna shot her a look, shocked that she didn't even feel the prick. She waited for Brendan to release her hand, but he didn't, and that thrilled her even more. She was experiencing so many more emotions with him then she'd ever felt with Toby. Sure, she'd loved him and was attracted to him. At least until he turned so mean. Then the attraction faded. But she'd remained determined to honor her vows and find a way to love him, no matter how he behaved. His death had released her from that obligation.

"Is Emory running DNA on all of these blood samples?" Brendan asked, shocking Jenna back into the present.

Sierra nodded and placed the sample in a bag. She bent under the counter to get out a swab and ripped open the package. "And she can use this DNA sample to compare to all the DNA tests she's running. I'll have it delivered to her."

"I'll take the swabs," Brendan said. "I'm stopping in to see her next."

"Please don't bug her." Sierra motioned for Jenna to open her mouth. "Emory's working as fast as she can."

"I know. I just want to see if she has a firm time for the DNA results, and since we're here, I'll stop by instead of calling."

Sierra ran the swab around Jenna's mouth then put it back in the container. She took part of the blood she'd recovered from Jenna and put it in a slide then handed the sample to Brendan, but her gaze remained on Jenna. "If he starts to get pushy, please rein him in."

"I'm not sure what I can do." She looked up at Brendan. "I have no control over him."

"Are you kidding?" Sierra nodded at their twined hands. "Brendan isn't usually a hand holder. You have more power over him than you can even know."

Brendan jerked his hand free and cleared his throat then told Sierra about Thomas Steele. "His blood could be the sample located by the hilt. He's a former police officer, so his DNA will be in CODIS."

"CODIS?" Jenna glanced at Brendan.

"It's the FBI's Combined DNA Index System."

"I'm sorry to hear about his death." Sierra frowned. "I'll run the samples against the database."

Brendan rested on the edge of a nearby table. "And the other forensics?"

"The piece of fabric you recovered matches Odell's jacket. Interestingly enough, I recovered several stray fibers from the jacket. I'm trying to identify them right now, but it's looking like asbestos."

"Asbestos?" Jenna asked.

Sierra nodded. "It's still found in older houses in walls, tiles, ceilings, and wraps for metal ducts. It requires professional remediation to remove it, but Odell might've been in a building that was being torn down or remodeled and not remediated correctly. Know of anywhere he might've come into contact with it?"

Jenna shook her head.

"Me, either," Brendan said. "His house is old enough to contain asbestos, but there wasn't any active construction going on. I can have Erik run an internet search on Odell and asbestos and see if we find a connection. Maybe there was a recent renovation, and we'll find building permits."

Sierra nodded. "Or perhaps he met his killer in an abandoned building."

"Maybe." Brendan didn't sound convinced.

"What about Shawn's clothing?" Brendan asked. "Have you found any connection?"

"Yes and no. His hair sample is a visual match to the ones found in the tent, but my equipment isn't advanced enough to positively match them and have it stand up in a court of law."

"Shawn said Odell was with him, so does matching it matter?" Jenna asked.

Sierra lifted her eyebrows but didn't speak.

Brendan shifted to look at Jenna. "Shawn could be lying."

"Oh, right." She should've thought of that.

"That's not what I was thinking," Sierra said. "As a scientist, I have to work each bit of evidence to its conclusion no matter what's happening in the investigation, and I don't feel like I've done as thorough of a job as can be done here. I have a friend who can take the process a step farther than I can. I'll see if he's available."

"You all have been so kind," Jenna said. "Always going above and beyond."

Brendan looked proudly at his sister. "That's how the lab

got such a good rep. Not quitting when many labs do and using cutting-edge techniques to advance investigations."

Sierra glowed under his compliment.

"And what about Jenna's clothes and nail scrapings?" he asked.

"I sent the samples I recovered to Emory. She has only so many machines, so she had to prioritize, and she's running the blood samples first." Sierra studied her brother. "You look like you were hoping for more."

"Sorry," he said. "I know you're doing your best."

"I'll get going on the fingerprint evidence next," Sierra said. "Not that I don't like seeing you both, but scram so I can get to it."

Brendan cracked a smile, but his expression was so mixed that Jenna had no idea what he was thinking.

Sierra suddenly pulled Jenna into a hug. "Brendan's falling in love with you," she whispered. "Don't you dare hurt him."

Sierra pulled back and gave Jenna a warning look.

Jenna wanted to say she wouldn't hurt him, but at the moment she didn't know if that was true.

20

In the hallway, Brendan looked over his shoulder at Jenna. "Mind jogging down a couple flights of stairs?"

"Not at all. It'll feel good to move around after all the sitting we've been doing."

He opened the door. "I'm a runner but figured while I was up at the cabin that skiing would take over for a few days. Not that I could've run with the snow anyway."

"But you've missed out on your ski vacation," she said. "I'm sorry. I didn't even think of that. That was so very selfish of me."

"No problem." He started down the stairs two at a time. "I can go skiing any time, and keeping you safe is far more important."

He heard her footfalls behind him but moving at a much slower pace.

"Do you ski often?" she asked, breathing a bit harder.

He slowed down. "Most years, yeah, but with getting the business off the ground this year, we've pretty much been working seven days a week."

"And the cabin was supposed to be a break for the whole

team." She paused, and he looked back to see her shaking her head. "I've imposed on everyone's time off."

He reached the landing on the second floor and waited for her. "They feel the same way as I do."

"Are you sure?" She halted her steps for a moment before resuming. "Have you asked them?"

"No, but we're all wired to prioritize helping a damsel in distress." He grinned.

She locked gazes with him and stumbled on the stair. He grabbed her arm. "Careful. Would hate to put all this work into protecting you just to have you break your neck in our stairwell."

"Maybe I just wanted to swoon into your arms." She grinned at him.

She was joking but he honestly wished she wasn't. Not that he would tell her that. No way. He unlocked the door and checked out the hallway then stepped out.

He pointed at the first sign on the wall, Toxicology and Controlled Substances. "That's Maya's lab. She's analyzing the heroin we recovered from the tent and from Shawn. She'll email her report once she's finished."

"But you don't think it's important enough to stop in and ask about it?"

"Her results might match Shawn's stash to Odell's. Or it could link to a supplier, who could be our killer, I suppose, but the DNA has a far better chance at identifying the killer."

He continued down the hall to the back of the building, where a sign announced Emory's DNA lab. He opened the door for the bustling place filled with long work tables and people in white coats.

Emory stepped out of a closet and brushed her hand over her shoulder-length red hair then pushed up her large black glasses.

Brendan marched right over to her, figuring Sierra had filled her in on the investigation. "Jenna Paine, meet Emory Jenkins."

Emory held out her hand. "I'm sorry to hear about your attack."

Jenna shook hands. "Thank you for running the DNA tests for us."

"Happy to do it."

"Do we have any results yet?" Brendan asked.

"Well hello to you, too." She laughed. "Let me check the machines and see how long before they finish."

She crossed the room to where six machines about the size of tall toaster ovens sat on tables affixed to the wall. She glanced at them and returned. "Should have something to you in two hours or so."

"That soon?" he asked. "That's great news. Thanks. "

He handed over Jenna's DNA swab and blood samples, explaining it all as he did.

"Don't suppose you could have these done in two hours too?" He grinned, knowing his request was ludicrous.

"You think you're joking." Emory held up Jenna's swab. "But I can use a Rapid DNA test for a cheek swab, and that only takes ninety minutes."

"Seriously?" Brendan's eyes widened. "Why didn't you do that for all the samples?"

"I knew you'd ask that." She wrinkled her nose. "Because the court only recognizes Rapid DNA for buccal mouth swabs at this time. And before you ask me to explain, it's because forensic samples recovered at a crime scene, like this one"—she held up the blood sample Sierra recovered from the knife—"often contain mixtures of DNA from more than one person and require interpretation by a trained scientist."

"Makes sense, I suppose, but sure would be nicer if everything could be run through the rapid system."

"And put me out of a job?" She mocked a shudder and laughed.

Brendan laughed with her and glanced at his watch. "We'll go ahead and grab something to eat at my condo and wait there for the results."

He gestured at the door for Jenna to go ahead of him.

She looked at Emory. "Thanks again. I really appreciate you fitting in my samples in your very busy schedule."

Emory waved off the comment. "You're most welcome."

Brendan headed for the door and opened it for Jenna. Her eyes were narrowed, and she dragged her feet as if she were heading for the gas chamber. She should be thrilled that they would have DNA results in a matter of hours, so why wasn't she? Or did her mood not have to do with the DNA at all?

Wait, did she not want to go to his condo? Or be alone with him? Could be. Or it could just be that he hadn't asked her. He'd been so used to calling the shots since they'd met, but this was one area she could have her way.

In the hallway, he looked at her. "Is it okay if we grab dinner at my place? It won't be fancy or anything. I'm not much of a cook. But it'll be edible." He ended by flashing her his best smile.

She met his gaze. "What about Clay? He's expecting us at your office."

Brendan's good humor evaporated. "I can call him."

"Maybe he'll want to have dinner with us."

"Maybe." Obviously she hoped that was the case. "Let me call him."

"Or we could have dinner at the office, right?"

"Sure." He tried to sound enthusiastic, but her desire not

to be alone with him chafed. He felt like saying something, but he swallowed the words.

He poked his head back in the door. "Change in plans, Emory. Call me at our office."

She agreed, and he headed for the elevator, where he placed his fingers firmly on the reader. He pressed so hard it returned an error, and he had to do it again. He was letting his emotions take control.

Since when had he become all about feelings? He'd never acted this way. Never.

He needed to gain control before he made a fool of himself in front of his brothers. Or worse, before he forgot that his purpose in life right now was to keep Jenna safe, and his carelessness could cause him to make a life-threatening error.

They boarded the elevator, and he selected the sixth floor. The space was rife with tension, and he had to say something. "Veritas has floors one through four, and we're on six. Five is empty. They're saving it for expansion, which it looks like they'll be doing soon."

He was rambling. Spitting out facts. Saying anything other than asking her to tell him why she didn't want to go to his condo. The bell dinged, and the doors split.

He stepped out and waited for her to join him. "The skybridge goes to the condos."

"When I first saw the bridge, I knew it would have an amazing view." She looked longingly at it, a look he would like to see directed at him, not some inanimate object. "Can we check it out?"

"Sure," he said, glad to have the tension gone. And even more, he would love to share the view with her. The sun set around four-thirty at this time of year, and the skies were clear, so she would get a spectacular night view of the city.

He led her to the bridge and stepped aside to let her

pass. She marched out to the middle and grabbed onto the railing. "It's so high."

Not what he'd expected her to say.

"An absolutely beautiful view, though." She sighed with contentment.

He agreed, but his thoughts were on her—the beautiful picture she made with her shining expression as she pinned her focus on the city skyline. She looked at him, and he had to grip his fingers into tight knots not to march closer and take her into his arms.

"Do you come out here a lot to absorb the beauty?" She kept her gaze riveted to him.

He did, but he was embarrassed to mention it, as it sure didn't fit with the bodyguard persona he wanted to project while she was under his protection.

She dropped a hand to her hip and tilted her head. "What's that look for?"

He didn't want to tell her, but if he truly wanted her to get to know him, and maybe consider a relationship, he had to be open. With all things. Not just the He-Man stuff. He only hoped she didn't hurt him in return.

"You're gonna think I'm nuts, but when I have a problem I don't know how to work through, I come out and do this at night." He dropped to the floor and laid on his back. "The glittering diamonds God put in the sky helps me remember how infinitesimally small I am. How, if He can fill the sky with stars, He can handle anything I'm dealing with, and He'll see me through my problem."

She moved closer, and he turned his head to look up at her. She searched his gaze, deep and unyielding, then without a word, she dropped down beside him and laid back. "It's awe-inspiring."

"It is at that." He turned to get a glimpse of her expression.

"God seems very present here." She bit her lip and turned her head to look at him. "Can I tell you the truth about something?"

"Sure."

"My relationship with God is suffering more than I've let on."

Not what he'd expected her to say. This was an important topic, so he took a moment to think about his response. "It's not surprising that you're struggling. You've had a hard past and then you lost your husband, leaving you with a financial burden too. A lot of Christians would struggle after all of that."

"It's not that. Though I wish I had a lovely family like yours and a marriage like your parents, I'm grateful for my experience. At least some of the time, when I remind myself how it has shaped who I am and made me stronger."

"I respect the way you're looking at your past, but why the struggle with God, then?"

"It's Karlie and her illness. She's so little. So helpless, and I can't do a thing about it." Tears wet her eyes. "I just can't see the loving God portrayed in the New Testament as one who would let a little child suffer."

He couldn't begin to imagine how hard it was for Jenna or Karlie to deal with this on an ongoing basis, but maybe he could help. Maybe he and Jenna weren't meant to be together, but helping her was the reason God put them together.

He took her hand, the softness of her skin against his calloused fingers reminding him how delicate she was, and yet she possessed an iron strength that he found so attractive. "I haven't known the two of you for very long. And I don't pretend to know about a chronic illness and what you both go through. But I do know from seeing Karlie that she has a special light inside of her. Despite the illness, she's happy and full of vitality. That's thanks to you as a mother supporting her and the faith you share with her. So, if people know she has a chronic illness and yet see that she's able to enjoy life to the fullest, they'll see that her faith is the reason, and that will bring glory to God."

Jenna didn't say anything for the longest time. "I hadn't thought of that, but I guess it will."

"Good will come from Karlie's illness. And maybe it will be the catalyst for people who are on the fence about God to embrace faith."

"I suppose." She looked up at the stars. "I still wish she didn't have to suffer, but I'll try to focus on the good that can come from her pain by starting to focus on her joy instead of her pain."

She turned back to him and smiled. "And thank you for noticing such a special thing about Karlie. After her father was so harsh with her, it's refreshing to see what you think of her."

He squeezed her hand then rolled to face her and propped himself up on his elbow.

She touched his cheek with her fingertips, her touch tentative as if she was afraid or shy. "You really are a special man, Brendan Byrd, and I'm honored to know you."

Jenna held her breath as she waited for Brendan to respond to her forward behavior. She knew that by today's standards touching his cheek was very innocent, but for her, making the first move and touching a man who wasn't her husband was an aggressive step. Especially after her limited experience with men.

She didn't have a clue how to flirt. Another thing she'd never really done. She'd been socially shunned in high school due to her family's finances and reputation, so guys didn't even give her a second look. When she met Toby, he came on to her and was straightforward about his interest. No flirting. Just bam—I like you and want to go out.

Besides, she shouldn't be flirting. Not after Sierra warned her not to hurt Brendan. He might take it the wrong way.

He held her hand between his rough fingers, his gaze riveted to hers. "Right back atcha on being special. Except you're not a man. Not at all."

He leaned closer, his intent clear. He was going to kiss her. Last time he'd asked. This time he just swooped in and pressed his lips against hers. She was probably giving him all kinds of nonverbal signals telling him this was what she wanted. And she did. How she did. At least for now.

She twined her arms around his neck and drew him closer. Boldly deepening the kiss and enjoying the warm feel of his lips against her. His were cold and firm and skilled in the art of kissing. He shifted closer, and the kiss turned heated.

She followed his lead and ignored how he must've gotten so good at kissing. He probably thought her a novice. Again, she didn't care but inched even closer, getting lost in the joy of caring for such a wonderful man.

A door slammed in the distance, and her fog lifted. She was here—in a public space, lying on the floor, kissing a man. She jerked free, scrambled to her feet, and bolted back into the hallway with the elevator.

"Jenna, wait," Brendan called out, but she didn't stop until she'd reached the elevator.

There, she drew in breath after breath to still her traitorous heart.

How could she have engaged in such a public display of affection? Sure, no one saw her. At least she didn't think they did, but someone could've come to the bridge then tiptoed away. Maybe the person who slammed the door.

Brendan caught up to her. "What's wrong?"

"That." She jerked a thumb over her shoulder. "We... we're in a public space."

"Not exactly public."

"But still. Your brothers. The Veritas partners. Guests. Anyone could've seen us."

He didn't look the least bit distraught. "And would it be so bad if they did?"

She grasped her hands together. "I'm sure you can tell that I'm not used to kissing men."

"I have no idea what you mean."

"My lack of skill."

"There was nothing lacking in our kiss. Trust me." He smiled, his eyes alight with joy.

Part of her was thrilled to hear his comment, the other part mortified. "Can we just go to your office?"

He took a step closer. "We should talk about this."

She flashed up a hand like a stop sign. "No, we shouldn't. Please. Your office."

He searched her face, his lips pressed tight. "Okay, for now. But I want to talk about this later. I'm not in the habit of casually kissing women. Public space or not. I have feelings for you, Jenna, and you need to know that."

She turned to face the hallway. "Is your office this way?"

"Fine, run from it if you have to. Ignoring my feelings won't make them go away. Trust me. I tried." He marched past her, and she had to nearly run to keep up.

She hated seeing his joy evaporate, his posture become rigid, and his steps urgent. She'd hurt him. The last thing she'd wanted to do. No. That wasn't right. The last thing she wanted was to get involved with a man. Or so she'd been telling herself, but was it still the last thing for her, or had Brendan changed her mind on relationships? Had his parents proved to her that a solid, loving relationship was possible?

This man, the one whose shoulders were set in a stiff line and hands fisted at his sides, racing away from her, was a remarkable man. He'd just demonstrated that with his insight into Karlie. He truly found her daughter amazing, an inspiration. Just the kind of man she would want as a husband, *if* she was looking for one.

He jerked open a door and stepped into the space. Even as angry as he was at her, he held the door open. Ever the gentleman. She only hoped she could raise Karlie to hold the same values and morals as the Byrd children.

He could help you with that.

She shoved the thought as deeply as she could into the recesses of her mind and looked around the large, open space. She should be thrilled to see his work space, but acid burned in her stomach. Still, she glanced at a reception desk by the door. No one sat behind it. She stepped in further to see a picture of a black lab.

"That's Stella's desk," Brendan said. "She's our receptionist, but she's done for the day."

Jenna shifted to look at a large table and chairs in the middle of the room. Made with rough-cut wood and metal legs, the table fit right in with the unfinished walls and ceiling with metal joists, beams, and ducts in full display. An office, with a floor-to-ceiling glass wall, was located directly ahead and cubicles lined the back wall. Clay sat in the middle one and looked up.

She turned her focus to Brendan. "This space really fits you guys. I like it."

Her compliment elicited a tight smile, but the hurt from her rejection still lingered in his eyes. Thankfully, Clay came to join them, so they didn't have to focus on what had just transpired between them in the hallway.

He glanced at each of them a few times. "Everything okay?"

"Fine," Brendan snapped. "DNA results in two hours. We're thinking about having dinner and hanging here until they come in."

"Sounds good." Clay seemed uneasy as he studied his brother. "If that's what you want."

"It was Jenna's idea." Brendan shoved his hands into his pants' pockets. "I can make something at the condo and bring it back or we can order in."

"Are you kidding? Order in for sure. I've had to sample your cooking far too many times." Clay grinned.

Jenna smiled with him, but Brendan's half scowl remained.

"I'll grab the menus." Brendan spun and went into the office.

Clay's gaze followed Brendan then shifted to Jenna. "You sure everything's okay?"

She nodded as she didn't want to lie to him. Plus, she hoped it would be okay soon. That Brendan would get over his anger with her, and they could be friends.

Right. Friends. Was that what she wanted? Hardly. But wanting and doing were two different things. She had to be careful. Assess things. Make a sound decision. She had Karlie to think about, and Jenna couldn't risk her daughter being hurt even more than she already had been at her tender age.

"Might as well sit while we wait for him to hunt down the menus." Clay pulled out a chair for her.

She took a seat and was glad she faced away from the office, or she might sit and stare at Brendan, giving Clay even more ammunition to question them.

He sat in a chair across from her and watched her.

Feeling uncomfortable under his study, she said the first thing that came to mind. "So, you were once an ICE agent."

He nodded, seeming wary.

"Did you like it?"

"Loved it." His excited tone didn't match his expression.

"You seem hesitant."

He folded his hands on the table. "ICE is getting a pretty bad rap right now. I never know how people are going to react to it, so when someone brings it up, I hold back. Assess. It's a shame. The bad reputation isn't deserved."

"Tell me about it from your side."

"There are so many different aspects of ICE, but the news only focuses on immigration issues. The agency's primary mission is to promote homeland security and public safety. For example, I was involved in stopping human trafficking. But that isn't often mentioned because people like to ignore the fact that other people are trafficked." He shook his head. "They think it doesn't happen in our country, but it's a big problem. Huge. And Portland is one of the hotspots for trafficking."

"Portland, really? I had no idea."

He sat forward, his eyes alive with interest in the subject, looking so very much like Brendan that it made her heart ache.

"The I-5 corridor running through the state makes it easier to move people and goods out of the state," he said. "And to bring trafficked victims into it. Most of them are women. Powerless. Victimized. And trapped. I was happy to be a small part in stopping that. And it gave me a chance to share my faith. Sure, the agency has rules against that, but it's who I am, so it was only natural to share, and I was prepared to take any consequences for it."

These women must've been so thankful for a positive

male role model in their lives when they'd witnessed terrible men who trafficked them. She was about to say so, but Brendan came back and dropped several menus on the table.

"Go ahead and choose, Jenna." Clay leaned back and draped his arm over the next chair. "We'll eat anything."

He smiled at her, but she could see the lingering pain from the memories of the trafficked women in his gaze. She quickly prayed for him and asked God to give him comfort and help him to not linger on the horrible things he must've seen.

She turned her attention to the menus. Toby never wanted to pay for takeout when she could cook for him, and her family never had the money for it when she was growing up. She didn't have the money now either, so she would find the most cost-efficient meals.

She thumbed through the menus and found a Mexican restaurant that seemed reasonable, and she could get a single taco for very little money.

Brendan sat next to her, and she slid the brochure to him. "This one, please."

"What are you going to have?" he asked as he opened it.

"I want a soft beef taco." She got out her wallet and put a five-dollar bill on the table, lamenting how far it would go to feed Karlie.

"I've got this." He shoved away the money from her. "That's not enough food to keep a kid alive."

She stopped his hand and met his gaze. "It's fine, and I pay my own way."

He studied her face for a moment then let go of the money, grabbed a notepad, and wrote down the number for the corresponding taco. Then he added a group-sized portion of nachos and rice, which she knew, when it arrived, he would insist she help herself to. He was just trying to be kind, but a pang of irritation formed in her gut. Mostly irritation at Toby for leaving her penniless, but irritation all the same.

Brendan finished writing down his meal then passed the pad and menu to Clay. Brendan's phone chimed, and he picked it up. "Text's from Maya. Shawn's heroin didn't match what we found at the tent."

"Which corroborates his story." Clay slid the notepad back to Brendan, who nodded.

Jenna let out a quiet breath. She was glad her brother hadn't lied to them.

"She also says the tent heroin was cut with powdered milk," Brendan added. "And she's asking her contacts for any dealers moving this kind of product."

The door opened, and Erik entered with a tired-looking Drake trailing him.

"Just in time," Brendan said. "We're ordering Mexican."

"Perfect." Drake practically fell into a chair by Clay. "Hospital food isn't the best."

Erik sat next to him. "Mom's not going to be too happy with us missing a meal this close to Christmas. She has it all planned out."

"I called to check in," Brendan said. "And let her know we were staying here until the DNA results came in. I promised we'd eat tons of dessert when we got back, and she's fine."

Now Jenna knew what had taken so long when he'd gone to get menus.

He turned to her. "She also said Karlie's feeling better. No fever and she has more energy. Mom's still keeping her involved in quiet activities."

"Thank you for checking." She gave him an earnest smile when what she really wanted to do was squeeze his hand.

His mouth started to quirk up but he quickly moved his focus to Drake. "So if you want anything, write it down, and I'll order."

"This on you?"

Brendan nodded but glanced at the money on the table and frowned.

She felt churlish now for insisting on paying when he was treating his brothers. Maybe she'd offended him. She almost sighed. She simply didn't know how to act around him.

When was she a client, albeit a nonpaying one? When was she the woman he was interested in? But most importantly of all, she wanted to know if she really wanted to return his obvious affections and begin a relationship with him.

Her questions left her quiet all the way through their meal and an update meeting to discuss where they were in finding Odell's killer. When the business phone on the table rang, she hoped for something, anything, to move them forward on the investigation.

Brendan grabbed the handset and punched the speaker button. "Nighthawk Investigations."

"It's Emory," she said. "The DNA tests have completed."

"And?" Brendan asked while Jenna held her breath.

"As expected, Odell's and Jenna's DNA were in the blood found on the knife."

"And the third sample?" Brendan asked.

"Matches to Thomas Steele, like you thought," she said. "One other thing. We recovered DNA from the handle too, and we have a match in CODIS for that profile."

Brendan met and held Jenna's gaze. "A match means Emory will be able to give us the murder suspect's name."

21

Everyone seemed to be holding their breath. Brendan included, but he couldn't very well speak without breathing. He riveted his eyes to the phone, a pen in hand. "Who are we looking at?"

"Sal Whitby." Emory rattled off an address in Woodburn, a suburb in the very southernmost metro area.

The same first name that Shawn and the restaurant owner had mentioned. Brendan jotted the information down then glanced at Jenna, who was frowning. "You know this guy?"

She shook her head hard, her hair whipping over her shoulder. "Never heard of him."

Erik pulled a laptop across the table and began typing.

Brendan looked back at the phone. "Do you have anything else on him, Emory?"

"No, but I could get Blake to run him through law enforcement databases to see if he can get more info on why his DNA was in CODIS."

"Do that. Now. Have him get right back to me." Brendan was shocked at the sharpness in his own voice.

"Okay." Emory sounded surprised too.

Brendan let out a long breath. "Sorry. I didn't mean to snap. It's just...we finally have a lead, and I don't want to waste a second in getting details on this guy."

"No worries," she said. "I deal with law enforcement types like you all the time. Every one of you wants your information yesterday." She laughed.

Looking at Jenna, he forced out a laugh he didn't feel. "Blake is Emory's husband and former sheriff, now the investigator for Veritas."

"Oh, great," Jenna said.

"Thanks for your help, Emory," Brendan said. "I owe you big time."

"You can thank me by paying your bill on time." She chuckled again.

"Thank you from me too," Jenna said. "I appreciate you prioritizing the tests."

"Glad to help, and I hope you find this killer."

Brendan hung up and looked at Erik. "We need to see—"

"His picture, I know," Erik answered without looking up. "Putting it up on screen one now."

The man's image filled one of two large flatscreen TVs mounted on the wall. He had a narrow face with a beard that ran up to a skinny strip of hair just like Shawn had described. The picture matched the guy in the restaurant video minus the cap.

Jenna gasped.

Brendan got it. She was shocked to see the suspect they'd only just heard about. He wanted to reach out to hold her trembling hand resting on the table, but she'd made it clear that she didn't want that from him. Instead, he focused on his brothers. "Matches the guy talking to Odell in the video from the bar. So we have our guy, and I need—"

"A look at his property," Erik interrupted again. "Aerial

view of his house is coming up on screen one, and an eye-level view on two."

Brendan looked at Whitby's house. The place was surrounded by a dense grove of trees. His property included a ramshackle red barn with metal roof and an old farm style house set back from the road, almost to the wooded tree line. Faded white paint, near gray now, looked as if it would flake off with the slightest of breezes, but the door looked new and was painted a glossy black. A collie dog lay in the dirt driveway.

"Does Whitby own this place?" Brendan asked.

"Searching property records now," Erik replied, his eyes remaining fixed on his computer.

The phone rang.

"It's Blake's extension." Brendan answered on speaker. "What did you find, Blake?"

"Whitby's got a long rap sheet. Mostly aggravated assault. Three arrests for suspicion of murder. All in Multnomah County. Charges are from six years ago, then nothing since then. Looks kind of like he fell off the face of the earth at that time."

"That's when he bought the place he's living in now," Erik announced.

"So he moves out to the country and suddenly stops being a thug," Brendan said. "I don't buy it."

"Maybe he just hasn't gotten caught since then," Drake suggested.

"That sounds more like it," Blake said. "Unless he suddenly had an epiphany of some sort. Maybe found God."

"And then lost Him when he killed Odell?" Brendan asked. "I don't think so."

"What about a military record?" Clay asked.

"Yeah, he's former spec ops. Army."

Brendan shared a look with his brothers but made sure he erased his worry before Jenna got a look at it.

"Thanks, Blake," Brendan said. "We owe you one."

"No sweat." Blake ended the call.

Jenna met Brendan's gaze, and her breathing increased. "We need to go there. Now. Quick!"

Brendan didn't want to disappoint Jenna, but this was one area where he would have to. "We'll head right out, but you need to stay here."

"But I—"

"Can't help, and you'll be in danger."

"Still I—"

"If you won't stay for yourself, stay for me." He gave her a pleading smile. "I'll be distracted if you're with us. I could make a mistake. Get hurt or worse, get one of these guys hurt."

She bit her lip. "Can I go out to the cabin?"

"I'd rather not take the time to drop you off. Whitby could skate if we don't get right out there."

She rubbed the back of her neck. "Okay. I'll stay, but you have to call me the second you have any news."

"I will." He smiled at her, but she didn't respond. "I'll ask Blake to stay with you."

"Is that necessary with all the security here?"

Nothing was too much for keeping her safe, but he schooled his voice so he wouldn't come across as harsh and demanding. "I won't take chances with your safety."

He looked at his brothers before she could argue. "Gear up. I have a few calls to make."

His brothers, fire in their eyes, jumped up and went to the weapons storage area in the back of the office. They were no longer law enforcement officers so approaching this guy would be tricky. He would likely be armed, and they had to be prepared for anything, but would only ever fire a gun as a last resort. Like if someone's life was in imminent danger.

Brendan grabbed his phone and dialed a deputy he knew who regularly patrolled the area where Whitby lived.

"Byrd?" Jake said. "You ready to leave civilian life and come back to the real world already?"

"Not a chance, but I could use your help. I need to get eyes on a suspect's house ASAP." Brendan shared the address. "I just need to know if he's home, and we'll take it from there. Can you do a drive-by?"

Silence filled the phone for an uncomfortable moment. "This gonna get me in trouble with Sarge?"

Brendan totally understood his buddy's hesitancy. "Not if you don't do anything but the drive-by. But you should know the guy's former spec ops, so play it cool, man."

"Okay. I'm a few miles out. Stand by for my call." Jake hung up.

Brendan grabbed the handset and dialed Blake's extension. "Are you free to stay with Jenna while we raid the suspect's house?"

"Sure thing."

"She'll head down to my condo on our way out, and I'll text to let you know when to meet us."

"Got it."

Brendan hung up and looked at Jenna. "I thought my condo would be more comfortable than hanging here. Is that okay?"

She nodded but didn't look happy about it.

He wanted to know the reason for her hesitancy but couldn't waste time trying to discover the reason. He had to get ready too. "Be right back."

He joined his brothers and grabbed his favorite rifle. Odds were great that he wouldn't need to use it, but they had to be prepared for anything. If the guy was home, they'd try to do a knock and talk and worm their way inside. If he was uncooperative, they'd detain him. If he wasn't home, they'd find a way in.

Brendan's cell rang. He answered the call back from Jake.

"Suspect's at home," Jake said. "Want me to keep eyes on the place until you get here?"

"Thanks, but no. I don't want to risk him seeing your patrol vehicle and getting spooked."

"You know I can make sure that doesn't happen."

"Yeah, but then you're gonna have to report your location to dispatch, and he could be listening to a scanner."

"I could go AWOL for a little while."

"And get in trouble? I don't want that to happen."

"Okay," Jake said, sounding like he'd like a little excitement in his day.

Brendan remembered those quiet patrol days and wished he could comply, but he didn't want to ruin a friend's career. "Thanks for the offer, though."

"I'll remain in the area. Let me know if you need assistance."

Brendan ended the call and shoved his phone into his pocket. He turned to Clay. "We need everyone on this detail. With the suspect at home, it should be safe to bring Aiden in. I'll grab his gear. Call him and arrange a place for him to meet up. Dad can take over protection detail for the others."

"Roger that." Erik made the call.

Brendan put on his tactical vest and loaded the pockets with extra ammo magazines and a few flash-bangs. Again, he didn't think he would need them, but his father taught him to always be prepared, and the army drilled in the preparedness requirements even harder. His buddies in Delta would've laughed him out of the unit if he'd come to an op without the gear he'd needed.

He grabbed a flashlight, switched it on to be sure it worked, and shoved it into his vest holder.

"Aiden's on his way," Erik said, picking up his comms unit. "We'll rendezvous near the target house."

Brendan nodded and tucked away his smile at Erik's use of tactical jargon instead of just saying Aiden would meet them. His little brother was pumped and in tactical mode for sure.

Brendan mounted his comms mic on his shirt and picked up the in-ear headset. The buds were heat activated, so he compressed the first one before putting it in his ear, and it expanded to fit as he adjusted the cable retainer over his ear.

The team had splurged on units with external microphones for natural hear-thru so they could hear everything happening around them while wearing the headsets. As he plugged it into the control unit, he looked at Jenna. She remained at the table, her fingers twisted together. He wished he could bring her along, but the reasons he'd given her were valid. If time allowed, he could've added so many more.

The chief one? He'd fallen for her. Big time. He didn't want to leave her care to anyone. He wanted to be by her side. But he also didn't want to leave apprehending this killer to anyone else either. Besides, she'd be fine in his condo.

Brendan surveyed his brothers. "Everyone ready?"

He received affirmative nods and grunts.

"I'll drop Jenna off at my condo and meet you in the garage." He looked at Clay. "You're in charge of team gear. Make sure we have everything we need."

Clay nodded and grabbed a bin holding glass cutters, a battering ram, and other items used by the whole team.

Brendan crossed to Jenna and sent Blake a text as he walked. He confirmed he was on his way.

She stood and ran her gaze over Brendan, a hint of admiration in her expression. "You look ready for battle."

"Ready, yes, but that's the last thing we want to have happen." He ignored the admiration, as he sure didn't need to get caught up in his feelings for her.

"Just tell me one thing."

"Sure."

"This guy is former special ops. That makes this more dangerous, right?"

"Could be, but Aiden and I've had the same training, maybe more. We can handle it." He led her to the door before she could ask additional questions that he would have to duck, since he didn't want her to worry.

They crossed the skybridge. Memories of their kiss tried to take over his brain, but he shoved them away. Took a strength he didn't know he had to ignore them, and even more so as they settled into the tiny elevator space on their ride to the third floor. Her sweet peach scent permeated the air, and he had to swallow to keep from commenting on it. How she managed to impact him like this, he didn't know, and at the moment he didn't like it. Not when he should be full-throttle concentrating on the upcoming op.

The doors opened, and he spotted Blake standing by the condo, kissing Emory. She had a hand resting on an orange-and-gray stroller. Their baby Amelia, who Brendan thought was around four months old, flung a stuffed bear to the floor.

Jenna rushed over to pick it up and knelt in front of the baby. "She's adorable. What's her name?"

"Amelia," Emory said. "And this is my husband, Blake, in case you haven't met."

Jenna looked up. "Sorry for ignoring you, but, I mean..." She pointed at the stroller.

"That's okay," Blake said. "I ceased to exist the minute she was born. But if that's the cost of having a daughter, I'm more than ready to pay it."

Brendan rarely saw Blake with his child, but pure love radiated from his eyes as he looked at Amelia. For the first time in his life, Brendan could imagine being a dad. He was sure it had to do with finding a woman he wanted to be the mother of his children and her adorable little girl.

"You're heading out now, I assume," Blake said.

Brendan jerked his gaze to the door and unlocked it. "Help yourself to anything."

Jenna stood. "Please tell me Amelia is staying with us."

"We were actually just saying good-bye," Emory said.

"But you can change your mind, right?" Jenna asked.

Blake shook his head. "Sorry. As much as I'd like them to be with us, you're in danger, and I won't put my family at risk."

Jenna cringed. "Not much danger here, though, right?"

"Right." Blake settled his hands on his hips. "Everything should be fine. But I won't take any chance with my family, just like Brendan won't take a chance with your safety."

She looked up at Brendan then, her eyes seeking something, but he didn't know what and didn't have time to ask.

That was for later. Much later. Tonight.

Then he'd tell her how he felt. Once Whitby was behind bars and that danger Blake mentioned was long gone.

"Please be careful." Jenna grabbed Brendan's arm before he walked away.

"Always." He placed his hand over hers, his gaze locking

on her eyes. "And you please listen to Blake. If he tells you to do something, don't stop to analyze it. Just act. Your life could depend on it."

She nodded, but her mind was still awhirl. What had he thought when Blake mentioned how her safety was important to Brendan like his family's was to Blake? What would it be like to have a family with Brendan? Wonderful, for all she could tell. Man, she'd fallen for him.

He gave her a long look then spun and marched down the hall, his shoulders back, a sense of urgency in his step. A sight to be sure. She could easily imagine him in Delta Force, going out on dangerous missions. She was very thankful that he no longer faced that extreme danger. Or even patrolled as a deputy. Sure, he was going to face a killer right now, but he had his brothers with him and the element of surprise on his side.

Keep him safe. Please.

"You ready to go in?" Blake asked.

Jenna took one last look at the child. "Amelia's beautiful, and I know you both are so happy to be parents. May God bless all of you."

"Thank you." Emory squeezed Jenna's arm. "I hope after all this is over we get to see you again. I can tell we'll be good friends."

Jenna smiled but didn't answer. "I'll give you time to say good-bye privately. And thanks for sharing Blake with me."

"Of course." Emory beamed a loving smile at her husband, and he blushed.

Jenna stepped into the condo, thinking about how fun it was to see a tough guy like Blake, once a sheriff in charge of a whole county of deputies, blush when his wife gave him such an endearing look. She could imagine Brendan and his brothers doing the same thing, but only the thought of Brendan remained as she stepped down a short entrance hall, eager to see where the man she was falling for lived.

The hall opened to a big space holding a living and dining area and an open kitchen along the back wall. The brown cabinets had flat fronts and were very contemporary. So was the furniture. Black metal bookshelves took up one wall and were filled with records. Lots and lots of records, plus an old fashioned record player. A gray sofa, a bright yellow easy chair, and a round glass-and-wood coffee table were placed on a fluffy gray rug topping the dark wood floors. The rug looked super soft, and Jenna could see Karlie wanting to cuddle up on it.

But what she noticed most was that the place was spotlessly clean. Not a typical bachelor's home, but then Brendan's clothing was always perfectly pressed too.

"Place is just like the condo Emory and I lived in here," Blake said, coming into the room. "But it was never this clean. You can tell Brendan served in the army for so many years."

"Ah, right. That explains it." Wondering if a neat freak like Brendan could live with a messy four-year-old, she turned to Blake. "You lived in the condos, huh?"

"Until Amelia was born and we found out how much stuff a tiny little thing needs to live." He shook his head. "They really should warn you."

Jenna smiled with him, remembering the years Toby had lavished Karlie with things. Then his perfect little girl got sick, and he couldn't handle it.

"Did I say something wrong?" he asked.

"Wrong?"

"You're frowning."

"Am I?" She shook off the memory. "I don't know what Brendan has to drink, but can I get you something?"

"A glass of water would be great, but you don't have to

wait on me. Emory's got me trained to get things myself and even serve others." He laughed and went into the kitchen. "Would you like something?"

"Water would be good." She set her purse on the counter and sat on the gray metal stool that matched the color of the couch.

Blake found glasses and looked at her. "Ice?"

"Please."

He pressed the refrigerator door dispenser, and ice clinked into the glasses. "I had no idea Brendan was into old records."

"Me either."

"Really?" He set the glass in front of her. "I got the feeling that you two knew each other before this."

"We just met." She took a long drink of her water. "How did you meet Emory?"

He rested his glass on the counter and smiled. "It was back when I was sheriff in Cold Harbor and I had a woman disappear on my watch." His smile evaporated. "I brought her DNA sample to Emory to process, and I about dropped to the floor. She was a dead ringer for the missing woman. Turns out the missing woman was Emory's twin, but Emory didn't even know she had a sister."

"Oh, wow. What a shock that must've been."

"It was. To both of us. So anyway, once I figured out she wasn't the missing woman playing some sick game with me, we worked the investigation together, and I fell for her." He turned his glass on the counter and ran a finger through the ring it left behind. "It was perfect timing for me. I was ready to hang up my sheriff's hat. I bought into the Veritas Center as a partner to coordinate forensics for investigations."

Jenna loved it when people found their happily-ever-after, something she'd once believed she'd found with Toby. "Sounds like God had a hand in bringing you two together."

He nodded. "And removing personal obstacles we had that at first kept us from getting together."

So they'd had issues too, and God helped resolve them.

Could He do the same thing for her and Brendan? Just as important, did she want Him to?

22

Brendan and his brothers fanned out around the house, where a single light from the front window spilled into the darkness and illuminated a large porch. Aiden was on overwatch this time as Brendan wasn't going to miss a chance at talking to this guy.

He crept onto the porch with Clay, cringing when the floorboards creaked. The front door had multiple deadbolts, and a *No Trespassing* sign was posted on the front gate. Could be paranoia from this guy's days in the service, urging him to live off the grid, or he could be up to something illegal. In addition to murder, that was.

Brendan signaled for Clay to hold while he looked in the lighted window. Whitby sat on a black leather couch, head thrown back, mouth open, in the living room. Brendan could hear him snoring through the closed window. He was a fit guy and the odd beard proved he was their guy. Empty beer cans were scattered on the floor around him. A rifle lay next to him. Drunk and dangerous.

Behind him, the drywall had been removed from the framing, and an air duct wrapped in white ran up the wall.

Asbestos. Had he not known about asbestos and accidently disturbed the hazard? Then Odell came by. Or Whitby transferred the asbestos to Odell's clothing. Either way, another factor pointing to this being the guy they'd been looking for.

"You're gonna want to see this," Aiden's voice came over Brendan's earbuds.

Brendan crept back from the window. "On my way."

He looked at Clay. "Guy's sleeping. Maybe passed out. Keep an eye on him and report any movement."

Brendan moved over the worn painted porch floorboards, his footfalls nearly silent, and joined Aiden, who stood by the other window. "It's our guy, all right. Just take a look."

Brendan glanced in the window. The room was illuminated by the blue light on a computer tower. One wall held an American flag and several service medals. He'd taped pictures of Odell at the bar on the wall above the desk. Pictures of him arriving at the bar. On his snowmobile. At his tent. And photos of Thomas Steele. At work. At home. In his car. At the store.

Below were pictures of Jenna at her cabin and outside the cabin with Karlie. But what chilled Brendan deep in his soul were the photos of Jenna with him. Lots of them spanning the past few days. The guy must've used a zoom lens because Brendan knew the creep was never close enough to take a regular picture. If he had been, Brendan would've known. The sixth sense he developed in Delta would've warned him.

He gritted his teeth and swallowed his desire to break into the place and pummel the guy.

"Whitby's getting up," Clay said over the comms.

"Everyone back off to the trees so we don't spook him," Brendan said. "We'll decide there how to handle him."

The team crept back across the lawn and gathered near a soaring spruce.

"We have a choice," Brendan said, his breath white in the chilly night air. "I go talk to the guy, or we call in law enforcement to make the arrest."

"Law enforcement?" Aiden eyed him. "Since when did you get so cautious?"

"I don't want to do something I'll regret that lets this guy get off on two murders. The last thing I want is for him to go free and set his sights on Jenna again."

"If it was me," Drake said, "I'd bust down the door and restrain him, then call in deputies to take him into custody."

"And let him claim I assaulted him?" Brendan shook his head and looked at the door that was opening a crack.

"Who'sh out there?" Whitby stepped onto the porch with a rifle in hand, his voice slurred. "Show yourself or I'll let it rip."

"Take cover," Brendan said. "And I'll step out."

Aiden lifted his rifle. "I've got your back."

"Relax," Brendan said.

"Not with a guy like this."

"But he's drunk. Biggest danger is he accidently discharges his weapon."

"Still, I got your back." Aiden eased behind a tree, his rifle poking out.

Brendan waited for his other brothers to take defensive positions. He wouldn't risk their lives.

"Coming out," Brendan announced. "I just want to talk to you."

"Thish is private property," Whitby bellowed, waving his rifle.

"Sorry for intruding." Brendan left his rifle behind and stepped out of the darkness and into the pale moonlight.

Whitby took a step and nearly face-planted.

"Careful with that gun." Brendan didn't have high hopes of getting information from a drunk man, and he sure didn't want to get shot by one.

Whitby swayed and stared at Brendan as he got within three feet of the guy. "Do I know you?"

"You have my picture plastered all over your wall," Brendan said, preferring to be direct as usual.

Whitby's eyes narrowed, seeming confused and not recognizing Brendan from his earlier surveillance of Brendan and Jenna.

"Whatcher name?"

"Brendan Byrd."

"Heard that somewhere." With his free hand he pounded his head. "C'mon think, man."

Brendan moved into a position slightly to the man's left, so if Whitby accidently fired his weapon the bullet would miss him. "You can put down the gun. I'm not here to hurt you."

"Don't know that." He firmed his hold on the rifle but swayed.

Brendan figured he could take two steps and disarm the guy without incident, but then what? If Brendan didn't restrain the guy, he'd head inside and lock the door. Brendan wanted to ask questions before that happened.

"Tell me about Lonny Odell," Brendan said.

A hideously happy smile crossed Whitby's face. "Not much to tell. Guy's dead."

"Do you know how he died?"

"Knife. His own fancy red one." He chuckled, his tone low and guttural.

The knife details hadn't been released to anyone, and there was only one way he could know about it. He'd wielded it. "And how do you know that?"

He blinked, swaying. "Heard it somewhere."

"Where?"

Whitby shrugged.

"Would it surprise you if I told you the police and my team are the only ones who know the details on the knife?"

Whitby's eyes flashed, but then they blanked, and the hazy drunk stare returned. "Doesn't matter. Guy's dead. That's all that matters."

"Why did he have to die?"

"None of your bishness."

"Was it your idea to kill him and try to kill Jenna?"

His face paled, and he cupped a hand over his mouth, looking like he might hurl. Then he dropped his hand and grinned. "Myles. Stupid Myles. Hired me to find the flash drive that broad has. I told him I'd find it, but no. Was taking too long. So he fired me. Me! I'm the best. He shouldn't have fired me. But he did and pop—he's gone. No need to find the drive now. The broad can have it."

He laughed so hard he swayed and wobbled. "But don't worry. Still got my money. Myles safe was no match for me." He dusted his hands together. "Job complete."

"Myles is gone?" Brendan asked, though he suspected Whitby had killed the guy. "Did he take a vacation?"

"A long one." He grinned. "Didn't get no further than my backyard. Just like what's waiting for you." He peered at Brendan, blinking hard.

"And the cash in Odell's place. Know anything about that?"

He snorted, and saliva dripped out of his mouth and down his chin. "Myles hired him first. Not the best move. Maybe cash is from that. Or Odell's a big-time drug supplier. Maybe from that." Whitby lifted his gun as if he intended to use it, but then he swayed, his eyes rolled back in his head, and he dropped to the ground. Passed out cold. Unmoving.

He'd as much as admitted to killing Odell and now this

Myles guy, but since he wasn't sober it would never hold up in court. Nothing he said would. But at least Brendan knew he was their guy. And now it sounded like he'd killed the guy who hired him to end Jenna's life.

"We should check the back yard," Brendan told his brothers. "Clay, you keep an eye on the guy, Aiden remain in position, and the rest of us will take a look."

Brendan waited for Clay to get a gun on Whitby then headed for the back. On his way, he dialed Londyn Steele and filled her in on the details. She promised to arrive soon with backup, and Brendan turned his attention to the yard.

He searched the overgrown grass, his gaze landing on an area recently dug and large enough for a body.

"You seeing what I'm seeing?" Drake asked.

Brendan nodded.

"Wish we could start digging," Erik said.

But they couldn't, and as much as Brendan didn't want to stand here and wait for Londyn to arrive, he did for the next thirty minutes as did his brothers. She arrived with a flourish and brought with her a large group of forensic techs.

"Got Whitby in a cruiser on his way to jail." She offered a tight smile. "Thanks for calling me instead of Grant."

"No problem." Brendan pointed at the grave. "You have people who can get started on digging?"

She nodded. "Let me get them on it."

She marched over to two white-suited males and gave them instructions. After a round of photos and measurements, they laid out a tarp by the grave and started to dig. They quickly unearthed the body buried just below the surface. One of the techs reached into the grave then joined Londyn. He handed her a wallet.

With gloved hands, she opened it. "Guy's name is Jensen Myles. Lives in Portland."

Brendan looked at Erik to tell him to get searching for information on this guy, but before Brendan could say a word, Erik had dug out his phone.

"What's the state of the body?" Londyn asked the tech.

"Dead for a few days at most. Stabbed in the chest. Thin wound. Maybe an ice pick."

"Thanks," Londyn said and the guy went back to work. She looked at Brendan. "Any idea why this Myles guy might be hunting your client?"

Brendan shook his head. They would get to the bottom of it, but all that mattered right now was with the guy who hired Whitby dead and Whitby rotting behind bars, Jenna was safe. Finally safe. But it also meant she was free to walk out of Brendan's life.

In Brendan's condo, Jenna threw her arms around his neck and held tight. "I'm so glad Whitby's been arrested and none of you guys got hurt. Thank you so much for giving us our lives back."

"No thanks needed." He relished the feel of her in his arms. He would give anything to kiss her again. He could too. They were alone, and he knew she would go along with it, but when he kissed her again—and he would—he wanted to be sure her feelings weren't mixed up with gratitude like they were now.

He stepped back and drew her arms down. "You're sure you don't know Jensen Myles? Erik said Myles owned a sporting goods company called Lids and Gears. Seemed like an upstanding guy and no idea why he would hire a guy like Whitby."

"I don't know him," she said. "With a name like that you'd think I would remember if I did. And I don't have a flash drive either. I have no idea why he might think I did."

"Maybe Whitby knows, and once he sobers up, he'll tell all. Though I have to say if he's a hitman for hire, I doubt he's going to talk." Brendan wished they knew more about the guy so they could figure out what the flash drive he wanted held and why he thought Jenna had it, but with the guy dead, that was going to take some time to figure out. "We should get back to the cabin and enjoy my mom's dessert like I promised."

"I wouldn't want to disappoint your mom. Not when she's been so kind to us." Jenna broke eye contact and grabbed her coat.

He escorted her to the door. Since she didn't need protection any longer, his brothers had already returned to the cabin, leaving the second SUV in the parking garage for Brendan. He walked her out there, and neither of them spoke as the chilly wind howled through the parking structure. He couldn't read her mind, but maybe she was thinking about where they went from here like he was, and the tension mounted. The wind did nothing to blow away the strain. It clung to them, thick and heavy. When he got the vehicle on the road, he searched for something safe to talk about for the drive but the thing that kept beating against his brain was that he was falling in love with her.

He knew they would be good together, and he could remove so many of her problems. If she would let him, he could support her financially so she wouldn't have to work and her dream of homeschooling Karlie could come true. But this wasn't something to discuss while driving. He needed to look her in the eyes. Take her hands. Kiss her. A deserted road in the dark was no place to declare his feelings.

Their conversation turned to the weather and other

meaningless topics, but the strain remained between them, and the drive seemed to take overly long. When they finally arrived at his parents' cabin, the cheerful lights from the Christmas tree shone out the window, a welcoming sight.

"Whose car?" Jenna pointed at the shiny red Jeep parked outside of the cabin.

"Reed's sister, Malone. She's an attorney in Portland. She often represents battered women, and our agency helps her out with investigations and protections. She's very outspoken but she also has a heart of gold so you'll like her."

"Good thing I'm freeing up beds by going back to our cabin." Jenna unbuckled her seatbelt. "It's going to feel odd not staying here anymore."

"You're returning to your cabin?" He'd expected this, he just didn't want to hear it.

She nodded. "I don't want to intrude any more than we already have. Especially with Shawn getting out of the hospital tomorrow."

Brendan couldn't believe she was really leaving. "But you're coming to dinner tomorrow night, right?"

"Karlie would never let me miss it." She gave him a sweet smile.

He wanted to linger there under the warmth of her smile, but he had to hope he would receive more of them in the future.

"Tonight I'll get it all cleaned up for Shawn."

"My mom and dad already had someone do that. They even replaced the mattresses."

"But I..." She shook her head. "I hope they're going to get reimbursed from Londyn's insurance."

"I'm sure they'll sort it all out." He waited for her to say something about paying for everything.

She simply frowned and got out. Out of habit, he rushed to catch up with her. It felt so odd that he didn't need to keep her safe. He still wanted to protect her from all of life's hurts and struggles, but that wasn't his job. Not yet, anyway. Besides, God used those hurts and struggles to grow and stretch believers, and, as much as Brendan wanted to keep her from having to go through them, it wasn't the right thing to do.

He opened the door for her.

"Mommy." Karlie came running across the family room, her little cheeks rosy and a hot chocolate mustache on her upper lip. "It's almost Christmas. One more sleep."

"Until Christmas Eve, not Christmas Day," Jenna clarified.

A little pout flashed on Karlie's face but quickly evaporated. "It's still special. Nana said so. They have a yummy dinner and get to open a present after church. We're going to go with them. I'm wearing my red dress. You can dress up too. Just like you promised."

"Of course I will." Jenna smiled at her daughter, but Jenna's eyes didn't hold the brightness that they usually held when she looked at her daughter. "We need to pack up and get to our cabin so Uncle Shawn can come visit."

They didn't have a room for him at a free rehab facility yet so he had nowhere to go.

"Yippee." Karlie raced from the room.

"Glad to see she's feeling better," Brendan said.

"Me too." Jenna looked at his mom. "Thank you for watching her. And for making sure our cabin is in good order."

"No worries."

"I'll coordinate with Londyn to get the insurance money to you."

"We'll take care of that after the holidays," his dad said.

His mother smiled. "Let's just enjoy the resolution of the investigation and embrace the Christmas season."

"Well, thank you for making that possible for Karlie and me."

"My pleasure. Now you'll be wanting to meet Malone." She took Jenna over to Malone, who was sitting at the counter with Reed. She was dressed in what looked like very pricey jeans and a white sweater bringing out her dark coloring.

Brendan remembered when Reed had brought her to meet their family. All the brothers had been captivated by her beauty and had even forgotten about the football game they were watching for a moment. Though nearly six foot tall, she looked kind of fragile and delicate from her very feminine attire. But then, she'd sat down to watch football with them and it was clear she was as tough as they come.

"Malone, this is Jenna," Brendan's mother said.

She swiveled and held out her hand. "You have the most precious daughter."

"Thank you."

"And I should probably go supervise her. Please excuse me." Looking like she might cry, Jenna rushed across the room.

Brendan watched her carefully, seeing her glance at the tree and frown.

What was wrong with the tree? She'd admired it before.

He took a long look at the spruce with all his and his siblings' childhood ornaments and multi-colored twinkling lights. What could her problem be? Did the ornaments that spoke to his family's memories make her feel left out? Nah, she'd commented on how special it was that his mom still hung the ornaments from when they were kids.

Duh! The presents. There weren't any for either of them or for Shawn. And Karlie wouldn't have one to open tomorrow night when the family gathered around the fire.

Brendan needed to rectify that, and he knew just the things to get.

~

Jenna took a sip of her tea in front of the fire she'd successfully built by herself and sighed. She could finally breathe. Not because she was away from the Byrds' cabin and out from under their feet but because she was away from Brendan. She didn't have to see him again until tomorrow morning. As Brendan had said good-bye after carrying their bags to their rental, he'd invited them to hit the slopes in the morning. She wanted to say no, but if Karlie was feeling even better tomorrow, it would be fun for her for a short time, and the rental had come with ski passes, so it would be a free outing for them.

She heard Karlie stir in the other room. Jenna had tucked her little sweetheart in for bed, but before Jenna had left the room, Karlie had slipped into the closet to sleep. Interesting that she hadn't felt a need to do that at the Byrds' cabin. Maybe she'd felt secure there, but she didn't feel secure with Jenna alone.

Jenna looked at the fire, her mind filled with concern for her daughter. Maybe Jenna was giving out vibes of insecurity over their finances. Sure, she never talked to Karlie about how close they came every month to losing the apartment, but her daughter could still be picking up on the stress. And what about tomorrow night when presents were opened? Jenna had scrounged enough money to fill Karlie's stocking with small items at the dollar store, but the area under the Byrds' tree was loaded with gifts.

Karlie was sure to feel left out. Jenna had taught her daughter that gifts weren't the true meaning of Christmas, but it was still hard to be a child and go without when others received gifts. She'd never been without as a young child, but later, when her parents started fighting and partying, presents were few and far between, and she'd witnessed Shawn's disappointment year after year.

A rasping noise sounded at the back door. She shot a look in that direction, her heart rate kicking up.

"Seriously, relax. Whitby's behind bars. The man who hired him dead. You're safe." She shook her head. Her unease was understandable after days of being under siege, she supposed. But now? The wind had picked up and was howling down the road, blowing snow and creating huge drifts, and apparently, rattling the door.

She still wasn't used to this cold, so she scooted closer to the fire and held out her free hand to the comforting warmth. Thankfully, the weather was supposed to change tomorrow to a sunny and less gusty day for their ski adventure.

Another noise sounded in the back.

She jumped. "Quit being so paranoid. You locked the door, for goodness' sake."

"Sometimes locks aren't enough." The deep male voice had her blood running cold.

She spun to find a tall, brawny man holding a gun no more than ten feet away from her.

She shot from the chair, her teacup sliding from her hand. It crashed onto the wood and shattered in an explosion of ceramic and liquid.

"Now, now. Stay where you are." He sounded so calm, and the hand holding the gun was rock steady.

She tried not to panic. He wore what appeared to be pricey ski attire and had a glittering diamond ring on his long bony finger. His grayish-blond hair was cut short and stylish, and his skin was tan, the outline of ski goggles around his eyes.

She had no idea who he was or why he would be standing there with a gun. "Who are you?"

"Don't you recognize me?"

Her throat was closing in fear. She swallowed but found only dryness. "Should I know you?"

"I'm Victor Emerson. You worked as a temp for my company, Emerson Helmets."

What? This man couldn't possibly have created the company with the wonderful atmosphere where she'd worked for three days. "What do you want with me?"

"I want the flash drive Thomas Steele gave you."

"What?" She gaped at him. "I didn't even know him. How would I have something from him?"

Emerson's cool blue eyes narrowed. "Do you take me for a fool? I saw him hand it to you on his way out of our offices, and you're staying at his family's cabin."

"I didn't know Thomas." Her voice shook. "This place... it's just a coincidence. I won a vacation here on a radio show."

"Hah!" His eyes tightened, the bronze skin wrinkling. "You expect me to believe that? Then explain this video." He dug his phone from his pocket, tapped the screen, and held it out.

The video showed her at Emerson Helmets in the lobby where she'd worked a temp job a couple of months ago. A man bumped into her. A file folder flew from her hand and spilled onto the floor. She remembered now. She'd been holding the folder, but it wasn't visible in the video until she dropped it. The man picked up the papers and handed them to her. Then he reached into his pocket and placed something small into her hand.

"I remember that." She looked at Emerson. "I dropped the file with my timesheets. He picked it up and apologized for bumping into me."

"A ruse to hand you the flash drive without the camera seeing it."

"No, he gave me a butterscotch candy and told me to have a good day."

"I don't believe you."

"It's the truth. Honest. Only candy." She boldly met his gaze.

He didn't seem impressed by her eye contact. "You're lying. You have the drive. Others may have failed to get it from you, but I won't."

Others. Like Odell. Whitby. That panic she'd held at bay ramped up, and her knees felt weak. She took several breaths. She had to stay strong for Karlie.

Karlie. Would this man hurt her? Use her to get information Jenna didn't have?

Jenna had to keep him talking to buy time so she could protect Karlie. "Why would he even give the drive to me?"

"Perhaps he was worried he'd be searched by the guards on the way out through security."

"But so could I, right?"

"Yes, but if you got caught, no big deal. If he got caught, it would end our company's affiliation, and he wouldn't have another chance to get the info. You were just a temp, very replaceable."

"What's on the drive anyway?" She tried to sound calm, but she heard the tremor in her own voice.

He glared at her as seconds ticked by. "Oh, what the heck. You probably looked at the drive and know anyway."

"Know what? I don't know—"

"About our helmets not meeting safety standards."

"Is that it? Safety standards? You had a man killed for *safety standards*?"

"Is that *it*?" His voice rose, and he took a step closer, looking like he wanted to drop the gun and use his bare hands to strangle her instead. "Fool. If word got out, we'd have to recall and replace the helmets. Millions. The business would go under, and so would I. I can't have that."

"How did Thomas get ahold of that information? I mean, he didn't even work there."

"He provided our security."

"I don't see the connection."

"We search all employee belongings when they arrive and leave to protect trade secrets. You remember that, right?"

She did. "I had to use that clear plastic purse thing and couldn't bring my phone in. But what does that have to do with the drive?"

"An inside whistleblower couldn't risk taking it out so she gave the drive to Steele to smuggle it out of the building."

"Then he must've hidden it somewhere."

"Or you did."

"If I had it, I sure wouldn't bring it on vacation with me. Besides, your guy tore this place apart."

"My guy?" He snorted. "I didn't have a guy working on this."

"You're not in this with Jensen Myles?"

"That unethical competitor." He spat on the floor. "He was up to his eyeballs in corporate espionage. Learned our helmets were defective. He wanted the information to ruin me. Wanted it bad enough to hire very unsavory men. Now turn it over."

"How many times do I have to tell you I don't have it?"

"Okay fine. You want it your way." He lifted his gun. "Let's go get your daughter. Maybe she can tell me where it is."

Panic flooded Jenna. She reached out for the wall to

steady herself. "If I had the drive—which I don't—I sure wouldn't tell my child where I put it."

"You have it, and I think you'll tell me where it is if your child's life is in danger." He flicked his gun at the bedroom in an irritated jerk. "Now move."

She couldn't let him hurt Karlie. She had to stop him. But how?

Think, Jenna, think.

Get him away from her. *Now! Hurry!* "You're right. I did hide it. It's at my apartment. I can take you to it."

A sick grin slid across his face like the slimy trail of a slug crawling through the garden. "I thought you'd see the light. We're leaving now. Get your coat."

Jenna didn't waste time. No way she'd give him a chance to rethink his plan. She didn't know what she would do once she got to her apartment and she couldn't produce the drive, but she'd deal with that when they were far away from Karlie.

Jenna shrugged into her jacket.

"Over here, hands on the wall," he commanded.

"But you said we were leaving."

"You don't think I'm dumb enough to take you without a thorough search, do you?" His voice was a deep growl of frustration. "The others I sent might've been too stupid to get the job done, but not me."

Please protect Karlie. Please.

Jenna placed her hands on the knotty pine. He pawed over her body and through her pockets. He found her phone and tossed it to the floor. The glass screen cracked, and he stomped on it, shattering the device.

"Let's go," he said.

Her heart sank. Not only did she lose her only method of communicating, but she could never afford to replace the phone.

Probably didn't matter. Not at all.

When she couldn't produce the drive, he was going to kill her.

Kill her very dead.

~

Head down against the wind, Brendan marched up the road toward Jenna's cabin. He couldn't stay away. He missed being with her. Missed everything about her. And Karlie too. They brightened up the cabin. Brought a light to the place —and to his life. That light had gone out since they'd departed. But he couldn't just barge into Jenna's cabin and ask to spend time with her. She'd made it clear she wanted to be alone. To have space. He would simply check in to make sure she was okay. Maybe not even knock on the door. Just look in the window.

Great. Now you're a Peeping Tom. Talk about hitting rock bottom.

He lifted his head against the blowing snow as the cabin came into view. No lights on. Not a single one. Jenna had never gone to bed this early when she stayed with them. But she was tired from all of the stress, so maybe she did. But it still seemed odd. Had something happened to her? To Karlie?

He plowed through a few snowdrifts to the front door. He stood for a moment, hand raised. If he woke Jenna, he was going to be mad at himself. If he woke, Karlie, Jenna would be mad enough for both of them. Maybe he should just go. But the lack of lights was bothering him. For some reason he couldn't pinpoint, it felt off. Wrong.

An image of Tristen's body when he'd found her, all twisted at the bottom of the steps, flashed into his brain. He hadn't been able to do anything to save her. He wouldn't make the same mistake with Jenna. If he didn't check on her, he might regret it.

He knocked on the door and waited. No answer. He pounded harder and tapped his boot as he waited.

Still no answer.

He tried the knob. Locked.

Fine. It was time to turn into that Peeping Tom. He vaulted off the porch and eased behind shrubs to the same window he'd looked in a few days ago when he'd seen Jenna held by a knife-wielding lunatic.

Brendan's stomach clenched at the memory as he lifted his body up to peer inside. Dying embers from the fireplace glowed and lit the area. Karlie stood alone in front of the fireplace screen. Brendan looked around the room, but it was too dark to see if Jenna was asleep on the couch.

He knocked on the window until Karlie turned to look at him.

"It's me, Brendan," he called out. "Open the door for me, little bit."

She stood for a long moment then started for the door, limping as she moved.

Had her arthritis flared up again? She'd been doing so much better earlier.

Brendan bolted for the porch and up the steps. He heard the lock click open, eager to push inside, but he waited so he wouldn't scare Karlie.

The door slowly groaned opened, and she looked up at him with big, terrified eyes. He dropped to his knees and ran his gaze over her. His heart stilled when he spotted blood on her foot. Fear nearly paralyzed him, but he swallowed hard to keep it in control. "What happened to your foot?"

"I cut it. Mommy's mug broke on the floor."

"Did you tell your mommy?"

"Mommy's gone."

That fear catapulted into high gear. "What do you mean?"

"She's not here." Karlie started to sob.

"Come here, little bit." He scooped her into his arms and entered the cabin, closing the door behind them. He scanned the blackness and found sharp shards from a smashed mug near the fireplace, Jenna's phone shattered beside it.

"Did you look for her?" he asked, his voice wanting to go wild with fear, but he controlled it.

"Too dark. 'Sides, the man said 'Let's go.'"

Brendan's veins turned to ice. "Man? What man?"

"He came and took Mommy." The little girl's sobs wrenched his heart. "She didn't want to go. Didn't want him to see me."

"When?"

"I dunno. I hid in the closet, but I had to go potty. Then I cut my foot. It hurts." She started to cry. "I need Mommy."

"Shh. It'll be fine. I'll find your mommy." Brendan held her tight while she sobbed, his mind racing with what to do. First, he had to be sure Karlie was taken care of. And then...

Then I'm going to hunt this man down and make him pay. Pay big time.

Jenna unlocked her apartment door and gasped. Someone had ransacked the place, tipping and turning everything over and spilling out the contents of her kitchen cabinets. Just like at the cabin. The refrigerator door hung open, and containers and jars of food were rotting in sticky and smelly mounds on the floor. How was she ever going to replace all of this?

Her heart sank, but she didn't have time to worry about

that. Not with Emerson there. He shoved her deeper inside and locked the door behind them.

"Someone's been here," she said.

"Clearly," Emerson replied. "Must've been one of the guys Myles hired."

His eyes flashed with evil. "Too bad they didn't find it for me to take back from Myles. But now you're going to turn it over, or I'm going to take you out. Can't have you telling anyone else about it after all."

She clamped a hand over her mouth to keep from gasping. It was the first time he admitted his final plan. He hadn't said he was going to kill her no matter what but that was implied. She knew his secret and could tell. He couldn't let that happen. Thankfully, Karlie was safe. At least Jenna prayed she was.

Now Jenna had to get free for Karlie.

Think. Think of how to get away.

She searched the small room, looking for something to help. Anything. Sharp knives were scattered across the worn linoleum floor. If she could get to one, she would at least have a weapon.

But the question was, could she use it? Could she stab this man?

Karlie's precious face flashed before Jenna's eyes. Was her daughter okay? Alone and sleeping, or had she woken up? Was she standing in that big empty family room, searching for Jenna?

Oh, her poor baby. She needed Jenna. Needed her badly. Always and forever.

And for that, Jenna could kill. And would kill, if it came to losing her life.

23

After questioning Karlie on exactly what she'd heard and searching the cabin, Brendan wrapped her in a quilt and plowed through the snow that wanted to take him down and bury him in the powder. But he prevailed and raced up the steps to shove open the door. He didn't bother taking off his boots but rushed over to his brothers, who were congregated around the large dining table with his parents, Sierra, Harper, and Reed.

"Jenna's gone," he said managing to keep his calm for Karlie's sake. "Karlie said a man took her. And Karlie stepped on a broken shard of Jenna's mug and cut her foot."

"It hurts," Karlie said.

His mother stood unmoving. He'd never seen her paralyzed before, and the sight brought even more worry, his gut feeling like battery acid was eating a hole in it.

"Then we best get busy." His father stood.

His movement must have spurred his mother into action as she jumped up and reached out for Karlie. Surprisingly, the precious child clung to Brendan. He looked her in the eye. "Can you go with Nana, little bit, so I can find your mom?"

Her big eyes filled with tears. "What if she went away like Daddy?"

"Oh, no, precious." His mother pressed a hand on Karlie's back. "Your mommy will come back. Now come here, sweetie, and Brendan can go bring her home."

Karlie looked up at Brendan, her chin wobbling. "Promise?"

"I'll find her. You can count on that." He couldn't promise anything else. Like finding her alive. Not when he had no idea where she'd gone or who'd taken her.

"Ready to go with Nana?" Brendan asked her.

"I love you." She flung her arms around his neck and hugged him hard.

"Love you too, little bit," he whispered to her. He wasn't a crying kind of guy. Never had been, but her strong hold and announcement wetted his eyes, and he had to blink hard before untangling her arms and handing her over to his mother.

Karlie circled her arms around his mother's neck. "I love you too, Nana. And you too, Papa."

"And we all love you too, sweetie," his mother said, her voice holding a deep tremor of emotions. "Now let's get your boo-boo fixed."

Karlie's tear-filled gaze as his mother carried her off broke Brendan's heart.

His dad clamped a hand on Brendan's shoulder, looking rock solid. "You call 911?"

"Not yet. I want their help, but I don't have much to tell them, and I'm not going to sit around and wait for a deputy to get up here. I have to do something."

"Tell me what you know, and I'll give them a call," his dad said.

"Karlie said she got up to go to the bathroom and heard a man in the family room say 'let's go,' and Jenna left with him out the back door, which I found unlocked. All Karlie could say was he was a big man. Outside, several footprints had disturbed a snowdrift. One smaller set, one larger. Heading up the drive to a set of large tire tracks. Big. Like from a pickup or full-sized SUV. Jenna's phone is smashed on the cabin floor. Her car is still covered in snow so she's not in there."

"Okay, I got this." His dad dug his phone from his pocket.

"Good. Thanks." Brendan got the words out over a throat that was closing and raw with pain and fear. The woman he loved was missing.

There. He'd admitted. He loved Jenna. All the way to the stars they watched from the skybridge and back. Wholly. Completely. And it was a paralyzing kind of love.

"Who do you think could've taken her?" Sierra asked.

"Not Whitby or the guy he was working for," Drake said. "That's for sure."

"Then who?" Harper asked.

"I have no idea," Brendan said, panic threatening to take him to the floor.

"So, how do you want to proceed?" Aiden asked.

"Maybe Whitby knows something we missed," Brendan said, his mind searching for clarity. "Erik, get with Nick and light a fire under him to crack Whitby's computer. Then check for any CCTV cameras that might've caught a vehicle leaving this area with Jenna."

"You got it." Erik grabbed his laptop and fired it up.

Brendan turned to Aiden. "Head to the jail and question Whitby again. Get him to talk this time."

Aiden nodded.

"Drake, you have protection detail here with Dad." He looked at his sister. "And Sierra, process the boot prints outside the cabin and look for fingerprints from the back door to the living area. And cast the vehicle's tire tracks. I don't know if that will help us now, but at the very least we'll need it for when I bring this jerk in, and he goes to court."

"Can do." She fisted her hands on the table, her eyes tight with anger. "Reed can help me."

"Yes, good."

"And me?" Clay asked.

"Come with me. We're going to Jenna's apartment. Maybe the guy who took her is also looking for this mysterious flash drive and thinks she kept it there."

"Stop playing me and give me the drive," Emerson said.

"I told you, it was in this drawer, but now it's gone. Someone either took it or dumped it out in all of this stuff." Jenna waved a hand over the room. "Let me get down and search for it."

He locked gazes with her, his eyes burrowing in and warning her that he would follow through on his threat to kill her. "You better be right."

She dropped to her knees to search through her belongings for something that didn't exist. She moved pictures of Karlie smiling at the camera. One at the beach, her lips dark from the cold and her body shaking. She'd been so chilly that day but loved every minute of their outing. One with Karlie and Toby when they were close. Jenna kept this one so Karlie didn't forget the good times with her dad.

Jenna set the frames back on the shelf where they belonged to keep stalling and made her way across the room as slowly as she could. She pawed through and righted toys, children's books from the library, and notebooks she was preparing for homeschooling next year.

Oh, dear God, please let Karlie be okay. I'm so worried for her.

She's just a child and needs someone. Send one of the Byrds to her to watch over her. Please. Please.

She reached the far wall and still hadn't been able to secure anything to protect herself. She needed to get to the kitchen. Get to a knife.

"Oh, wait," she said. "I forgot I moved the drive when Karlie found it and wanted to play with it. It's in my kitchen junk drawer."

Emerson marched across the room, kicking her precious memories out of his way. He grabbed her shirt collar and jerked her to her feet then dragged her to the kitchen and shoved her down. "You have five minutes to produce the drive, and then we're done here. You either leave dead or alive. Your choice."

Brendan tossed Clay the keys. No way he could drive with his gut churning and his hands shaking. Besides, he wanted to be free to answer calls.

They piled into the company SUV, and Clay got them on the road while Brendan looked up Jenna's address in Gresham and plugged it into the GPS.

Finished, he glanced at his brother. "Faster. Go faster."

Clay gave him a quick glance. "You chose me to drive for a reason. Now let me concentrate before we plow into a drift."

Brandon couldn't see more than two car-lengths ahead due to the wind blowing snow piled up alongside the road. The headlights illuminated the white powder, and Clay flipped on the wipers. The rubber whisked across the windshield.

The scraping noise was a final irritation to Brendan, and

he slammed a fist into the dash. "Why did I let her go back to that cabin?"

"Because you didn't know there was someone else in on this." Clay's tone was far too calm for Brendan's liking. "The person who hired Whitby is dead. How could you know someone else was involved? None of us did. So stop blaming yourself and focus."

Brendan tried to swallow, but his mouth was too dry. He'd left his water bottle in the vehicle from the earlier trip and took a long drink, nearly choking on the liquid when he thought about Jenna in the clutches of a madman trying to get something from her that she didn't have to give.

Brendan tapped his foot, and Clay wound down the mountain roads and onto flatter land. They made fast progress once they reached the bare roads outside of Gresham, giving Brendan a glimmer of hope.

His phone rang. "What do you have, Erik?"

"Nick found Jenna in a truck on the road nearly an hour ago. Truck belongs to a Victor Emerson. He was heading into Gresham from Highway 26. He's driving a black Ford F150." He added the plate number, and Brendan memorized it.

"Also texting you his picture."

Brendan's phone dinged, signaling the photo. "Anything else we need to know about him?"

"He owns Emerson Helmets."

"What? Another sporting goods company? Can't be a coincidence."

"Emerson's fierce rivals with Lids and Gears. Maybe because Lids and Gears is so successful. Emerson Helmet's not so much. I also got Emerson's finances. He's so deep in debt that it'll take a miracle to pull him out."

Brendan didn't like the sound of that. Didn't like it at all.

"Which makes him desperate. And maybe the flash drive has something on it that will save him."

"Your destination is on the left," the GPS voice said.

"Arriving at Jenna's apartment. Gotta go." Brendan hung up and searched the lot for the truck. "There, outside the third building. Move on it slowly so we can get a look at the plates."

Brendan's pulse pounded as their SUV inched forward until Brendan could make out the plates.

"It's him," Brendan called out. "Emerson's truck. He's here."

"What do you want me to do?" Clay asked.

Brendan quickly ran his gaze over the area. "Pull past him and turn around. Let's get eyes on the apartment and make a plan."

Clay had no sooner shifted into park when Jenna's apartment door opened.

"Look!" Brendan said. "It's her. Emerson's got her."

"And a gun at her side," Clay added.

Brendan sucked in a breath. "We can't rush them. If he's been involved in this from the beginning, he knows who we are. So we can't even act like we live here and walk up to them."

"What do we do?"

"Follow them," Brendan said, adrenaline flooding his body. "That's all we can do without taking him out and going away for murder."

Jenna wanted to cry under the pressure of Emerson's hand, which felt like a vice. She was thankful when he opened the passenger door on his truck and released her arm. "Get in. You're driving."

"But I—"

"Shut up and get in." He gave her a shove.

She scooted across the seat to the steering wheel, and he climbed in after her.

"Where are we going?" She'd been at this impasse with him once and already knew there was no way out, not with him pointing that pistol her way.

"None of your business. Now drive."

She turned the key, and the engine rumbled to life, vibrating the cab. "I promise not to tell anyone about this if you'll just let me go."

"Hah! Like I believe that." He waved his gun.

"If you're planning to kill me, you should rethink that." She tried to sound confident when her insides were shivering.

He glanced at her, his face illuminated by his dashboard lights. "Why?"

Yes, why? Think, Jenna. "You haven't actually killed anyone yet, so when you're caught, you won't have to go to prison for so long. But killing me? That could mean life." She backed out of the parking space.

"I don't plan to kill you. At least not until you tell me where you hid the drive. We're just going somewhere where people can't hear your screams while I persuade you to talk."

She shifted into gear, and the truck leapt forward. As she drove, she imagined the torture he had planned for her, and her stomach churned, the acid burning a path up her throat. She swallowed and prayed for calm. "You know my body-guards are after you?"

"Really?" He cast her a sardonic look. "Then why don't I see them?"

She was striking out here, but she had to try harder, because Brendan and his brothers weren't coming after her.

They didn't even know she was missing. "They're well trained. They're not about to let you see them."

He laughed. "If they were still protecting you, you wouldn't have been alone at the cabin. You were easy prey."

A point she couldn't argue with. At least not logically. But why did she have to be logical? Her life was on the line here. And she was panicking. "They just had to step away, but I know they're coming for me."

"They have no clue where you are. I'm certain they don't know about me." He gave her a sharp look. "Maybe they'll show up at your apartment, but we won't be there if they do, now will we?"

24

"You're too close," Brendan said. "Back off so Emerson doesn't get wind of us."

Clay waved a hand. "I know what I'm doing."

Brendan trusted his brothers most of the time, but right now he couldn't trust anyone but himself.

Not God?

Did he trust God? Was that what this was all about? Remembering that God was in control? In charge?

From the day he'd spotted Jenna, had God been telling Brendan that he could do only what he could do to protect the people he loved and the rest was up to God? His training and experience gave him the skills to do the job. But he'd failed to protect Tristen. Failed to protect Jenna.

Still, he'd done his best in both cases. He couldn't have done any more. Not with the information he possessed at the time. So he needed to cut himself some slack like Clay said. And more importantly, he needed to ask God to be with them and then trust that, whatever the outcome, it would turn out in everyone's best interest.

He closed his eyes and offered a prayer but still couldn't accept that today might turn out badly.

Save her, please. If not for me, for little Karlie. She needs her mother.

"He's turning off," Clay said. "Looks like a driveway."

Brendan popped his eyelids open. "Slow down."

The SUV slowed to a crawl as Emerson's taillights disappeared down what wasn't more than a dirt path lined with scrub brush and trees.

Clay pulled off the road and killed the lights, blanketing the area in darkness. "What now?"

"First, I call in this address to Erik so he can look it up and get surveillance photos, then we go on foot." Brendan fired off a text, and Erik responded. "He's on it. Let's suit up while he works."

Brendan got out and went to the back hatch. Clay joined him, and they slipped into their vests.

Brendan grabbed his rifle, the memory of countless times he'd used a similar gun coming back to him, but now he was with a brother. Not the first time the team had run such an op, as they'd gone after Harper's stalker a few months ago, but this time it was just the two of them.

Clay picked up an assault rifle and shoved in the mag, then they both put on their comms units in case they had to separate. Last up was a pair of night vision goggles for each of them. Having clear night vision could mean the difference between success and failure in freeing Jenna.

Brendan perched the goggles on his head and dug out his phone buzzing in his pocket to look at the text from Erik. "Place belongs to Emerson. A hunting cabin. Or at least that's what it appears to be."

Brendan held out the phone and showed Clay overhead views of the property that had likely been taken by a drone. They studied the layout. The large log cabin was to the right. Further down on the left sat a large outbuilding, all of it located in an immaculately kept clearing.

"No cover between here and either building," Brendan said.

"We can follow the tree line behind the property."

"That's what I was thinking too, but once we reach the clearing, we need to figure out how to get eyes on the cabin without exposing our location." Brendan lifted his rifle. "Let's get moving."

He lowered his goggles and led his brother into the thick woods running parallel to the driveway. A soft breeze carried the scent of wood burning in a fireplace or stove. The clearing might be well-maintained, but this patch of land was rough, the scrub thick. Still, Brendan moved as silently as he could, ignoring the stinging branches snapping at his face and arms.

As they approached the building, he ducked to keep from showing himself, and Clay followed suit. When Brendan was directly across from the cabin, where lights glowed from several windows, he squatted. Clay joined him.

"Looks like our best bet is to head to the outbuilding and cross there," Brendan whispered. "Should be out of view from the rooms with lights on."

"Agreed."

Brendan stood but remained hunched over as he moved forward. A dog's frantic barks sounded from inside the cabin. Brendan dropped to the ground. He couldn't risk talking so he signaled for Clay to halt. He squatted, and they shared a pointed look.

The cabin door opened, and Emerson held a powerful German shepherd back by the collar. "What is it, boy? Another rabbit?"

The dog danced and whined.

"If I let you out, you'll come back covered in burs."

The dog looked up at Emerson and whined as if he knew what Emerson had said.

"Not tonight, boy. I'm busy." He jerked the dog back inside and closed the door.

Brendan let out a long breath. He hadn't planned to encounter a dog. They moved on, staying low and silent. The dog continued to yelp, but hopefully Emerson would believe it was sensing rabbits.

Brendan reached the outbuilding and looked in the window. Emerson's truck was parked inside along with a fishing boat and flatbed trailer.

He looked at Clay. "You stay here on overwatch. I'm going to the cabin."

Brendan wished he could just lift his rifle and shoot the guy, but he couldn't just shoot some guy, even if he had kidnapped Jenna. Sure, if it looked like her life was imminently in danger, like a gun to her head, he would do so, but until that happened, he had to take less violent steps. He got as low as he could and still maintained top speed then bolted across the lawn. The dog's barking ramped up, going high and howling.

Please, don't let him out.

Brendan reached the house and heard the front door open.

"Fine," Emerson said. "I'll get your leash, and we'll take a look."

The door closed.

"Did you hear that?" Brendan asked over his comms.

"Affirmative."

"Shimmy up a tree and do it quickly. I'm going around back to slip inside while Emerson is out. Let me know when he leaves the cabin and when he heads back to the door."

"Roger that."

Brendan bolted around back of the building and reached into his pocket for his glass cutter. He chose a window without any lights on and peeked inside. The room held a large bed and a dresser. No one was in the room. Perfect. He put the cutter to the window near the latch and made a hole in the first pane then a hole in the second one.

"Emerson and dog on the move." Clay's voice came over Brendan's earbuds.

"Got it."

He slid his hand in the hole and released the latch then lifted up the window. He slipped inside and raised his goggles as he headed for the lighted hallway. He crept ahead and stopped at the kitchen to search for some meat to occupy the dog. He found a container of ham lunchmeat that should do the trick.

He pocketed it and moved down the hall, inch by inch, being extra cautious to keep silent. He reached the living room and took a long breath before casting a look around the corner. Duct tape held Jenna to a chair and bound her wrists and ankles. Another strip covered her mouth.

He jerked back and stifled his fury. He wanted to pummel Emerson when he came into the room. Or cold-cock him at the very least. But that would be stupid. The guy was armed and could get off a round before Brendan could get even a few feet into the room. He needed to remain calm, not only to think straight so he could best Emerson, but to support and encourage Jenna too.

"Emerson's on his way back," Clay warned.

Brendan had no time to free Jenna, but he could tell her he was here.

He slid around the corner. She looked up. Locked gazes. Relief flashed in her eyes.

His anger churned even more, but he swallowed it down. "I want to free you, but I don't want to risk Emerson seeing me."

Her eyes misted.

"Don't cry, honey." He ached to go to her. "You'll be free as soon as Emerson comes back, and I take him down."

She said something behind the tape, and he wished he could understand.

"Does he have a weapon?"

She nodded.

"A handgun?"

She nodded again.

"Clay, make sure you tell me if Emerson has his gun drawn when he comes back."

Clay didn't respond. Brendan didn't worry something had happened to him. Emerson was likely in hearing distance.

"Clay's outside. And Karlie's with my mom and dad."

"'Ank you," he thought she said.

"She heard Emerson take you, but she's fine. She'll be glad when we get back home. Then we can begin celebrating Christmas for real. All of us. Together at my parents' cabin."

She didn't respond, and he wondered if she didn't want that or if she just wanted to be free and put this behind her.

"Emerson heading your way," Clay said. "No weapon drawn."

"Roger that." He looked at Jenna. "He's coming back. I'll be in the hallway waiting for him."

Brendan got the ham from his pocket and made ready to act.

He heard Emerson approach the door then chastised the dog outside. "I can't stand your incessant barking. You're staying here."

Brendan dropped the meat package on the floor and lifted his rifle.

The door creaked opened, and Brendan's heart rate skyrocketed.

Emerson stomped inside. He jerked his jacket over his shoulders and it slipped down to trap his arms in the sleeves.

Perfect. The guy couldn't get to his gun.

Brendan stepped out. "Hold it right there, Emerson."

He froze and glared at Brendan.

"On your knees," Brendan directed. "Slowly."

"But my jacket."

"Will have to stay as it is," Brendan said. "Now drop."

Emerson lowered himself to the pine plank floor one knee at a time and nearly face-planted before righting his body.

Brendan gave the guy a wide berth and circled around back. A quick shove with his boot, and the creep went down face first on the floor. He tried to free his arms, squirming like a worm trying to bury itself in the dirt.

Brendan planted a boot in his back. "Don't move."

Brendan turned his attention to his mic. "We're clear, Clay. Need your assistance in the cabin."

"On my way," Clay replied.

Brendan glanced at Jenna and smiled.

Outside, the dog's barking ramped up, his rapid cries telling Brendan that Clay was approaching the cabin. The door opened, and Clay stepped in. He took a quick look around the place. His gaze landed on Jenna, and he grimaced.

Brendan's gut held that same turmoil, only a thousand times greater. "Restrain Emerson's wrists and search him."

"You have no right," Emerson said.

Brendan and Clay ignored him. Clay took zip ties from his pocket and secured the guy's wrists then gave him a thorough search.

"You're not cops anymore," Emerson snapped. "You have no right to restrain me."

"Um, let's see," Brendan said as he couldn't ignore the guy any longer. "You're holding a woman against her will. Pretty sure that gives anyone a right to restrain you."

Clay pulled Emerson's gun from his belt and shoved it into his own. "He's clean."

"Keep an eye on him and call it in. I want this guy behind bars, and the sooner, the better."

Clay took over with his foot on Emerson's back and made the call.

Brendan hurried across the room to Jenna. He knelt and dug out his pocket knife.

Tears were now freely flowing from her big eyes, and he got angrier and angrier at Emerson with each tear. Good thing Clay was in the room or he'd be tempted to throttle the guy. It might feel good for now, but Emerson could press charges, and that would only let the creep win.

Brendan pulled the tape from her mouth. She moaned in pain. He stopped because he didn't want to continue to hurt her, but he had to.

"Sorry," he said softly. "I don't want to cause you pain."

She mumbled something, and he thought she was telling him to go ahead.

He pulled the tape until her mouth was free. He would let her remove the rest when she had use of her hands.

"Thank God you came," she said. "How did you find me?"

He sliced through the tape on her wrists while he explained what had happened.

She rubbed her wrists. "I can't ever repay you."

"You don't need to." He cut her ankles free.

She slid forward on the chair and threw her arms around his neck, groaning as she did, likely from having her arms restrained. He inhaled the peach scent of her shampoo and clung to her as if she was his lifeline, not the other way around. And maybe she was. Brought by God to stop him from drowning in his fear of getting involved again.

Because he *was* involved. Deeply involved.

"Thank you, Brendan," she whispered. "I'll never forget what you've done for me and Karlie."

Jenna might as well have thrown a bucket of ice water on him. It sounded like she didn't plan on seeing him in the future. His heart ripped to shreds, and he wanted to talk to her about it. But no way he would bring up their future in front of Emerson and Clay.

Later.

Brendan would get her alone, and they would talk. Had to talk. Once and for all.

Jenna held onto Brendan. She didn't care if Clay and Emerson were in the room. She wouldn't care if the room were brimming with people. Brendan was her knight-in-shining-armor for the second time this week. Her hero in plain clothes. And the man she'd fallen in love with. Or at least she thought she was in love with him.

The emotions were all mingled with the terror and the fear for her daughter. Sure, Jenna knew Karlie was safe, but her need to hide in the closet said she still had residual fear, and Jenna wanted to eliminate that from her life. Having Brendan with them would make them both feel secure. She just couldn't tell if her emotions were due to his rescue, his kindness for the last few days, or because she really did love this man. And that's why she pushed away from him. For now. Until she could think.

She swiped away her tears, and he gently touched her cheek. "I'd love to give you a glass of water, but we can't disturb anything."

"I understand."

"As soon as a deputy arrives to take charge of Emerson and take our statements, we can leave." He shifted back and looked at her. "What's on Emerson's flash drive?"

"It holds proof that his helmets are defective." She told him about the video and needing to recall them. "I don't have the drive. Never did. I'll bet Thomas hid it somewhere."

Brendan's eyes dark with anger, he glanced at Emerson. Brendan scrubbed a hand over his face and took a breath then faced her again, his expression filled only with compassion. She didn't know how he could wash away his anger like he had, but she appreciated his ability to do so. Toby had always let his temper fly.

"I'll give Londyn a call and let her know to look for it," Brendan said. "That way this guy will go away for abducting you, but also for putting lives in danger with his helmets and choosing to hide it."

She clutched her trembling hands together. "This is really over, isn't it?"

"Yes. For sure this time."

"Then I can go back to my cabin with Shawn and Karlie."

"I would like you to stay with us."

"We'll still come for Christmas Eve."

He took her hand. "You know I care about you, right?"

She nodded and held tightly to his hand. "And I care about you too."

He locked gazes with her, the intensity unsettling. "Then why is it so wrong for you to stay with my family?"

She almost said she would, because that was what she wanted, but she had to behave like the independent woman she wanted to be and come to a clear understanding of her feelings. Didn't mean she couldn't or wouldn't choose to be with him. Just meant she would be making a sound decision. "Because I need time. I don't know what I feel. It's a jumble in my brain and heart. I need to pray and figure it out."

He withdrew his hand. "Sounds like you plan to say good-bye after Christmas."

She instantly missed his touch and almost reached out to him. "I don't know what I might do, and that's the whole point of having time to think about it."

A siren sounded in the distance.

"All I want to do right now is give my statement to the deputy and get back to Karlie," she said. "That's as much as I can commit to."

25

The tree sparkled in the family room lit by the glowing fireplace. Brendan stood by the hearth, his parents sat on the sofa with Clay, and Erik and Drake had dropped into easy chairs with plates filled with appetizers. And Jenna and Shawn stood by the table, looking at the platters like they didn't know which item to take first. Sierra, Reed, Aiden, and Harper had taken plates to the kitchen counter and were talking to Malone.

Brendan rested against the hearth and could hardly breathe for being in Jenna and Karlie's company again. Due to the abduction, Jenna had chosen not to go skiing, plus Karlie needed another day of rest so he hadn't seen them since he dropped them off last night after the abduction. Today had been the longest day Brendan could remember. The moment they'd climbed into the SUV with Shawn to go to Christmas Eve service, Brendan felt every worry, every pain, everything other than love leave his body.

But what if Jenna planned to say goodbye tonight? He didn't know if he could be without her or Karlie in the future, even with such an amazing family of his own to support him. He glanced at Karlie, who played with her

Legos on the coffee table but she kept sneaking peeks at the Christmas tree.

He knelt down beside her. "You see something interesting by the tree?"

She looked up, her big blue eyes so much like her mother's that it put an ache in his heart. "Do you think there's a present for me?"

"Oh, right. We get to open a present tonight." Brendan faked not remembering to make light of things so she didn't feel so badly about it.

"Did you get to open them when you were a kid?"

He nodded.

She frowned. "Mommy says I need to be a big girl tonight and not cry when presents are opened. She says we only had enough money to come here. This is my present."

He was about to take her to the tree to show her what he'd bought when Jenna joined them.

"Remember, honey," she said. "Christmas isn't about presents but about baby Jesus."

Karlie peered at her mother, her expression puzzled. "Was baby Jesus a secret?"

Jenna tilted her head. "A secret? Why would you think that?"

"'Cause Sierra's baby is a secret. She said so to Reed in the hallway. So I thought baby Jesus might be too."

"Sierra!" His mother's shrill voice cut through the conversations as she gaped at Sierra. "What baby? What secret? Are you pregnant and didn't tell me?"

Sierra cringed. "I'm sorry, Mom. With everything going on, we wanted to wait. We were going to tell you tonight."

Brendan didn't know how his mother would respond, but her mouth fell open, and she whooped with joy. "A baby. Honestly? You're really pregnant?"

Sierra nodded, and Brendan's mouth dropped open as did his other brothers. But then congratulations rang out.

"This is too wonderful." Malone grabbed Sierra in a hug. "I'm going to be an aunt."

"Um, I had something to do with it too." Reed grinned.

Malone released Sierra and hugged her brother. "Congrats. Let the spoiling begin."

"Ah, Sis, the baby has to be born first."

"No." Malone waved a hand. "I see massages and plenty of spa days for Sierra until the little one is born."

"But that's spoiling Sierra," Reed said.

Malone rolled her eyes. "And the baby by virtue of the fact that she's carrying it."

"I'll be glad to take you up on that spoiling." Sierra winked and went to the tree to grab a small box and handed the brightly wrapped gift to their mom. "Open it."

She ripped the paper off and lifted out a small one-piece baby outfit that Brendan didn't know the name for. His mother held it up. The fabric was covered with a moon and stars and read, *Love my Nana to the Moon and Back.*

"Oh, Sierra, sweetie." She grabbed her in a hug then moved to Reed. "Congratulations."

When their mom released Reed, he beamed and took Sierra's hand. "She's due in June."

"Gender? Name?" his mother asked.

Sierra held up a hand. "When we know either of those things, you'll be the first to know."

Karlie looked up at them, a pout on her face.

"What's wrong, little bit?" Brendan asked. "It's okay that you told Sierra's secret."

"Nana got a present." A big tear leaked from her eye.

He stood and held out his hand. "Why don't we check for a package with your name on it?"

She got up slowly and put her tiny hand in his. His heart

swelled at her touch and trust. He'd never done anything more important than buy a gift for this deserving child. They went to the tree, and Jenna gave them a suspicious look.

Brendan squatted and pointed at a package he'd wrapped himself in bright striped foil paper. As he looked at it, he realized he didn't do such a hot job, but Karlie didn't care about the stray creases and the excess tape.

She grabbed it. "It says my name." She looked at him with awe. "Who's it from?"

"The tag says Mommy."

She bolted out of his arms and over to Jenna. "You had 'nuff money to get me a present."

"What?" Jenna bent down to look at the package. "But I..."

Brendan winked.

Her eyes glistened with tears, and she clutched his hand so tightly she was cutting off the blood supply. "That's the nicest thing anyone has ever done for me."

He met her gaze and held it. "I can top that in the future if you'd only give me a chance."

A little hand tugged on his arm. "Can we open it now?"

"Sure thing, little bit." He got out his phone to take pictures as she ripped off the paper, her petite face alight with joy.

He'd put that joy on her face, and his insides flooded with warmth. He was warm and proud and giddy all jumbled together. He wanted to spend a lifetime of making this little girl and her mother happy.

Karlie opened the box and squealed. "Mommy. The books. You got me the books I wanted."

Jenna glowed with the same happiness, and he captured it with his camera. If she was going to say good-bye, he would at least have pictures to remember them by, but he fully intended to stop that from happening.

Karlie took out the top book and held it up for everyone to see. She set the box aside and grabbed Brendan's hand. "Read, please."

He didn't hesitate but moved to the couch and lifted her onto his lap.

"Honey," Jenna said. "Maybe the others would like to open their presents before you read the book."

Karlie frowned, but it disappeared quickly. "There's one for you too, Mommy. But it's not from me 'cause I don't have money."

Everyone laughed, and Karlie looked confused. "Do you want me to get it for you?"

"Sure," Jenna said looking uncomfortable.

Karlie slid down and grabbed the package Brendan had wrapped for Jenna, and the one for Shawn too.

"One for Unca Shawn too."

"Me?" He tilted his head.

"You open first," Jenna said.

Shawn took the package from Karlie and dropped onto the hearth. "From you, Sis."

She shot Brendan another look. He just smiled.

Looking nervous, Shawn sliced open the box and pulled out the envelope Brendan had enclosed within. Shawn slit it open and removed the card. For a long moment he didn't move, but then looked up at Jenna, tears swimming in his eyes. "Man, oh, man. I can't believe you did this for me. And I thought you didn't have any money. Thank you."

"Maybe you should tell everyone what it is," Brendan said to Shawn, as Jenna didn't know.

"She paid off a debt I owed to a creep who I should never have borrowed from." He waved the card. "But even better, she got me into a rehab center. A free one, but a really good place."

His family applauded, and she looked at Brendan, her eyes brimming with tears now. He desperately wanted to hold her but settled for smiling.

"Go ahead, Jenna," Drake said. "You're holding things up."

She blushed and tore the paper from her package. She took out the envelope Brendan had put inside and read it. "I...oh, I can't even put into words how thankful I am."

"What is it, Mommy?" Karlie asked.

"Someone hired people to clean our apartment for us."

Karlie frowned. "But we weren't there to mess it up."

Jenna didn't seem to know what to say as she couldn't very well say that the apartment had been trashed, so Brendan looked at Karlie. "I want the very best for you and your Mom, starting with a sparkling clean place to live."

Her inquisitive eyes narrowed. "I wish we could stay here with you forever."

He wished the same thing, but he wouldn't put any pressure on Jenna. And he definitely wouldn't do so in front of his whole family. He had to hope his plan for the night succeeded. If not, he might have to learn to live with a broken heart.

Jenna watched everyone open their one present for the night, but she couldn't keep her mind off Brendan's generosity. Not only the money he'd spent on the books, the cleaning, and Shawn's debt, but his generosity of thought in taking the time to choose the perfect present for each of them.

He really was the most amazing man. She'd spent the

day praying. Asking God to make it clear if Brendan was the guy for her, and it looked like God had just done so. Now, what was she going to do about it?

"Can Brendan read the story now?" Karlie asked.

"He can read it while we clean up the paper," Peggy said, sliding to the edge of her chair.

"Please." Jenna stood. "Sit, and I'll take care of it."

"Nonsense. You're a guest."

"That's funny because I feel like family." She looked at Brendan.

He gaped at her.

"That's probably because we all think of you that way too." Sierra put an arm around Jenna and gave Brendan a pointed look.

"Gotta finish the book first," Brendan said.

Jenna looked at Brendan then back at Sierra. "Do you two have something planned?"

"Planned?" Sierra asked, sounding all innocent, but didn't say anything more and started grabbing paper.

Jenna helped her, and together they filled the paper recycle bin and returned it to the kitchen.

"What's going on?" Jenna asked.

"Just wait, please," Sierra pleaded. "It's good, I promise. I shouldn't have said anything."

"No, you shouldn't have," Brendan said as he carried Karlie to them.

"Brendan said I need to get my boots and coat on. You too, Mommy." Karlie held out her hands, and Brendan shifted her to Jenna.

"She's right," he said. "Jacket and boots."

Sierra stood back and clapped her hands, her face a mass of excitement. Reed joined them and put his arm around her. She looked up at him with such love, it had to be blinding to Reed.

"Come on, scoot." Brendan placed his hands on Jenna's shoulders and gave her a gentle push. "Boots and coat."

"C'mon, Mommy, hurry. It's a s'prise."

Jenna took Karlie to the door and got her ready then tugged on her own boots. Brendan had quickly dressed for outside, and he held out her coat for her. She slipped into it, and he lifted her hair free, sending delicious tingles over her body.

He opened the door, and they stepped out. A horse drawn carriage with wreaths, pine boughs, and twinkling white lights sat at the road.

"Horsey," Karlie called and ran for the road.

"Better catch up to her." Brendan swept Jenna into his arms and bounded down the steps. He put her down and took her hand, pulling her up the driveway so fast she could hardly keep up. He nodded at the carriage driver then lifted Karlie onto the seat and helped Jenna settle next to her.

"Want to sit by Brendan," Karlie said.

"Me too," Jenna said.

His smile broadened at her words, and she patted the seat between her and Karlie. He climbed in and scooped Karlie onto his lap then settled a blanket over the three of them and slid his arm around Jenna. She scooted closer and linked arms, and his mouth formed an O of surprise.

She loved that she could impact him this way.

"Ready," he told the driver.

He flicked the reins, and the carriage climbed up the hill toward her cabin, the clip-clop of hooves the only sound in the quiet night.

Most of the cabins were dark, but colorful lights shone from a few windows, glistening off the snow in a myriad of colors.

"Thank you for the presents," Jenna said to him.

"He only got you one, Mommy," Karlie corrected.

He winked at Jenna, and she smiled at him, then sat back to enjoy the moonlight ride with her daughter and the man she loved.

"This is fun," Karlie said and turned to look at Brendan. "I love you, Brendan."

He didn't hesitate but kissed her forehead. "I love you too, little bit."

Jenna's heart sang at the happiness in her daughter's voice. At the smile on her face. Jenna wanted to declare her love to Brendan now, but she wouldn't do so for the first time in front of Karlie.

The carriage reached the cul-de-sac and started back. Jenna wished the ride could go on and on, but this was what fairy tales were made of. Not real life. And that was what she wanted with Brendan. To have him in their everyday lives. Waking up together. Having breakfast with her and Karlie. Him coming home each day from work. A kiss. A hug. One for her. One for Karlie. A life of togetherness with more joys and fewer sorrows.

They reached the cabin, and the driver drew the horses to a stop. Sierra and Reed stood at the road, likely ready to take the carriage for a spin themselves. After all, they were still newlyweds, and this would be a perfect moonlight ride for them, too, where they could ponder the upcoming birth of their baby.

Brendan looked at Karlie. "Time for you to go with Sierra and Reed."

"Aw," she said.

"I need to talk to your mommy about something really important."

"We'll read your new books with you," Sierra said.

Karlie's sadness evaporated, and she slipped out from under the blanket and into Reed's arms.

"See you later." Sierra waved, and a knowing smile slid across her face as she stepped back.

"Go ahead," Brendan told the driver.

The carriage jerked forward. Jenna lost her seating, but Brendan steadied her. His touch sent her heart racing, and she shivered.

"Cold?" he asked.

"No." She looked up at him. "It's you. Touching me. I like it."

His mouth dropped open.

"And I shouldn't admit it, but I like surprising you too."

He shifted to face her but kept a hand on her shoulder.

"Does this mean you don't plan to say good-bye after tomorrow?" He sounded so unsure, which wasn't like him at all.

She hated that she'd put him in that position. "I'm sorry I couldn't tell you how I felt sooner. I just had to work through things and pray."

"And have you worked through them?"

She took his hand and held it on top of the blanket. "I'm pretty sure I'm in love with you."

"Pretty sure," his words came out on a squeak of emotion.

"No. I'm sure. You're an amazing man. Kind. Generous. Thoughtful. And tough and stubborn too."

He chuckled. "I'm guessing you don't like the last ones."

"Stubborn has its good points." She smiled. "Like stubbornly pursuing me even when I put you off."

"I had to. I'm in love with you. I couldn't do anything else." He smiled, a broad glorious smile that formed the dimple in his cheek. "Besides, my mom told me to go after you, and I always listen to my mom." He laughed, the joyous sound ringing through the quiet night.

She laughed with him, and she felt happiness bubble

out of her body. She never thought she could be this happy and carefree.

"Where do we go from here?" he asked. "Because I don't like being apart from you or Karlie for very long."

"You really love her, don't you?"

"Surprised me, but yeah. I do. I want to spend my life making her happy. And you too."

She leaned back. "Is that a proposal?"

"I don't know, honestly." His lips quirked. "I didn't plan to ask you to marry me. I just wanted to convince you to give me a chance. But you changed things right off the bat." He ran a hand over her hair, his fingers gentle. "I spent the day working out what I was going to say. Word for word. How to convince you not to leave me. But now...now it's all unimportant. We can talk about marriage later if that scares you. As long as we start dating right away."

"Marriage doesn't scare me. Not with you, but I think we need to give Karlie time to adjust to having you around more often."

"That sounds like a good idea."

The driver stopped at the cabin.

"I didn't even notice the ride," she said.

"Me either." He slid his hand around the back of her head. "But before we get down and go in, there's one last thing."

He pulled her close and kissed her. His lips were cold but soon warmed, and her heart soared again. This time with love for this man. She twisted her arms around his neck, pulling him even closer, and kissed him back, making sure he knew how much she loved him.

He drew back. "Wow. We should definitely do a lot of that while we're waiting for Karlie to get used to having me around."

The driver shifted on the seat.

Jenna realized they weren't alone. "We should probably get back inside."

Brendan stepped down and whisked her from the carriage. They walked arm-in-arm up the walkway to the cabin. He opened the door and stood back.

Karlie came running across the room. "Are we a family yet?"

"What, honey?" Jenna asked.

"Sierra said she hoped Brendan convinced you to join the family." She peered up at Jenna. "Did he convince you? 'Cause I want to. I love all of them." She flung her arms out to encompass everyone and spun in a circle.

"I love all of them too." Jenna smiled at his mom, dad, and siblings.

"Yay!" Karlie danced and then grabbed Brendan's leg.

He picked her up, and she hugged him. "Does this mean you're going to be my daddy?"

"Would you like that?" he asked.

The room went quiet, and Jenna held her breath.

"Yes, please," she said so quietly the rest of the room couldn't hear. "You'll be a nice daddy and not care if I get sick."

"I'll care if you get sick." He brushed back Karlie's hair. "Because it will make me sad, and I'll want to help you feel better."

"Mommy does that too. I like it."

Peggy crossed over to them, and Karlie swung into her arms. "Welcome to the Byrd family, sweetie."

Brendan put his arm around Jenna and drew her to his side.

Karlie frowned.

"What's wrong, little bit?" he asked, hoping she didn't dislike his arm around Jenna.

"I want to be in the Byrd family, but my name's not Byrd."

"It could be." His mother gave Brendan and Jenna a pointed look.

"Yippee." Karlie clapped. "If I'm a Byrd, then I'll be able to fly."

Brendan smiled at the little bit of a thing and chuckled to himself.

Jenna looked up at him. "Are you sure you're up to explaining this and a million other things to Karlie?"

He turned Jenna to face him and kissed her nose. "I'm looking forward to each and every one of them."

She arched a brow.

He couldn't imagine why she'd question him, and then it hit him. Karlie wasn't always going to be this little girl. She was going to grow up and have boyfriends. The thought brought terror to his heart.

"What?" Jenna asked. "You look like you want to run for the hills."

"I won't run, I promise." He tugged her closer and held on for dear life. "And I'll do my fair share of explaining. I might be a Byrd, but I'll leave the birds and the bees talk up to you."

ENJOY THIS BOOK?

Reviews are the most powerful tool to draw attention to my books for new readers. I wish I had the budget of a New York publisher to take out ads and commercials but that's not a reality. I do have something much more powerful and effective than that.

A committed and loyal bunch of readers like you.

If you've enjoyed *Night Vision*, I would be very grateful if you could leave an honest review on the bookseller's site. It can be as short as you like. Just a few words is all it takes. Thank you very much.

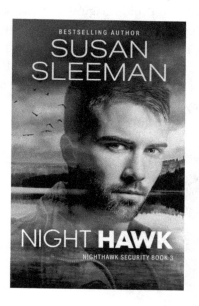

She's determined to find her father's killer...

FBI Agent, Toni Long lost her father a year ago when he was killed in a joint FBI and ICE investigation led by Clay Byrd, a man Toni had found herself infatuated with. Unfortunately, the killer escaped, and if Toni hadn't been distracted by her attraction to Clay, maybe her father wouldn't have died. When she receives an anonymous tip on the killer's identity, she follows the lead and an attempt is made on her life. Clay, having received the same tip, comes to her rescue. Thinking he can help find her father's killer and keep an eye on her safety, he quickly offers Nighthawk Security's help.

But she first has to face down her own dark past.

She fights the idea at first, but she will stop at nothing to find her father's killer, even if it means partnering with a guy she has feelings for. But as the investigation unfolds, they unearth deep, dark family's secrets, that are more dangerous than anything Toni could imagine, and she suddenly finds her life on the line. Problem is, Clay is right there by her side, offering her comfort and support, and protecting her from menacing danger. She soon has to fight feelings she's developing for him when her focus should be on the investigation and staying alive.

Pre-order Now!

NIGHTHAWK SECURITY SERIES
Protecting others when unspeakable danger lurks.

Keep reading for more information on the additional books in the Nighthawk Security Series where the Cold Harbor and Truth Seekers teams work side-by-side with Nighthawk Security.

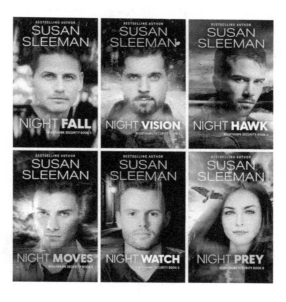

A woman plagued by a stalker. Children of a murderer. A woman whose mother died under suspicious circumstances.

All in danger. Lives on the line. Needing protection.

Enter the brothers of Nighthawk Security. The five Byrd brothers with years of former military and law enforcement experience coming together to offer protection and investigation services. Their goal—protecting others when unspeakable danger lurks.

Book 1 Night Fall – November, 2020
Book 2 – Night Vision – December, 2020
Book 3 - Night Hawk   – January, 2021
Book 4 –Night Moves – July, 2021
Book 5 – Night Watch – August, 2021
Book 6 – Night Prey – October, 2021

For More Details Visit -
www.susansleeman.com/books/nighthawk-security/

THE TRUTH SEEKERS
People are rarely who they seem

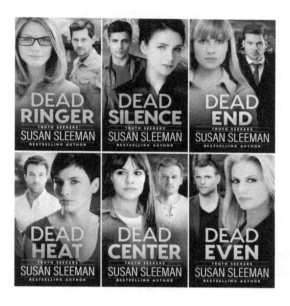

A twin who never knew her sister existed, a mother whose child is not her own, a woman whose father is anything but her father. All searching. All seeking. All needing help and hope.

Meet the unsung heroes of the Veritas Center. The Truth Seekers – a team, that includes experts in forensic anthropology, DNA, trace evidence, ballistics, cybercrimes, and toxicology. Committed to restoring hope and families by solving one mystery at a time, none of them are prepared for when the mystery comes calling close to home and threatens to destroy the only life they've known.

For More Details Visit -
www.susansleeman.com/books/truth-seekers/

BOOKS IN THE COLD HARBOR SERIES

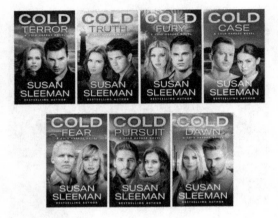

Blackwell Tactical – this law enforcement training facility and protection services agency is made up of former military and law enforcement heroes whose injuries keep them from the line of duty. When trouble strikes, there's no better team to have on your side, and they would give everything, even their lives, to protect innocents.

For More Details Visit -
www.susansleeman.com/books/cold-harbor/

ABOUT SUSAN

SUSAN SLEEMAN is a bestselling and award-winning author of more than 35 inspirational/Christian and clean read romantic suspense books. In addition to writing, Susan also hosts the website, TheSuspenseZone.com.

Susan currently lives in Oregon, but has had the pleasure of living in nine states. Her husband is a retired church music director and they have two beautiful daughters, a very special son-in-law, and an adorable grandson.

For more information visit:
www.susansleeman.com

CPSIA information can be obtained
at www.ICGtesting.com
Printed in the USA
LVHW092233271120
672639LV00008B/443